The Conductors

The CONDUCTORS

NICOLE GLOVER

A John Joseph Adams Book

MARINER BOOKS

HOUGHTON MIFFLIN HARCOURT

BOSTON   NEW YORK

2021

For information about permission to reproduce selections from
this book, write to trade.permissions@hmhco.com or to Permissions,
Houghton Mifflin Harcourt Publishing Company,
3 Park Avenue, 19th Floor, New York, New York 10016.

hmhbooks.com

Library of Congress Cataloging-in-Publication Data

Names: Glover, Nicole, author.
Title: The conductors / Nicole Glover.
Description: Boston : A John Joseph Adams Book,
Mariner Books, Houghton Mifflin Harcourt, 2021.
Identifiers: LCCN 2020009019 (print) | LCCN 2020009020 (ebook) |
ISBN 9780358197058 (trade paperback) | ISBN 9780358181798 (ebook)
Subjects: GSAFD: Fantasy fiction. | Mystery fiction.
Classification: LCC PS3607.L687 C66 2020 (print) |
LCC PS3607.L687 (ebook) | DDC 813/.6 — dc23

LC record available at https://lccn.loc.gov/2020009019
LC ebook record available at https://lccn.loc.gov/2020009020

Book design by Emily Snyder
Illustrations adapted from constellation images by
Iron Mary / Shutterstock

Printed in the United States of America
DOC 10 9 8 7 6 5 4 3 2 1

*For my grandparents who taught me everything I know,
and left me with questions I'm still answering.*

The Conductors

REWARD FOR TWO FEMALE NEGRO RUNAWAYS

A pair of sisters fled the 18th night of November 1858.

ESTHER aged 14, fine looking with chestnut coloring and a birthmark on her right cheek. Bring back untouched and alive for $50.

The other, HENRIETTA, aged 15, with chestnut coloring. If examined will find raw ringed scars wrapped around the neck, three fingers wide. Approach with caution and bring shock collar to subdue any magical attack. Reward is $20 dead or alive.

WANTED!

Five Negro males fled the Lea Farm in Pond County with false passes. HARRIS, 42, missing right eye. JON, 20, mulatto with collar scars. LUKE, 22, also mulatto, tall and stout. OBIE, 35, with an R branded on left cheek. BEN, 16, able to read and write.

$125 reward for all five, $20 per head.

Posted: December 24, 1858

WANTED, $1000 DEAD OR ALIVE FOR STEALING SLAVES!

A Negro man and woman were spotted by the subscriber on the 15th of January in the company of persons belonging to Mrs. Edna Reynolds. The criminals are BENJAMIN, dark coloring with a muscular build. Speaks well and can read. Last seen posing as a blacksmith. With him is HENRIETTA, dark coloring, fine looking despite scars around her neck. Dangerous magic practitioner.

$500 for returned property, $1000 for either criminal dead or alive.

Posted: January 16, 1861

Article XIII

Amendment of 1866

To define the rights of Negroes in regards to spellcasting.

SECTION 1. All persons heretofore known as slaves and free persons of color shall have the right to perform acts of magic and other permitted forms of spellcasting.

SECTION 2. These acts of magic are permitted as long as they are performed within the constraints defined by local authorities.

SECTION 3. It is unlawful for any former slave or free person of color to possess or use a wand. Any person or persons so offending shall face imprisonment no less than one day or more than ten days in the discretion of the Court or jury before whom the trial is had.

— CONSTITUTION OF THE
COMMONWEALTH OF PENNSYLVANIA

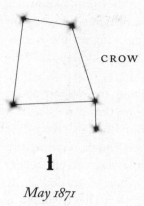

CROW

1

May 1871

PHILADELPHIA, PENNSYLVANIA

WHEN THE WAGON ROLLED into view, Hetty took another small step along the tree branch. Lookout was not a role she would have chosen, but Benjy had argued a trap was useless if it wasn't sprung in the right moment. Someone needed to watch the road, or trouble would be the only thing they caught.

If the stars were so willing, Elle could have made a proper lookout. But at the sight of the wagon, the girl clutched her branch so tightly that it was a challenge to find where girl ended and tree started.

The younger girl was one of the dozen or so people who had gone missing over the course of two days, and so far was the only one to have escaped. Hetty and Benjy just thought the missing girl's trail had gone cold when Elle stumbled out of the woods, frantic for help. Not realizing they had been looking for her, Elle told them everything without hesitation, confirming what they already knew. She had been approached by a kind face, led out of safety, and trapped before she even knew a trick was in play.

But the only thing they didn't know was carried in her breathless words. Details that changed their approach entirely.

After years of ferrying people to safety from white slave catchers, they assumed these kidnappers were cut from the same cloth.

They were wrong.

The men driving the wagon could have been one of their neighbors, someone they'd seen as they went on their business throughout town. Although Hetty did not know these particular men, not even their names, learning this detail stung like a friend smiling as they told your secrets to your worst enemy.

Below her, the bushes rustled as Benjy hurried to finish the last of his spells. Hetty silently urged him on as the wagon drew nearer.

If they had been working in tandem, the spells would be primed and ready.

But as this was not the first time they'd done this, Hetty knew that stopping the wagon was the least important part.

The driver's head had just passed under her feet when Hetty let a crow's caw escape her throat.

She projected her voice as if she had a crowd eagerly listening as she spun tales for their enjoyment. Trees some distance away stirred with confused crows, but farther along the road, the bushes stopped moving.

Benjy stepped to the side and slammed his hammer onto the sigil scratched into the dirt.

Light flashed from the strike and dust flew into the air. The trees across from Hetty's hiding spot swayed until three of them dropped like dogs onto a bone.

Wheels squealed and the horse cried out in alarm. The wagon veered to the side, and the driver swore as he did his best to avoid the pile of trees.

The moment it shuddered to a stop, two men jumped out of the back of the wagon to yell at the driver.

As the dust settled, Benjy tucked the hammer away. But before he approached the trio, he reached up and tugged his left ear.

Hetty rolled her eyes.

Clearly he still remembered the last time they pulled a stunt like this. But she would have lingered on her perch a bit longer even without his warning.

Their plan had not accounted for three men being on the wagon. Nor did it consider the guns the men held in their hands.

The swearing stopped when Benjy drew near. One of the guns turned his way, but Benjy grinned and greeted the trio with a rolling drawl he brought out for these occasions. For some reason, it seemed to put people at ease. Hetty's husband was imposing even when he tried not to be. He wore his past labors on broad shoulders and held his head high with full confidence as he made his way in the world.

"You fellas look to be in a spot of bad luck," Benjy said. "Need some help getting those trees out of the way? Can't move them, but my pappy taught me a good chopping spell to turn them into firewood."

While Benjy held the trio's attention with a rambling story Hetty had invented, she launched into the next stage of the plan. Hetty swung off the branch, soundlessly dropping from the tree to the ground.

The wagon's doors were partially open when she reached it.

With care, Hetty nudged them a bit wider so she could slip inside. Beams of dying sunlight caught the eyes of the dozen men and women seated around a log. Like a fat spider in the middle of its web, ropes sprouted from the log to bind each person's hands together so that not even the smallest of fingers could twitch.

This was not as terrible as she expected, but it came mighty close.

Hetty took another step into the wagon. Her appearance sent a shiver through the group.

When the man closest to her made to speak, Hetty raised one finger to her lips.

The only noise she heard was Benjy's rambling, so she drew the Crow star sigil into the air.

A simple square with a short line extending from one corner, the sigil shimmered in the air for only a moment before Hetty gave life to the constellation. Suddenly, instead of lines and vertices, a crow hovered in the air, silently flapping its wings. Unlike a true crow, this one did not have ink-black feathers. The star sigil was a deep midnight blue from its beak to its tail feathers, speckled with starlight that twinkled even when it stood still.

The star sigil looped circles inside the wagon, slicing through bindings and unraveling the web of ropes.

As the crow did its work, Hetty held out a coin with the Dipper emblazoned on one side. Gesturing toward the open door, she pointed at the road back to town. Most blinked back at her, but an older woman stood up and took the coin from her. She gave Hetty a hearty wink and then held the coin toward the sky. The coin flashed at once.

Ursa Minor took form in front of the woman before shifting into a shower of pale purple light. At the sight, the reluctance in the group melted away. They might not have seen Hetty before, but they had heard the stories of people like her. They knew they were not the first people Hetty had freed.

The older woman held her hand toward the man closest to her. After Hetty urged him with a look, he took it. Others followed, grabbing each other's hands. One by one, the magic of the coin vanished them from sight—like a veil of invisibility had been tossed over them.

When the last person disappeared into the woods, Hetty directed the crow upward. With a swish of her hand, she imploded the spell, letting loose the magic in a blazing light.

The men outside swore. There was a thump, and then a gun-shot split the air.

The horse started at the sound, and its neighs added to the sudden chaos. But it was the second flash of light that got Hetty moving.

She ducked around the wagon, holding out a sharp hairpin.

A bullet struck tree bark inches from Benjy's head. He ignored it and flicked his fingers into a series of star sigils, forming them so quickly that Hetty got only a faint impression of their shape. The spells shot from his hands and struck the man in front of him. Another man was already on the ground, moaning as he clutched a hand more in pieces than whole.

And the third . . .

The third man was frantically cramming bullets into a pistol.

Hetty jammed the hairpin into his arm. The man yelped, falling to his knees. Hetty jumped back. She ran a finger along the cotton band at her neck, calling on the Taurus star sigil she had sewn into the stitches.

Wrenching out the pin, the man stared at it and then at her. His mouth was still twisted over some crude word when Hetty's spell sent him flying into a tree.

The man slipped to the ground, out like a snuffed candle.

"Too bad you can't do that spell from a distance," Benjy said, tossing the knocked-out men to join the third. The pair hit the tree trunk with a thud. None woke up.

"If I could do anything from a distance," Hetty reminded him, "I would have pinned them with a sleeping spell from the start and we could have avoided all this trouble."

Her husband snorted. "Certainly would have made things easier."

A star-speckled wolf loped over, carrying in its mouth the binding ropes from the wagon. It stopped near the three men and shook itself briefly before vanishing. The ropes fell on the men and then knotted together, binding wrists and ankles with a precision as sure as if done by hand.

"Plan still worked," Hetty said.

"We've done this before," Benjy said, shrugging, "and this time we didn't need to be as careful." He cast a glance around the clearing. "Everyone on their way?"

Hetty pointed upward.

"Except for one."

Up in the tree, Elle had a death grip on the branch, but a new wariness entered her eyes as Hetty approached.

"Who are you people?" Elle stammered. "You summon birds, walk into gunfire with little pause, and make people vanish into the air. I thought when I ran into you it was luck—"

"Hardly luck," Benjy scoffed. "We were looking for you!"

The girl emitted a small squeak and pressed her face back into the tree bark.

"A friend of ours sent us looking for you," Hetty called up to Elle. "Miss Penelope."

The name did the trick.

Elle's eyes opened and her grip relaxed so she merely held the tree instead of squeezing life from it.

"Who *are* you?" she repeated. Curiosity bloomed in her eyes, overshadowing the fear.

Hetty held out a hand to the girl, much as she'd done many times before, and said, "Someone here to help."

When they brought the girl back home, Elle's mother's face shone wet with tears. Elle barely stepped through the door before her mother drew her into a crushing embrace.

Hetty stood aside watching the reunion as envy prickled her with each word and gesture.

"Thank you for bringing back my girl," Elle's mother said

when she finally released her daughter. "Come inside—can't have you out there after all you done."

The room was tiny, surprisingly so, given how grand the boardinghouse appeared on the outside. This room must have been partitioned to create more rooms for renters. Hetty's eyes fell to the paneled wood to her left. It was a shade lighter than the rest and allowed muffled noises to slip through from the next room. But these were small things. The family had a small window to let in the light, a hooked rug spread across the floor, and wilted flowers in a vase on a round table. It wasn't much, but it was well cared for and filled with love.

"It was no trouble." Hetty took a few token steps inside. "We were lucky. She escaped them on her own. I don't think they expected her to have a talent in magic."

"You taught her, didn't you?" Benjy asked.

The mother nodded, pride filling the soft curves of her face. "First thing I did once freedom came. Didn't dare teach any of my children back when we were slaves, but now times are different. Now they'll have all the tools they can get."

"She learned well."

"Not well enough." Giving Elle a stern look, she said to her daughter, "You should have known better."

"Those men, they said they knew where Daniel was, said they'd bring him here if I brought the money. I thought . . . I thought it wouldn't hurt to try. It's my fault he got sold and I just wanted to see my brother again!"

"We will," her mother said, "but these things take time."

"Sometimes too long," Hetty murmured.

"How did you even know about this at all?" Elle's mother asked. "I barely told anyone, and none that would know you."

"Penelope Jones is a friend of mine," Hetty explained. "She saw a few things that concerned her and got word to me."

"The choir teacher? I'll be sure to thank her. I'm in her debt. All your debts."

Elle's mother thanked Hetty again and, as they were attempting to leave, offered up payment in the form of an inky black candle. Reeking of herbs more mundane than magical, it was a candle of protection, although Hetty suspected the only protection it offered was from the darkness.

Not very much of that, either, Hetty thought as she turned it over in her hands. But they didn't take up this work expecting payment.

Their first case, if you could call it that, started when they fished a body out of the Schuylkill River with a slit neck and a week's wages in his wallet. It was disturbing, it was strange, and, above all, it was curious. But only to them. The police—who patrolled the streets looking for trouble to stir up—weren't interested in the dead man. When Hetty and Benjy pressed too hard, suspicions fell on them. So instead of the police, they directed their questions to people who might actually come to their aid.

That dead man wasn't the first to be murdered in this city, but he was the first that drew their attention. Hetty and Benjy realized similar deaths would keep occurring and no one would do anything about it.

It became their job. And it still was after five very interesting years.

Whether it was bodies found chopped up in a trunk, missing cauldrons, or cursed teakettles, they poked and prodded until they made sense of the senseless. They found nightmarish things tucked away in the quietest of homes. Revealed culprits and caught thieves. And they found lost loved ones.

The day spent looking for Elle was no different, except this one had a happy ending. Most of their cases ended in death, especially ones like this. Being able to bring that girl home, alive and only slightly shaken, was a delight in every fashion.

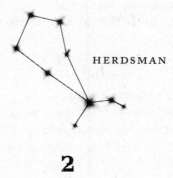

HERDSMAN

2

Aₛ ᴛʜᴇ ɴɪɢʜᴛ ᴄʀᴇᴘᴛ ᴜᴘ on them, they left toward home. At the street corner, Hetty turned right instead of left. Benjy turned with her, although he was not quick to follow.

"I want to pay Penelope a visit," Hetty said. "Let her know what happened with the girl. You can wait downstairs. I won't be long."

"I think I hear thunder." Benjy cupped his ear. "It's very distant, but it's there."

"I won't be long," Hetty repeated.

He scoffed and started naming all the times she said this before.

Benjy had listed a dozen examples by the time they arrived at the house, and if the day hadn't been such an eventful one, she might have considered prolonging her stay just to be petty.

It was a cool spring evening without a chance of rain. She could leave him waiting for half a night and not feel guilty, especially considering he would wait for her. He always did.

The windows of the schoolroom that took up the ground floor of the building were dark. But the second level was quite the opposite. Even before Hetty reached the top of the stairs, she heard muffled laughter, and voices that threatened to spill out into the hallway.

This apartment belonged to Darlene and George, and while lights flickering in the windows were expected, such rambunctious noise was not.

"Are they having a party?" Benjy asked.

Benjy stood a few steps below her, curiosity drawing him near despite his greater reservations.

"I would have heard," Hetty said, though she couldn't be sure.

Darlene and her husband, George, taught letters and numbers in the schoolroom below. Daylight hours were for the fifteen children that attended regularly, but two evening classes for adults met each week. Devoted educators, the couple lived very simply, forgoing most pleasures in their private lives. However, to help raise the prestige of their little school, they had gotten themselves wrapped up with the rich elite—people who enjoyed fine dining, gossip, and filling their homes with trinkets that could have fed a family of four for a month. While Darlene claimed the rich elite of the city were a trial to contend with, she made no effort to curtail George's ambitions.

"Why don't we ask Penelope together?" Hetty suggested. "Or you can ask, since you're curious."

It was too dark to fully make out his expression, but she smiled anyway, imagining the displeasure on his face, since he had stumbled into a trap of his making.

The stairs went up for one more level to Penelope's apartment. She lived in a small set of rooms filled with plants on every possible surface and space. The fewest number was in the kitchen, where a dozen plants were spread across the windowsill and the counters, waiting to be used in a potion or poultice. The air always held traces of freshly cut leaves, and there was always a half dozen herb bundles suspended over the sink by a wire, drying for some later use.

Although Penelope rented from Darlene, she paid no money, and instead taught music lessons or performed small favors.

Hetty knocked once and heard the slight tinkle of mugs. She knocked a second time and heard chairs move. On her third knock, the door swung open.

"Hetty!" Penelope pulled the door open wider, urging her to come inside. "I didn't expect to see you so soon! It's just you, isn't it? No one behind you causing trouble?"

"No one," Hetty replied. "Except for my husband."

"Benjy's here?" Penelope called out to the shadows with a broad grin. "Well, he can stay outside and out of the way!"

Despite being her opposite in most things, Penelope was Hetty's closest and dearest friend. While Benjy was willing to entertain her complaints, gripes, and fears — not to mention numerous other ills — he lacked a certain sensitivity about certain matters. In Penelope, Hetty had a listening ear, a companion to perform hijinks with, and someone who took her blunt words without insult or annoyance.

Penelope had thought herself alone in the world, until her mother's sister found her through the theft of records from a burned-down sugar cane plantation. With five children of her own — three married with families — adding Penelope into the mix was no trouble. But while Penelope loved her newfound relatives, she chose to live apart for reasons she never quite explained. Skilled with herbs and brewing magic, she worked at the best herbalist shop in town, providing remedies and charms alike. While she took pride in this work, her true passion was singing. Penelope lent her voice to contests and traveling shows, and she ran the choir at church as a labor of love. If she could make a living off her voice, Hetty had no doubts Penelope would drop everything to try.

"Did you find Elle?" Penelope asked.

"Yes, she's back with her mother. This" — Hetty held up the candle — "is our reward."

"I knew you'd find her!" Penelope clasped her hands together.

"I was so worried. I keep seeing her talking to that man after practice. I should have done something when I saw him pull her out of sight. I just stood there and watched."

"You did do something," Hetty assured her friend. "You told us and set us searching. What you call nothing meant Elle and the others lured away would not be sent to have their magic harvested."

"Magic harvesting?" cried a voice from inside. "That can't be going on!"

"Darlene," Hetty said, spying the other woman seated at Penelope's table. "What are you doing up here?"

Darlene's appearance on its own wasn't strange. Penelope's large round table was the place they gathered to gossip and discuss various matters in and around town. But Darlene should have been in her own apartment given what Hetty had seen as she came upstairs.

Instead, Darlene sat hunched over her sketchbook, gently rocking a basket with her foot to keep the little baby swaddled inside in the arms of sleep. Her glasses slipped off her nose, and as usual there was a smudge of charcoal along the right side of her face, like a beauty mark against her skin. Reserved and quietly elegant, Darlene was often the voice of reason in their little trio.

Together her friends presented an interesting contrast, vividly expressed in their attire. Penelope favored bold colors, pumpkin orange, canary yellow, and even rose pink, all paired with frothy lace and ribbons. On anyone else it would have been overwhelming but with Penelope's fuller figure and flair for dramatics it all suited her rather nicely. Darlene, on the other hand, stayed with earthy brown and maroon and was quite keen on buttons. Buttons on her sleeves, to be precise, to keep the fabric from ruining whatever painting she was working on.

All their dresses were made by Hetty. While a few times she was bribed to make something, like the butterfly-themed dress

Penelope had wanted for one Easter Sunday, Hetty took on the work without much fuss and without asking for payment. Her dresses were worn by some of the richest people in the city, but her greatest pleasure was working away on a new dress for her friends.

"We're just having a bit of a chat." Darlene's lips pressed into a thin line. "What's this about magic harvesting?"

"Nothing to worry about." Hetty handed the candle to Penelope and slipped inside the cheery kitchen.

Something had driven Darlene up here. It didn't look to be the baby. Since she had adopted the child last month, Darlene took every sniffle, cough, or sneeze as a precursor to doom. With Penelope's proximity and talents with healing remedies, she was the first stop for Darlene's frantic queries.

But instead of worry, irritation creased Darlene's face.

Whatever brought her up here?

"Magic harvesting sounds like a great deal to worry about," Darlene replied. "Given it's not herbs."

"Don't mind her. When we don't know why people suddenly vanish, she calls it magic harvesting." Benjy moved out of the shadows. He didn't come inside but leaned against the door frame. "Don't understand why."

"Because that's how it was back in slavery times." Hetty kept her voice earnest. "Magic users were snatched up so their bones could be ground up into wands."

"That's only a story," Darlene said, but her eyes flicked around. "Isn't it?"

"The stories have to come from somewhere." Hetty took a seat across from Darlene. "Why do you think"—she tapped her thumb against her neck and at the scars hidden from sight—"we were collared?"

Hetty had her for a moment, like she knew she would. Darlene was the most imaginative of her friends, which meant with the right story Darlene was easily tricked, especially when Hetty weaved in bits that were true. People did disappear suddenly and without reason, but magic harvesting wasn't likely the cause—or even a true practice.

Darlene shook her head, breaking the power of Hetty's words. "Now I know you're telling tales again. Why do you persist on making up stories like this? Wands are just made of wood—they aren't rubbed with bone dust!"

"I never said anything like that," Hetty teased.

"I don't know anything about wands," Penelope admitted, too lost in her thoughts to pay attention to either of them. She turned the inky black candle over in her hands as she leaned against her counter. "But it's no worse than what I feared might have happened to Elle."

"You must have an idea why they snatched her," Darlene said, jumping to turn the tide of the conversation, "or why they were doing such a thing?"

"We don't know yet, but we're going to make sure it doesn't happen again." Hetty reached for Darlene's sketchbook. "May I?"

Darlene nodded, pushing the book across the table. Hetty turned to an empty page and drew a horseshoe.

"These men all had the same mark on their hands. It's worth keeping an eye on."

Darlene looked away. "I told you, the past is behind me."

"You know people," Hetty persisted, "and some of them aren't fond of me."

"With good reason." Darlene attempted a smile. "I'm sorry."

So was Hetty.

Freed at a very young age, Darlene had been an agent with the Vigilance Society, acting as a point of contact in the city. When Hetty got involved with conductor work, Darlene familiarized her with the procedures of the organization and provided assistance beyond the city's limits. With slavery abolished, others in the Vigilance Society turned their hands toward making freedom more than just words on a piece of paper, but Darlene retreated from the work. She had reasons for it, some of them good, but to Hetty's ears they sounded like excuses.

"Don't be sorry." Benjy's words drifted in, paired with a pointed look at Hetty. "This is a task for us to handle."

Taking the hint, Hetty pushed the sketchbook back to Darlene.

"That's all I came for and—"

"Stay for a bit," Penelope pleaded. "It's not that late."

From his spot in the doorway, Benjy shook his head. "What should I do while you chatter on?"

"You can go downstairs," Darlene huffed. "Plenty to keep you occupied."

His curiosity about the excitement in the apartment below was greater than Hetty had anticipated. Eager as he was to go home, Benjy slipped inside instead, joining them in the kitchen.

"What is going on downstairs?" he asked.

"George is hosting a group of people from this political club he joined, E.C. Degray." Darlene turned a page in her sketchbook, the paper snapping with the action. "There's an excursion later this week across the river. They're finalizing details now, or so they claim."

"E.C. Degray?" Hetty echoed. "Is this another one of those secret societies?"

"I couldn't tell you. George keeps shying away from giving me a direct answer. I can certainly guess what they're about, but I like to be told things!"

Hetty nodded along but hid a bit of a smile. She did not have this problem. Her marriage to Benjy hadn't been a love match, but theirs was an agreement that suited them rather well. She often thought their understanding made a stronger marriage. Hetty had seen the pain love matches caused in both the past and the present. She was glad to be spared it.

"I suppose it's about voting." Darlene tapped her pencil against the table. "But isn't it too early to be talking about elections? October is so far away."

"It's good to know who our husbands will be voting for," Hetty said. "Benjy, what do you think?"

"It's too soon to tell," he murmured as he sat down, drawing up a chair next to Hetty.

"About the candidates?"

"About this club. Charlie waxed on about it the other day but didn't tell me anything of value."

"You should join." Penelope placed mugs in front of them. Swirling steam lifted fresh mint into the air. "You'll bring sense into that group. I heard from my cousin Sy that there's talk of recommending people for public office. He didn't like some of the names being suggested, but thought you'd do a good job. Is that not a good idea? You were saying that there were many things you wanted to fix."

"I don't disagree there," Benjy replied. "But the job does not suit me."

"Surely better than *Charlie*," Darlene grumbled. "He shouldn't be in a position to make decisions about anything more important than the cut of his coat!"

Penelope laughed at this, although with a hesitation that Hetty shared. Charlie, the husband of one of their friends, fretted about the cut and style of his clothes so much that they'd taken to calling him Peacock—until he learned about it and took all the fun out of a good joke. But even before the joke was ruined, Darlene never used it. It was unbecoming and rude, she said, with a stiffly held chin that didn't waver despite their insisting it was harmless fun. How odd for her to say different now.

"Do you think George would be better suited?" Penelope asked.

"Me? The wife of some politician!" Darlene exclaimed. "Who do you think I am? I'm not—"

Darlene's words stuttered to a halt. Her face filled with a panic Hetty had seen quite often in the months since that last disastrous tea party with Marianne last winter.

"Marianne," Hetty supplied. "She's downstairs, isn't she?"

It was as if she'd spat out a hex into the room. Penelope and Darlene both drew back, and Benjy shot Hetty a look filled with more concern than when they'd concocted the plan to strike at the kidnappers.

That look stung the most.

Hetty nursed less than kind feelings for Marianne these days, but if they were expecting her to storm down there and turn Marianne into a frog, they were wrong. Such magic wasn't possible.

"Darlene," Benjy said in the silence that fell in the room, "do you know if anyone by the name of Randall is down there? George told me the fellow had a job for me, but we couldn't find the time to meet."

This was a lie. Made worse by the excessive details. And Darlene snatched it up eagerly.

"I don't know." Darlene reached down and pulled out the bundle that was her baby. "Why don't we go find out?"

With her daughter cradled in her arms, Darlene led Benjy out of Penelope's apartment, presumably in an effort to keep Marianne away from Hetty.

"Not going with them?" Hetty asked, as the door slammed shut. "Or are you here to keep me out of trouble?"

Penelope settled into Darlene's empty chair. "We all have our tasks to play in this world. Although, this is the perfect time to show you what I found. I think you'll find it interesting."

Penelope waved a hand. The Arrow star sigil whipped past and struck a cabinet drawer. Under Penelope's guidance, a squat green vial floated across the room and landed on the table.

Hetty recoiled at the sight.

The last time she saw a vial like this, she'd had to break the fingers of a dead woman to pry it free.

Hetty picked it up. The more she studied it, the more she had to stop herself from smashing the bottle onto the table.

"Where did you get this?"

"A customer at work showed it to me." Penelope's mouth curled into a wry smile. "Wanted to know if we had something similar on our shelves. It was lucky she showed it to me. Miss Linda would have lost her temper. We got enough trouble without charlatans cutting up our trade. It's the same kind, isn't it?"

"It's the same."

Penelope expelled a breath. "How dreadful."

Dreadful was not a big enough word. People sold the moon and the tides as far back as anyone could remember, winking and laughing as they cheated people out of their hard-earned money. Doing it with brewed magic was just the latest variation.

But brewed magic was a finicky beast. It required patience, time, and access to ingredients and tools that often proved hard to gather. Penelope worked at a herbal shop that provided such things, but she often lost customers due to frauds offering cheap remedies and faulty herbs. These swindlers sold potions and brews to straighten hair, lighten skin, even to make a womb comfortable for a child. However, as with most claims, the small promises delivered but the big ones didn't.

With a heart full of hope, a woman named Emily Wells had drunk an entire vial of a potion just like the one Hetty held. It brought the woman to death's arms. It was a simple case, the culprit easily found. But solving the mystery was not enough for Hetty. The death was an accident, but Emily Wells would have not died if her mother, her husband, and even her friends didn't pressure her to have a baby her body could not carry.

But that wasn't the only reason Penelope showed this to Hetty now.

Darlene had nearly been the next victim. Darlene had been trying for ages to have a baby. No miscarriages, thank the stars, but no luck. In fact, a twin of this very same bottle was in Darlene's pocket when one of her students approached her after class. The girl had a hand pressed on her heavily pregnant belly and asked if Darlene would like to raise a baby that would otherwise be unwanted.

The simple act saved the lives of the young student, the baby that would become Lorene, and Darlene.

"I know where this con artist is," Hetty said. "She promised to stop, but she must have forgotten."

"Must have," Penelope echoed. "What do you plan to do? Remind her of that promise?"

"And a bit more."

Worry crossed Penelope's face. "This is why Darlene and Benjy rushed to usher Marianne out the house. You say things like this and we all wonder what will happen next."

"Why always bad things?" Hetty laughed as she tucked the vial away.

"Don't you know five different stories about preparing for the worst?"

"What's the worst in this case? There's nine stories I can tell, and one has a good ending." Hetty stood, heading for the door. "I'm off to collect my husband. If I do happen to meet Marianne, I apologize for any smoke."

"That's not funny, Henrietta!" Penelope called after her, her voice carrying even through the closed door.

Still chuckling, Hetty headed back down the stairs. She had just placed her hand on the doorknob to Darlene's apartment when she heard someone call her name.

It wasn't Penelope or anyone she wanted to have her name on their lips.

"Henrietta," said Charlie Richardson. "I need to talk to you."

"You may talk." Hetty swung around to face Marianne's husband. "That doesn't mean I'll listen."

Faint light illuminated his surprise. "You're still mad about the dresses?"

"I am mad you took what was meant to be a gift and sold it to others! Maybe it's my fault for thinking gifts could bridge a peace between Marianne and me, but that doesn't mean you weren't wrong!"

"Your work is worth the price I charged. Did you want to be paid?" Charlie reached into his pocket. "I can get you the money and more if you like. Name a figure."

She paused, taken aback by this generosity. "Any figure?"

"Any."

Hetty's answer was on her lips when she saw the gleam in his eyes. He'd tossed bait at her feet, and she'd nearly taken it like a fool.

"No. No money. No listening to a word you have to say."

Charlie grabbed her arm.

"You must! It's important. At the elm —"

Hetty coolly meet his gaze and held it until Charlie wisely removed his offending hand.

"Please," he begged. "You must listen."

The words were a rasp from the back of his throat, raw and stripped of his usual airs and whimsy.

The man who said these words wasn't Charlie Richardson, the peacock with eyes toward the next bright shiny thing. The man stooping to beg his case was a Charlie in a raggedy coat and split shoes, with eyes darting to shadows.

Charlie sought her out for trouble he couldn't handle. But if it was truly dire, he wouldn't waste time talking to her — he'd go to

Benjy. Talking to her was a delay. Unless of course that was the point. She was here to field his request, since he seemed to think Benjy wouldn't even consider it.

"Can I do something about it right now?" Hetty asked.

"No, but—"

"Then it can wait." She opened the door. "Tell us together. It's the better choice."

"Only choice, you mean."

"Why, yes." Hetty paused in the threshold, letting conversation in the next room wash over them. Beams of light striped his face into patches of light and shadow. "Did you think you would get special treatment?"

He didn't have an answer, or if he did, hadn't found the right words when she shut the door behind her.

Hetty spotted Marianne right away.

It was hard not to. Marianne was resplendent. She stood in a crimson dress from Lord and Crown. The bright color and the overly complicated waste of fabric was a stark contrast to the dark suits of the men and their wives clustered around her.

Of the group of friends Hetty had formed over the years, Marianne was the only one that did not talk about the days when she had been enslaved, skipping over that chunk of time as if nothing mattered before she arrived in Philadelphia. Darlene claimed it was because of painful memories, but Hetty knew it was tied to Marianne's ascent into the insular upper class of the city.

Wielding the gifts she was born with, Marianne used her golden-brown complexion, dainty features, and softly curling hair to fit right in with the elite of the city. What she was aiming for was hard to tell. At first Hetty assumed it was a better life, but these days Hetty wondered if it was to forget the past. If that was true, Marianne was doing an astonishingly good job of it.

As Marianne held court, Darlene tiptoed about with a pitcher held in her hands. She weaved through the crowd, refilling drinks, ignored by all until Marianne snapped her fingers. Marianne's glass floated in the air, all but shoving itself into Darlene's face. Marianne said something Hetty didn't hear, but she could guess the gist of the words in the way Darlene's polite expression curdled into contempt.

But Darlene was a better person than Hetty. Instead of tossing the drink at Marianne, she returned to the kitchen. Darlene paused at the door, and when she looked back her eyes locked on Hetty.

Don't, Darlene mouthed. With her chin, she pointed in the direction to Hetty's right, and then disappeared through the door.

When Hetty turned, she could see why Darlene felt confident to leave Hetty in close quarters with Marianne. Benjy was across the room.

Like Marianne, he too stood apart from the crowd around him, due to his rough and muddied attire. He seemed perfectly at ease despite being locked in a conversation with Darlene's husband, George.

While Charlie had climbed up into society with a skip and jump, George had clawed his way upward inch by inch, enduring taunts and gentle rebukes from all sides. He had fought with the 43rd regiment, witnessing everything from the horrors of the Battle of the Crater to the surrender at Appomattox. George's experience during the war, as well as his classical education, inspired him to do something great in the world. The classroom that sat below this apartment was the fruit of that inspiration, and his motivation to force himself into the high society world that wasn't all too welcoming.

"I'm not surprised to see you," George declared heartily as Hetty approached. "Everyone," he slurred, "this is Benjamin's lovely wife, Henrietta. She's going to be a teacher at my school."

"I think someone told you a lie." Hetty eyed George's flushed face, unsure what brought these words about.

"Why not?" George said. "You know your letters and numbers, and your stories charm children. You're good with people."

"Doesn't matter," Hetty said as the men around them chuckled. "I'm not teaching anyone anything."

"Not even magic lessons?"

There was a small outcry at that. Even Benjy's eyebrows lifted. George's opinions on magic ran pragmatic and practical—the old mindset that came from the plantations. Back in the old days, magic was a handful of star sigils to till the land, to aid in picking the cash crop of choice or sweeping nettles out of the way. In George's view, there was no room for inventive or cleverly done spell-work. For him to even float the idea meant one of two things. He was either desperate for teachers, or drunk.

Hetty leaned toward the latter.

"She's exceptionally good with magic." George spun around to the crowd, waving a hand about. "Every story you heard about these two, they're all true!"

When he didn't get the response he expected, George blathered on. "You haven't heard of them? Have none of you heard? Benjamin and Henrietta Rhodes worked as conductors for the Vigilance Society when it was still up and running. You know of Joseph Mills or Della Reynolds? These two brought them up north, and a slew of others. Some that are even in this room right now!"

Eyes went to Hetty and Benjy, but as always, greater doubt swung back around to her.

"Tell them about the barn," George pressed, staring into Hetty's general direction. "And the dozen white folks you had to shoot. Or the boat you stole. Or even the cat that saved your skins. To think—all these adventures happened because Henrietta went looking for her sister!"

"Is your sister as pretty as you?" one of the men called.

"That's a story for another day."

Hetty forced out a laugh she nearly choked on. She needed to leave this room; she needed to leave now. In moments, they would ask the question people asked when learning of this sliver of her past. And she was in no mood to spin a pleasing lie.

Hetty pushed her way through the group. Benjy followed close behind, whispering what he thought were consoling words.

"Don't mind him, he was drunk."

"Anyone could guess that." Hetty stomped down the stairs, welcoming the rush of cool air against her face. "With him acting as if I was going to be one of his teachers! What was he thinking getting that deep into his cups! Can't imagine it makes him a good host."

"George always has some at gatherings like this," Benjy said. "Thinks it makes people like him. I'm not sure if he does it due to experience or Richardson putting the thought in his ear."

The mention of Charlie made Hetty forget all about George, as she recalled her earlier conversation.

As they headed down the street, Hetty glanced up at the dimly lit streetlamps over their heads and considered her next words.

"Did you see Charlie earlier?"

"I got a glimpse." There was a long pause. "Why do you ask?"

"Charlie twisted my ear with a tale of trouble. Said it was important and seemed to think you wouldn't listen to his ramblings."

"That's one thing he's right about." Benjy's words were quiet, but they snapped and crackled in the air with an anger that couldn't find its target. "Is someone in danger?"

"He didn't say." Hetty kept her words light and airy, but underneath her curiosity stirred.

Her falling-out with Marianne had been looming on the horizon for some time, but Benjy and Charlie met regularly to play cards. Or at least she thought they did.

"Then he was right," Benjy said. "I won't listen to him."

"What if I convince you otherwise?"

"If you cared about what he had to say, we'd already be talking to him."

"I didn't, but now that I know you're against it, I do."

"Not tonight."

"Not tonight," Hetty echoed, not wishing to wage a battle when she didn't care about the outcome. There would be plenty of other chances to talk with Charlie.

After all, Charlie never gave up without a fight.

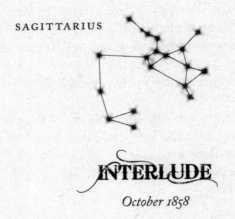

INTERLUDE

October 1858

BOYKIN FARM, SOUTH CAROLINA

BEFORE HER SISTER had come back from the Big House to tell her, Hetty knew good and well someone had run off.

"You heard the alarm?" Esther asked as she plopped down on her pallet.

"Didn't have to," Hetty grunted. The heat of flames ran along her neck, and it was all she could do to keep from tugging at her collar. "Punishments started. Don't look at me like that," she added when Esther's head whipped around. "This ain't nothing that hasn't happened before."

Esther settled, running a finger through the dirt floor of their cabin, her next words soft and filled with resentment. "It shouldn't be happening at all."

The silver collar at Hetty's neck, at the neck of every slave that could do magic, was always on Hetty's mind. There was no way it couldn't be. It was always there. Pinching as she slept, rubbing her skin raw every time she moved, and leaving her shivering when cold weather reared its head. The overseer took pleasure in grabbing it whenever she looked at him funny, jerking her head up so he could blow stale smoke in her face. The collar marked her. It told everyone that set eyes on her she was magic enough to be trouble. And the ones that didn't know that would know she was a runaway when the collar started ringing like a bell.

This was all very bad, but not as much as the Punishments.

The Punishments sent sharp pricks like needles jabbing into your neck, or made your skin burn like fire that seared until you couldn't breathe.

Hetty got enough of them that she knew how to push down the pain—to reduce it to a dull ache, one that never quite went away. But usually she had time to prepare. Just like you knew you were going to get slapped for saying the wrong thing. You do magic, you hurt for it.

But this morning was too new for her to have done anything wrong. That meant the pain she'd just felt was from someone else kicking up dust.

"Who was it? I know it was someone magic."

"Solomon ran off last night," Esther said. "I heard them talking as I left Little Miss's room. I hope he makes it to freedom."

Hetty could only grunt, not wanting to tell her sister it was his only option if he wanted to live.

Usually, Hetty worked in the weaving room, stitching and sewing the day away. To keep their mother's garden patch, she had swapped places with Nan for the change of a moon. That put Hetty working in the kitchen under Tilly's blistering tongue, but it was a worthwhile trade. Esther had been worried they'd lose the patch, which still had plants their mother had touched and cared for. This arrangement put that worry aside until the spring. But Esther was happy, and that was all Hetty cared about.

Hetty kept thinking about those plants and her sister's smile all morning as she helped prep supper. Her pleasant thoughts made a strong barrier against the rough side of Tilly's words.

The pain at her neck was harder to ignore. With each breath it got sharper and sharper, until Hetty put down the knife—before she lopped her thumb instead of the carrot.

"Stop your cloud gazing," snapped Tilly. "You might be Connie's girl, but unless you got a bit of her skill, you don't get to sit around. Shoo—get that pan into the fire. You can do that, can't you?"

Biting down on her tongue, Hetty held the pan over the flames, shifting and shaking it as needed. When she lifted it to shake it once more that fire kissed her skin. The pan slipped right out of her hands, and fear plunged her forward as she saw every terrible thing that would follow if she burned Master's breakfast. When her hands grabbed the bottom of the pan, relief was her most prominent feeling—before flames lapped against her palms.

She didn't scream.

Others did. But somehow the noise never left Hetty's throat.

She felt the pain but nothing else. Everything flowed around her. People pulling her back, the hot pan being stepped over, Tilly's horrified face. And then, finally, Esther was there to do something about Hetty's red and bubbling hands.

The wrappings hadn't been replaced twice before Hetty was summoned into the parlor the next day.

Mistress lounged on a chaise, rubbing the ears of the evil creature in her lap. The dog didn't growl at Hetty, not like it usually did. Perhaps it found something to pity with the bandages.

The room was full of beautiful things: the curtain, the rug on the floor, the pictures hanging on the wall. Painted pictures, she remembered. These folks called it *art*.

The only thing that wasn't beautiful in the room was the overseer. He was perched on the edge of one of the dining room chairs, sweat dripping off his forehead and mud clinging to his boots.

"Mister Tibbs," Mistress said. "Take a look at her hands. See those bandages? She got burned because you went above and beyond your place."

"She's collared." Tibbs stumbled over his words. "I was told—"

"Yes, I know," Mistress sliced into his words. "My husband gave you orders to punish the collared slaves. I have no problem with that. But this girl is mine. I came into this household with five slaves, and any children they bore became my property. I can't breed her since she has too much magic, but she's the best seamstress in the county. I've gained favor by lending her out to my neighbors and gotten invitations I only dreamed about. You best pray her hands heal properly, for you've cost me a great deal of money."

"But she wasn't supposed to be in the kitchen," the overseer stammered. "She switched her placement around—"

"Doesn't matter. You're still fired."

"Mistress, I—"

A wand slid into her slender, milk-pale hand, though no words came to light it with a spell. "You're fired. Leave before I have my husband forcibly remove you. And you," Mistress said to Hetty as the overseer stumbled out. "If your hands are not healed by the end of winter, you're going to the fields. Your mother was my favorite. I took good care of you on account of her. But if you can't sew, you're no use to me."

Hetty said the right things, mumbling and stumbling over words just as Mistress wanted her to, all while staring at one of the paintings on the wall. And as she did, she realized that it wasn't just art. It was something far more important.

It was a map.

"The healing salve won't work if you keep drawing in the ground with your fingers," Esther said as she tended the little plants in their mother's patch, keeping her body in the way of anyone who might look over at Hetty. "You ain't drawing star sigils?" She paused and considered something worse. "Or words?"

"No," Hetty said. Esther's shoulders had just relaxed when she added, "This is a map. I saw it in the parlor. It shows the land around here and beyond." Hetty pointed at the messy marks. "I don't remember most of it. There are lines and colors, and words. I need to get it all in my mind, tell it over and over like a story, and then I'll—"

"Run?" Esther whispered.

They talked about running after Mama died over the summer, but it was just talk and wishes.

Grown men couldn't make it past the edge of the farm without being dragged back beaten to the edge of death's door. What chance did *they* have? The few words she had learned to read wouldn't be enough. The magic she knew was of no help either, not with this collar on her neck.

Hetty turned her hands over to stare at the blood and dirt mixed on her bandages.

Papa had played the fiddle at fancy dinners in the Big House and got paid plenty by the white folks who liked his music. He was even lent out to play at nearby farms. When Mistress found out he was saving to buy them all free, she pointed her wand at his hands and broke every single bone. She must have slipped a curse in as well, because his hands wouldn't heal right no matter how many healing balms and prayers Mama wrapped around them. When he couldn't even lift a hoe without it slipping from his curled fingers, they sold him the next time a minor debt needed settling.

The day her father went away was the only time Hetty had seen tears in her mother's eyes. Not because he was gone, but because they couldn't do a thing about it.

"Yes, I'm running," Hetty said. "And I'm making a plan for both of us."

"It should be just you." Esther shook her head. "I'd just slow you down."

"I'm not leaving you here. Even when Mama was bleeding everywhere and crying out in pain, she grabbed me, looked me in the eye, and made me swear to look after you."

Esther stiffened. "Don't make up stories about things like that."

"No story," Hetty said. "It's the truth. She asked me with her dying breath. I promised I would. That's the sort of promise you don't break unless you want something bad to happen."

The moon had grown full once and then halfway again before Hetty's hands fully healed. During that time, she slipped into the parlor whenever she could to study the map, spending each night tracing it back into the dirt. She even started to make sense of the words. She kept in her mind the letters of each word and matched them with words she saw in other places. They didn't all fit, but the bits and pieces started to make something.

Nan did poorly in the weaving room during this time. Mistress complained about the poor quality of her dresses and linens, while still threatening to sell Hetty if her hands didn't heal properly. Out of spite, Hetty kept the bandages on a full week more, taking a tip from a housemaid who complained about stomach pains each month to get out of work.

Even though she waited on purpose, the day Hetty chose to take the bandages off for good was the very day Solomon was dragged back to the Big House, more dead than alive.

"How can someone be *mostly* dead?" Hetty asked later that night. Esther crept back into their cabin after hours spent healing the dying man.

"His spirit was already leaving," Esther said. "It was being pulled away by the Great Spider."

"Not *spider*," Hetty corrected, dragging her left finger to make new lines in the dirt. "The Great Weaver is the one who creates the thread of life, measures it, and cuts it when your time is done."

"Don't matter who it is." Esther turned over, her eyes reflecting the light of their candle stub. "Solomon should be dead. He's got nothing but horrors waiting for him."

"They're selling him?"

Esther shook her head. "They're going to do to him what they did to Martin."

Martin had been gone from the plantation for several years before Mistress came here as a young bride, but everyone knew what had happened to him. He was wrapped to a post with chains, and Master's father had slashed a knife in his flesh until a carving of the Cursed star sigil was left in the wood. This was the final punishment for the Collared who dared to use more magic than what they were allowed. Many with the mark died within days—the lucky ones by nightfall. Martin lived on for weeks, forcibly given water and food to prolong his suffering. Whispers in the quarters said only his body lived, that his spirit had been long since snatched. But that did little to change the end of the story.

"Solomon broke his collar and fled. They can't sell him now. Price is too poor, and when that happens ..." Esther fell silent for a moment. "I don't think he'll make it," she said. Then added hopefully, "His heart is weak, and his spirit is confused. He keeps mumbling these things that don't make a lick of sense. Like this bit: 'Ask the Aspen on the Hill and check the gourd in the little bear.'"

Hetty stopped drawing.

"What? It's just nonsense," Esther said.

"No, it's not."

Sketched in the ground before them was not the outline of the county. It was a world bigger than Hetty could ever imagine.

"Aspen Hill." Hetty pointed to a space where she had only attempted to draw out the letters. While in the dirt it was nothing, she saw the words as they appeared on the map. "That's a place near here. What else did he say?"

"Lots of things." Esther drew back. "Funny names and such. It's a song of a confused spirit."

"It's a song, but he's not confused. Tell me the rest."

Esther still frowned, but she repeated the bits and pieces she remembered. Her confusion turned to wonder as Hetty pointed to each place on the map.

"It's a song that tells us the way to leave. It's probably how he left in the first place. This tells us how to stay away from the traps and safeguards!"

"It's not a good one."

Hetty's excitement faded. "No, it ain't."

Still, Hetty studied the map far longer than usual before she swept it away.

Solomon wasn't made an example in the end. He died a few days later, writhing in pain from a sickness Esther claimed was too far gone to be cured with any herbal remedy.

No one questioned Esther too hard about that truth.

As Solomon died, he screamed out curses and a jumble of words at such a frightful pitch, Master actually had Mistress and Little Miss sent away so the house could be checked for any evil curses cast with a dying man's last breaths.

"Not sure how they know what to find," Hetty said as she sewed up the tears in Esther's good dress. "White folks don't understand a thing about our magic."

"Both the stars and the herbs," Esther added with a laugh as she wound string around a bundle of herbs.

"The skies and rivers, and rain and sunlight," Hetty recited.

"The wind and soil, the storms and the calm," they said together, repeating the words their mother had sung to them. "The magic is the world and it moves through us. There are words and rhyme and—"

Hetty's words cut off with a cry as the collar turned iron hot against her skin.

"What's wrong?" Esther crouched next to her. "You didn't do any magic!"

"Something else," Hetty spat. "*Words* have magic!"

"Hetty," Esther said, and what else Esther had to say was lost as the pain reached the point where Hetty couldn't breathe. This was just like what happened in the kitchen—but to make matters worse, now it was happening in front of Esther. Esther had never seen her like this. Never saw her crouched over in pain and unable to do more than let it run over her like rain. Hetty had always tried to keep this from her sister, to protect her like Mama had made her swear to. She was failing. Failing the only thing she could do in this terribly cruel world.

"*Stop,*" Hetty said, as she grasped at the collar, pulling uselessly against it, her sewing needle prickling against her skin. "Stop!"

Hetty kept pulling and pulling, and then the pain was gone.

The metal cooled and Hetty's hands fell away . . . and so did the silver collar.

It fell into the dirt. Perfect twin halves spotted with blood.

If it had been a snake, they couldn't have moved away faster.

"What did you do?" Esther whispered. "Was that magic?"

"Don't know." Hetty prodded the closest half to her with her sewing needle. It didn't spark. No bells rang. "Don't care. Did it glow when it came off?"

Esther shook her head.

"Then it's dead. We have time. They can't use it to follow us."

Esther swallowed hard, but her voice didn't tremble. "Where?"

"North." Hetty clawed at the packed dirt. "We follow the stars."

"That's not a place," Esther said rather seriously. "That's a direction."

Hetty almost laughed. She could always count on her little sister to find humor in the most terrible of times.

"It's not. I don't know where I want to go. I just know we can't stay here."

"I know a place," Esther said. "I heard it healing some sick folks in the next farm over. They were talking bad about it, so that means it's a good place for people like us."

"Where's that?"

"Philadelphia."

"I don't know where that is," Hetty said as she buried the collar. "But let's find out."

3

At first, Hetty had ignored the whispers around the lone attic window. The trio of young women situated there always managed to find an excuse to stop the work on their dresses, especially on late Saturday afternoons. But the longer they lingered, the more curious she became.

The window overlooked an alley, where passersby—unaware they were being watched—would engage in all manner of activities. Innocent actions attracted little attention. A bit of kissing between a couple half hidden in the shadows brought about giggles. But whispers came around only when there was something interesting sitting out there for some time. Usually a man, whose many attributes were remarked and sighed over.

As the whispers continued, Hetty kept her eyes focused on her stitches. She had no time to spare. Not if she planned to arrive at the telegram office before it closed for the evening. Distractions from her fellow dressmakers would only delay that task.

But when she walked across the room to pick up some trim, Hetty happened to pass by the window and let her eyes glide toward the glass, and she stopped right behind the group.

Benjy sat in the short alleyway next to the upholsterers. He must have been watching for her, since she had peered for only a few moments before he waved.

The trio of busybodies looked at each other and then toward Hetty, astonishment showing on their faces.

"How do you know a fellow like that?" Lily asked.

"I married him," Hetty said.

"You're married to the blacksmith on South Street?" Julianna asked.

"You didn't know he was married?" Hetty presented this question on a knife's edge, with a friendly smile that stopped Julianna and Margo's whispering in its tracks.

"Not to you," Lily said rather carelessly. "If I was married to a fellow like him, I'd be too busy raising babies to work anywhere."

"Sorry to disappoint you." Hetty glanced once more at Benjy. Content to know he had been seen, he turned his attention toward the clouds, deep in thought.

She could see why the trio had lingered at the window. They were flies lured into his web, caught up in his attempts at charm. Though to be honest, Benjy didn't have to exert himself for this lot. Handsome by most standards, no visible scars to upset a dark brown complexion, and a bearing that held confidence and pride, with little arrogance. Hetty was accustomed to him, after all these years. It was hard to be impressed when she still remembered the scamp of a boy who had yet to grow into hands, ears, and the unwieldy and unfamiliar words that tumbled out his mouth.

As nice as it was to see him, Hetty couldn't help but be annoyed. The dress shop was not on the way home from the forge. He didn't normally just leave early to see her. This meant trouble. Maybe not for her, but trouble enough to keep her from sending a telegram like planned.

"What are you doing here?" Hetty greeted him when she finally escaped the shop, her sewing kit swinging from her hand.

"Came to ask a favor," her husband said. "But it will disrupt your plans to badger that woman making dodgy potions."

"Maybe," she said, eagerly staking a claim to that excuse. "But that can wait. I know you wouldn't come without a reason."

"That is true." He didn't quite meet her eyes. "I need help breaking in to Moya Prison."

Hetty's smile fell off her face.

There went all her plans.

Breaking in to the prison wasn't merely sneaking Benjy inside, but also helping make sure he could leave without stirring any suspicions.

They did their best to avoid the police. Thieves, liars, and other miscreants they handled on their own. But murderers were left bound and unconscious on the police station doorstep, with carefully worded notes. Even then they took care not to let anything be traced back to them.

"This about those kidnappers?" Hetty asked.

Benjy nodded. "We need answers about those men, to understand why that girl and the others were snatched. I should have asked before I dropped them off like Christmas presents at the station. But it was more important to take that girl home."

"They weren't exactly willing to talk last night," Hetty observed. "That might not have changed after a day behind bars."

"I'm sure," Benjy said with a most unpleasant smile, "I can loosen their tongues."

Getting Benjy inside Moya was no trouble.

On the cusp of an evening to cap a very fine spring day, the police at the station were distracted. Just distracted enough that Hetty needed only a simple glamour. One that would muffle sound and make Benjy an uninteresting sight. She sewed those into his clothes, whipping her needle quickly along the cuffs of sleeves as if a button had fallen off.

As he slipped toward the buildings, Hetty drew Libra against the brick wall. It flared gold. The scales tilted from side to side, dampening the jail's magic nullifier so Benjy's entry raised no alarms.

The last bit of magic she cast took the form of a crow. She left the star sigil in its raw form so the star-speckled bird could perch on top of the building. If there was trouble, it would provide Benjy some cover. It would also give her a warning.

Settled a block away on some upturned boxes, Hetty placed her sewing kit on her lap and rifled through it. Instead of mending work, she pulled out a bundle of papers.

The small stack held fragments of news regarding her sister. Heavily creased and folded, some of the papers were illegible, even the ones Hetty had written herself. They were newspaper clippings, telegrams, and ticket stubs. They were years filled with dashed hopes, wishes, and last chances. And they all led nowhere. Yet these papers were all Hetty had of her lost sibling.

The night she had broken her collar, she had escaped with Esther, using the map and song she'd memorized. It got them far. It got them far enough that it seemed like they would make it.

Then their luck ran out. Dogs caught their scent. They crossed paths with their pursuers. When all their troubles came thundering after them armed with wands and guns alike, a roaring river blocked their path.

Then Esther had pushed her into the river.

That's all Hetty knew for certain. Her memory of the rest had been shared with too many dreams in the years since. Dreams and accompanying nightmares that whispered the worst of her fears.

Plucking out the note she received from a woman in Colorado who owed them a favor, Hetty copied the address. She took great care forming the words of her message, keeping her request simple and short and unburdened with the weight of her hopes.

Hetty was nearly finished when the crow flew back to her side.

She reached to stroke its head, and it melted into a puddle of starlight.

Benjy emerged moments later just as Hetty slipped the papers out of sight.

"What did you find out?"

"Enough. A farmer was looking for hands to help and didn't question where the hands came from. The trio saw an opportunity to make quick money. It worked rather well in Maryland and Virginia. This was their only attempt up here."

"Only attempt?" Hetty asked.

"Yes." A rather unpleasant grin filled his features, glittering with a sliver of the malice the unlucky men must have seen. "I made sure of it."

"Good," Hetty grunted, pleased at the neatness of his efforts.

"Shall we head home?" Benjy asked. "Or do you have another errand? If you want me to stand there glowering, I'm up to the task."

Hetty was sure he was, and she almost wished she could claim such an errand. It was a good excuse, and one that needed little explanation. But instead of a vial of dodgy potion, she had only the telegram tucked away in her sewing kit. Telling him about that was not an option. Especially as she shouldn't even have the telegram with her in the first place.

Things were so chaotic in the South that Hetty had stopped traveling to look for Esther. The roads that hadn't been blown up, cursed, or left in shambles were guarded by raiders of the nastiest disposition. Papers spoke boldly of the federal forces helping to rebuild the South. But more trustworthy reports suggested that the New South under construction seemed to be the old one, just remade with a different pattern.

With that avenue closed, Hetty turned to others. She worked with the Freedmen's Bureau at first. They had promised assistance in tracking down family members, but their efforts — strained by lack of funds, resources, and belligerent forces—made it hard to deliver results. In time, she relied on her own devices, sending letters and telegrams and even placing newspaper advertisements. Throughout the years all those efforts went nowhere.

Last summer, Hetty had sent out eight letters to eight places around the country that Benjy felt was the best place to look. All but one letter had returned.

Usually this was not noteworthy, but this time Benjy had made Hetty promise that she would not send for any more information until the last letter returned.

She agreed without much care at the time. It had been late September and she was certain the letter would arrive soon.

It never did.

Over time the lost letter shuffled into the corner of her mind. In the past winter their lives had been disrupted both by cases and by antics from their friends. With so much excitement going on, it took the idle chatter from the men crowding Darlene's apartment last night to bring the lost letter back to her attention. Now Hetty couldn't let it rest until she did something.

Even if it meant breaking a promise.

"No," Hetty finally said, giving him an answer. "It can wait."

Sunday passed quietly. There was church, a few short visits with their friends, and the long walk they took simply because they had time to fill. Hetty knew where the woman with the dodgy potions lived, but she hoped to find the woman out in the streets. However, there were familiar faces selling magic and other charms, but not the face she was looking for.

As evening slipped away into night, they returned home to the boardinghouse and settled in their room.

While Benjy was keen to discuss more about the kidnappers and similar crimes, Hetty sorted and spread the mending on the table, giving only absent answers.

Realizing he wasn't going to get much conversation out of her, Benjy lay on top of their bed and disappeared behind a book.

Just as Hetty had planned.

New books were rare and precious things in their little room. Even when they were stories he read before, once he picked up a book it often took breaking a glass to get his attention.

Once she was certain any question she would ask would be met with a grunt, Hetty put aside her mending and withdrew her telegram. She filled out the rest and then checked for errors. She tried to keep it simple. Unlike most of the people they met through their travels, this contact had scant knowledge of Hetty's sister, and little motive to help.

"What are you doing?"

Hetty dropped the mending over the papers, just as Benjy drew near the table. "Just seeing what I need to work on before I go to bed." Hetty picked up the sleeve of a worn shirt and pretended to examine invisible tears.

Benjy fell into the other chair. His fingers rapped against the cover of his book, and the air around him grew pensive.

"You were pulling this mending out a while ago and it looks like you haven't even touched a stitch."

"Only," Hetty said, grabbing the first thing that came to mind, "because there are no pins."

Benjy turned to the far wall.

Depicting the city and surrounding areas, the map hung there was prickled with pinholes. Benjy had put the map up after a rather interesting case with some barbershops. Since then, the map became the best way to visualize cases. Using Hetty's old sewing pins with colored strings looped at the ends, they marked out the places where information had been found. Small cases and incidents were often clustered in pockets on the map, making a patchwork of color.

"I don't see what the problem is."

"You used my good sewing pins." Hetty pounced on the subject, her ready complaint not entirely faked. "You're supposed to use the old ones I put aside. They're in separate boxes and you still forget."

"I didn't." Benjy held his hand over the mending, catching her eyes with his. "If you were that upset about them, you would have said something before. You're trying to distract me."

"What I'm trying to do is explain—"

Hetty was saved from figuring out how that sentence would end by a knock on their door. A knock that was as fast and erratic as a runaway rabbit.

"Someone's come to call." Benjy dramatically lifted his hand away. "How lucky for you."

"Yes." Hetty took the mending and scooped it up so she picked up the telegram as well. "Very lucky."

Benjy answered the door and Hetty scarcely paid attention to the conversation. The knock, the lateness of the hour, even the frantic fear in the man's voice were all too familiar to her. People who came this late weren't coming about missing trinkets or stolen treasures. They came about the dead.

"Who died?" Hetty asked, as Benjy grabbed their lantern from atop the wardrobe.

"A drunk, in an alley not far from here." Benjy tapped Orion onto the metal lid. The sigil flashed red and light bloomed inside the lantern. "The man at the door says the pump near his building was broken so he went to the closest one to get some water. That's when he stumbled across the body. I told him to go on ahead since I know the place he described. You can stay here. Sounds like the usual sort of thing."

"I still want to see." Hetty reached over to the nightstand, running her fingers across an assortment of cotton bands embroidered with star sigils. She sifted through them before selecting one trimmed with ribbons to tie around her neck. "You're not as observant as you think you are."

The man, Alain, led Hetty and Benjy toward an alleyway that ran along the rougher edges of the ward, though only a few streets kept it apart from more respectable homes and businesses.

When they neared the alley, Alain Browne stopped at its mouth.

"There." Alain's hand trembled as he pointed. "That's where I found him."

With the lantern held before him, Benjy led the way. A mixture of old cigars, booze, and sweat that not even the rain could wash away rose up and nearly overwhelmed Hetty before it all faded into the background. Tiny claws scurried as the lantern light bounced off bricks and crates. In the middle of all this was the body.

Benjy whistled a few notes under his breath before handing the lantern to Hetty.

Not expecting it, the lantern slipped in her hands and light scattered before she had a chance to correct her grip. By the time she managed to do so Benjy was already taking measured steps around the body, mumbling disjointed words under his breath.

She'd never understood why he always found the bodies so interesting. The body only held the secret to a person's death. The surroundings were what told you how it might have happened.

Hetty swung the lantern around and a beam of light passed over Alain. He stood there, his arms wrapped around himself despite the spring night hardly holding a chill.

Up ahead, past Benjy and the dead man, was the water pump, light glinting against the dull metal. All around her was garbage —discarded furniture, matted papers, broken glass shoved hastily in corners, and much more, lost in the shadows at their feet. Not the sort of place one lingered. Not even if you spent all your time staring into the bottom of a bottle.

However, the dead man couldn't have been a drunk.

If he had been, they would have found him slumped against the wall. Instead, he lay sprawled on the ground like a bag of hay tossed off a wagon.

No wonder Alain had stumbled across the dead man. Anyone crossing through here would have found the body. There wasn't a single way to avoid it no matter which entrance to the alley was taken.

"He was left here to be found," Hetty said as she stepped deeper into the alley. "This was planned."

"Murdered," Benjy grunted as he kept up his slow pacing. "This might take longer than I thought."

Hetty lowered the lantern and the motion reflected light off the body. "What was that?"

"It looks like a bottle," Benjy said. "Hard to tell in this poor light."

"Let me brighten it."

Hetty sketched the Aries sigil on the side of the lantern, the magic trailing from her fingers as she drew the long lines and tapped dots onto a single panel. The star sigil burned in the metal until the light brightened and a stream of stars flowed to the ground.

Splotches of garbled spells swirled by her feet, creating a chaotic mosaic of bright colors muddied together in places where the mixed magic was the greatest.

Hetty didn't see any traces of magic on the body. Just a man in an ill-fitting suit of clothes so threadbare, the patches required patches. He lay in an unnatural supine pose, with his fingers clenched around an empty liquor bottle.

Her gaze moved upward. Gashes split the dead man's face with ribbons of rust. Eyes that would stare out at nothing for the rest of time. Yet there was something familiar about it.

She brought the lantern closer and then saw a face she would have been happy never to see again.

"That's Charlie!" Hetty dropped the lantern. "Stars above, someone's killed him!"

"Charlie?" Benjy echoed. He turned Hetty toward him, his fingers pressing into her shoulders. "That's not Charlie!"

"Look closer."

Benjy let go of her and knelt. He picked up the lantern and waved it over the body. The light brightened once more, intensifying to the strength of a sunny day. Then it faded and metal met the ground once more.

"Stars, it *is* Charlie." Benjy's voice cracked on the edge of the name. "Why didn't I notice that first?"

When Charlie had approached her the night before with fear in his eyes, had he sensed this death coming? Or was it something else? Something that surprised him just moments before he took his last breath?

"You know Charlie?" Alain's tentative voice crept in, welcome and unwanted at the same time.

Hetty's laugh squeezed itself out, brittle in the night air. "Who doesn't know Charlie Richardson in this town? Why didn't you say who it was?"

"He was my landlord. Now he's dead. Who he was doesn't matter anymore."

Benjy's head turned with such speed, the younger man jumped backwards into the grimy wall. "That's where you're wrong. Men like Charlie Richardson don't just disappear when they die."

Hetty bent to pick up the lantern but froze as the beams of light revealed something else along Charlie's chest. Something worse than the sickening mess made of his face.

"Benjy." Hetty tried to keep her voice steady, but it trembled despite her best efforts. "Tell me you see this too."

A star sigil was carved into Charlie's chest. The vertices were coin-size holes and the lines that connected them were as thick as cords, forming a man wrestling with an unruly snake. Any sigil seared into flesh would have been terrible, but this was Ophiuchus—the Serpent Bearer—and the one star sigil so terrible Hetty never used it.

"The cursed sigil," Alain wailed from behind them. Pressed against the wall, it was hard to say if a single noise would have him sprinting off into the night or collapsing in a dead faint. "I touched him. I was near him. I'm going to die, aren't I?"

"There's no curse," Benjy said, though he brushed his hands against his shirt as if to brush the stain away. "Other wounds caused his death. Oliver should be able to tell which one." He paused then, his gaze moving along the alley for any more signs of trouble. "We shouldn't linger here. Whoever did this might come back."

"Go. I'll be right behind you after I take care of the residue."

Hetty waited for a protest to pass his lips. While they took equal share in their messy and sometimes dangerous work, Benjy rarely suggested parting ways. When Hetty suggested it, they always wasted time arguing until someone's hand was forced.

One look into his eyes and she knew tonight there would be no argument.

Magical residue had helped them find murderers many times before, but if they weren't careful to erase their own, it could lead a murderer straight to them.

Benjy hoisted Charlie's body into his arms and called for Alain to follow.

"Make sure," Benjy added, "to come straight to Oliver's. I don't want to light up the city looking for you."

4

Hᴇᴛᴛʏ ʀᴀɪsᴇᴅ ᴀ ʜᴀɴᴅ to the band of fabric at her neck, tracing a finger along the raised stitches of the star sigils hidden among the floral flourishes. At her touch, the sigils unbound themselves from the fabric, flowing into the form of a woman.

Her eyes were the black of the night sky, and twinkling blue composed her skin, her long braided hair, and the pouches dangling from her waist. At her feet, two hunting dogs strained against their leashes.

Hetty nodded at the Herdsman, and the woman made of stars released the dogs. The beasts ran along the alley. They bounced off walls and stone, erasing all traces of the lingering spells as they made contact. What they didn't touch the Herdsman cleared away with the sweep of her staff.

In any other situation, Hetty would have directed the Herdsman to define the boundaries of the residue. Then slowly she would slice, crumple, smash, and otherwise destroy the traces remaining of the magic she and Benjy had performed. In alleys such as this, all sorts of enchantments littered the ground. Erasing them all would be as telling as patching a lace dress, but there was no time for the fine work required. This drastic measure was a necessity, especially after what she had just seen.

The Serpent Bearer.

Something like bony fingers glided along her arms.

Benjy might not believe in cursed sigils, but Hetty had seen that sigil with her own eyes many times before, and each time it had been in close quarters with death.

This time would be no different—if they weren't careful.

With a flick of her hand, Hetty dissipated the spells and a burst of light flooded the alley.

That was a bit dramatic, but it would also blind anyone skulking around.

There was no one about, however. No one rubbing their eyes frantically at the alley's opening. No one lingering on the street corner with a knife. No one following her along the street as she hurried as quietly as she could to Oliver's.

Hetty took twists and turns, roundabouts when she could, and even jumped a fence that wouldn't tangle her skirts. The only time she looked away from the patch of street in front of her was to look upward at the glittering stars to regain her bearings. The pinpricks of light were dimmer in the city, but they gave her guidance all the same.

Only when Hetty caught sight of the abandoned cigar shop that stood on the corner of Oliver's street did she breathe easily.

Opening the unlocked door and entering, she was greeted by cutlery and dishes left in piles on every available surface in the kitchen. Trousers hung from the ceiling, and one of the lamps flickered like a twitching eye, drawing moths that fluttered inside. Though she wasn't sure which was the worse sight: a pair of mud-caked shoes sitting on a counter, or the *Eventide Observer* serving as a tablecloth for a bowl of congealed stew.

Hetty remembered a time when this place didn't look like a

hurricane blew in and parked itself in place for a few days. But that was a time before Thomas left to open a school in Texas for the newly freed.

Thomas left at the top of last fall, and everything about his leaving was a surprise. He wasn't a teacher, having only recently learned to read. His only talent in carpentry was handing tools to Benjy, and not always the right ones. The day before he told them about Texas, he was making plans to open up a barbershop. And most importantly, Oliver did not go with him.

Thomas and Oliver had been an inseparable pair ever since Hetty matched them up at her wedding. In the years since, they had been a rather steady source of comfort and good sense in their circle of friends. When Hetty first learned of Texas, she assumed they would both be leaving. However, when Thomas carried his bags onto a train headed south, Oliver hadn't even come to the station to say goodbye.

In fact, Oliver, who freely complained about the slightest upset, had yet to acknowledge Thomas's departure in any manner. Not by speaking his name, or even cleaning the mess that engulfed the house.

The mess that thankfully hadn't drifted into his work.

Oliver worked as an embalmer, which made him the perfect person to take in victims of murder and other violence. He always fussed about it, but he never turned them away. Oliver even put on funerals for people who would get pauper's graves otherwise. Although, that only started because of a few misunderstandings and Hetty spinning a tale about Oliver's gladly taking on the work.

In the cellar, Benjy peered down at the table with Charlie's remains.

With a candle floating nearby, it was easier to see the exhaustion that weighed down Benjy's broad shoulders. A shadow of grief touched his eyes, and perhaps a touch of guilt.

On the opposite side of the table, Oliver sat on a stool, stirring a spoon into a cup of something that was probably too strong to be considered tea. Although the hour was late, he hadn't changed out of his stained and wrinkled clothes.

But then again, these days he rarely made it to bed at a reasonable hour.

"I'm sure you're right about that." Oliver tugged at his beard. "I'm just more concerned that whoever killed him might find their merry way to my home."

"No need to worry." Hetty placed the lantern on the bottom-most stair. "I took care of it."

"As I told you she would," Benjy said, giving her a strained smile. "Hetty is true as the North Star."

Oliver huffed as he shoved his glasses up his nose. "You mean your wife insisted and you didn't argue for a change."

"There wasn't time." Hetty approached the table. "Once we saw this."

Oliver waved a hand over the wounds that the brighter lights only made more grotesque. "You mean this carving on Charlie's chest?"

"You've heard about the cursed sigil, haven't you?"

"It's hardly a curse," Oliver replied, though he absently rapped his knuckles on the table. "Nat Turner used it in his uprising. It was the only sigil he knew, and he burned it into land and flesh alike. What makes it a curse comes from the part of the tale where white folks get their revenge. They don't know a whit about our magic, or even how the sigils work, but they know enough to memorize that one."

"And use it to bring destruction," Hetty said.

"Do you actually think it's a curse?" Oliver's smile was bitter and brittle and made him appear even older than what he was. "I can't believe Benjy hasn't changed your mind."

Hetty stepped around the table and drew the Leo sigil in the air. A star-speckled lion lunged at Charlie's body, only to meet a wall of silver light head on. It vanished on impact.

"I see you set boundary protections." Hetty found the sigil Oliver had drawn on the table. Pisces pulsed against the wood. "Yet you say you aren't worried about a curse?"

"These are just the usual protections," Oliver blustered, nearly sloshing his drink onto his clothes. "I had to set them up after the last man you brought me nearly burned my house down."

"We learned to check for latent magic." Hetty met his gaze and only saw her scowling reflection in his glasses. "We wouldn't have brought him here if it wasn't safe. You don't need the boundary."

"I most certainly do." Oliver stood, using what little height he had over her to his benefit. "I need to find out how he died. Given the circumstances, I wish to be a bit cautious. Or maybe I won't be here to collect dead bodies the next time you come around."

This bit was directed over her head at Benjy. Hetty snapped her fingers to bring Oliver's eyes back down to her. "You don't need protections. I already know how he died."

"You do?" Benjy asked. "You didn't get that close to the body."

"I didn't. But you're covered in blood. It's hardly a big mystery."

Benjy looked down at his shirt and stared a bit too long at the dark splatters across his chest and arms. The location as well as the shape had given Hetty pause when she first noted them, but hardly enough to worry. She was more surprised he hadn't noticed. Benjy was usually three steps ahead of her. Was Charlie's death that shocking that he could have missed such an obvious thing? Or was the failing on her part? Now that the shock had passed, she found herself annoyed by the mess that remained. In some ways, it felt like Charlie's last laugh.

"This happened when I carried Charlie here," Benjy murmured.

"That can only mean one thing." Oliver put his mug aside

and rubbed his hand across the sigil drawn onto the table. The boundary faded, and Oliver reached to turn Charlie over.

The light revealed a large dark spot between Charlie's shoulder blades. "He was stabbed in the back."

"He wasn't wearing these clothes when he was killed. Yet he bled again."

"It might not be blood," Oliver said. With a jerk of Oliver's hand, Charlie flipped back onto his back with a small thump. "It could be the sigil. Perhaps you might want to try a purification spell on yourself. It could be poison."

"I doubt that's the case." Benjy touched the splotches on his shirt. "It's trouble — not curses — that seems to follow Charlie."

"It certainly does." Oliver's shoulders sank. "What are we going to do about him? Surely you're not going to leave him with the police?"

"No," Hetty interjected. "Not with that mark on him. It'll cause a panic."

Oliver looked to Benjy.

"It will," was Benjy's simple reply. "I don't want to draw attention."

"I can't see how you'll avoid that," Oliver said. "This is Charlie Richardson, not some old man you found in a park missing his hands. People will notice he hasn't been seen around town for several days. You can't keep this quiet."

"This was never going to be quiet." Benjy shook his head. "Someone killed Charlie with great deliberation, and we need to find out why."

"Then he needs a funeral," Oliver said.

"Are you offering to put together services?"

"It will give me a reason to keep him here longer, to discover all I can."

"I think you're both galloping after a star that hasn't fallen yet," Hetty interjected. "Marianne needs to be told about Charlie. I'm certain she'll have a few opinions about you handling the funeral, especially if she has no say in the matter."

"That's right." Benjy nodded. "She needs to be told. I'm glad you agreed to do it, Hetty."

"Me?" Hetty crossed her arms over her chest. "I never said anything about that!"

"Who else would do the honor? You're so much better with words. Marianne will appreciate hearing the news from you."

Marianne would not, for a variety of reasons, but Benjy always said the wrong thing when talking to mourners—and Oliver was even worse.

"Should I tell her about the sigil carved in his chest?" Hetty asked as Oliver pulled a sheet over Charlie. The light of a preservation charm shone as fabric touched skin. "She might know something."

"I wouldn't." Benjy shook his head. "I want to keep that bit quiet. I don't believe in curses, but if we're going to find out who did this, we don't need to make a monster out of a mere mortal."

"Too late," Hetty said. "Only a monster could have done this."

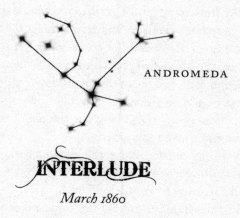

ANDROMEDA

INTERLUDE

March 1860

ROCK CREEK FARM, NORTH CAROLINA

SHUT UP IN THE COFFIN, Hetty couldn't do much more than lie there, listening to the roll of wagon wheels against the packed earth. Hours in darkness taught her every creak the wagon made as it bounced along, yet she still waited for the moment when the bumping, rolling, and creaking would cease and the next sound she'd hear would be her last. Although she paid the undertaker enough money to trust him, she remained as jumpy as a frog caught on dry land. Despite the spells she knew and even the knife shoved in her boot, if the night patrol opened the lid she would die in this coffin—and that was if she was lucky.

If she wasn't, well, she was certainly never going to see her sister again.

Planning a route that would take her to the tobacco fields of North Carolina was hardly any trouble. As luck would have it, the older couple who gave her a bed in their attic were station masters. Their home was not just a hub for the Vigilance Society, but the point at which all communications in and out of Philadelphia went through. After Hetty learned how to read, it was easy to find the time to sift through the missives, learning names and important codes, as well as whom to contact for her journey. The rest was simple. She saved her coins, gathered supplies in secret, listened to the stories of the conductors whenever they passed through, and sent a series of messages down south. Once she got a response regarding the whereabouts of her sister, Hetty set off.

And now here she was, living out the plan she made.

The wagon slowed to a stop.

Hetty heard creaks along the wagon bed, along with soft mumbling. Only when she heard the rhythmic taps on the lid did her hand slip away from the knife at her side.

"End of the line," grumbled the undertaker as he opened the coffin lid. He chewed on a stick, eyes darting around as Hetty sat up. The lantern dangling on the wagon swayed, making shadows jump along his bearded face. It wasn't a kind face, and the darkness did little to soften his features. But he took her aboard without a word.

Hetty lifted her head toward the stars dancing over her head, breathing in and out slowly.

"Do you need any more money?"

"Your companion took care of that," the undertaker said. "Shoed my horses before we left. If I had the means, I would take him on. Best work I ever seen, even for a Negro."

Hetty climbed out the coffin, ignoring the pinpricks in her feet and calves as she lurched toward the other one on the wagon. She knocked on the lid just once before yanking it open.

"Get up," Hetty said, "or we'll be late."

Benjy yawned, slowly rising to a sitting position. "Aren't we there already?"

"On the outskirts," the white man said. "It's as far as I can go. Hurry now. I need to be on my way."

Hetty jumped off the wagon and Benjy followed a breath later, his bag of tools jingling behind him.

The undertaker departed with his empty caskets, the light on his wagon shrinking down the road until shadows swallowed him up.

Hetty and Benjy likewise vanished, leaving the road for the protective embrace of the woods.

Above their heads, the stars blinked in and out of sight depending on the stretch of the branches. The woods went on for several miles according to Old Annie, and to avoid getting lost they needed to find a tree with a dipper gouged into its bark. From this tree they would go east, drawing near to the quarters where they would meet their contact. Any other direction would put them off the path and into danger.

Hetty walked to each tree, rubbing her hands along the bark, going up, down, and around as her fingers sought the carving.

Nearby, Benjy pressed his hand against a tree but didn't circle it like Hetty. He stayed still, and it was hard to tell if he was pushing it or letting it support him.

"I don't like this," Benjy murmured. "Danger catches up when you stand still."

"This is the plan." Hetty absently touched her neck. The bumpy, scarred skin remained even after a year of applying healing salve to it. "The contact gave us a spot to meet, and we'll be there at the right time."

"If he's not there? Do you have a plan for that?"

Hetty stayed quiet, moving to the next tree.

After a few moments, Benjy's voice came from behind her.

"You don't have a plan." His voice was flat, but there was no accusation in there, nor surprise. "Did you ever have one?"

This stung. Not because it wasn't true. She had a plan, but he'd ruined it.

Benjy was never supposed to come.

The blacksmith's apprentice followed her out of Philadelphia because she'd stolen a broken collar from the forge. He claimed he would be blamed for the theft. If theft was his concern, Benjy would have returned to Philadelphia once the collar was in his hands a long time ago. Instead, he traveled with her like a grim disapproving shadow, his mere presence requiring her to make hasty arrangements with contacts who weren't expecting two people.

The further they traveled it was clear she wasn't going to get rid of him.

"You didn't have to come." Hetty's nails dug into her palm. "You chose to not turn back. Why come all this way? You didn't even know my name when you set off."

"I knew you were doing something I didn't have the courage to do."

This was not the answer Hetty had expected. Her surprise left a pause long enough for him to barrel on in a rush of words.

"I left people behind too," Benjy continued. "Not blood kin like you, but we were as close as that near the end. I was the only one who made it. I thought that to honor that sacrifice I needed to stay safe and free. I was a coward to think that was the only thing I could do."

"I'm not brave." Hetty shook her head. "I'm scared."

"You should be," Benjy said. "It would be dangerous if you weren't."

She grunted, acknowledging his words, before she returned to her search. After a few moments more of running fingers along rough bark, Benjy called out to her.

"Here." Benjy patted the tree. "This one has the mark. Where do we go next?"

Hetty put her hand on the dipper mark and then looked up at the sky. The stars aligned, and her fears faded as she saw the path made from the stars. "We go east."

• • •

East they went, conversation falling by the wayside as they drew near the plantation. The stars guided them around traps left by overseers in the woods—from simple snares such as bells strung to the branches of trees, to complex spells hidden under fallen leaves. Eventually the stars led them to a man sitting in a pool of moonlight, whittling a piece of wood into the shape of a bird.

Hetty tugged at Benjy's arm, and Benjy whistled out a bird's song like their contact had instructed them to do. The man's knife stilled, and he pitched his voice toward the shadows.

"Just like Old Annie said," the man said rather cheerfully. "You must be the conductors."

"You're the one we're supposed to meet?" Hetty asked.

"Yes." the man beckoned them forward in the light. "You're in luck—there's quite a to-do up at the Big House tonight."

"A party?"

"Much better than that. The young miss wants to elope with her fellow . . . and he's Irish. Missus fainted dead away."

The man led them to the quarters. The cabins were arranged in neat rows like the tobacco their occupants picked, but that was the only neat thing about them. The cabins were tightly packed and squat structures, some with the look of rotting wood. Firelight flickered in a few windows, while others were dark as the night. Hetty and Benjy followed the man past most of the cabins until he entered one at the very end of a row. Hetty took a deep breath, exhaling slowly, before slipping inside.

A dying fire illuminated the cabin, casting light and shadows unevenly around the room. As Hetty's eyes adjusted, she saw a living space that had much in common with the one she left behind in South Carolina. The same walls—so close together you need only to stretch out your arms to touch both sides at once. The only difference was this one had wooden floors instead of packed dirt.

The man that led them there moved towards the fire, where

a gray-haired woman sat darning a shirt. The man bent over to speak, and the woman's hands stilled.

Benjy placed himself by the doorway, half in the room and half out the door. Hetty ignored his watchful gaze, just as she ignored the hurried whispered conversation across the room.

Her attention went to the young girl sitting on a pallet with a bundle clutched to her chest. Her face remained in shadow until she looked up at Hetty.

The age was right, as were the delicate features that held a certain sweetness and charm. Taken together, however, none of it was right.

"This girl isn't Esther," Hetty said, staring into the face of a stranger.

"Esther was here until a moon ago," the older woman said. She carefully placed her mending aside as she stood. "She was sold with a few others to settle a debt."

"To who?"

"I don't know. But far from here," the man said. "The buyers weren't local."

Hetty almost stopped breathing.

She had traveled all this way and was no closer to seeing Esther.

"That means," Hetty rasped as the floorboards lurched and shifted under her feet, "we have to go."

"You'll still take Poppy with you? Won't you?" The older woman's voice cracked in the air. "I'm sorry she isn't the girl you're looking for," she said, without a trace of sympathy gracing her deeply lined face. "She can't stay here. You *must* take her."

Hetty looked back down at the girl, who was clutching the bag even tighter now. She wore no collar around her neck. She likely didn't know magic, or if she did, not enough to be punished for it. She was pretty, delicate, and young, and Hetty suddenly understood why the news about Esther not being here anymore didn't reach her ears.

"You're about to be sold, aren't you?" Hetty asked, although it was hardly a question. "To the breeding farms?"

Poppy nodded. "Buyer will be here in a few days. You coming here is a blessing."

"It's just luck," Hetty said, looking away from those bright, hopeful eyes. "Stand. You're coming with us. Your mother, too."

"I'm not her mother," the woman said quickly. "I just want her safe."

"She'll be safer if you come along," Hetty said quite reasonably. "To look after her."

"In that case, mind if I come along too?" the man drawled. "I hate to be left out."

Hetty glanced over at Benjy from his position at the door, waiting for the protests he would surely make.

They had planned to take only one person back with them. This scenario had never entered her mind at all. A girl that was not her sister and two grown adults. Not to mention an eager buyer arriving in a matter of days who would give chase. Surely Benjy would protest this.

Yet when Hetty found Benjy's eyes, she saw no complaints, only a steady gaze eagerly awaiting her next move.

Leave them, take them—no matter her choice, he would support her.

If these people were willing to run, how could she refuse to help them? How could she refuse anyone with the courage to walk down this dark and twisting road?

"Just be ready to listen," Hetty said with a confidence she didn't feel. "That's the rule. Listen to me and keep up, because otherwise we'll leave you behind. Do you understand . . . ?"

"Charlie," the man said, a slow grin filling his features. "Name's Charlie Richardson. Or at least that's what I plan to call myself once I'm free."

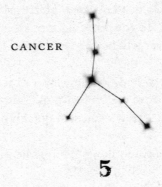

CANCER

5

Unable to sleep without disturbing dreams, Hetty read an old newspaper, tidied up their small room, finished the laundry, and, just before dawn, started sewing charms into Benjy's shirts.

She was just rounding off a rather nice piece of work with Canis Minor and Canis Major when a shadow fell over her.

"Did you even go to sleep?" Benjy asked.

"For a moment," Hetty admitted. When he poked at the pile of his clothes on the table, she called out, "Wait, you should take this one."

Benjy held up the sleeve, studying the fading light as the magic settled into the fabric. "It's not your fault," he added softly.

"What?"

"It's not your fault," Benjy repeated as he pulled on the shirt, running his fingers along the new stitches. "You told me Charlie wanted to talk, and I put it off."

"I could have listened to him," Hetty shook her head, "even if it was just for a moment."

"Even if you had, it might not have changed the course of events. Charlie was deep into something. He was only reach-

ing out a desperate hand when it was too late for anything else."
They were both silent for a moment, and Hetty's eyes fell onto
the vial on the table.

There was one more thing she needed to do before they started
investigating Charlie's death. Although dodgy potions were no
longer that important to her, Hetty still needed to speak with the
woman, if only to prevent it from becoming a larger problem in
the later days. "I'm going to pay Geraldine a visit before I go to
the dress shop. Hopefully this time I won't have to threaten to
hex her seven different ways."

Benjy answered her words with a small grunt.

"Visit Marianne first. I'll be going around town spreading the
news about Charlie. It wouldn't be good if she heard the news
through gossip first. Unless you want me to tell her?"

"I will visit her," Hetty said quickly. "But afterward. She'll be
busy with her children. I don't want to tell her the news while
they're around. It won't be a waste of time." At his raised eyebrows,
Hetty added, "Geraldine lives near the alley where we found
Charlie. I can check if there are any clues sunlight will show."

"You could find something if you looked again," he admitted,
"and it might be a good idea to talk to Geraldine anyway. She's
married to Alain."

He let this revelation drop like the winning card in a game of
noughts.

As Hetty gaped at him, he only smiled.

"Did he tell you this?" she demanded, already knowing the answer.

"I remembered his face from the last time we were at the building. He remembered us enough to come here for help." Benjy
reached for his bag. "If you have time, could you see if the water
pump is truly broken?"

"You don't trust Alain's story?"

"It's a key detail. If the pump was fine, I can only wonder who would have discovered the body instead."

Charlie owned three buildings he rented out in the Seventh Ward. A fact he mentioned proudly at various gatherings. Ownership of a home—let alone several—was rare in their community. Those that did either were wealthy or had taken on many debts to make the purchase. This success was just another mark of pride for Charlie, to show how far he came in so little time.

Hetty suspected no one who cheered him on had ever seen the properties themselves.

Water was streaming from the main entrance of the recently renovated building—a muddy river that flowed with a current strong enough to send bits of brick and toys bobbing into the streets.

With reluctance, Hetty entered, stepping around the rushing indoor river. She climbed the stairs, her shoes slipping and sliding on the sludge until she passed the third landing.

This level was the source of the flood. A young woman was frantically creating star sigils over a cauldron, trying to slow the rush of water spilling out of it. Her defunct enchantment only seemed to encourage the contents to spew out faster.

As Hetty turned to continue up the stairs, she waggled her fingers to shape Capricorn. There was a splash, and the flow of water stopped.

The woman looked down at the cauldron and fell backwards on her heels with the relief of one who had just won a hard battle.

Although the river was gone, the building's appearance did not improve. In fact, it grew worse. For without the distraction she could see all the scuff marks, mouse droppings, and chipped paint.

Reaching the top of the stairs, Hetty rapped on Geraldine's door just once before it swung open.

A child stared balefully up at her.

"I'm supposed to say no one's home," the girl declared. "Even though it's a lie and a sin."

The girl was yanked out of sight.

"If you can't do it right— Oh, Henrietta!"

Geraldine let go of her daughter's arm and shooed her away.

With a slight gap between her teeth and a button nose, Geraldine still held the vestiges of youthful innocence. If she had ever been innocent, Hetty didn't know. Geraldine had been charming people away from their money ever since she arrived in Philadelphia three years ago looking for a life that had nothing to do with sharecropping. Brewing and selling magic with the promise of bottled miracles. Hetty had turned a blind eye to such operations. Geraldine had a daughter to support, and she couldn't help fools who willingly parted with their money. Hetty's willingness to leave things be ended when the death of Emily Wells came to her attention.

Geraldine's part was an accident, but she showed no remorse for what had occurred. She continued to sell her little potions, and one of them had ended up in Darlene's hand. The one thing Hetty could never forgive.

"I hope you aren't here about my little brews," Geraldine simpered, "because you threw out my last batch, my equipment, and nearly all my supplies."

Hetty eyed the room behind the alchemist. "Don't act as if you didn't hide some away."

"I have nothing," Geraldine insisted. "Whatever you found, it's not mine."

Hetty plucked out the vial, waving it in front of the younger woman. "Don't lie to me. This is your handwriting. I warned you about what would happen if I saw this again."

"Go on, I got nothing for you to ruin."

"I'm sure I can find a few things." Hetty's hand was primed to start drawing spells, but footsteps in the room drew her attention.

"Geraldine, who is at the door? What, you," Alain stammered, "what are you doing here?"

"Bothering me is what she's doing." Geraldine turned to him. "Be a good husband and get rid of her."

"I don't think I should." He gulped.

"What do you mean, 'should'? You put our high-and-mighty landlord in his place yesterday! If you can do that, you can get rid of her!"

Alain shushed his wife, who only ignored him as she detailed the promise Alain had extracted from Charlie regarding the water pump.

Alain had lied to someone.

If to his wife, it meant he claimed victory over a dead man. If to Hetty, it changed the sequence of events from the previous night.

Alain had motive and opportunity. Which was, as Benjy always said, key in finding a murderer.

The only thing that gave Hetty pause was the fear that had gripped Alain like a beam of sunlight on a cloudless day. His horrified reaction at the cursed sigil was too genuine to be faked. He hadn't seen it before Hetty pointed it out, which meant he couldn't have carved it. However, his wife gleefully lied to people's faces; maybe Alain learned a few tricks from the woman. They might have even worked together.

She considered the pairing for a moment and then disregarded it. If someone died by Geraldine's hands it would have been through one of her dodgy potions first.

"I wondered if there was a problem," Hetty said, her voice

raised over their chatter. "I saw a river flowing out of the building as I came up."

"It wasn't me," Geraldine said quickly. "Though it would be nice to be able to wave our fingers and make water appear."

"Don't say such things, Mommy. It's a sin," the little girl called from the other room. The clink of glass drew Hetty's ear and she peered over just enough to see the girl grinding something with a mortar and pestle at the table.

"Seems you are in business," Hetty said.

"The potion you have there. I didn't sell that." Geraldine shifted to block Hetty's view. "All I made lately is gifts for some friends. I'm not sure how it ended up in your hands."

"What does this 'gift' do?"

"It's just a bit of tea to help stop common complaints. Bad dreams, bad tempers, and ugly moods. You can have some. It'll be my gift to you, as a reminder of all our little chats."

"Don't need any," Hetty replied. "I'll be keeping an eye on you. If someone gets the slightest cough from a strange potion, you'll be hearing from me again."

Geraldine snarled. "Why can't you just leave things be?"

"Not in my nature," Hetty said, and turned her back on Geraldine and her apartment filled with lies. "Good day to you."

Hetty had made it back down to the street when she heard her name.

When she turned around, she was only a bit surprised to see Alain scurrying after her, lunch pail in hand.

"You won't tell her the truth?" he gasped.

"She's going to find out," Hetty replied, hardly sympathetic at his plight. There were better lies he could have told that weren't so easily undone.

"I had to. That pump's been a beaten-down mule for two weeks now! Nothing's been done. Everyone complains and that's all we talk about. Gerry's been on me to do something. When I got home last night, I told her I confronted him about it. I figure with him dead and all, he can't call me a liar!"

Hetty resisted the urge to roll her eyes.

Why were other people's husbands like this? Benjy didn't act like this at all. Shuffling about to hide things that weren't a problem to begin with. It was needlessly tedious, and showed just how little they cared for each other.

"Don't you think she'll find out, since it's not going to be fixed?"

"Could you do something about it?"

Hetty thought of the children living in the building. Thought of the sick. Thought of the elderly. "Is it a mechanical or a magical problem?"

"You're going to have your husband fix it? Bless you! I'd ask him myself, but I don't think he likes me very much. But if you convince him, he'll do it."

"I'll tell him," Hetty said, and held up a hand before Alain could start. "As long as you keep quiet about Charlie."

"I'm not a gossip," he said, rubbing his nose. "But aren't people going to notice when no one sees him around town?"

"I mean stay quiet about the unusual things you might have noticed last night."

"Ah." His eyes widened. "You don't have to tell me twice! It's a curse, that was, and—"

"It's not something that should be spread around. We can't find out who did it if there's excitement all over town about it."

"I can manage that." Alain grinned at her and left, whistling a merry tune, as if this would be the last he expected to see of her.

Which would be true, until she had other questions for him.

Now for the pump.

A closer glance told her everything she needed to know. The broken handle drooped like a despondent dog. With her fingers, she traced Aquarius on the metal handle. Blue light intensified at the vertices, and the magic spread from the sigil to wrap around the pump all the way to the ground.

The handle jerked and clicked into place. She pressed down on it, pumping it until a gush of brown water sputtered out. Hetty jiggled the handle a few times more until it ran clear.

The water spilled past her boots, and she found herself wishing the task took a bit longer. Not too long, but just enough to delay her next errand.

The Richardson home was not far away. Hetty had only to walk a few blocks before the streets widened and the houses had more space to breathe.

That wasn't the only change.

Her dress, which had been too neat and clean for the neighborhood she'd just left, was now too shabby and faded. Hetty tugged at the band around her neck, if only to assure herself it hadn't moved and exposed her scars.

Most of the people who lived in these rowhouses were born free. A few had families that lived in Philadelphia for generations. They owned barbershops, restaurants, and grocery stores. They were caterers, clerks, and teachers. They printed weekly papers and preached virtues to those not as fortunate. And they all belonged to the same beneficial societies and clubs, creating an insular circle of support that seldom benefited anyone outside of it.

These people usually had nothing to do with Hetty and Benjy until a child went missing, strange magic crept into drawing rooms, or someone found a finger in a cigar box and did not know where it came from. Then suddenly, these people considered Hetty and Benjy their dearest friends.

Hetty arrived at the Richardson house just as Marianne was sending her children off to school. The older girls clutched their books while Marianne straightened her youngest's collar.

"Remember to mind your teacher, and I'll—" Marianne's

words slowed as she caught sight of Hetty on the sidewalk. Marianne patted her son's head. "I will pick you up after school."

Rising to her full height, Marianne's gentle maternal smile took on hard edges. So that answered one lingering question. Marianne still remembered Hetty dumping a cup of tea onto an expensive rug.

Ten different excuses for her presence here this morning fluttered in Hetty's mind. Some of them were even believable, and only one was a completely outlandish story. There was even one that had her walking away without a word.

Instead, Hetty stayed the course. This was a case like any other, she reminded herself. She just happened to know the people involved quite well.

"There is something I need to tell you," Hetty said. "And it cannot wait."

Marianne went completely still, and her hands clenched together.

Her children, still lurking nearby, locked their gazes on Hetty. They must have recognized her. She had little to do with them lately, but she had been there to mark their births and subsequent birthdays.

"Come inside," Marianne said. "Children, you need to leave or you'll be late."

The eldest of the girls tugged her siblings forward. While Hetty didn't look back to check, she could feel their gazes only added to the burden that clung to her back.

Little had changed in the Richardson home since Hetty was there last December. The rooms were still tastefully decorated with rich and warm hues, and the faint scent of flowers filled the air like a half-remembered dream. On the mantel, a small portrait of the family peered down from above, showing the youngest child still a babe in swaddling clothes. Yet what stood out to

Hetty, more than the ornate rugs or the crisp wallpaper, were Charlie's slippers neatly placed near the door.

Marianne clutched the back of her husband's chair, her eyes fixed on Hetty. "What happened to my husband? I know something did. Charlie did not come home last night. I expected he would stumble in this morning, but you are here instead."

"We found him," Hetty began, and at the sight of hope flaring for a moment in Marianne's eyes, she forced out the rest. "It was too late for anything to be done. He's gone. I'm sorry." Hetty tacked on those last words like embellishments vainly placed on a dress too ugly to be improved.

If Marianne heard that bit, Hetty couldn't tell. Her friend swayed on her feet. She didn't faint, but Hetty rushed to her side and led her to the couch. As Marianne collapsed onto it, Hetty found her handkerchief.

Marianne's face disappeared behind the cloth. The sobs started slowly but grew louder and louder as the woman's shoulders rose and fell. Hetty reached out to touch her shoulder but stopped short. Instead, she waited until the tears slowed.

"Is there anything I can do for you?" Hetty said.

Marianne's head jerked up. Tears dripped along her face, but a familiar sharpness had returned to her eyes.

"We brought Charlie to Oliver's," Hetty confided. "He offered to prepare the homegoing services, if you don't mind. I'll go around to the church, make sure there's a collection set up for you. I'm sure Mrs. Evans would be more than happy to assist. I expect she'll insist on it."

"Don't you worry about me. I'll manage well enough. Charlie's mother—" Marianne paused, shutting her eyes briefly before she continued. "Charlie's mother will be arriving this week! We got the telegram the other day. It would have been the first time they would have seen each other since she was sold back when he was a boy. After all these years apart, and he misses her by just a few days. Imagine that! What shall I say to her? What can I possibly have to say?"

Marianne turned to Hetty for an answer, but Hetty had none to give.

Of course Charlie had found his mother. Hetty had spent years looking for Esther and was no closer than when she'd first set out with a cobbled-together plan and a stolen collar. Meanwhile, Charlie Richardson sends off one telegram and everything falls into place.

She shouldn't be jealous. She shouldn't be mad. Charlie was dead. His reunion with his loved one would not take place in this world, whereas Hetty still had a chance. Still, at least he died knowing what had happened to his mother.

"Just tell her stories about her son," Hetty said finally. "Tell her of the good times, the bad times. Tell her things to make her laugh, to make her cry, or to shake her head at his foolishness. She'll want to hear such tales. It's probably the only thing you could do for her."

Just as there was little that Hetty—or anyone—could do for Marianne and the grief that swallowed up her heart.

"Who could have done this?" Marianne handed Hetty the sodden handkerchief, only to pull out a lacy bit of fabric that passed itself as a handkerchief and dab her eyes. "He was always so careful. Always tipped his hat, kept his voice down, and minded his words. Not like Benjamin." Marianne blew her nose. "I'm sorry, I didn't mean—"

"Don't you worry. It's not news to me that my husband has the least amount of sense in the world."

Marianne dabbed her face once more and she seemed herself again. Cool and opaque, like a frosted mirror. "How did you come to find him?"

"The usual way. Someone knocked on our door in the middle

of the the night saying they found a dead man. I promise you, Benjy and I will do our best to find out who did the deed and why."

"Why would you need to do that? I know why Charlie was killed."

"You do?"

Hetty leaned forward, hoping her eagerness would be mistaken for mere curiosity.

There was a reason Hetty was the one that always told newly minted widows about the demise of their husband. Not only was Hetty better with words, but she was a better judge of character. Cora Evans had given her lessons on how to be a lady. The lessons didn't take, but Hetty remembered all the silly rules and social cues. Using them, she sifted through words, gestures, and inflections of tone to peel away lies, find truths, and see the core of a person's character. When that didn't work, she relied on her gut. Trusting that strong surge of feeling never steered her wrong.

"Yes. I know what killed him," Marianne repeated. "He was in the wrong place at the wrong time. If only I'd stopped him from leaving when he did. If only I'd tried harder."

"Leaving from where?"

Marianne hid her face in the handkerchief. "A party with the Waltons." She said the name as if Hetty should have known them, or even been impressed by the connection. Hetty didn't know the name, of course, or if she had heard it before, she had long let it slip away from her memory.

"Dinner," Marianne continued, "had just been served, but instead of going into the next room, Charlie pulled me aside and told me we needed to leave earlier than expected. He'd forgotten something important, he said. I told him that surely if it was so important, he would have remembered while he was having a cigar with the other men. But he insisted, and said I could stay if I liked, and that no one at the party would miss him."

"Why didn't you go with him?"

"It would be rude to leave a party. I'm not you. I can't make the same excuses."

"Not even out of concern for your husband?"

Marianne's trembling lip stiffened into a thin line, and Hetty wished she kept that last bit from slipping out.

Provocative questions like that might work on strangers. Most were slow to trust and very reluctant to talk. Ignoring the chains politeness put on conversation helped get a few answers she might not get otherwise. But that tactic had just crumbled whatever ground had formed between them.

Despite the arguments that had chilled their friendship, Marianne still expected special treatment.

"Out." Marianne's murmur grew to a roar when Hetty started to protest. "Leave, get out of my home! You always bring trouble when you come. Get out. Leave me alone!"

Hetty took the yelling without comment.

She deserved it, even though it was an honest question and hardly the worst she could have asked.

Still, it stung when the door slammed behind her and the sobbing grew even louder on the other side.

There was nothing Hetty could say to temper Marianne's grief, but still her hand hovered over the door for a heartbeat before dropping away. She had done what she came here to do, so why did she feel like she had done something wrong?

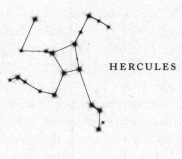

6

HETTY'S TENURE AT MRS. HARPER'S dress shop outlasted all her previous jobs despite being the one she despised the most.

She could not justify to herself *why* she disliked it so. Mrs. Harper was decent. The other girls crammed in the attic with her, with one lone exception, were pleasant. The pay, while a pittance to some, brought no complaints from her. And it was steady work, for Harper's attracted clients that were flighty, fickle, and fashion conscious.

Hetty supposed the real reason she disliked working at the shop was that very few dresses required enchantment. Straight sewing was favored by most of the shop's clientele despite the current trend toward enchanted garb. Not because their work was subpar. The work of Hetty's fellow employees was some of the finest she'd ever seen. But while the general trend favored clothing with enchantments, certain people cared more if the method of enchantment was Sorcery or Celestial magic.

There was a long history to the art of Sorcery, with convoluted rules about wand waving and chanting strange words that sounded made up. It started in Europe, but as it spread around the world with conquerors, pilgrims, and missionaries, it took on different forms. One thing remained consistent: Sorcery was for

white folks. Mostly because there were laws that prevented anyone who wasn't white from learning. Some of those laws were
formalities that confirmed what generations of spilled blood already made taboo. A wand in hand, a whisper of an incantation,
or even a glance at a spellbook meant losing everything you held
dear — and if you were lucky, you died before that happened.

It was like that everywhere, as far as Hetty knew.

Yet Hetty had heard stories of Quakers who taught Sorcery
to runaways and the freeborn. And even now there was pressure
from certain groups to overturn the law. But for Hetty's neighbors it was a waste of time. Few would dare to learn if the law
changed. Laws, after all, were only words printed on paper. The
consequences of ignoring them were left up to interpretation.

No laws stopped white folks from trying to use Celestial magic,
just jeers and taunts. There were stories of the genuinely curious
who attempted to learn, and books written by well-meaning ab-
olitionists talking about what they called Primal magic found in
the quarters. In these same books the writers were often puzzled
by this branch of magic. But that was their own fault. They had
this idea that magic existed to make their lives easier.

But magic was more than that. It was in everything that made
life. It was life itself.

The magic Hetty's mother taught her was a mixture of lore
brought over from Africa, from the West Indies, and even from
the native peoples of this land. Mingled together, it created a
magic system that was greater than the sum of its parts. It in-
corporated traditions that found ways to brew magic with herbs,
to enchant candles for protection, to use song to rejuvenate, and,
most important, to develop sigils from the constellations.

With Celestial magic you memorized the shapes, lines, and
vertices of the night sky. While the magic worked well enough
when drawn into the air, these sigils were even stronger once
grounded on a surface, whether it was drawn in dirt, carved in

wood, or pounded in metal. It also kept the magic alive longer to be used at a later time. This was why Hetty sewed sigils into the band at her neck. Doing so kept a reserve of magic at her finger-tips ready to be drawn on no matter the circumstance. A trick that saved her life on more than one occasion.

"You're late," Julianna muttered as Hetty slipped into the attic. "Don't you want to keep your job?"

"You should worry about keeping yours," Hetty replied as she settled on a stool. "Given how often I have to clean up your stitch-work."

Snickers floated around the room.

Air hissed out between Julianna's teeth, but good sense for a change led her to duck back over the dress she was working on.

"Mrs. Harper didn't notice," Margo said as Hetty placed her sewing kit on the floor. "She hasn't been up here all morning."

"In that case," Hetty replied, "let's not give her reason to do so."

Hetty's skill with needle and thread gave her the ability to change employers as she saw fit, and a way to merge magical talents. With her hands busy, her mind was also free to dwell and wander on various topics, such as the elements of a case before her. A few times she pieced together a crucial part of a mystery while stitching tiny flowers onto a bodice.

This morning, instead of a case, her mind kept returning to the fragments of her half-remembered dreams—a dead body sprawled on the ground and her too afraid to look and see who it was. She wanted it to be Charlie, but she knew it wasn't him at all.

"Henrietta, which dress are you working on?"

Mrs. Harper stood above her, her usually kind face creased with short lines between her brows. A prim and tiny white woman, she had been left a widow and childless by the war. Losses that would have made her a sympathetic figure, if Mrs. Harper didn't say her menfolk didn't die in Union blues for her employees to be lazy and ill-mannered. She saw the younger girls as charity cases and looked after the older ones with pity. Mrs. Harper spoke to Hetty only about jobs, but something in her manner told Hetty that wasn't the case today.

"This is a quick hem job for the Clarks. I'm almost finished."

"Julianna can finish it."

Drawing out her wand, Mrs. Harper sent the dress floating into the air. With a flick of her wrist, Mrs. Harper removed Hetty's stitches so hard that the thread flew out of the dress as if it were yanked by an invisible hand. The dress floated over to Julianna, who took it but otherwise remained frozen like everyone else in the room.

"We shall speak in my office. Bring your things."

The flurry of needlework halted as Mrs. Harper left.

Nothing good would come out of that combination of words, and everyone in the stuffy attic knew it.

"I suppose you aren't that needed after all," Julianna hissed. "What will you do now? Mind house and hearth for your husband?"

Hetty packed up her sewing kit, carefully tucking her needles so she could find them easily.

With no answer from Hetty, Julianna barreled on, her voice rising to a taunt.

"Unless house and home aren't where you're wanted. After all, if you travel for weeks at a time with one man, he's likely to be the only one that'll marry ruined goods!"

Hetty snapped the kit shut and turned to Julianna.

The other woman's sneer trembled and fell away. Julianna had gone too far and she knew it. But she had said nothing new. Hetty had heard variations of this gossip time and time again. In some ways, it provoked her marriage in the first place, even though it was an arrangement made to best suit their interests. Still, it stung to hear such words. Hetty expected this of the rich and snobby luminaries, not of someone she worked with side by side.

"Without me to clean up your stitch-work," Hetty said, "you'll be called into the office next. I'm not the one that's here because she couldn't find a job elsewhere."

In Mrs. Harper's office, a dress draped the wire dress form, its voluminous skirts spread out as far as it could go. The dress drew on the colors of the morning sun, with soft gold embroidering along the bodice. The Sea Serpent and the Dragon, designed to draw the eye from any distance away, easily blended into the hem, granting protection from stains and wrinkles, keeping the colors vivid.

So much of Hetty's attention was focused on the dress, she nearly overlooked the two other figures in the room. A young miss sat in a chair like a statue, her limp blond curls falling into her face as she stared down at her clenched hands. The other person faced the window. A tall and spare white man, with a small balding spot on the back of his head. He turned as the door shut, and his features echoed the girl's in some areas, but were sharp instead of round.

"Mr. Whitmore, this is the one that made the dress." Mrs. Harper shoved Hetty forward. "Everything she did, she did without my direct say. I try to give some responsibility to these girls to teach them how to act properly. She came highly recommended, so I thought I could loosen my grip. I'm sorry."

"There's no trouble," Mr. Whitmore said. His smile sought to envelop Hetty, but it contained little warmth. "I have no complaints about the work. It is rather excellent." He moved toward the dress and tapped his wand against the hem. As the tip ran along the stitching, a spark appeared. "I take offense to enchantments being placed on it without my permission."

This stirred the girl to life.

"Papa, I said I wanted—"

"If you wanted an enchanted dress," Mr. Whitmore said, interrupting his daughter, "you should have asked me first. Especially if you got it from here. You never know what sort of hocus they'd put in the dresses. Primal magic is nothing but trouble."

"None of my girls enchant regularly, only by request," Mrs. Harper said. "This one did it all on her own. I gave her too much freedom, it seems."

"I don't mind that bit," Mr. Whitmore said. "It's good when they think for themselves. Means I don't have to explain things over and over. This is better work than any I'd gotten from New York, and if it weren't for the magic, I'd keep it."

"I'm so sorry about that. Perhaps she could remove it."

"No need. I can just borrow her. Victoria, didn't you want a new ball gown? We can even talk about new dresses for fall."

"Mr. Whitmore." Mrs. Harper's voice dripped like honey off its comb. "We don't have fall fabrics yet."

"We wouldn't be buying from here." Mr. Whitmore laughed as if Mrs. Harper had claimed horses could talk. "A dress is good as its maker, and judging by the quality of this one, she is the best."

Mrs. Harper laughed as well, and there was a strain keeping it in the air. "I would loan her out to you, but I'm afraid she sneaks magic into everything she sews, even items she promises are plain stitches. Not worth your time."

"I see." Mr. Whitmore's gaze returned to Hetty. One moment he seemed to study her closely, the next he looked right through her. "What a pity. I suppose we'll have to go elsewhere."

"I have others—"

"Not interested."

The Whitmores left despite Mrs. Harper's arguments, or maybe because of them. She trailed after them, rattling on about others who could take Hetty's place, but the father and daughter didn't even glance back.

The door shut and Mrs. Harper whirled around toward Hetty.

"How dare you add enchantments to the dress! I give you liberty with select clients. Now you lost the biggest fish I'll ever catch. Do you know who these people are? They'll tell everyone what happened and no one will come here anymore." Mrs. Harper slapped a hand on the dress. It swayed and nearly toppled over. "Do you know how much money you just cost me? It will come out of your salary. The fabric, the lace, and the jobs I shifted around so you could focus on this. You'll have to pay it all back!"

Mrs. Harper went on and on, and all Hetty could see were her hands plunged into a cook fire, trying to grab a pan as it fell.

This woman was going to loan her out like a pair of scissors to a man who was only halfheartedly indulging his daughter. Hetty had endured this before, but that was back when she'd had no choice. Now she did, and she knew exactly what to do.

"Take my wages," Hetty interrupted. "For last week and today. You earned them."

"Excuse me?"

"You told me to enchant the dress—you wanted to impress them. It's why you hired me. But if it's such a problem, then I can find better work elsewhere."

"How dare you—"

"I quit." Hetty smiled, further rendering Mrs. Harper speechless. "Thank you for the opportunity."

Hetty exited through the front of the shop, scandalizing the finely dressed ladies who milled about. Hetty stopped to speak briefly to a pair of white women studying a lovely russet gown displayed in the window.

"You'll find more fashionable dresses just up the street," Hetty said to them. "Better prices, too."

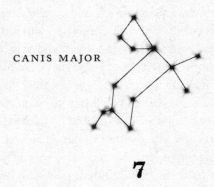

CANIS MAJOR

7

After leaving the shop, Hetty found herself standing in the alley not far from the spot where Charlie had been lying the night before. Despite her earlier conversation with Benjy, she had not planned on returning. But with hours she suddenly had to spare, her boots brought her here as if by an enchantment.

Her eyes skimmed along the grime and the dried brown spots that speckled the ground.

No footsteps broke up the grime. Although, it was hard to say if someone had returned. The chaotic mess appeared unchanged, and there were no magic traces after her work of the previous night. The band around her neck didn't even prickle against her skin. This wasn't a trap waiting for her.

Hetty almost wished there had been.

A feeling of unease had kept her up most of the night. Charlie being dead was troubling, the carved sigil in his chest worse, but it was downright terrible how they found him.

Strewn in an alley, dressed in ragged and torn clothes and mistaken for a drunk. Yet despite the wounds on his face, he was not unrecognizable. Anyone acquainted with him would have known him at once.

So why the alley?

Why not leave Charlie in a more public place, like a park? If he was meant to be found, why tuck him somewhere to be stumbled upon by accident?

What did the murderer want?

As always, the answer to that pertinent question was the thing they found out last, even if it would be the most useful starting point.

Tired of staring at garbage, she left with no helpful insights. Hetty crossed over a few streets to avoid passing Marianne's house. This turned out to be a wise move, because once she did that, she realized it was only a few blocks to Cora's home.

Most days following work, she spent a moment or two speaking with her old friend, exchanging the latest news and gossip. Sometimes they spoke of the past, and more often than not, she came here for reassuring words as soothing as any balm.

When Hetty first arrived in Philadelphia she stayed with Pastor Jay Evans and his wife, Cora. As station masters for the Underground Railroad, they took in runaways, but they did more than just provide shelter and safety. They gave directions, they found jobs, and they taught the interested how to read. Hetty herself had been one of their many boarders, but instead of staying for a few days or weeks, she called the snug attic room her own until her marriage.

She had thought both Jay and Cora would have been upset when Hetty snuck out of their house in the middle of the night on that first failed trip to find her sister. On her return with Charlie and others, she feared their anger and disappointment. Instead they informally inducted Hetty into the Vigilance Society. Cora even gifted Hetty with a pistol and proceeded to teach her how to shoot.

While their station master days were long behind them, Cora and her husband were still prominent voices in the community, through both the church and their other acts of philanthropy. If anyone could help raise funds for Marianne at the drop of a pin, it was Cora.

Her old friend smiled when she opened the door, her silver-streaked hair pulled back into a neat bun. Tiny round glasses dangled from a beaded chain around her neck, and her ivy green brooch contrasted with the cream of her ruffled blouse. Because she ran a kitchen in the church's basement, her attire was always serviceable blouses and skirts. But on the rare occasion, and Sundays, Cora could be spotted in one of the sedate dark blue dresses Hetty had made, paired with a single strand of pearls.

"I was wondering when I would see you," Cora said as she welcomed Hetty inside. "I heard about Charlie."

This didn't surprise Hetty. News reached Cora's ears at great speed, even under normal situations.

"It's terrible, isn't it?" Hetty said. "There's so much to do—"

Muffled noise at the other end of the short hallway, coming from the parlor, caught her attention.

"You're not alone?"

"Not for the last few hours. Once word got around, I've been entertaining people who want to help. It's astonishing, really, but the Richardsons endeared themselves to many people over the years. I must say I'm rather impressed with Eunice Loring. She's spearheading the collection that will be going around. And has everything under control."

Hetty's smile froze on her face, killing the question on her lips. Suddenly she wished she was anywhere but here.

Eunice Loring was Hetty's reflection in a warped mirror. As much as Hetty tried to deny it, she couldn't entirely blame people for mistaking one for the other at social gatherings. They were close in age, and had a similar height and the same deep brown complexion. Like Hetty, Eunice had a collar forced on her until freedom came, although Eunice's scars were easily hidden by simple ruffs and ribbons. That was where their similarities stopped.

The beautiful wife of a caterer, Eunice was adored in the community, and for good reason. Eunice played a crucial role on a number of committees devoted to supporting children, widows, and the poor. She had held poetry readings in her home. And her work with the veterans of the United States Colored Troops went well beyond the efforts of most.

Hetty could have tolerated Eunice's goodness and shimmering perfection with nothing more than a groan, but Eunice had infiltrated Hetty's circle of friends.

It started with Marianne, who traded hostess duties for parties and teas with Eunice. But Eunice soon charmed the others, playing the piano for Penelope when Benjy wasn't available. Dropping off entire meals for Oliver. Eunice even performed a tricky bit of magic to save one of Darlene's paintings from ruin when it got left out in the rain.

Eunice had done nothing wrong—she just filled all of Hetty's friends' stories with cheery exploits and charming escapades Hetty could never match.

"I can still help," Hetty insisted, determined she could do this small thing.

"There are better ways for you to help," Cora assured her.

"What have you heard?"

"I heard Charlie died in an accident, which is how Benjamin phrases everything that is a bit unusual."

"All sudden deaths are unusual," Hetty said.

Cora's gaze sharpened. "Charlie Richardson was a healthy and lively young man who spent an hour yesterday at the Waltons' dinner talking about buying buildings and his plans for them. *Unusual* is the first and last word involving this."

"Benjy wants to keep this quiet."

"Charlie's been murdered, then?"

"Attacked, at least," Hetty admitted. "We don't know what happened exactly, but we'll be looking into it."

"Be careful. I know you always say you will be, but you must mean it this time. You've taken risks with your life before, but at least back then you did it in the shadows."

"People knew who we were then."

"They knew about the conductors. A couple, older than their years and with magical talents that were things of legend. Despite your extraordinary gifts, you're still flesh and bone."

"Mrs. Evans"—Hetty took on a teasing tone—"are you trying to encourage me or warn me off?"

"I'm saying take care. There's all sorts of trouble around and you must figure what trouble is worth getting down in the mud for. Sometimes," Cora added as the door to the next room opened, "trouble is going to roll in regardless."

Cora patted Hetty's arm and left her in the hall. Hetty remained where she stood, almost in a daze.

Did Cora just hint that Charlie deserved what happened? Charlie chased after shooting stars while still scrambling after seashells to make his riches so quickly, but did he really deserve a cursed sigil carved into his chest?

"Henrietta," Eunice Loring called as she strode into view, a collection of papers clutched in hand. Startled, Hetty had no choice but to force a polite smile onto her face.

Another factor that made Hetty less than keen to be in Eunice's presence was a professional disdain of Eunice's wardrobe. Her gowns either were in cool colors like pale green that didn't suit her, or had unflattering cuts that were more distracting than horrible.

Today's offense created a new category: excessive ribbons flowing from her sleeves.

"It's terrible about Charlie, isn't it?" Eunice cried. "Marianne and those poor children of hers!"

"Yes, indeed," Hetty said. "You're doing the collection?"

"Along with a few other things. I wasn't very close to Charlie, not as close as you were, but it was such a shock to hear! I can't believe this happened! Things are supposed to be different now. Our friends aren't supposed to die so brutally. We're free. We should only die of old age in our beds."

"I don't believe that's how the world ever worked."

"It should be." Eunice shook her head. "It's the only proper thing!"

"I don't disagree," Hetty said softly.

"The next few days will be difficult, but I'm grateful to have so much work to keep me occupied. I'm also glad Charlie and Marianne were part of the burial society."

"Burial society?"

"The Southgate Burial Society." Eunice nodded. "We collect a small monthly fee, and in return you are guaranteed a funeral plot and money to cover your homegoing services."

Hetty recalled this now. There had been notices in the paper a few times, announcements at church, pamphlets put in her hand, all of which Hetty ignored. The fee was reasonable considering the service, but it was too much money to spend in preparation of dying.

"I know you think it's silly, but it's a nice certainty to have. We aren't slaves anymore. No more slipping away in the night to hastily dig graves and whisper prayers. We should be able to take care of our dead. If we can't do it alone, we should band together to help each other." Eunice's eyes had brightened as she gave her pitch. "You and Benjamin are the only ones in our circle who haven't joined. I would feel so much better if you did. You aren't exactly as well off as the rest of us. What would you do if something happened to your husband?"

Hetty didn't hear what else Eunice had to say.

What would she do if something happened to Benjy? She saw an outline of such a life, but the thought, the mere thought—

"I'm so sorry!" Eunice's voice cut through the fog that whirled around Hetty. Alarm flashed through Eunice's gentle features, and her papers crumpled under her grip. "I didn't mean to say that! You don't have to join."

"It's fine," Hetty lied. "We haven't really thought that far into the future."

"You should start," said Eunice's husband, Clarence, as he drifted up to them. "No one knows the form the future may take."

Eunice turned to him, but Clarence didn't seem to notice as he greeted Hetty with a stiff nod. The round frames of his glasses gave him an owlish look, which was the only interesting thing about his appearance. He had inherited a thriving catering business from his uncle and used his wealth to shower Eunice with expensive gifts, while his clothes remained poorly fitted and ten years out of fashion. Although tall, his stooped shoulders and quiet manner made him much like a turtle, one that wouldn't even notice when spring blossoms fluttered past.

Hetty had met Clarence in line at the Freedmen's Bureau, joining dozens of others looking for information about missing family. She was there for Esther of course, and when the white man at the desk asked her to describe her sister, she had burst into tears. Clarence had been standing behind her, and he helped her string a few words into a sentence. It was that memory and that small kindness that kept Hetty from fully dismissing Clarence as the dullest person she ever had the misfortune to meet.

"This is a terrible way to convince me to join," Hetty replied, glancing between the couple's faces.

"It's a fact," Clarence said. "You're very fond of facts, aren't you?"

"Benjy is."

"Then tell your husband there are few facts in life you can escape, and death is not one of them."

Eunice laughed at what her husband had said, and it was a

mighty effort, since there was nothing funny in his words or his delivery of them.

"I'm so sorry about him," Eunice whispered, drawing Hetty aside. "Don't listen to a word he says. He's been out of sorts since hearing about Charlie's death."

"We all have," Hetty murmured as Clarence said something to another person passing in the hall. "In different ways."

As Hetty swung around the corner, she spotted her landlord banging nails into the main door of the building. She lingered there, debating if she wanted to turn around before he saw her.

Her landlord was a lean man with an impeccable memory of just how short of the rent they were. Although born free, he held little sympathy for them or the people who came knocking on their door for aid. In fact, those visitors had led to the sudden increase in their rent. When they couldn't pay, he let it carry over into the next month, with an added fee. A fee they couldn't cover, which got carried over for another month, which meant over time they owed a great deal more money than they should have. They should move. But Hetty resisted the idea. The tiny room wasn't the best, but over the years it had become theirs.

Before Hetty could scramble away, her landlord looked directly at her. Instead of the dour expression she was often greeted with, McKee beamed.

"Good evening, Mrs. Rhodes! How is everything? Any complaints about the room?"

McKee kept smiling. She wished he would stop. The strain behind it made her wonder if he was hexed.

"No complaints."

"If there's any trouble, let me know. I'm always here to help." He even bobbed his head at her as if she were a proper lady.

Hetty hurried into the boardinghouse, stopping only to glance over her shoulder briefly. Their landlord only made to speak to them when they were late with the rent, and scarcely wasted a breath on anything else.

Had good fortune suddenly dropped on his head?

Did she even want to know?

As she checked the mail, one of her neighbors peered out of the communal kitchen.

"The word going around is he's been cursed." Her neighbor juggled the youngest of her four children on her hip. "One of the new boarders said we should let it run its course."

"What curse?" Hetty said, shutting the box. "I see only a blessing. What's for dinner tonight?"

"You just missed it, although it might be good you did. Whoever's turn it was, they didn't even clean the collards properly."

"It was Mrs. Samson." Hetty nodded. "She eats them raw."

Her neighbor made a face of such disgust, Hetty didn't need to fake a laugh. She let it roll out of her, relieving the strain that had started last night and stayed coiled inside her all day.

Hetty shuffled the letters in her hand and a ripped scrap of newspaper fell to the floor. Picking it up, she gave it a closer look. At first glance, it was an advertisement for a nearby store. But as her fingers settled on the edges, Virgo blazed in the far-right corner. Inky words appeared on the edges of the ad, as if written by an invisible hand:

I am in dire need of your aid, please help.

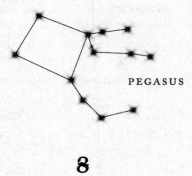

PEGASUS

8

Mᴍʏꜱᴛᴇʀɪᴏᴜꜱ ɴᴏᴛᴇꜱ ᴡɪᴛʜ ᴜʀɢᴇɴᴛ ᴘʟᴇᴀꜱ were not unusual. Hetty had them pressed into her hand while crossing busy streets, stumbled across them in job postings, had them slid to her across the bar at a saloon they visited on special occasions. She had once received a note coded in a bouquet of flowers. That one had been her favorite, although she had needed Penelope's help with identifying the flowers to discover its true meaning.

This scribbled note was a bit cleverer than the others. The mark only activated when she touched it, which meant the magic didn't leave even the faintest trace of residue. While that was clever, if a bit overdramatic, there was no name attached to it. The place to meet the writer was obvious. The advertisement was for a goods store in town, and the scribbled numbers were tomorrow's date with a time marked right underneath it.

And there was something else. A crescent moon scrawled in the corner.

Hetty's eyebrows lifted.

The crescent moon was her mark, and it noted sensitive cases that needed a delicate touch. A sun drawing would have made a case Benjy's, and would lead to places shrouded in vice and ruin.

Hetty was still studying the paper as she pushed open the door to their room. She swished her fingers to form the simple jutting line of the Canis Minor sigil. Distracted as she was, she had already finished the spell before she realized the lights were already on.

Instead of lights bursting to life around her, she was thrown into darkness.

"Hetty!" Benjy called. "You need to pay attention!"

"Sorry," she said, but before she could reverse it, Pegasus flew into the lamps, the discharge of magic lighting the glass orb inside. There it would bounce inside the glass until it faded or they disrupted the charm. Although Benjy had made them, he hadn't yet patented their design. These two lamps were the only ones that didn't catch on fire after three uses. After months of tinkering with glass, three small fires, and turning her favorite dress into ash, Benjy hadn't figured out how to bottle lightning twice.

"You are usually not home this early," Hetty said as she shut the door. "Did you manage to—" She stopped and pointed to the cradle at Benjy's elbow. "That doesn't belong here."

"Of course it doesn't." Benjy studied the edge of his knife before striking it against a stone. "This is kindling." He nudged the cradle and it rattled like a set of bones. "Although I couldn't set it on fire even if I wanted to. Did you eat yet?"

Hetty hadn't. On the table was a plate kept warm by an array of spells. She ate dutifully, even the forsaken collards, for she learned a long time ago never to turn down freely given food.

As she ate, Benjy continued to sharpen his knife in measured strokes.

"My boss's daughter is having a baby. He purchased this cradle and asked me to carve enchantments into it."

"Amos asked you for another favor? You should have said no."

"You're sewing christening gowns." Benjy nodded at the tiny pile of baby clothes in a basket on the floor.

"Penelope's cousin Maybelle asked me to sew protective charms into the hems. I only agreed because she offered to pay."

Hetty looked over to her husband expectantly, but he didn't meet her eyes.

"Benjy," Hetty said softly, "what have I told you about taking on things out of the goodness of your heart?"

"It's just a little fix," he replied. "I only brought it here because I wanted your opinion on what charms to use. The ones I know wouldn't be quite right."

There was enough truth in those for Hetty to take his explanation at face value. Although Benjy often pounded spells into the things he made and mended at the forge, his work was different from hers. His spells were the forest to her trees. Where her protection spells would protect a person directly, his spells were focused in broader scope around the person.

Hetty drew a sigil into the air, and a gust of wind picked up one of the little gowns and sent it in Benjy's direction. "Use this one as a guide."

Benjy held up the gown and brought it close to study the star sigils she'd hidden in the hems. "You're not going to show me?"

"Show you?" Hetty echoed. "I thought you liked figuring things out on your own?"

"Not always," he said, but his tone was rather strained.

Hetty waited for him to continue, but when he said nothing more, she took the opportunity to move the conversation to a more interesting territory.

She held out the advertisement. "This was in the post."

Benjy's eyes darted along the paper.

"A plea for help," Benjy said, shrugging. "No mystery there, other than how you would meet this person when you're working at the shop."

"No trouble. I quit."

Benjy didn't even blink.

"What's your reason this time?"

"An enchanted dress. The work was perfect, but the only thing wrong was me. I did everything I was asked, but the clients and Mrs. Harper had complaints. I decided I didn't want to listen anymore."

"I suppose that's fine," Benjy said as he lined up the stitches of the little gown against the wood.

"What about rent?" Hetty asked, surprised at this quiet reaction. "I won't get my last wages."

"I'll take care of it. You worry about that note. That woman must be very desperate to go through all that trouble. It's your case to solve. Keep your focus on it."

Hetty found herself nodding until she recalled the last time he had encouraged her to pursue a case without his assistance. She'd solved it without issue, but the case he took on without her ended up with him locked up in a lighthouse.

"I don't have to take this on," Hetty said, watching him very closely. "Small cases can become distractions that could limit my time in making inquiries about Charlie's murder."

"I never said a word about that."

"But you aren't keen on me getting involved. Even though you suggested that I confirm Alain's story."

"I did," Benjy began, and then deftly avoided the trap she'd laid for him. "What new insights did you discover?"

"Alain's story about looking for the water pump is true. The pump at his home was broken, and it's been broken for weeks without Charlie doing a thing about it. Geraldine said something about him exchanging words with Charlie, but it might have been a lie, since he never mentioned it before."

"His wife is the one selling dodgy brewed magic." Benjy hooked a thumb along one of his suspenders, as he nodded along. "So there's a good chance they're both liars and you can trust nothing they said."

"Although the broken pump is just one reason for murder. The building is in poor shape, worse than it has been in the past. Or maybe I never noticed. I can't believe Charlie let the place get into such a state. It makes me want to take the money they're collecting for Marianne and give it to those poor tenants."

"What did you tell Marianne?"

"Not a word about the sigil. I should have, perhaps." Hetty frowned. "She thinks he was in the wrong place at the wrong time. Charlie left early from a dinner party last night."

"Why?"

"Marianne didn't put it to words, but I suspect they argued."

"Were they having trouble?"

"Marianne would never admit it, even if Charlie was having an affair. Especially to me. She likes the façade she put together far too much."

Benjy's face twisted and Hetty forgot her petty annoyances with Marianne as she recognized his expression.

"You believe Marianne might have something to do with his death?" Hetty asked.

"Do *you*?" he countered. "You neglected to mention her reaction to the news."

"She was devastated," Hetty replied, sharper than her words merited. "I didn't think such an obvious fact needed to be mentioned. She all but sobbed on my shoulder. I don't think she's involved."

"I need a better reason than that to discount her," Benjy said. "Not," he added hastily, "that I don't trust your judgment. But in this particular case I think it's clouded."

Hetty stood up from the table, bristling at each offending word. "How kind of you to say that."

She started to cross the room only to be stopped by a gentle tug on her arm.

"Hetty, I didn't mean—"

"What *did* you mean?"

At the snap of her words, Benjy let go but didn't retreat. He stood there and replied in a measured tone, "You tend to discount people for very odd reasons."

"Odd reasons," Hetty echoed, stepping forward as her anger raised the volume of her voice. "I believe Marianne couldn't have killed Charlie. She loved him. How is that odd? The oddness is the circumstance! Marianne loved Charlie. If she killed him, it would have been a passionate move done in a moment of distress. She would not take the time to carve symbols into his chest and then deposit the body in an alley. Nor would she take care to dress him in a drunk's clothes. Marianne would have stabbed him in the neck or the chest and probably been too startled to think about what to do about the bleeding body on her floor."

"What about magic?" Benjy prompted.

"That requires thinking." Hetty curled her left hand into a fist, raising it high. "Especially when Marianne can't work even the simplest spells quickly! A knife, on the other hand, doesn't require thinking to make its mark!" She made to swing her hand down, but Benjy caught her wrist.

They stood there, locked in this oddly intimate pose. There was no knife in her hand, or murderous intent in her heart. But in the moment he touched her wrist, she remembered the knife he had once given her.

It fit her left hand perfectly, and instead of a tool it was an extension of herself.

He had given it to her knowing she didn't trust him. When his words of assistance in helping find her sister were met with suspicion. Back when his touch on her arm got the knife's tip pressed to his throat.

At some point it all changed. But he never took the knife from her, even when it almost cost him an eye.

"I think you proved your point." Benjy released her wrist.

"Though you forget he was stabbed in the back first. It must have been *two* knives."

Although he faced her as he spoke, his words weren't meant for her. Benjy's gaze had gone beyond her to study their map, his mind whirling as if powered by clockwork pieces.

Benjy was smart in a way Hetty did not have words for. It was something greater than the books he read, or his ability to craft something out of metal. It was in how he saw the world, not just for what was there but what it could become. When things fell apart, he saw how the pieces moved back into place. He figured solutions to problems that hadn't occurred yet.

Benjy tried to explain it to her once, and she did her best to listen, but Hetty never fully grasped it. In a way, she didn't need to. People saw the world in a hundred different ways. Benjy's view was no better or worse than any others.

So when he got quiet and lost in his thoughts, Hetty just settled and waited for him to come back to her.

"If there are two knives," Benjy resumed, "It could complicate things. Two means another person. We can't know for sure."

"Oliver would, if he found different marks. I will make time to see him tomorrow. I have plenty of it now."

"What did you do once you quit the shop?"

"Nothing much." Hetty sat back down at the table and began to pull out the pins that kept her hair in place, grabbing most by touch and chance. "I stopped by to see Mrs. Evans on the way home . . ."

As Hetty tied down her hair for bed, she outlined the conversations and events of the evening. Benjy made all the little comments she knew he would make, including scowling at the mention of the burial society.

"We're not doing that," he grunted as he focused on the map. "How can you enjoy living if you're saving for death?"

"I think it's about peace of mind."

"You want to join, then?"

"Of course not. I just realized I don't have a plan if you died before I do."

"I'm not going anywhere."

Those simple words unraveled a knot in her chest crowded with more fears than she realized. Fear—not of death, but of the loss of the many moments that would follow.

She had lost so many people over the years. She couldn't do anything about those losses then, but she could do a bit more to prevent losses now.

"I wouldn't want it any other way," Hetty replied airily.

She dropped a bent hairpin into his hand.

He started, clearly not expecting the small gift. His reaction tugged a small smile out of her. "Can you put this on the map for me?" Hetty said. "I think this mysterious note is going to be quite interesting."

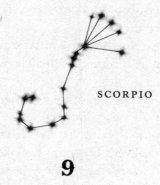

SCORPIO

9

Although hetty walked through the doors to the telegram office the moment they opened the next morning, she found herself waiting longer than she'd expected.

The white clerk took his time straightening papers, polishing the machine, and adjusting eyeglasses, until he very slyly placed his wand within arm's reach.

"What can I do for you?" the man asked when it was clear she was the only person in the tiny office.

"I would like to send a telegram." Hetty slid the coins and the note across the counter.

The man didn't even look at the slip of paper.

"You'll need a bit more if you're sending it this far," the man remarked.

"The price changed?"

"Yes, just last night."

Hetty knew the price hadn't changed, not recently and not for long distance. However, little would come of an argument this morning.

She reached into her purse and pulled out a few more coins. Without clarifying or asking for a certain sum, the man snatched her coins and her note.

This was the last bit of money she could spare, and now she doubted it would even make it.

How ironic, she thought with a bitter smile. She went through great lengths to hide working on the telegram, and it might just come to nothing.

Her jaunt to the telegram office took her away from more familiar streets, but she was in no rush.

She headed south, leaving behind Twenty-Second Street to make her way to Oliver's house on Juniper. It was a long walk, and to walk it was to see nearly every face the Seventh Ward had to present. Everything north of Twenty-First Street was white and bright, filled with businesses, offices, and places where people like her were only brought in to clean. But south of there, things changed for the better. More places had brown faces, as well as the immigrant populations: the Chinese who recently settled along Race Street, and the Italians and Russians on the east end.

There was a stretch along Lombard where gambling and political clubs got on with their business, hiding in plain sight. They were the same caliber of places found in the worst of the slums, only with a gleam of respectability. Hetty had been to her fair share of saloons and gambling dens, and she favored the places where she was likely to get stabbed over those where she might face a professional con man trying to sell her a bridge that went nowhere.

A streetcar rolled to a stop in front of a knot of people at the corner. With the sky turning a concerning gray, Hetty elbowed her way through the crowd. At the last moment, she jumped up and grabbed the outer rail.

In her haste, she had leapt right into a group of men who had the same idea as her. They called out to her in playful cheers as she found her footing along the metal edge.

"You know, miss," called a grizzled man, "we're allowed to sit inside now. Some very fine people went through a great deal of fuss so the likes of us can ride with no trouble."

"I like the fresh air." Hetty hooked her arm securely around the bar. "It's a lovely day."

"Looks like rain to me," called another on her left. "Why do you think people are crowded together?"

"Don't you worry, miss. We'll make room for you if the skies open up."

But the skies stayed temperamental as the streetcar lumbered southward, stopping only to shift its burden. While she could have moved, Hetty stayed where she was for a bit longer, soaking up the strands of conversation nearby. She might only hear bits of the stories, but those bits were interesting and sometimes got woven into her own tales.

"I saw it in the *Eventide*. They went straight up to the prison and dragged him from his cell. Ain't it something when a man can't expect to be safe behind bars? And I heard—"

". . . I'm sure proud of my little girl, but ten dollars for a year of schooling ain't easy to part with . . ."

". . . can't find any work here, I'm going to leave town. There's jobs up here, but if you aren't turned out for your color, they boot you right quick for having a touch of magic . . ."

". . . if you want the best stuff you go to Miss Sal's, best fried chicken around, so fresh it's practically still kicking . . ."

"There's a show tomorrow evening," a young man at Hetty's left called to his companion. "It's supposed to be a real hoot. They got these ladies that—"

"Shut your mouth." His friend swatted him on the back. "We got a lady right here listening in. Excuse him, miss," he said with a gap-toothed smile. "He ain't got much sense."

At the next stop, enough people got off that it was silly for Hetty to cling outside any longer. Slipping inside, she adjusted her sewing kit in her hand and walked through the lurching car.

She had a few choices for seats. Some right behind the driver, some further in the back, but once she saw a familiar face, the adjacent seat was the one she chose.

"Well, well, looks like you're traveling my way," Hetty said to Maybelle Lewis. "Is this chance or fate?"

Maybelle was the eldest of Penelope's five cousins, and she had a warm, cheerful air. There was little resemblance between them, except for dimples in the exact same spot in their cheeks. A so-called contraband of the war, Maybelle escaped slavery with her two young children to a Union camp. There, under the dubious protection of the army, she cooked and washed laundry, often to her great peril. Maybelle always said her prize for such hard labor was her husband, and the shoe shop they ran together.

"If I knew I would see you today," Hetty said, "I would have brought the christening gown."

"No need to worry about that!" Maybelle brushed a hand along the curve of her stomach. "This baby will not come for some time. So I have plenty of time for my other baby. I should have asked you from the start to make Annabelle's wedding dress. You should see what we were given. It's a star-forsaken shame."

"I could fix it for you," Hetty said. "Or make a new one."

"I hate to ask that of you," Maybelle said, "and a new dress from scratch—"

"Will be easier than fixing a downright mess," Hetty interjected. "I can start on it right away. I know her measurements and her tastes. I just need materials."

"Truly?" Maybelle's eyes filled with sudden hope. "Even by the end of the week?"

"Yes," she promised. "Sooner, even."

"That would be lovely." Maybelle paused and then frowned. "Won't you be busy at Harper's?"

"I no longer have a job there."

Maybelle grinned. "Which explains your eagerness for this job."

Hetty's protests were cut off with a wave of Maybelle's hand. "I'd do the same in your place," Maybelle said. "Though I expect people will be asking all sorts of orders from you once they find out you're a free agent. Why, I see this as getting to you before you become too popular."

As the streetcar rolled through town, Maybelle rambled on about the shoe store's business and passed on harmless gossip and chatter. Hetty had long passed the stop she should have gotten off, but rain tapped against the window, so the conversation was welcome.

When the car emptied of enough people so no one sat nearby, Maybelle stopped in the middle of her own chatter and leaned forward. "Are you stopping at the hospital?"

Hetty had been waiting for this. Maybelle had also missed her stop, and not because of the rain. While their conversation had been pleasant, she could tell Maybelle had been drawing it out as she waited for the right moment.

"Why would I go to the hospital?" Hetty asked.

She knew why Maybelle had made the suggestion. But Hetty liked to ask such questions anyway. It gave her a sense of control over the events that would occur next.

"My son is working nights as a cleaner," Maybelle said. "And one night he saw Samuel Owens on a slab."

"He died from breathing too much smoke," Hetty said. A building on Ninth Street had gone up in flames two weeks ago. The fire was quickly contained and no one died. Except for Samuel, who'd returned multiple times to the building to look for anyone still inside. He seemed fine besides a few bruises, but when he went to sleep that night, he didn't wake the next morning.

"It's not that he died unusually," Maybelle continued. "But that he was there at all. He was buried. I was at his funeral."

"So was I," Hetty recalled. "We put that on with Oliver's help. It was a small affair. He didn't leave much family behind. I suppose that makes it easier for people to dig up his body and sell to students. No need to ask permission of anyone."

"Can't anything be done?"

"Grave robbers will keep coming as long as hospitals make it worth their while," Hetty said, repeating what Benjy had told her as they watched a group dig up a body one summer night.

They could do something about *this* group of men, *that* woman, *that* lone man, or *that* couple sneaking about, but neither Hetty nor Benjy could be around to stop it completely. After all, grave robbers were not the problem. It was the value placed on Black bodies and circumstances that allowed theft to occur in the first place. Unlike white cemeteries where even simple tombstones were dusted with enchantments to protect the dignity of the dead, a series of laws forbade enchantments in the few cemeteries they were given access to. These were laws that gnawed at even the most conservative and placating members of their community. For without those protections, the dead remained vulnerable to harm from the living.

"This is worth looking into," Hetty continued. "Can't say if it'll be soon."

"Oh yes, I heard about Charlie Richardson. There's been chatter these past few days." Maybelle's face grew thoughtful. "Did he ever pay you back for the dresses?"

"No, but it was never about the money," Hetty replied. "I'm grateful that you told me about them."

"It was nothing." Maybelle waved her hand. "My daughter just happened to be wearing the dress you made, so I had a nice comparison to the other dress. You have such distinctive work. Anyone who knows it can recognize it later. It's why I thought your friend foolish to sell them."

"He did many foolish things."

And one of them got him killed.

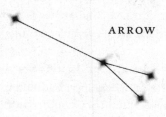

ARROW

10

Standing on oliver's doorstep, Hetty lifted her hand to knock. It only took a moment for her to realize there was no need for such action, as it would not be heard.

"For the last time!" Marianne's voice rang out through the open door. "I want to see my husband! And if you protest even a word more, I'll take him out of here on my own, and you can't stop me!"

Hetty coughed, stopping the argument in its tracks.

Using the surprise to skirt around Marianne, Oliver greeted her as if they had parted many moons ago. "Hetty, I need to talk to you!"

"You will not!" Marianne stomped her foot on the polished wooden floor. "I want to see my husband!"

Oliver turned pleading eyes to Hetty.

Hetty did her best not to sigh.

She should have turned around at the first sign of yelling. Because she hadn't, she was now required to do something or risk the situation going further off the rails.

"Would you like some tea?" Hetty said, and without waiting for a word of protest, she ushered Marianne into the kitchen.

Thankfully, there was no congealed stew on the stove, or muddy shoes lying around. The surfaces were clear, the papers stacked tidily, and there were even clean mugs waiting in the cupboard.

Penelope must have visited. In the first weeks after Thomas's departure, Hetty and Penelope had taken pity on Oliver and cleaned up the house when they could. Hetty lost patience with him around January, but Penelope still came by.

The prospect of tea appeared to soothe Marianne, and as Hetty placed a steaming cup in front of her, her old friend sat there as if she hadn't been screaming at Oliver mere moments before.

Their last conversation hung in the air between them. Hetty sat there sipping her tea unable to find the right words to keep the calm. Anger, after all, was an endless resource. Forgiveness was not.

In the end, she kept things simple.

"I'm surprised to see you here."

"The funeral is tomorrow and I need to make sure everything is in place."

"That is quite soon," Hetty admitted. Seeing how Marianne's gaze sharpened, Hetty added, "Do you need any assistance with arrangements?"

"Oh, no need for your help — Eunice has taken care of matters. Although, there is something you can do for me."

From her pocket, Marianne pulled out a watch.

"I was going through Charlie's things, putting them away, seeing what could be left aside for Junior, and I found this in the drawer. He always had it with him. First thing he bought after gaining his freedom. When I found it, I began to wonder . . ."

"About what?"

Marianne's voice was almost a whisper. "What was he up to that night?"

Hetty glanced at the watch, uncertain if there was any residual magic that could tell her a tale. "All from a pocket watch?"

"Not just the pocket watch. From the man who came to leave a wilting bouquet of flowers." Marianne placed the watch on the scratched table, her hand shaking just a bit as she did. "I never seen that man before this morning. He said he came to pay respects to Charlie, but I suspect he'd come about gambling debts."

This would be the first Hetty heard of such a thing, but she was hardly surprised. Charlie was the one that taught her how to play various card games, and he always upped the stakes by adding money into the mix.

"I didn't know he gambled," Hetty said, deciding to take a lighter approach this time around. "Was it on horses?"

"Why would I know? Gambling is such an ugly pastime. Filled with nothing but lazy men and loose women."

"Do you have money to pay the debts?" Hetty asked.

"My husband took care of me!" Marianne slammed her hand on the table, and Hetty quickly changed course.

"I meant"—Hetty swallowed a few choice words—"if someone like that shows up again—"

"He won't."

"But if he does, please be careful. This business might have caused Charlie's death. If he had debts, you'll be the one to pay now."

"I told you—wrong time, wrong place."

"You only hope that." Hetty spread her hands. "If he's tied to gambling, it might mean more trouble for you and your children. It won't go away if you pretend otherwise."

Marianne met Hetty's gaze, but instead of anger there were tears in her eyes. "None of this will ever go away."

As Hetty reached to comfort her old friend, Oliver rapped his knuckles against the door frame.

"Would you like to see him?" he asked.

Marianne closed her eyes and placed the teacup firmly on the table.

She held her head up high as she went down into the cellar, Oliver following closely behind.

Content to remain where she was, Hetty reached for the watch Marianne had left behind.

The first time Charlie had shown it to her she had thought it enchanted. While it certainly was accurate in telling time, it was also an astrolabe. It could point out stars and determine their location, which was useful for travelers and even practitioners hoping to increase their knowledge of the stars. It was an object of many ironies. Such a watch would have been invaluable in its assistance in escaping to freedom. But for a Freedman, it was just a pretty token.

Hetty opened the watch. The clock face's hands were locked in place. Just like its owner, she couldn't help but think, before her fingers moved to wind it up. But the knob nearly popped off when she met resistance from the gears.

"It needs to be fixed." Marianne strode back into the kitchen. Her eyes weren't red, but they shimmered with unspent tears. "Could Benjamin repair it? I won't have it buried with Charlie, so he can take as long as he needs to make the fix. Charlie always said something worth doing is worth doing the right way."

Behind her, Oliver nearly choked, making it doubly hard for Hetty to bite back a smile.

Said earnestly by his widow, Charlie's words took on a regal air. Yet all Hetty could hear was Charlie yelling at them before jumping into a wagon with the horses flying at a full gallop, and other times the man went off and did something dangerous, unwise, or both.

"I'll take my time then," Hetty said, tucking the watch into her sewing kit.

"As for other business," Oliver said, "I don't wish to insist, but Charlie was my friend. The least I can do is his homegoing services."

"You insist?" Marianne queried. "I already—"

"I'll do it for no fees. It isn't much, but I insist on the honor."

Marianne nodded. "I'll bring a set of clothes. Is there anything I need to do?"

"You've done enough. Let me take care of the rest."

Marianne sniffed and threw her arms around Oliver.

Oliver stood as straight as a rod as Marianne sobbed into his collar. At Hetty's beckoning, he lowered one arm and stiffly patted Marianne's shoulder until she released him.

"Thank you," she repeated, this time to Hetty. "Both of you."

The moment Marianne slipped away, Oliver sighed loud enough to rattle pots.

"You insist on the honor," Hetty echoed.

"Not out of the kindness of my heart. But it shouldn't be too hard with the beneficial society ladies helping."

"Do you need me and Benjy to—"

"No, I can handle it," Oliver interrupted. "I'm well practiced. All these bodies you bring here for me to poke at. I end up burying a third of them!"

"You can refuse, you know."

Oliver snorted. "If I did, you'd find someone else to hand off your dead bodies to. There are plenty of hospitals that will turn a blind eye to bodies as long as they are whole."

His words sparked her interest, bringing her back to what Maybelle had told her.

"Have you heard of new cases of grave robbing?"

"No more than what Benjy told me. Why?"

"Just an odd word or two. From Maybelle."

"That busybody," he scoffed.

"You're thinking of Jobelle," Hetty said, "she's the one that gleefully spills gossip. Maybelle's the one with the shoe shop."

"I thought she owned a cigar shop."

"That's Clarabelle. And it's her husband's shop."

Oliver sank into a chair. "Penelope has too many cousins. No wonder she comes here to escape them."

"She was here?" Hetty asked innocently.

"Don't act like you don't know." Oliver nudged Marianne's abandoned mug aside. "She stopped by to chat. I told her about Charlie. She got so upset, she started to clean. I left her alone because it would be my only chance to have a clean kitchen this week."

"You are a terrible person." Hetty shook her head.

"I'm an understanding one. You all have your quirks, and I know how to deal with each of them." He studied his fingernails. "I'm not sure how you'd manage without me."

"With great difficulty, I suppose."

"Isn't that why you're here?" he asked. "Come to see the body and to admire my work?"

"I would like to," Hetty said, spying the clock in the kitchen. Unlike the pocket watch, that one was still ticking away. "But I have to leave. I need to meet someone for a different case."

"I'll come with you," Oliver suggested. The words seemed to surprise him as much as they did her. "I found a few interesting things I wanted to tell you in detail."

"Did you notice if the knife wounds were different?"

"No." He blinked. "They aren't. Should they be?"

"Just a theory we can lay to rest." Hetty stood up then. "That's all I came to ask about."

Oliver tried to hide it, but like a stormy sky brightened by lightning, an emotion buried under late nights and copious amounts of alcohol was revealed.

Loneliness.

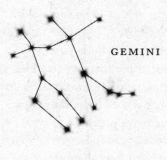

GEMINI

11

HETTY ARRIVED AT THE GENERAL GOODS store a few minutes earlier than the marked time. This was fortunate, for it allowed her to familiarize herself with the shop. While the selections of most of the goods were far more expensive than she cared for, she only came here for fabric, since the shop had the highest quality. When she had commissions from the rich ladies up on Society Hill, Hetty came here to purchase fabrics, knowing the good quality would only further elevate her work.

She was studying a roll of golden pink, wondering if it would be suitable for an underskirt, when footsteps approached and stopped right next to her.

"Will you be buying this?"

A shop assistant stood right in her shadow. The same one who kept her in sight as she moved toward the more expensive side of the store. Although he was not tall enough to look down his nose at Hetty, he made a fool of himself trying.

This was vexing, but she knew how to handle people like him.

She held up the fabric in her hands. "Yes," Hetty said. "I will be buying several yards."

"Who is this for?" the assistant said, his eyes clearly taking in her plain dress as much as her brown skin. "What name shall I place on the tab?"

"Alice Granger."

A white woman approached them. Her gray dress was plain, but the fabric was of a quality equal to the ornate butterfly brooch at her neck. A few curls of light brown escaped a neat bun, and her smile was distant yet pleasant.

The shop assistant, who looked ready to toss Hetty out of the shop just moments ago, was all smiles now.

"Miss Granger," the shop assistant said, "you'll be wanting . . ."

"Everything she just said," the strange white woman declared. "Although, double the order. I didn't tell you earlier," she said, turning to Hetty, "but I changed my mind. I will have several dresses made with the material. It is so versatile."

Hetty went along with this ludicrous statement, enjoying the shop assistant scrambling even as she kept a wary eye on the stranger.

Continuing with the ruse, Hetty followed the woman out of the shop. On the street awaited a cab driver, who jumped down from his perch to help them inside.

Hetty pressed the package close to her chest, less of a shield than a ready weapon to throw if needed.

"Thank you for purchasing this for me," Hetty said, with her eyes lowered to the ground. "I'm very grateful."

"It was no trouble," the woman said. "It looks ready to rain again. Come, I can take you to where you're going next. Hop inside."

"Oh, I couldn't."

"I insist. I have a favor to ask of you."

Those simple words stopped Hetty's protests. Not because she believed them, but because they explained her circumstances quite clearly. With this clarity, Hetty broke her rule about not entering a wagon with strangers and climbed inside without any more protest.

"A favor from me," Hetty asked after the woman tapped on the side closest to the driver. The wagon lurched forward. "I'm not sure about that." She looked the woman straight in the eye and dropped all pretense. "I am not in the habit of helping white women. Though I suppose it does not matter, since you are not one."

Alice sat back, more than slightly stunned.

"What gave me away? Was it that I helped you?"

"No." Hetty tapped her nose, and the act made Alice touch her own in horror. "If you know what to look for you can see the truth."

People who could pass for white often did. Many of the runaways that escaped the plantation leveraged their light complexions to hide in plain sight. While it was often a temporary act dropped the moment trouble ended, some chose to live their lives out in full this way. For most, it was not an easy choice. Passing meant cutting ties to family and friends and living in fear of the smallest mistake that could end everything. While some used that privilege to aid others, some passed purely for personal advancement.

Given that Hetty sat across from Alice in a cab with a package of fabric worth several months' rent bundled next to her, she suspected the latter to be the case here.

"I heard stories about you," Alice said. "About what you do, what you have done. Amazing things, remarkable rescues, escapes, all right under people's noses."

"Don't believe everything you hear. It's often exaggerated."

"You are the only one that can help me."

"Help you how? You appear well off."

"I'm exceedingly well off," Alice admitted. "But it's not me that needs your help. There is—" she paused, and started again, "There is someone teaching servants Sorcery."

"Good for them. Though rather risky, given the laws. But, as there isn't a citywide uproar about it, I don't see how this is a problem."

"It might explain her disappearance."

"Whose disappearance?"

"My sister. Judith Freeman. I haven't heard from her in several days."

"Do you talk regularly?"

"Only through letters," Alice laughed. "Though she has visited me on occasion, pretending to be a servant on an errand."

Hetty's hand curled into a fist, and she shoved it into the folds of her skirts. "If you're worried, why are you wasting time talking to me?"

"I can't seek out my sister," Alice admitted, stating the obvious. "I would lose everything!"

"I think you already have."

Alice's lips pressed into a thin line. "I'm not asking for your help. This is a job. I just purchased several reams of fabric for you. Consider that your payment."

"I have a right to refuse this job."

"You do not." Alice smirked like every rich girl Hetty had seen before. "Or we'll have to bring others into this conversation. Some of them might be curious about the fabric in your possession."

And who, Alice's smug smile seemed to say, would people believe if Alice claimed Hetty had stolen it?

Certainly not Hetty.

"We have our differences," Alice went on, "but my sister would never have willingly disappeared like this. I'm worried. The rich have ways of making problems quietly vanish when they desire it."

Hetty grimaced. Despite the protests on her lips, she knew in the end what her answer would be.

She already said no to someone else who had been desperate for her help, and he ended up dead. Benjy might say she bore no blame for Charlie's death, but that was a lie. Charlie's death was on her back. Alice might be exaggerating her sister's plight, but Hetty would take no chances this time.

"I'll take the case. But I need information to help me start."

Alice gladly gave Hetty the information she wanted. It wasn't much. An address for Judith's apartment, names of a few friends, an abridged history of the sisters' separate lives in the city. Information full of holes that needed filling if Hetty was going to get any use out of it. All of this paled compared to Alice's reluctance to give Hetty any easy way to contact her.

"If you need to talk to me," Alice said when they arrived at the address Hetty had given her, "I sell perfume at the store on Grand. Slip me a note saying it's an order from your mistress and I will meet you in a place where we won't be seen."

So much caution for such a lie. Hetty couldn't help but wonder if Judith had disappeared simply to stop playing her sister's games.

The unkind thought lingered in Hetty's mind as she turned the corner to the blacksmith's shop.

Sy Caldwell stood in the front, fumbling with a horse's tack as Hetty entered. The lanky young man fought a losing battle, and it slipped out his fingers the more he worked at it.

"You need to unbuckle it," Hetty pointed out.

"It's fused," Sy said, just as his elbow bumped against the table.

One of Penelope's younger cousins, Sy had run off the plantation to join up with Union soldiers at the tender age of fifteen. Not wanting to spend his time doing laundry or playing nurse, he cut his hair and changed his name. Doing this left him tasked with leading supply wagons instead, and he soon discovered that what had been a disguise was something that reflected his true self. In his transition to civilian life, he took night classes at Darlene and George's school, where his interests ran toward numbers. However, his best skills didn't lead to any employment until Penelope persuaded Benjy to take him on as an apprentice. Sy was practical, easily excited, and still had the job at the forge only because the owner was seldom there.

"Looking for Ben?" Sy asked. "He's around back making horseshoes."

"That shouldn't keep him busy," Hetty observed.

Sy lowered his voice, "It's for one of those folks uptown."

"Are they there watching?"

"No."

"Then," Hetty said, "I shall not bother him too much."

Sy's protests followed Hetty as she slipped into the back of the forge.

She heard the banging of a hammer long before she saw him. Clouds of steam rose up around Benjy, obscuring him partly from sight even as Hetty drew near. The heat pushed her back, and she could see his work shirt tossed haphazardly on the stool, covered in soot and drenched with sweat.

Hunched over the forge, Benjy struck the metal over and over with a hammer hard enough that sparks flew. The fire behind him cast long flickering shadows that made him loom even taller in the room. He was drenched in sweat, and each movement only served to emphasize his well-formed muscles — the product of working in the forge since he arrived in Philadelphia.

Several things came to mind at the sight, but the foremost was one of her favorite stories, in which the hero met the god of the forge and asked the master blacksmith for items of great power. When her mother told it, the items were humble tools like hoes or kitchen pots. Since Hetty was married to a blacksmith who made clever things with many uses, over time the items became a key that could open any lock, a coin that cast a spell of invisibility, a lantern that needed no oil to burn, and a compass that pointed to your heart's desire.

"Hetty." Benjy absently dabbed his face with his apron. "How late is it?"

"Not late at all," she said, eyeing the stack of horseshoes. They were stacked high enough to nearly topple over. "How long have you been at this?"

"Forever, it seems," he remarked. "Still more to do."

"I can wait until you finish. I don't mind watching you work."

These teasing words led him to roll his eyes, but Benjy couldn't fool her. She saw a smile tug at his mouth and knew that even if he had a large and complex work order to finish by the day's end, she wouldn't be sent away. He might try to convince her to work the bellows, but he would let her linger around the forge even if she was nothing more than a distraction.

There was a box that once held some matter of tools, and she placed her package on top with care.

Mindful of the flames, she walked to the workbench. It was rather empty today, with only a few tools scattered across the surface. Usually there was a long line of work across it, from repairs to drawings of new work. She even came here once to find a sword among his work for the day. But there was nothing on the workbench to make diverting conversation, so she sank onto a nearby stool and rolled one of the chisels along the surface in front of her.

"Is something the matter?" Benjy dropped another horseshoe onto the stack.

"Do you know someone named Judith?"

He picked up a hammer and proceeded to wag it at her. "You should rephrase that question before I give an answer that gets misunderstood."

"Oh!" Hetty laughed. "I was just wondering if the name was familiar."

"It's not. Who is she? No," he corrected himself, "what is this about?"

"The odd note that was in our post. I met the writer, and the lengths she took to meet me was because she's passing. It's also why she sought me out. Her sister Judith has gone missing. According to her, Judith taught Sorcery to others and recently disappeared. But she's only worried because there's a chance Judith's activities will be connected to her, even though it shouldn't matter. This is her sister and she is more concerned about being caught living a lie."

"Then don't take the case."

"I can't." Hetty's protest was scarcely off her lips before she saw her hands were shaking. She shoved them behind her back, but it was too late.

Benjy had dropped his hammer, the half-formed horseshoe, and everything else he was doing to come around to where she sat. He exchanged his apron for the abandoned work shirt, her stitch-work glowing for a moment as the fabric brushed against his skin.

"This isn't about my sister," Hetty said in answer to his unspoken concerns. "This woman, Alice, she bought all this expensive fabric for me. I can't refuse, or she'll have me arrested."

Benjy didn't reach out to touch her, but loomed overhead like a thoughtful cloud, as if touching her would bring on a storm of tears.

She wasn't sure she wanted him to grab her hands and say everything would be fine and he'd take care of it, but this wasn't much better. Looming over her with concern just made the distance between them greater than what it was.

"I wouldn't worry," Benjy said, looking more at the arrangement of tools on the walls than at her face. "This woman considers you her only hope to find her sister."

"If I'm her only hope, it's only because she doesn't want to look herself!"

"But you do. And you will." He paused before adding, "Would you like help?"

"What happened to 'This is your case, Hetty'?" she said, mimicking his voice. "Now you want to *help?* Is it because it involves a missing sister?"

"Yes, that's exactly my reason," he replied. "This is your weakness and it skews your judgment. You'll lose yourself in this case."

"I haven't before."

"It only takes one time."

She heard an echo of their conversation last night about Marianne, and her dismissal about naming her friend as a suspect. Just like then, he was casting doubt on her judgment, but this time she wasn't nearly as vexed to hear such words.

He had the right of it.

Her love for her sister led her to see that relationship echoed in other sibling pairs and to be surprised when the bond wasn't strong. He was right to warn her. But it was already too late.

"Why do you have to be right about that?" she grumbled.

"Sometimes I don't wish to be."

Benjy's face was carefully blank, which made his words an even greater puzzle. She was still considering what to make of them when footsteps filled the thoughtful silence.

"Am I interrupting?"

Darlene stood in the doorway with her daughter cradled in her arms. She eyed the room hesitantly, as if she was uncertain if her dress or baby could come to greater harm.

"There's nothing to interrupt," Benjy said as he stepped toward the workbench, abandoning Hetty as he tucked his concerns away.

Darlene, deciding to take a risk, moved forward in the space, nodding briefly at Hetty as she did. "I've come to ask you a favor. It's a bit short notice, but I am only a messenger. Benjy, will you play the piano at the repass tomorrow? Eunice thought it would be a grand idea since it'll be hosted at her home."

"Repass?" Benjy echoed. "At the Loring home?"

"Charlie's funeral is tomorrow." Darlene frowned. "Didn't Hetty tell you?"

"I didn't get a chance," Hetty admitted, speaking directly to Benjy. "Marianne insists on services as soon as possible. Oliver is busy getting ready, but he's not asking for help."

"Then I should change his mind," Benjy replied.

"Will you play the piano?" Darlene asked again.

He nodded.

Then, strangely, he made a show of looking at the horseshoes. "I think I got the number of horses wrong. Excuse me, I'm going to talk to Sy." Rather abruptly he left them, but not without giving Hetty a peculiar look as he passed.

It happened too quickly for Hetty to catch his meaning. But it had to be something about Darlene.

Her friend would not have come to ask Benjy about the piano. A piano needed only to be present in a room and he would play. No, Darlene came here for something else.

True to form, Darlene lingered, biting her lip as she glanced around the forge.

"I'm sure he'll be back," Hetty said, collecting her package. "Just wait a few moments."

"I didn't come to talk to him. I mean," Darlene added, "I came to talk to him because I wanted Benjy to pass along a message to you. I went around to the dress shop and they said you weren't there."

"I quit—the usual story."

"Ah." Darlene stumbled at this. If Hetty wasn't already curious, she would have been now. Like a berating elder sister, Darlene always had a few choice words when Hetty announced she was looking for work. Usually to the tune of tossing aside perfectly good opportunities on a whim. "Good, then you'll have time to talk," Darlene said. "I need to tell you something. I went to see Marianne. There's something about Charlie's death that she's hiding!"

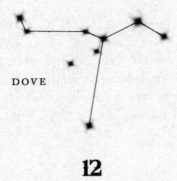

DOVE

12

Such a conversation could not be done so openly, even in the back of the forge. With little effort, Hetty convinced her friend to walk the few blocks to the boardinghouse, where they could finish their conversation. The moment they went inside, however, Hetty realized she made the decision a bit too hastily.

Darlene, who had said nothing other than whisper a soothing word to her daughter, grew wildly animated at the sight of the cradle.

Darlene peered into it, and even the baby appeared to assess the piece of furniture for its quality and use.

"That's not ours," Hetty said, when an utterly delighted Darlene turned back around. She placed the package of fabric on the table. "It's just a job Benjy picked up."

"I should have known," Darlene replied as she walked around it. "It's too poorly made to be his work. Although it does look rather nice in here."

"It takes up too much space," Hetty grunted as she reached for her scissors. With a simple snip, she cut open the brown paper to free the fabric. It spilled out along the table like a river of moonlight.

"You can always make room, especially if you gave this away." Darlene pointed to the tiny plant on the shelf.

Moonleaf was the only scrap of herbal lore Hetty still remembered from her mother. A plant whose leaves eased the pains of monthly bleeding and kept a baby from growing. The only protection her mother could give. It didn't protect from unwanted attentions, but it did prevent a baby being born from violence and pain.

"Give it away?" Hetty remarked. "To who?"

"To Eunice Loring." Darlene lightly bounced her daughter on her hip. "Eunice told me she wanted some to ease her monthly pains, but I think she wanted it for its other properties."

"Why tell *me* about this? Penelope has access to far more herbs than I do."

"Apparently the wares at the store are already allotted to customers. The other shops in town don't carry the herb at all, even in limited qualities. It's the most effective means, which makes it the most expensive. I don't have anything she could use," Darlene continued. "My trouble was I never could manage to get pregnant. But I knew you had some. I'm not suggesting you give her the whole thing, just asking if you could spare her some. She's been rather listless lately. I think she had a miscarriage."

"And doesn't want to risk another pregnancy." Hetty took the herb mostly out of habit, but had no pressing need for it. "I can spare some. Maybe even seeds for her to grow her own later."

"I'm glad to hear that. She has this silly idea you don't like her."

"Not her directly," Hetty said as she pounced on the chance to bring the conversation back to why she brought Darlene here in the first place. "Marianne rubbed their friendship in my face."

Darlene drooped at the mention of Marianne's name, and a worried frown replaced her brief touch of glee.

"Why don't you put Lorene in the crib?" Hetty suggested.

"She looks ready for a nap. It'll be a good way to test if the charms Benjy put in actually work."

"You don't trust it does?"

"I trust he made a good attempt at copying my spells."

The baby went into the cradle and made gurgling noises as some of the sigils carved into it lit up.

Relieved of her precious burden, Darlene settled into a chair. She held herself still as the reason for her coming suddenly flowed back into her.

It was a nervousness Hetty recognized, which was why she busied herself with the fabric. The illusion of occupation would make this feel more like a conversation.

"When did you see Marianne?" Hetty asked.

"This morning. I went alone. She was glad to see me. Marianne apologized for the other night, but we didn't talk much. Just about the arrangements for the funeral, and things people had contributed. Then someone knocked on the door. I thought it was Charlie's mother, who was due to arrive at any moment. But there was this man instead. Marianne tried to shoo him away. It took some time for her to succeed. I asked her about him, and she told me she had never seen the man before. I was ready to forget it when she added the man might be someone that Charlie had known through business. The way she said it was very odd."

"Charlie had fingers in a number of things." Leaving the fabric aside, Hetty went to fetch her dress form.

Since their room was small, instead of standing in the corner, it stood upright in her tub sharing the space with blankets, winter coats, and a few other things that couldn't quite fit elsewhere. Gripping her arms around the headless wire figure, Hetty lifted it out. "Did Marianne say which business?"

"Gambling."

The dress form hit the floor hard enough that it might have added a new scar to the wood.

Marianne had lied to her!

Hetty had believed her without question because the woman had just lost her husband and would be too distraught to make up lies. How could have Hetty forgotten Charlie didn't earn his money by himself? Marianne was right there next to him with pointed advice and suggestions.

"I thought you should know," Darlene went on, "so you could follow up on the gambling. You are investigating Charlie's death, aren't you?"

"He died in an accident." The fib came quickly. "It has nothing to do with us."

"Hetty." Darlene's hands were flat against her knees, and when Darlene looked up there was nothing quavering or trembling in her expression. Her eyes were sharp and attentive as they had been in the days when she was an agent of the Vigilance Society, tasked with moving people in plain sight of bounty hunters. "Everyone knows what you and Benjy do. Why, even George said that Charlie's death is so much of a shock that you couldn't *not* investigate. Benjy has gone poking about on less."

He had, in fact, with her right at his side doing her fair share of poking.

"That's all very true," Hetty said, "but I thought the past was past."

As expected, Darlene didn't challenge the reminder. She pursed her lips, though, clearly wishing she could press further.

Hetty held up the fabric against the dress form.

"I didn't realize you have a commission to work on," Darlene said in an attempt to shift the conversation.

"Not a commission," Hetty said. "It's for Maybelle. Her daughter needs a new wedding dress. I'm not even sure where to start," Hetty added with an exaggerated sigh. "I have more fabric than I need, but not enough for two dresses."

"Do you have an idea of what you want?"

Hetty considered the polite request. While she could make the excess of fabric work, she wanted to keep Darlene here a bit longer.

Darlene knew something more about Marianne, and not necessarily from this morning. Charlie's death had not been a random thing—it had been the final play in a game already in progress. Hetty had an idea of what that game might have been, but she had been on the outside of the Richardsons' social circle since the start of the year. The same could not be said of Darlene.

Darlene had to know something helpful, and Hetty was going to keep her talking until she found it.

"I don't have a single idea," Hetty lied. She shuffled the items along the table, pushing aside papers until she pulled out a battered bound book. In between half-written notes and maps in and around the city were Hetty's own sketches of dresses and Benjy's rough designs for machines. She turned to a blank page and held out a pencil to her friend. "Can you draw something for me?"

"When have you ever needed to ask that?"

Darlene put pencil to paper, and Hetty kept up her questions as she continued with her own work. As she cut fabric and pinned pieces together, she kept up a steady flow of conversation. She learned the Waltons were owners of a candy store and that the husband was a member of the same secret society of masons as Charlie. Darlene and George hadn't been at that dinner. But Darlene was very upset that Marianne's children had been enrolled at a different school instead of theirs. She didn't admit it, of course, but she returned to the subject more times than it merited.

"Where they ended up going is very good, but she made it seem like they would come to us. She promised!"

"You know how Marianne is with promises."

"But she promised me and—" There was a sharp snap behind her. Darlene let out a small cry as her sketchbook tumbled from her lap, and she held up a hand with the broken end of a pencil jammed in her palm.

"I'm so sorry," Darlene sputtered as blood began to pool. "The pencil just snapped and I . . ."

"Don't touch it! Don't move it at all. I have something that will help."

Hetty opened the door to the wardrobe and withdrew a box from the top drawer. Penelope had gifted Hetty with a collection of healing salves. A collection they put to great use. Still, when she reached for a jar, she was surprised to see that it was mostly empty.

Returning to her friend, Hetty summoned a chipped bowl to her side, and a pitcher.

Darlene had removed the pencil from her hand, and she sat there with a trembling lip as Hetty carefully cleaned the wound. A little healing salve covered the cut, and a bit of torn fabric became a makeshift bandage.

"You'll be fine in a moment," Hetty said. "Penelope made this, after all."

"I wouldn't have expected anything less." Darlene turned her hand over. "She makes them special for you, given all the trouble you find yourself in."

"Not that much trouble."

"Oh, it's plenty enough." Darlene said this without her usual cheer. It could be the pain radiating from her hand, but if the healing salve was working, something else drew away the mirth from her features.

Was there something else Darlene hadn't told her?

Hetty went to the dress, resuming her work. As she mulled over how to frame her next question, the door opened.

"Good, you're here! You won't believe what I found out." Benjy strode in pausing only when he saw Darlene perched on a chair.

"Hello, Darlene," he said cheerfully, and he eyed the dress form Hetty worked at, "and Catherine Anne."

"Catherine Anne?" Darlene giggled.

"It's what he calls the dress form," Hetty said around the pins in her mouth. "He thinks it's funny since the dresses are always for fancy white ladies. But you're wrong this time," she informed her husband. "This is for Penelope's cousin."

"Which you're doing out of the goodness of your heart," he teased. Benjy stood on the other side of the dress form, his hands resting on the wire shoulders. "I went to see Oliver," he began.

"Hold this." Hetty thrust the end of the fabric into his hand.

"I ended up having to fix the casket," Benjy soldiered on.

"Maybe it's a sign you should have been a carpenter."

"That's not funny at all."

"I should be getting home." Darlene shut the sketchbook. "I've stayed far too long. It'll be dark soon."

"Would you like me to walk you home?" Hetty asked. "I know we don't live in the best part of town."

"I can manage." Darlene placed the sketchbook on the table. "The past may be past," she said, meeting Hetty's eyes, "but you don't forget certain things."

She went to the cradle and picked up Lorene. The little girl didn't make a sound as Darlene settled her in her arms. "Sound asleep!" Darlene declared with a surprising amount of relief. "It looks like the charms worked."

She left then, her skirts rustling as she bade them goodbye.

"There's no charms other than protection on it," Benjy said once the door shut. "I barely started on it."

"You should finish it," Hetty said, and when the fabric slipped, she tapped his hand. "Not at this moment. Tell me what you found out. Because carvings on a casket aren't that interesting."

"Charlie, it seems, had ingested a number of herbs before he died."

"So that was what Oliver wanted to tell me." Hetty pushed back his arm so the fabric went taut.

"I'm surprised he did. It was gruesome."

"This whole thing is." Hetty summoned her scissors to her hand once more and placed the tip to her throat. "He found it here?"

"No," he said, "but close. Stuck between the teeth. He chewed it like it was Winged Whispers. But it's not Whispers. Oliver says the herb was something else, but didn't know what. Penelope should have an answer?"

"Yes, but having her ask at her job might get her in trouble, so take it to a different place. They'll know what it is, and maybe who might have sold it."

"Brilliant," he exclaimed.

"Hardly," she laughed. "You can let go now."

Hetty made a decisive snip with her scissors. The fabric parted. Catching the end, she wrapped it around the wire shoulder of Catherine Anne.

Holding on to the scrap fabric, she placed it back onto the table next to the sketchbook. Remembering Darlene's intent work, Hetty opened the book.

Darlene's drawing captured the folds and play of the fabric quite well. While it was pretty on the page, it was hardly practical once put on a person. But she could make changes as she saw fit. Hetty flipped through the book and the ragged ends of a torn page flopped out in front of her.

Did this happen when it fell?

"What did Darlene have to say?"

"Not much." Hetty closed the book. "Although she revealed Marianne lied to me when I spoke to her earlier."

"You spoke to Marianne?"

"She was at Oliver's home, giving him grief about seeing Charlie. While I was there, she gave me this."

From her pocket Hetty pulled out Charlie's watch. It swung around on its short golden chain like a tiny captured sun.

At the sight of the familiar token, Benjy held out his hand.

"This old thing? Spent all the money he had at the time." He flipped it open and then frowned. "It's broken."

"I know. Marianne hoped you might be able to fix it. She said she didn't need it soon."

"That is good, because I'll need some time with this."

"Truly?"

"Charlie never let me touch it," Benjy said. "An astrolabe as small and functional as this is rare. It's lucky only the clock's broken."

"Someone wouldn't agree."

"It's funny. I was looking for this the other night. Charlie always had it with him. I thought it might have been stolen."

"Clearly he put it away for safekeeping. Marianne told me a man was at her doorstep looking for money to settle some debts."

Hetty expected Benjy to nod along. Instead he swallowed rather hard.

"Did she know who it was?" he asked, but then muttered, looking past Hetty, "No, don't ask her. It's best not to get her even more involved. I should have put wards on their home, just to be safe."

Hetty reached for his arm, his vague words having brought a sudden chill into the air.

She never liked seeing him spooked. Even less so for reasons she barely understood. "Why are such protections needed?"

"I need to speak to someone." Benjy shook off her hand, leaving her holding empty air. "I'll see you later tonight."

Hetty stared at her hand and remembered sitting next to Marianne as she sobbed heavy tears.

I let him go.

"Wait!" Hetty called after Benjy. "I'm coming with you!"

He stopped and turned back to her. "Not dressed like that. I'm going below Seventh Street. You'll draw too much attention even this early in the evening. I want to slip in and out without notice."

Hetty glanced at her skirts, mindful that half his words were about propriety and the rest was a riddle. "Well, it's a good thing I still have my trousers."

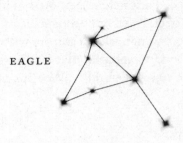

EAGLE

13

Saloons and illicit magic ran amuck below Seventh Street. It was the part of town where luck had long fled and people went without even on the finest summer days. There were far too many boardinghouses packed to the brim with people who never stayed longer than the change of the moon. In alleyways, foul magic came in flasks, cracked vials, and in fine powder poured from one hand to another. Most streets didn't have streetlamps, causing shadows to be mistaken for people. Although the grisliest of murders occurred in these streets, night or day, Hetty had never fretted. She had her magic and she had her hairpins, not to mention enough common sense to avoid fools. And most of the people, even those with pinched faces that betrayed their taste for crime, did not bother strangers who didn't prod fingers where they didn't belong.

None of this explained why she needed such a flimsy disguise. One of Benjy's shirts tucked into her trousers, and her hair hidden under a hat, did make her appear less conspicuous, but so far she saw nothing to need such caution. Benjy had told her nothing, even after resigning himself to her clever solution. He hadn't even said one thing about where they were going or even what to expect. Only that it was related to Charlie's gambling.

Their walk took them past a number of gambling houses, brimming with loud laughter and music.

Benjy stopped at none of these places. She was almost certain they were going to keep on walking until they reached the river when he stopped at a squat and unassuming saloon. The doorman was ignoring a poor sap searching his pockets for a coin, but as Hetty and Benjy drew close, the doorman stepped aside to let them through, nodding at Benjy as he did.

The Smoked Hen was much more spacious than it appeared on the outside. In the dimly lit space she could tell its occupants were mostly men. Men from the docks adorned in stained uniforms. Men in neatly pressed suits. And men in faded rags fingering their empty flasks.

No matter where they stood, folks kept one eye on the raised platform in the center. Hetty thought it a stage at first, until she saw the ropes were slung between the posts at each of the four corners.

"Is this a duel?" Hetty whispered.

"Not with magic but with fists," Benjy replied. "It's a boxing match."

"A magic duel sounds a bit more interesting."

"Harder to have those underground," he said, almost absently addressing her. "The real appeal is betting. The sport takes second place to it. Which is funny, considering such bets might not be legal."

"When did I ever care if something is legal?"

He didn't smile at her little joke, looking deep into the crowd. "They won't be placing bets for tonight, but for Sunday's match."

"What makes Sunday the bigger draw?"

"Some idiot is going toe to toe with an Irishman. He has to lose. If he wins there will be a riot."

"Why host the match at all?"

"Money" was all Benjy said, as if that explained nearly everything.

She watched more of the crowd and noted a few women here and there. They dangled off the arms of their companions, whispering secrets and laughing into the men's ears. It wasn't just one or two, but at least a dozen and a half. More than enough that one more wouldn't be noticed.

Unless of course the concern wasn't that they would notice her, but who she was with.

Benjy had come here directly and was let in by the doorman with a nod.

That was familiarity, not courtesy.

"You came here with Charlie," Hetty said. "Did you place bets on the matches?"

Benjy didn't answer.

Instead of her husband, there was only an empty patch of air.

Hetty poked at the space, just to be certain.

This earned her some odd stares from those nearby, and since she found no sign of Benjy in disguise, she quickly moved on from the spot lest she draw more attention to herself.

It wasn't like Benjy to disappear without a word, unless he saw someone he couldn't let slip past. He had been on his way to this place and delayed because she'd insisted on coming along. Now that she was here, though, she was disappointed.

From his manner, she thought he was going somewhere dangerous to meet some ruffian who might have been responsible for killing Charlie. Though they were in a corner of town she wasn't fond of, it wasn't worth the bit of panic that had taken hold of her.

Still, she wasn't about to go looking for Benjy. When he was done, he would find her. For now, she was occupied with why he knew about this place at all.

Over her head, a clanging bell sounded and the din in the

room receded. A man jumped into the middle of the raised platform.

"Welcome, one and all, to tonight's main event!" boomed the man, his voice magically enhanced, so all could hear. "Fighting for your viewing pleasure are two fellows you should start getting to know. In this corner, we have longtime favorite Tommy 'Thunder' Jones, and in this corner, we have newcomer Max Stallion!"

Cheers rose up from the crowd as the names were spoken, with boos peppered in as two men climbed into the ring. Stripped to the waist, the men in the ring bore scars and bruises from other matches. They acknowledged each other with curt nods. They pounded their hands together so a cloud of magic circled their fists. Blue for the man on the left, red for the man on the right.

Another bell clanged, and the men hurled themselves at each other.

Around her, the audience howled with each blow, excitement riveting the crowd as flesh met flesh, and blue light bled into red light.

The pacing, the posturing, the back-and-forth. It just kept going even when blood arced into the air.

What a brutal sport, Hetty thought, and the people involved in organizing such a thing were probably even worse.

As the boxers grappled, Hetty caught sight of Benjy on the other side of the ring. He bent over and leaned his head toward a grizzled man at his side. The old man said something and Benjy laughed, free of the concerns that brought him to this place.

Maybe it was the angle or the shadows, but from her vantage point, it almost looked like he was in the ring with the other men. In fact, considering him once more, clothes aside, he almost looked like he belonged there.

Her mind stuttered to a stop as the pieces slid together. Benjy was familiar with this place, familiar with the people inside and even the upcoming matches.

Not because of the bets, but because he was boxing alongside these fools.

Could it be true?

The idea wasn't entirely silly. Benjy had gotten into brawls before, in far less structured situations than this. He was strong and fit and could outwit his opponents without trying. She could just see him punching, ducking, and dodging in the ring before her. Winning matches, of course, and—

"Too bad Ross isn't in the ring tonight."

A man strode up next to Hetty, but his eyes stayed on the match instead of her. He was older, and scars not only crisscrossed his face but looped around his neck as well.

"Ross?" Hetty echoed, deepening the timbre of her voice.

"Yes, Bender Ross—that's him over there." The man gestured toward Benjy. "Doesn't often show on nights he doesn't have matches. People like to talk, but I think he's shy. Stays to himself mostly. It might be the fans. Why, there's a gaggle of—"

"He's popular, then?" Hetty cut in, sharper than she should have given her disguise, but the man scarcely blinked.

"More than that. Why, he's been the highlight since winter, winning matches and causing previous champions to bow out as if they were still wet behind their ears. Word has it he only started because a friend of his owed some money. Him winning that match evened the score, and he just kept going. I won so much money placing bets on him, I'm not even upset he'll fall on Sunday."

"How can you be so sure? Can you divine the future?"

"I can." The man tapped his nose. "White folks won't let it happen. Either he'll be pressured to fall in the last few rounds, or he uses the good sense he was born with and gets as close he can and then loses. Most of the bets going on are in that vein."

"Maybe you should bet differently," Hetty sniffed. "Just because people expect one thing don't mean it'll happen."

"This your first time here," the man drawled. "Won't find anything fair here, 'specially not fights. The winners and losers are already decided, the fix made before the opponents are even cast."

"Thinking like that keeps the system in place. Change your bet. He won't lose," Hetty said with confidence.

"You sound as if you know him." The man's eyes narrowed and seemed to cut through her flimsy disguise.

"I don't," Hetty said, as the grappling boxers blocked Benjy from her sight. "Least, not as well as I thought."

The man must have been eager to talk. He filled her ears with chatter about the matches, giving Hetty more details than she ever wished to know about the brutal sport and its spectators.

If she had any lingering doubts, they were gone at the man's mention of the last name. Ross had been the surname Benjy had considered taking for himself before Hetty suggested a superior option. As for the rest . . .

A friend with bets settled by a match—that was certainly Charlie. Going on since the winter, too? It was amazing Benjy had been able to keep this from her.

Or maybe she simply hadn't noticed.

The thought froze her in place.

She hadn't noticed a thing.

A week or two she could dismiss. But a month? Several months? There was a feeling welling up inside of her, and it wasn't anger, it wasn't disappointment—it was something else. Something she couldn't even name.

That feeling grew and grew until she found she couldn't stay in the room a moment longer.

Hetty pushed through the crowd, nearly losing her hat as she ran through, the noise and clatter falling away as she threw herself out the doors.

The brisk night air struck her face. Stars popped into the air around her. Hetty took a deep breath, but it did little to clear her head of the lingering smoke.

Months of deception? How was that possible? He had been out late a few times. She thought he was playing cards. He played them often enough with Oliver and Thomas. What did she think he was doing now that Thomas was gone? Did Oliver still play cards these days? How could she not notice a change? The fighting, too. Even if he did miss every strike, he couldn't always be lucky to leave uninjured. Unless that was the reason the jar of healing salve was nearly empty. Every wound, every bruise, wiped away before she could see them.

Why didn't he tell her?

That thought lingered the most, until Hetty dismissed it.

They had lived separate lives before they married and did so more or less afterwards. It was how she wanted it to be. She had her amusements and he had his, and there were spots that aligned together rather nicely. But otherwise, but otherwise . . .

It wasn't important.

The boxing and Benjy's business with it was not important. This was about figuring out why Charlie was killed. Nothing else mattered.

Hetty took another deep breath, and as she had done many times in the past, she pushed down her thoughts and feelings until they were tucked away and out of sight.

Her spirits greatly improved, she continued home and turned her attention to more important matters — like how much money Charlie must have gambled to get himself killed.

When she rounded the corner to the boardinghouse, she stopped as she passed the streetlamp. Benjy stood directly under the light, his left foot tapping out a pattern, though there was no music to be heard.

When she drew up next to him, the tapping stopped, but he made no further move.

"You disappeared," he said.

"So did you," Hetty replied, thrusting her hands into her trouser pockets. "But you had questions to ask. Like how much money Charlie placed on your match on Sunday."

"Did Quentin tell you, or did you guess?" Benjy asked with none of the shame he should have had.

"That doesn't matter. You should have told me months ago!"

When he didn't say anything, Hetty pressed on. "If Charlie hadn't died, would you have told me at all?"

Benjy opened his mouth, but the words, whether they were an apology or explanation, never materialized.

Concern rippled through his features as his head jerked in the direction of the boardinghouse.

"You need to go around the back," he said.

The words to ask why were already on her lips, but they vanished as Hetty noticed what Benjy already had.

The wards on their room had been breached.

AQUARIUS

14

THE WARDS PLACED on their room were basic spells. They got rid of deeper protections after the time their landlord banged on their door early one morning and was greeted by a rush of ice water. Not wanting to be evicted in the future, they set protections that warned when the wards were breached. From the outside, this took the form of Aries nervously tapping its hooves on the lamppost next to the boardinghouse doors.

"Whoever is inside wasted their time," Hetty said. "We have nothing to steal."

"Maybe," Benjy answered, his attention fully on the building. "Go through the window. I'll go in the regular way. We can trap whoever is in there."

Given his temper, Benjy was likely to charge in there. If the intruder was smart enough, they would run. If they were even smarter, they would run right into her so she wouldn't have to chase after them.

Working her way around the building, Hetty found the window that aligned with their room, and then started to climb.

The bricks and window ledge made an untidy stair, nearly unbroken except a place or two. While she had climbed it in skirts, it was far easier to maneuver in trousers without the added weight and rustle. Hetty climbed quickly, her boots slipping against the bricks as she did.

She lost her grip only once. As her foot met only air, she hit the wall hard enough that it made the light turn on in a nearby window. Her nosy neighbor peered out into the darkness. Hetty hung there for what felt like an age until the neighbor and the light finally disappeared.

Hetty hung on to the sill for a moment, counting her breaths, before she put her hand on their window.

Through the glass pane she could feel the hum of the wards. They were still intact. Just as she was about to grumble about Benjy being wrong, a ripple of light along the bottom of the window-pane changed her mind.

Her wards were intact, but *his* were shattered.

Which meant . . .

The window popped open and the barrel of a pistol leveled it-self right between her eyes.

"Be a dear and jump right back down or I'll shoot," said a familiar voice. "From this distance I can't miss."

Hetty rolled her eyes. "Penelope, move out of the way!"

"Hetty?" Penelope squinted in the moonlight. "Is that you?"

The lamps flicked on. Penelope jumped and nearly dropped the gun.

"Of course it's me." Hetty swatted Penelope aside. "Who else would climb up this way?"

"Thieves?" her friend declared. "Murderers? Someone who wants to leave a trap for you? Should I go on?"

"You made your point." Hetty pulled herself through the window and rolled neatly inside.

She wasn't the only one who had made it in.

Benjy had his back against the door. His arms were crossed and his scowl told her he had figured out how someone was able to slip into their room.

It went without saying, he was not pleased by this discovery.

"Put that gun away," Hetty said to Penelope, glad her friend provided a distraction. "You shouldn't wave it around."

"It's safe." Penelope tilted the pistol to the side. "I don't have any bullets."

"It's hardly of any use without them."

"I'm only following your example," Penelope replied demurely. "Make a great show but never actually intend to shoot anyone."

"I'll have you know I've *always* intended to shoot people," Hetty said. "At least the ones that deserved it." Hetty looked Penelope up and down, taking her in.

Her friend had tossed on a rain cape over a worn and faded house dress. Hetty didn't see any signs of injuries or wounds, but there was a certain fright lingering in Penelope's wide brown eyes under all her playful banter.

Penelope was always welcomed for a long evening chat, but tonight she hadn't come for gossip.

"Was there something you wanted to talk about?" As Penelope's mirth vanished, Hetty added, "If it's delicate, I can send Benjy out the room."

"Benjy should hear it too." Penelope turned to him, still clutching the pistol. "I've been thinking about the night Charlie died. I think . . . I think I'm sharing a house with murderers!"

"Potential murderers," Benjy said, not even blinking at this statement. "Everyone is a suspect until proven otherwise. Good thing you have a gun with you."

Penelope swallowed hard and her knees wobbled.

"Do you seriously believe—"

"No, he doesn't." Hetty placed a steadying arm around Penelope. "He's throwing out ideas again."

"It's not an idea," Benjy scoffed. He settled on the end of the bed, flipping open his book. "But it's a possibility."

"Which can also be wrong," Hetty said. "Darlene is our friend, and George, is, well, *George*. Neither had any reason to murder Charlie."

From behind the cover of *From the Earth to the Moon*, Benjy snorted before turning a page. "Are you about to explain they couldn't have murdered anyone because they have a baby? Because there are several flaws in that logic."

His words bristled and seemed poised to irritate. But even as they did, Hetty recalled his manner when he returned after visiting Oliver. How he spoke nonsense about a coffin until Darlene had left. He wasn't just messing with Penelope. He believed it. Just like how quick he was to consider Marianne as a suspect. Just because one of their friends died didn't mean the rest of them were murderers!

"All possibilities need to be proven." Hetty guided Penelope to a chair. "Penelope, what did you hear?"

"I heard nothing, actually." Penelope's words came out slowly as she placed the pistol on the table. "The night Charlie died I was looking after Lorene while they were out. It wasn't their usual night and it was so sudden, I nearly refused. But Darlene begged and promised she'd make it up to me. They didn't come back until quite late. Since then, there's been whispers. I haven't been invited down to dinner. And when I do come downstairs, conversation stops and they watch me very carefully. Like they want to ask what I heard, but if they do it'll give everything away. It's possible, isn't it?" Penelope peered up at Hetty. "We saw how upset they were about that party forced upon them."

"That is a motive," Benjy interjected. "Not a strong one, but plausible. Wouldn't be the first time we've taken a case about someone killed over a terrible party."

Penelope's face filled with an unspoken question.

Hetty nodded. "Last winter someone stabbed their host with an ice pick."

A burst of nervous laughter escaped Penelope as she clutched her arms. "I can't do this. I can't spend the night at home. I shouldn't have come here at all. I was hoping you would say there was nothing to worry about, but now I think I should have gone to Oliver's instead, or even to my cousins'—"

"You're not going anywhere." Hetty patted Penelope's shoulder. "Especially not on your own." She glanced over at Benjy.

When he didn't respond, she swept her fingers about and brought his book flying into her hand.

"Yes, stay," Benjy remarked as he leaned against the bedpost. "You won't end up with a slit throat come morning."

The neat stack of blankets on the chair was the only sign Benjy had even spent the night in the room. He had gone for a walk after his last remark sent Penelope into hysterics. And when he returned, Penelope was curled up in their bed, with Hetty lying on his side of the bed pretending to be asleep until he settled into the chair.

"Looks like someone pulled a vanishing act," Penelope yawned.

Hetty moved her gaze from the blankets, back to the bed where Penelope sat rubbing sleep out of her eyes.

"He's only gone to work. I'll make him apologize to you later. He was extraordinarily rude."

"I may have deserved it," Penelope said. "I did surprise you."

"It's not just that," Hetty admitted. "He didn't know I gave you a key." Hetty sat down on the bed, running her fingers along the quilt. "There's also the wards I changed without him knowing."

"So it's you he's mad at?"

"No need to sound so eager," Hetty snapped, bristling at the uncomfortable truth tucked into her words.

Penelope's face took on a rather thoughtful expression. "I didn't just surprise you—I surprised you in a middle of an argument!"

"Not an argument. A disagreement about a silly little thing."

"You say that," Penelope said, "but I'm worried about the quilt under your hands."

Hetty loosened her grip on the quilt square. It hadn't come loose, but the fabric was much more wrinkled than it once had been.

"Dare I ask the cause? It can't be about you quitting the dress shop. This isn't the first time you did such a thing."

"How did you know about that?"

"Maybelle." Penelope gestured with her chin toward the dress form draped with fabric. "Tell me, it can't be that horrible."

"It's not," Hetty admitted. "I thought Benjy was out playing cards with friends when instead he's been boxing in matches held below Seventh Street. Not only that, Charlie might have placed some bets on an upcoming match. Bets we think caused his death. But the part that bothers me the most is that I didn't know a thing about it until he brought me there. He never lied about it. I just never noticed, for months."

"Since last November?" Penelope asked.

That question brought Hetty's attention squarely on her friend. "You knew?"

"No!" Penelope declared empathically. "I would have told you the moment I did. Around that time Benjy started asking questions about my healing salves. I have a special recipe. It's why Miss Linda hasn't fired me from the shop. She can't brew anything to match. When Benjy started asking, I was afraid he was going to do the same but unlike Miss Linda he'd figure it out. So I made him a batch that was three times what I usually give to you, made him swear up and down that he'll never try to figure out the recipe, and admitted I mistook the number on a card the last time we played noughts."

"Did he make you promise not to tell me?"

Penelope shook her head. "It was only that one time. I figured he used it at the forge. Or for Sy," she added. "My cousin is not suited for any trade that involves heavy or sharp things. I'd take him on at the shop, but Sy doesn't even know what lemongrass looks like."

"Not many do," Hetty said, then jumped up. "But you reminded me of something that requires your expertise."

From the mantel, Hetty picked up the vial of the strange herb that had been found on Charlie's body.

"Do you recognize this?"

Penelope lifted the vial to her eye. "I don't know for certain, but if I had to guess it's related to thornapple. Most people use it for sleep potions, but add anise and nettle, and it gains protective abilities. Something for the body, maybe even spirit, depending on the other herbs involved."

"Protection from what?"

Penelope chuckled and handed back the vial. "I hope you're not expecting me to answer that."

"If only it were that easy." Hetty scowled at the herbs. "I hate brewed magic. There's never a simple answer."

"Hetty," Penelope said as she went searching for her shoes, "you use five different star sigils to do the same spell."

"That's different," Hetty retorted. "I know what I'm doing."

"Do you? I used to think I knew how Celestial magic is supposed to be, but Eunice has a system with unique sigils for each type of magic. It's very clever. And it might help me figure things out."

"Eunice has plenty of time to waste to make up such things," Hetty snapped. "And you wouldn't want to learn from her. Her spells might be neat, but she's too slow making them."

"I don't care about that."

"Well, you should, if you're going to put your magic to good use. It's not window dressing, Esther. It's all about protection from the worst."

Penelope stopped pulling on the laces of her shoe. Her hand

tightened before she gave them a mighty tug. "Now there's some-thing new I've learned," Penelope said cheerfully. "Your sister is as terrible with magic as me!"

"Worse," Hetty replied, nodding until she realized why Penel-ope said that. "Stars, I didn't mean—"

"Don't worry." Penelope laughed as she moved on to her next shoe. "You didn't sleep well last night. You kept tossing and turn-ing, like a fish out of water. Did you have that nightmare about your sister again? The cliff and the river?"

"No," Hetty admitted, embarrassed at how easily Penelope had brushed off her slip of the tongue. "I've been having bad dreams since we found Charlie. I've seen my fair share of the dead, but this was the first time it felt personal. The person most likely to have done it was someone he knew, which means we knew them as well."

Penelope's fears of the night before were nowhere to be seen as she thoughtfully frowned. "No wonder Benjy is willing to see our friends are murderers. I bet he'll think even sweet Eunice Loring might have killed Charlie." Penelope deepened her voice in a bad imitation of Benjy. "Everyone is a suspect until I prove they're not."

"Not everyone. He tends to think the people close to a mur-der victim have the greatest motive and opportunity. That list, I'm afraid, is going to include people we know quite well until proven otherwise."

"Well, if it includes me, tell me. Then I can start questioning my own memories!" Penelope picked up the rain cape and pulled it over her shoulders. "I'll see you at the funeral," she sighed. "I might be late. I had promised to close the shop today."

With the room to herself, Hetty finished dressing for the day and pinned up her hair.

Reaching for the small box she kept the pins in, she paused for a moment. Inside was a pile of pins that weren't there yesterday.

They were curved and shiny with sharp tips sure to stay in place no matter how she dressed her hair. The one pin that caught her eye was the only straight one among them. It was longer, and one end of the metal was twisted so a bird perched on a branch.

Hetty held this one, marveling at the little curves and bends.

It was just a hairpin, and not even one that would stay in her hair for long. Yet she loved it all the same from a single glance.

Or was it, a small voice urged her, because of who made it?

Benjy had made many things for her, but this was the first that made her linger for several moments. It was a pretty thing, something that someone like Marianne would show off as a symbol of her husband's affections.

Or wear to show off her own affection.

The pin slipped from her fingers and joined the others back in the box.

In love? Her?

The idea was ridiculous. Her friends had love matches, and everything she'd seen only made her glad her marriage was nothing like that. Her friends worried and fretted at the slightest change in the wind, but Hetty always knew where she stood with Benjy.

She was respected, she was cared for, they had delightful conversations about odd things, and he left thoughtful gifts when she wasn't looking because she liked surprises. They were family, they were partners, they were companions, and—

Hetty remembered jumping out of bed the other night to sew protections into his clothes, because every time she closed her eyes Benjy met a different grisly end.

She thought those dreams were a reaction to Charlie, but those were just her own fears. Fear of his dying, fear of her losing him, fear of her having to live without him in a world that would be a little less bright.

She loved him.

Not as a friend. Not as family. But differently, in a way that all the words she knew weren't enough.

Was this a temporary feeling? Would it fade away along with the shock of Charlie's death? Or would this feeling remain stubbornly for months and even years?

And if it did, would that be a bad thing?

Yes was the answer she wanted to give. Such romantic feelings were a distraction. She could name seven stories where one half of the couple died in a gruesome way because of romance. And then there were her friends. In the name of love, Darlene and Marianne gave up their own goals and wishes for their husbands and didn't seem to notice how small their lives had become. More important, these feelings complicated matters between them. Hetty's feelings may have changed, but she knew Benjy's had not. If they had, he would have said something. He would have done something more than just leave her new pins as a surprise.

Staying quiet was probably for the best. She liked how things were, after all. They were simple and pleasant and—

The door opened and Benjy appeared with bowls of steaming porridge floating in behind him as he carried mugs for tea and a pot of honey.

"Good! Penelope's gone. I brought breakfast."

Wonderful. Things were already wonderful.

Frozen like a statue, Hetty remained seated at the table as Benjy made room for the bowls, pleasantly explaining how he got a jar of honey from one of their neighbors. He could have been explaining how he solved Charlie's murder based on some strange smudge he found and Hetty wouldn't have given it a second thought.

She spiraled in a mess of her own creation. If he had gone on to work, she would have had time to stitch herself together and pretend these stray thoughts had never occurred to her.

But Benjy had returned, which meant she had to face an even more unpleasant truth before she fully accepted the first.

Benjy was not in love with her. He had stated it numerous times, to her and others when they asked why he joined her on that very first trip south. They were companions and partners, he always said, working together in mutual agreement. This was something Hetty agreed with. *Companion* had been a good word to describe their marriage, and now Hetty saw it as a lovely but plain dress that needed something to draw out its quiet beauty. Though while she could easily find suitable fabric to add, she was certain that if she asked for Benjy's opinion, he would either reject it kindly or tell her something he thought she would want to hear.

"These gifts, of course, are probably credit against the future," Benjy said. "The honey certainly seems like it, since Mr. Owens has hives in his room."

"Hives," Hetty asked, turning her attention to the swirl atop her porridge. "As in more than one?"

"I was surprised he managed to keep them at all." He tapped his spoon against the side of his empty bowl before he spoke again. "I'm sorry about last night."

"Penelope will forgive you. You often tease her after all."

"I mean you. I should have told you about the boxing."

"I am not angry," she said, and there was a dull lurch in her stomach as she now realized what her muddle of feelings last night meant. "I'm just surprised. I would've gone to the matches if you'd told me."

"You would have?"

"Even if it meant Charlie would be my only company. Plus I probably could have won money—" She noticed the alarm in his face. "Not by betting, but by playing the onlookers' false. I'd make a show of it, by acting worried or concerned at the right moments."

"You would have told people you were my wife," he said as he caught the trail of her words. "You would have used that to make them change bets. That's the most duplicitous thing I've ever heard!"

Hetty didn't know what that word meant, but his soft and thoughtful smile was more than an adequate answer.

"It's not just a possibility," Hetty said as she picked up her spoon. "I can start at your next match. It'll make sense that for such a big match your wife will be there. I'll introduce myself as Lottie Ross and I'll be there to cheer you on when you win."

"I can't win that match," he began, and then stopped, more than slightly aghast. "You picked Lottie for a name?"

"Yes. Doesn't it sound like the name of a successful dressmaker with an established shop in Baltimore? Lottie posed as a dressmaker for Confederate ladies during the war, listening in on all the gossip related to the Lost Cause. The person she passed important military plans to was the man that would become her husband, Ben Ross. A name," Hetty added rather pointedly, "that doesn't sound like someone who gives up so easily."

Benjy pretended to glare at her. "I'm not giving up. It's just not worth the trouble."

"Of what? Messing up people's bets? Or do you really think there will be a riot?"

"I want to make a quiet exit," he protested, not answering her question directly. "If I win, it won't be. My only other option is not to show, but I can't. With the bets Charlie placed, I have to be there, if only to see if the murderer will be there to collect."

"So you're going to lose. I don't like that."

"I lost matches before."

"Oh, you have?" Hetty said, deliberately prodding him. "Now I understand why you never told me. Lottie Ross doesn't like being married to someone who loses."

"Like I said, it's not worth the trouble. And can't you pick a better name than Lottie?" He squinted as if the name had personally offended him. "It's not that interesting."

"Said the man who just cut his name down a few more letters."

"It's for Benedick," he said, rather dramatically, "from the play we did before Thomas left for Texas?" When she stared at him, he recited: "'When I said I would die a bachelor, I did not think I should live till I were married.'"

"Oh, that play!" Hetty nodded, recalling it properly now.

After Oliver complained that his house had too many empty rooms that weren't being used, Thomas got the idea to stage plays. The ludicrous idea brought all their friends together to take part, plus others that were mildly curious. The scripts were mostly what they could afford, which meant most were old plays from England, although they did manage to find a few that had traveled up from Haiti. With Thomas directing the overall vision of the plays, they picked a set of rooms to be the stage, chose parts, decided on which illusions to set the scene for the play of choice. A little play called *Much Ado About Nothing* had been the last one they put on before Thomas left. And while it was very humorous at times, a particularly strong bit of laughter erupted from Oliver, Thomas, George, and Charlie at the lines Benjy recited for her just now. The interruption had actually stopped the play, because Benjy refused to continue until his friends brought the laughter down to a reasonable level. Hetty learned later that Thomas had picked the play as a rather pointed jab at Benjy, due to similarly asserted claims of perpetual bachelorhood right up to the day he asked Hetty to marry him.

"I miss those nights," Hetty sighed. "It was fun. So much laughter, silly arguments, and no one thinking any of the others might be a murderer."

Not taking the bait, Benjy leaned back in his chair. "I think it helps prove it. Weren't you paying attention to *Fire at Dawn*?

George is a poor actor, but he was the vision of a cruel tyrant king."

"Wasn't he annoyed you kept correcting his lines?"

Benjy waved a hand about. "Details, details."

He liked this theory too much, and Hetty thought it best to hold back an observation of her own. Thomas often cast them as lovers, from feuding fairy royalty to revolutionaries in Haiti. What Benjy had to say about that was not something she wanted to know at this moment.

Instead, Hetty turned back to her food. "Not that this hasn't been pleasant, but why aren't you at the forge?"

"I'm not going in today. Oliver needs our help."

The spoon, halfway to her mouth, fell back to the bowl. This breakfast wasn't an apology—it was a bribe!

Oddly enough, that put her at ease. Tallying up favors was much better than dealing with grand gestures.

"I thought he was taking care of things on his own?"

Benjy went on to explain, describing the scene at the house, where preparations were in every sense thrown together. Although Oliver had put on funerals before, they had not been often, the deceased less well known, and there hadn't been a rush to observe all the proper rites.

"Did Oliver ask for my help?" Hetty interrupted.

"No, but I need you. I can't do this without you."

Benjy said this easily, the same words he said when he teased her about doing some chore that needed doing. Hetty usually rolled her eyes, unswayed at these lighthearted words, but this time . . . this time, she hastily asked, "What can I help with?"

ORION

INTERLUDE

September 1862

DUSTY COUNTY, ALABAMA

HETTY SHUT THE DOOR to the safe house, one ear listening for gunshots. They were distant, and growing more so. She ran her hand along the weathered wood of the door, over the dipper carved there. They would be safe for now.

They had to be.

She glanced over where Lou lay on the ground, a hand pressed to his shoulder. His older brother, Cassius, hovered nearby, distracting Penelope as she pulled bundled leaves from pouches in her dress.

Hetty had initially considered leaving the younger girl behind. Penelope had wasted precious time muttering prayers over a stub of a candle before they slipped out of the quarters. But when bad luck had them stumbling into the guns of men eager to get their hands on coin, Hetty was glad they hadn't left Penelope behind. Without her quick thinking, the younger boy would have bled out by now, and his brother would have lost his head.

"We stay here long enough to get him settled and not a minute more," Benjy said.

"Not through the night?" Hetty asked. "That wasn't the plan."

"Plans change. The supply cache is low and the sigils have been copied instead of drawn with skill." He gave her a sharp look. "Someone's been here since the last time we came through."

"You'd know all about that." The scarf tied around Hetty's face hid her smirk and made her words harsher than she meant them to be. Benjy didn't appear to notice. Although he could read well enough to make sense of tightly packed words filled with denser meanings, he copied the star sigils she made without knowing how they worked, and it was a miracle that before he finally admitted this to her he hadn't gotten them killed.

"If you're worried," Hetty said, "poke fingers around and see what jumps out of the corners."

"I'm more afraid about who's outside. Might be One-Eyed Jack out there with his boys."

Hetty resisted the urge to box his ears. If he simply thought it, that would be one thing. Speaking it aloud meant it was true. Suddenly she knew why he'd insisted she wear trousers. It wasn't to make it easier for them to travel—it was to disguise her. One-Eyed Jack was mighty sore she'd put a gun to his head and left him trussed up to a tree stump like a young chicken. "We just got to keep ahead and not get ourselves tripped up by anything. Then we can—"

Hetty stopped speaking as she recognized a ringing noise. She felt it more than she heard it, and without thinking, she strode forward and placed her pistol at the base of the older brother's skull.

"Give me one good reason not to drop you like a sack of hay."

"What are you doing?" Penelope said, her voice rising over Cassius's protests and his brother's weaker cry.

"I've done nothing." Hetty slid the pistol down until it reached the tarnished silver collar. "He, on the other hand, is going to get us killed with this collar around his neck! Don't you know they can find you with it?"

"It's been quiet," Cassius protested.

"Well, it's not quiet anymore," Hetty growled, "and once it starts it won't stop until you're dead."

"Don't hurt him," Lou cried out, struggling against Penelope's hands. "Leave him alone!"

"Sparrow isn't going to shoot your brother." Benjy approached, giving Hetty a mild look of reproach. He had a nail file in hand, and a smaller tool she didn't recognize. "It'll be too loud. We just need to take it off."

"We don't have the time for that! We need to get out of here," Hetty said, keeping her arm steady. She never shot anyone before and wasn't keen to start with a spineless coward.

"We don't leave anyone behind."

The snap in Benjy's voice cut through all the protests in the room and even Hetty's best argument.

Leaving people behind was not an option for Benjy, even when it was the most troublesome path.

"They *will* find us here," Hetty protested. "We got an injured boy and we're too far south to cross the river—"

"You can cross it."

The new voice that entered the room got Hetty's pistol pointed at it.

The man seemed unbothered by it as he stepped out from the shadows that clung to the corners of the room. He was older than Hetty by at least ten years. The right side of his face was a wrinkled mess of burned flesh that extended from just below his eye to his chin. A deliberate meeting of the wrong end of a candle to rid himself of something nasty. A runaway brand, most likely. He was not the first Hetty had seen to take to such drastic measures to hide that mark of shame, nor would he be the last. His clothes were as rough and threadbare as the other three, but he was much thinner than what suited his broad frame.

So someone did sneak into the safe house after all.

"There's a boat," the man said. "When the moon hides her face, I take it to get fish."

"Why haven't you taken it further upstream?" Hetty demanded.

"It's not mine."

Benjy shrugged and turned the nail file to the collar at Cassius's neck.

Gunshots were growing louder now, and as much as Hetty wanted to fight with this man, she made a choice — the only one she could make.

She lowered her pistol.

"Show me the boat. You two come with us," she added to Penelope and Lou. Penelope looped an arm around Lou's shoulder, helping him up. As they scrambled off, Hetty glared at the stranger. "If you're lying, this will not end well for you."

He spread out his hands. "I got nothing to lie about."

"There's always something," Hetty said, and urged him forward.

The boat was exactly where he said it would be, tied up near a farmhouse with a set of knots that fell away as Hetty ran her sewing needle along them, her magic giving the needle a sharper edge.

She and the man carried the boat to the closest part of the river, where Penelope shivered with Lou's arm slung across her shoulders.

"Is the boy still alive?" Hetty asked, sliding the boat into the water.

"I think so."

"Keep him like that."

Gunfire sounded much closer now.

"They're coming!" Penelope squeaked.

"Quiet." Hetty put a hand on Penelope's shoulder. "You're safe with Sparrow and Finch."

Something like a laugh escaped her lips. "Are those really your names?"

"They weren't my idea," Hetty said. "Get the boy in the boat. You," she said to the man, "stay where I can see you."

"I have a name," he interjected. "It's Thomas."

"Well, *Thomas*," Hetty said. "Stay put."

Gunfire blew the bark off the top of a tree, followed by the tell-tale flare of wand light.

In that light, Benjy and Cassius came running to meet them.

"Go!" Benjy called out, shoving the boy forward. "Both of you get in! They're not far behind us!"

Thomas didn't need telling twice. He bounded forward, shaking the boat with his efforts.

"You got the collar off?" Hetty asked.

"Part of his neck, too," Benjy said with a grimace, handing her his bag of tools. "Those things are tricky."

"I'll make sure he doesn't die too." Penelope appeared at Hetty's elbow.

With her help, Hetty brought the stumbling Cassius into the boat, then jumped in herself. She held out her hand to Benjy.

He stepped back.

"I'm going to lead them in a circle, get them off our trail." He held up the broken pieces of the collar. "Or they'll be waiting for us."

"That's a terrible plan."

"I know." Benjy shoved the boat into the river. "You know where to meet me."

"I'm not waiting for you," Hetty called. "I'll be gone at dawn!"

If he heard her, Benjy didn't show it.

He was already running along the muddy banks even as something bright whizzed through the trees.

In that flare of light, Hetty saw men astride horseback with flaming torches. The ones not firing guns spat out curses that blew chunks of earth into the air.

Hetty yanked the scarf off and ran her fingers along the fabric's stitching. At her touch, Pegasus escaped. It flew at their pursuers on the riverbank, bringing with it a rush of wind as it went in a direction opposite where Benjy had fled.

Yelling split the group apart, as some went east and others west.

"Are you all still alive?" Hetty called back into the boat.

"Mostly," Penelope said as she tended to the brothers. But her simple answer was overshadowed by a gasp.

"You're a woman!" Thomas stammered, pointing at Hetty as if this was the most remarkable thing he'd seen all night. "But how—"

"Spells sewn into the cloth to mask my voice," Hetty said, retying the scarf around her neck. Hetty tilted her head backwards, studying the stars and trying not to look at the coast. "We have other worries. Pick up an oar—we need to row to shore while we still got cover."

"Or you'll shoot me?"

"You're not worth wasting a bullet on."

Thomas and Penelope took turns rowing with Hetty, neither complaining as she steered them along the river. There were some complaints when they banked near some shrubbery and left the boat behind for the hard-packed road. Low grumbles about how they should stay in the boat the whole way.

Hetty ignored her charges, and in time they grew quiet once more.

Their detour had taken them a roundabout way that diverted them from their destination, but thankfully not too far. Once they got back on the road, it wasn't too long before she spotted familiar landmarks. Her stride became more purposeful as she grew confident that her path went to safety instead of danger.

Pushing through the brush and bramble, she spotted the doctor's house, set back some distance from the road. A light in the attic window danced like the rest of the stars in the sky. The sight the first good thing she'd seen all night.

Hetty went up to the back door and knocked once, and then twice.

"Who's there?"

"Sparrow with four."

The door opened, and light framed the only person who could help them that night.

"You're early," Oliver grumbled.

"Plans change."

"I see that." Oliver opened the door to let them in. "Where's Finch?"

"He'll be here. We leave at dawn."

"Dr. Gardner is out delivering a baby, so you can stay up here instead of the cellar. I'll bring up some spare clothes."

Oliver peered at the others. His eyes moved from the injured brothers to Penelope and then lingered on Thomas. His frown deepened. "You said three in your last message."

"Plans change," Hetty repeated. "This one was hiding in the safe house."

"Smart move if he meant to catch a ride going north," Oliver said. "But I think he was planning to hide until the president makes good on his threat to free slaves."

"Is that what you plan as well?" Thomas shot back.

Oliver coolly turned his way. "At least I'm doing some good. Have you helped any of the people that came through there, or did you just stay hidden the whole time? Don't say you helped to-night," Oliver said. "You're only here because you're riding with good people." Thomas staggered backwards, but Oliver was sniffing about for a kill. "Are you the reason we're one conductor short?"

"Stop it," Hetty hissed, pushing Oliver back. "He's a passenger and needs help."

"I'll help them," Oliver said, and with a gesture, he urged the runaways into the next room.

Hetty settled at the table and picked at the stitching in her scarf with her sewing needle. She had unraveled most of them when Oliver returned.

"You should rest." Oliver pulled out a train schedule and spread it across the table. "I can wait up for Finch."

"He'll be back soon enough." Hetty eyed the schedule. The tiny printed words blurred before her eyes, before she gave up on it. "I'm glad you're here. I was worried we'd be too early."

"You're lucky this time." He paused. "Can't promise I'll be here next time you pass through. The doctor signed up for war, and I'm going with him. If I make it through the other side with him, I'll be free."

"The doctor is a good man."

"You think he's lying?"

"He won't admit he's your brother. Though none of them do, even when their father's faces are staring right back at them."

Oliver shook his head. "You can't just wish me luck?"

"You'll need more than luck," she said, "but when you're free, we can find a place for you in Philadelphia."

"Is that city so wonderful?"

"It has been for me."

Dawn slipped through the shutters the next morning, and Hetty watched as sunlight tiptoed into the room. The brothers and Thomas were still asleep, but Penelope was awake.

She entered the kitchen just once with a question she never asked once she saw Hetty's face.

The scarf had holes in the places where she'd ripped out the stitches and used the thread to a new purpose. She was finishing off the last set when a bird flew through the wall—a dark blue bird glittering with the sheen of the stars.

"Pack the wagon!" Hetty called as the bird flew away. "We're leaving!"

Voices called back in alarm, but she didn't hear them as she ran out to where the wagon was waiting.

But someone was already there.

Benjy lay stretched out in the wagon's bed. He was covered head to toe in mud and one of his sleeves held on by the barest of threads.

At the sound of her approach, he lifted his hand off his face and grinned at her.

Hetty tossed his tool bag into the wagon. It bounced and nearly struck him, but that cheeky grin didn't fade.

"You're late!" she grumbled.

"I got here before dawn," was all Benjy said. "Where were you?"

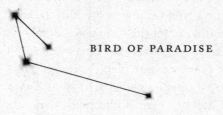

BIRD OF PARADISE

15

THE FUNERAL WAS LOVELY.

The mourners echoed those words as they trekked into the cemetery in pairs or in clusters, each pleased by the beautiful service honoring the deceased.

Hetty didn't know if this was true. She hoped it was. While she had been there the entire time, she was not truly present. Throughout the entire service she moved from place to place, unable to sit down once, not even for the eulogy Pastor Evans delivered. From the moment people entered the church she was there, helping people find seats, find fans, move something out of the way, hand out the spare Bibles to those that could read them, and anything else people stopped to ask her for.

Then there were the candles.

Five large white candles spread around the church dressed with special oils and with important sigils carved into their sides. They were not there to add light but to observe rites that would help provide safe passage of the departing soul.

They were gorgeous candles, but she had to keep lighting them as the press of people kept causing them to flicker out. No matter how quietly she did it, with or without magic, people glowered at her for the distraction she presented.

For all she endured, she was luckier than Benjy.

He didn't even make it inside the church.

Oliver did not let the cemetery caretaker know that burial services were to be performed later that day. This meant nothing had been prepared, not even the digging of a grave — a task that fell squarely on Benjy's capable shoulders along with whatever else that had been left undone. All that entailed was something they didn't know either, for Oliver had vanished like the wind after passing the casket into their hands.

The whole thing had left her so filled with rage that when everyone went to the cemetery, Hetty was glad she needed to remove the decorations. Anger roiled in her chest as she ripped things away, but it was only when she blew out the last candle that she realized it wasn't just at Oliver. Yes, she would have words with him the next time they met, but the anger wasn't for him.

It was for Charlie. Not for dying. But for dying with her still so angry at him that she couldn't shed a single tear.

Charlie had been the first person they had rescued from slavery. He had married someone Hetty had called a friend, in a match she arranged. He was the jokester in the group, the one whose good fortune everyone aspired to even when they disliked him for it. He had been a friend, even when he hadn't been kind to them in the end.

And he didn't deserve this death, not before she had gotten a proper apology from him.

"Don't run," Cora said when Hetty finally arrived at the cemetery grounds. A bit of a smile took the sting out of the reprimand. "Charlie is not going anywhere."

Cora stood at the fringes of the group, and while she faced the procession of the casket, her attention had fallen to Hetty.

"I thought I missed something."

"Like the rest of the service?" Cora asked. "I had to look to see if you were there at all. When I did, I only saw a swiftly moving blur. I've just seen Benjamin now, and he was here waiting for us. Was he even there for the service?"

"There were things to take care of."

"I'd say," said another voice.

Recognizing that particular voice, Hetty looked beyond Cora to see Bernice Tanner sitting atop a gravestone.

A regal woman with a mane of pure white hair, she leaned against a polished cane, her round dark spectacles glinting in the light.

An old friend of Cora's, Bernice had also worked with the Vigilance Society but in a vastly different role. From the time before she lost her eyesight and long afterwards, she was the source of all information that went in and out of the city. News came to her, and from it she charted routes for conductors, made sure the cargo also made it to their chosen destination, and provided assignments for retrievals down south. A few of those assignments ended up in Hetty's hands, although they were undertaken rather reluctantly, because helping Bernice took away from the search for Esther.

Despite the old woman's friendship to Cora, Hetty was surprised to see Bernice here. Bernice did not suffer fools lightly, and Charlie had been one of the biggest, even on his best days.

"You hit all the right notes, but it was sloppy. If you ran a proper funeral home." Bernice stood up, planting her cane into the ground with care. "You'd never stay in business long, based on today's performance."

"I heard no complaints."

Bernice shrugged. "Because they don't care about the dead, just the show. You'd been better off letting things fall apart so you could properly mourn."

Cora nodded along with her friend's words. "You didn't need

to do all this. You're Charlie's family as much as anyone. You deserved to have a moment to mourn, and have that time respected without people asking for assistance."

"I've mourned."

"You have not had even a spare moment to do so. They expect you to be strong, to not show a bit of weakness no matter what you're going through." Cora held Hetty's gaze, the affection in her eyes softening what could have been stern words. "Don't accept the burdens they cast onto you. They don't take them on themselves for a reason."

"Someone has to take them on," Hetty said. It was a fight to keep her voice calm, to neither hurt her friend nor gain the scorn of Bernice Tanner. Cora's words had the air of an observation. An observation held back until it could be delivered at the right moment without dismissal. "If not me, who else?"

"Plenty of others," Cora said. "Unless this is the path you choose."

"It is."

"Then I hope you do so for the right reasons."

"And get your just rewards," Bernice added. She pointed her cane toward the graveside, the brass tip uncannily landing on the burial party. "You do too much work and no one knows it."

The pallbearers that brought Charlie's casket to the graveside were all unfamiliar, except for George and Clarence. Benjy stood in the background. Even from a distance, she could see smudges of dirt he hadn't managed to hide. His jacket wasn't as dirty as the rest of him but was still mussed.

No one seemed to have noticed. They probably thought he was the cemetery caretaker.

As things progressed, Hetty finally got her first clear look at Marianne. She stood flanked by her three children with an older woman in her shadow. While her black dress was unremarkable,

it was paired with a lace veil, making her a beautifully tragic figure, trembling as Charlie was lowered into the grave.

Then one of the pallbearers started to draw star sigils in the air.

Cora gasped along with a few in the crowd. "They're going to
use magic to bury him," she said, voicing their unspoken horror.
"That's not right!"

"By the stars, it isn't," Bernice growled. "You bury the dead
with your own two hands, and nothing else."

Benjy was already moving forward with his shovel even before
George turned to the first man and said a few stern words.

It was brief, but Hetty saw anger in the man's face. She didn't
know him, but he had the face of someone who knew he was
handsome and made sure everyone agreed. That flash of anger
was hardly flattering, although he backed away as Benjy stepped
forward.

Together, Benjy and George buried Charlie, with only token
shovelfuls of dirt from the others.

The crowd dissipated as they did their work, heading out of
the cemetery to the repass that waited at the Loring home.

Hetty lingered a bit, watching as the man who dared to shift
dirt with magic moved behind the graveside and bent over to—

"Henrietta," Cora called. "Are you coming?"

"I am," Hetty said, forced to turn away before she could see
what the man might have been up to. "I'll be right there."

At the Loring home, Hetty was promptly abandoned by Cora
and Bernice for other conversation.

Left to her own devices, Hetty milled around, making polite
conversation. From the people that knew her, she received compliments on her work for the funeral, condolences for the loss,
and questions about what would happen with Marianne and the
children. While none was a conversation she wanted to have, par-

ticularly since the compliments of the funeral service skated close to insult, these interactions were much preferable than when Alice Granger called her name.

At first Hetty thought herself mistaken.

Many voices sounded alike in this crowded room, but at the sight of the butterfly brooch at Alice's neck, Hetty knew what she saw was the truth.

Alice stood there in a dark gray dress wearing gloves of a similar shade. Between the coloring of the dress and her hair twisted into a style that was a growing fashion around town, she looked like she belonged in the room. She certainly was at ease, even more so than the last time Hetty had seen her.

The shock of seeing her was enough that Hetty didn't even try to hide it. "Why are *you* here?"

"Everyone knows Charlie Richardson," Alice said with a little shrug. "I didn't know him personally, only by reputation. He was a young healthy man who died suddenly. I grieve his loss. I heard he'd gone missing before he died. If only he was found sooner."

"You're quite impatient. You just hired me yesterday."

"Time moves fast," Alice reminded her. "I wouldn't have contacted you if I had plenty to spare."

"What about the will to search? Do you not have that, either?" Hetty asked. "Like a lizard, you can change your colors to blend in with your surroundings."

"And it always suits me," Alice replied. "Try to shame me all you like. My sister did much the same, and she knew where to cut. But it's not my fault. People see what they wish to see, and often with little effort on my behalf."

"Did you come here because you thought your threats failed?"

"I'm not here for you," Alice said. "You're just a nice surprise." To prove her point, she turned her back on Hetty and walked right into the crowd of mourners.

Hetty considered following, but strands of piano music tugged at her ear. She listened for a moment until she made a connection to its sudden appearance.

Seated at the upright piano in the corner, Benjy danced his hands along the ivory keys, and slow, melancholy notes drifted into the air.

The first time Hetty heard him play was when they disguised themselves as traveling musicians to gain access to a plantation. While Benjy dazzled the room, Hetty sneaked into darkened corridors looking for a ledger of some importance. She nearly missed her cue. Music had been noise to her for so long, that she was surprised to find herself nearly lost in the gentle melody. Although she could now admit it might not have been the music at all.

Hetty leaned against the piano's lid, and Benjy's eyes flicked up in her direction.

"Did you see her?" Hetty asked.

"See who?"

"Alice. The woman with the missing sister."

Benjy shook his head. "Impatient, isn't she? Though I'm surprised she was able to blend in with this crowd."

"Why are you surprised? Look at who's here." Hetty waved a hand at the smartly dressed men and women, many of whom were born free in the city, or had come into some fortune that let them hide every trace of any unsavory past. These folks were rich, powerful, and tended to associate only with each other.

"I'm not sure what you mean," Benjy remarked.

"We don't belong here. We belong to the past Charlie tried to scrub away. There was no mention of him being a runaway, not even once throughout the ceremony. It was struck from his personal history, and that means he struck us away too. You weren't even a pallbearer."

"It doesn't matter."

"It matters to me," Hetty said. "We knew Charlie better than anyone, and I've got people asking me to fetch them water."

"You should have changed into a better dress."

Because she knew he was only teasing, Hetty let that comment pass unremarked.

She wasn't even sure why she was so upset. This wasn't anything she didn't already know. At some point over the years, her friends started associating more and more with the luminaries of town, and only Hetty and Benjy's past as conductors kept them even on the periphery of that circle.

"Can we leave early?" Hetty asked.

"You're asking?"

"Don't want to disappear and leave you to the wolves. After all, you're convinced all our friends might be tied to Charlie's murder."

"Not all," Benjy said, rather earnestly. "Penelope would have poisoned him and made the death look natural. Pastor and Mrs. Evans—"

"You *can't* consider them!" Hetty exclaimed.

"They were at the same dinner with the Waltons." Benjy grinned. "But they're implausible as well. They had a deathbed vigil they attended shortly afterwards. No time at all for murder. Oliver has no motive that would make sense. And Thomas, of course, is impossible, as he is not in town."

"Why not add Marianne and Darlene to this list?"

Benjy didn't stop playing, but his hands moved slower as he considered his next words. "Because it's an emotional choice instead of a logical one. Especially when they are more involved in this than the others. This case was never going to be easy."

"Which is a reason we should do this together," Hetty said. "Burdens lessen when they are shared. Or will you better understand this with a story?"

He snorted. "I'm curious at how you'll tell it. Would it be a story told with animals? Of mice banding together to scare off a lion? Or ants that carry a bounty of food home? Oh, I know just the one: It'll be about birds that roll a pumpkin home?"

"It'll be a story about three impossible tasks the husband can't figure out until the wife shows him the trick."

His lips twitched up into a smile. "You just made that one up."

"Where do you think my stories come from?"

"You heard them in the quarters and at your mother's side as you shelled peas. You collected them from old aunties and uncles with more dreams than memories of African kingdoms. And most of all, you gathered them from the fancies of others wanting nothing more than to pass the time."

"That's one part," Hetty murmured, "and it's a very small part. A story is a living creature, and they need a personal touch to live on. You breathe in your woes, your loves, your troubles, and eventually they become something new. They aren't the books you love so much. Stories change with the tellers."

The music had stopped. Not for long, but long enough for her ears to note it before it started again.

She waited for him to protest, to offer up some argument, but he only shook his head.

"You win," he said as his fingers glided into a new song. "I won't make another move on this case without telling you first. A promise I can start fulfilling right away, as the next suspects on the list are fast approaching."

As she questioned how he even saw them, Hetty fixed her face into something suitable for the occasion.

Darlene and George slowly made their way to the piano. Darlene's glasses glinted in the light, but her eyes were as dry as her husband's.

The last time Hetty had seen the pair together was the evening she and Benjy had visited their home — the night Marianne and Charlie had turned an impromptu gathering into a so-cial event that had reduced Darlene and George to guests. The event itself was little reason for murder, but maybe it was a spark sprung from tinder composed of grievances. Grievances Hetty would have little idea about. These last few months had passed with Hetty spending as little time as possible in the Richardsons' company. She had no idea of any of their interactions, not even from a reliable secondhand opinion. Penelope was not fond of Marianne, and Oliver had ceased to attend any social event once Thomas left.

George and Darlene stood at an angle from the piano so they could easily speak to both Hetty and Benjy.

"I would say it was a pleasure," George said, "but these are not the best stars to meet under."

"Though we've met under worse," Benjy replied.

"Yes," George said with a small laugh, "that's true. Luckily those days are long behind us and we're free to meet under good, bad, or worse circumstances."

"George," Darlene interjected softly.

"Oh yes, that sounds quite rude, I apologize," he said. "Have you had the opportunity to speak with Marianne?"

"Not today," Hetty said. "You wanted to talk to her?"

"Just a few questions about a matter she was privy to."

"If I see her before you do, I'll tell her exactly that," Hetty said. "Vague words and everything."

"It doesn't involve you." George bristled. "You made it clear you don't want anything to expand your horizons with the aid you give back to the community."

"For the final time, George, I am not teaching at your school."

"You should consider it. You might get paid well working for that dressmaker, but wasn't part of the reason you ran away to avoid serving others?"

"George!" Darlene protested. "Don't be rude!"

"I'm not wrong, am I?" George swung toward his wife and then back to Hetty as he spoke. "If you're going to slave away—"

"I thought you had plenty of teachers," Benjy interrupted, playing louder now. "You and Darlene, plus two others."

"One is no longer with us." George stopped scowling at Hetty long enough to look in Darlene's direction. "We let her go. Not a good fit."

Hetty was growing bored talking about the school. She understood its importance. Learning her letters and numbers opened up the world for her. But while George's heart was in the right place, he was going about it the wrong way. The students were taught various subjects, but they did not learn. Nor were they inspired to seek knowledge unless they already had the taste for it. Like Sy Caldwell, or the shy poets that caught Darlene's eye. Telling George all this was a mistake, one she dearly paid for each time he asked her to teach a class. Still it didn't stop her from giving him her opinion.

"Poor teachers are what you end up with when you get recommendations from your rich donors. They always have a younger sibling that fancies themselves knowledgeable of the world because they took some fancy courses."

"You think you're better than them," George snapped.

"I think you're so worried about running the school, you've forgotten its purpose. When you are not doing that you're chatting up people who would never look your way if you didn't have something to offer. I bet—"

"Why, there's Clarence," Darlene called rather desperately. She waved and called his name until he turned their way. "Clarence, thank you for hosting the repass."

"It was all Eunice's idea." Clarence's eyes went around the little group at the piano. He drew close but remained on the edge of the circle. Clearly he had heard bits of their conversation. "Nothing to do with me. I preferred it be held at the church, especially with all these people. It's such a mess."

"You're a better man than me," Benjy said. "With all this, you won't have your home to yourself for quite some time."

"It's expected," Clarence said. "We are celebrating the life of a great man who knew so many."

"Many is an apt word," Hetty said. "Who was that man that tried to shift dirt with magic? I don't know him."

"That was Isaac Baxter. He's the president of E.C. Degray," Clarence said.

"That doesn't give him the right to do such a thing," Hetty huffed. "It's not proper."

"Funny for you to say that when you sew magic into clothes simply because you can," George grumbled.

"Some things you just don't use magic for. That's one of them."

"Have any of you met Charlie's mother yet?" Clarence asked. "She's quite a character, much like he was."

Darlene shook her head. "That poor woman. She finally learns where her son is only to miss him by days."

Hetty stiffened even before the piano music halted after an earsplitting crash.

"Charlie's mother is here! He found her?" Benjy declared, half rising from the piano bench.

"Didn't your wife tell you?" Clarence asked as Darlene and George swung toward Hetty, both equally confused. "Letters got lost in travel, which was part of the delay. His mother was not far from where he knew her last to be. Terrible all around for everyone, and they're the lucky ones."

"Not always lucky," George pointed out. "When people were sold, they were good as dead. You'd likely never see them again, so you moved on with your life. When the past shows up it causes problems. That puts me in my mind one of my night classes.

Class was interrupted when a student's wife showed up. Let me just say it was not the one he was currently living with!"

Darlene hissed. "Don't tell that story here!"

"Charlie would enjoy this more than anyone." Ignoring his wife, George turned to them. "This student of ours had been married back in the old days, but he'd gotten sold, and so they lost track of each other. He comes here after the Surrender and marries a new woman, starts a new life. Never looks for his first wife, or says he does, but I don't believe it. Neither does the first wife. She listens to all this and starts throwing books at him."

"It's not funny," Darlene said. "It's horrible. How would you like it if I had a husband that showed up, claiming rights on me?"

"Well, you would have been too young for that," George said with confidence. "You were a child when your father bought your freedom. Although Hetty would have been old enough for such a thing. What do you say? Does Ben have something to fear?"

"You do if you don't stop treading on dangerous ground," Hetty said.

This didn't seem to dissuade George. "It's a simple question."

"I don't know how it was on the farm you ran off from," Hetty said, "but on the plantation I was at, marriages only happened to make more hardworking slaves." She ran a finger along the cotton band at her neck, pressing against the scars the fabric hid. "I was too magic for that to happen."

"Some marriages were by choice," Clarence said, rather thickly.

Their gazes turned to him, and Clarence cleared his throat, but he did not say a word more.

"What happened with the student?" Benjy asked George. "Did he choose his past or his present?"

"From what I can tell he's taking time to choose his future carefully."

"Wise man," Benjy said, and the music started up again.

Clarence mumbled excuses and disappeared without anyone trying to stop him. With him gone, it left Darlene and George to linger uncomfortably, unable to make the same excuse to leave. George nudged Darlene's shoulder and whispered a word into her ear. Darlene gave an almost imperceptible nod, then said to Hetty, "Shall we get something to eat?"

Leading her away from their husbands, Darlene waited until they were by the laden table before speaking.

"Why didn't you tell him about Charlie's mother?"

"It wasn't an important detail," Hetty admitted, staring at the piles of good and hearty food.

"Does he know of the other secret you're keeping?"

"What secret?"

"Trouble." Darlene snatched a plate from the table. "Trouble that places you in a situation that has nothing to do with you. No matter what you heard, you need to leave it alone."

"I can't leave it alone," Hetty said at once, even though Darlene's words could mean so many things. Some harmless. Some terrible. "You can't expect me to."

"Leave it alone. This is my advice. Do with it what you wish."

Darlene went on to fill a plate with food, but Hetty stood there rooted in stunned silence.

She wanted to take Benjy's suspicions with a laugh. That naming their friends as suspects was all part of the process of him discovering Charlie's murderer. But those words. Those were damning words that couldn't be explained away.

One thing was clear. Darlene might be her friend, but until they found Charlie's murderer, she had to question as much as she could.

Like the story Darlene told her yesterday about Marianne and the strange man. It matched up in some places with the spiel

Marianne had told her, but it was also different. And there were Darlene's reasons for telling her in the first place.

Darlene, who the other night was quick to say let the past be past, and stay out of Hetty's investigations, was now suddenly very eager to drop information into Hetty's lap. Were there other reasons than just being helpful? What about the missing page in the sketchbook? It could be a drawing Darlene wanted to keep. Or maybe something less innocent. What if it was a spell?

At this twist of her thoughts, Hetty welcomed the sight of Penelope across the room. But only for a moment. A second glance found Penelope stuck between an awkwardly placed table and a man who moved forward every time she leaned backwards.

He turned his head slightly, and once Hetty saw the beard, she recognized him as the man from the cemetery who'd tried to enchant Charlie's burial dirt.

"I must insist," he was saying. "It may be short notice, but this will be well worth your time. You're such a beautiful singer."

"I have work." Penelope leaned as far back as she could. "Mr. Baxter, I can't—"

"Call me Isaac," he said. "And I trust you can do more than just sing on your own. I felt the Holy Spirit through your singing, and that is a gift that must be shared."

Penelope smiled. "Don't let Pastor Evans hear you say that."

"Sing for me, for all of us—you won't regret it."

"I'm afraid I must decline. I have other engagements that day, Mr. Baxter—"

"Isaac," he corrected Penelope, once more grabbing ahold of her arm.

"Penelope!" Hetty cried, elbowing her way through the crowd toward them. The first moment she could, she grabbed Penelope's arm, pulling her from Baxter's clutches. "I'm so glad to see you! I need your help with something urgently! Remember what we talked about earlier?"

"Oh, yes." Penelope nodded rapidly. "I'm sorry I forgot. Another time, Mr. Baxter."

Baxter made noises of protest, but Hetty whisked Penelope away into the crowd before he could stop either of them.

"What was that about?" Hetty asked.

"Isaac Baxter wanted me to sing at this excursion tomorrow." Penelope waved a hand. "It's too sudden for me to make any sort of promise."

"Nothing worse than a man who can't take no for an answer. I wouldn't have been as polite as you."

"You have a shorter fuse than I do," Penelope said, her smile fading a bit. "And you have a husband to shelter you."

"I suppose there are some advantages of being married."

"And plenty of disadvantages." Penelope downed the rest of her drink. "You should hear my cousins. From their talk you would think they were considering sprinkling arsenic in their husbands' coffee."

"I can see Clarabelle and Jobelle complaining but not—" Hetty stopped, remembering the strands of gossip Maybelle often brought her. "Penelope, is Maybelle here?"

Penelope pouted. "Is my company not good enough for you?"

"It's just with that shoe shop of hers, she knows so many people, and I wanted her to ask around about a missing person."

Penelope nodded. "You wanted her help in looking? Who is it? I'll tell her."

"A woman named Judith. A servant, maybe a former servant?"

"It's quite a common name, and quite a common profession. You only have that?"

Hetty nodded. "And the fact she's teaching Sorcery."

"That's quite risky." Penelope frowned. "Is she in trouble?"

"That's what I'm trying to find out. Anything your cousin

hears will be useful. I'm sure Maybelle will find something. She's good at this sort of thing."

"And if she can't, I'll ask myself. It'll keep me busy."

"The shop is not busy enough?"

"It's plenty during the day, it's just those evening hours." Penelope dropped her eyes. "I know I overreacted last night, but the thought is still there. What if they were involved—what would you do?"

"I'd be impressed by their acting ability. Considering neither are particularly convincing no matter what play they are cast in."

Her friend would not be deterred. "If they did do it, what will you do about it? What should I do?" Penelope persisted.

"Nothing I would tell you here."

Penelope swallowed, and then nodded, understanding at once.

"Then you must tell me later. I promised a visit to my aunt. Rosabelle is sick again."

"I wish her well," Hetty said, "and, Penelope, if you can't stay in your apartment with peace, you can always stay with us."

"I appreciate that," Penelope said, "but I would try Oliver first. There is more space in his home."

"You might not have the choice." Hetty wrinkled her nose. "After he left us scrambling about, it might be his funeral you'll be attending next."

A small laugh lightened Penelope's features, even though Hetty had not meant her words as a joke.

Parting with her friend, Hetty headed back to the corner occupied by Benjy and the piano. Halfway there, she spotted Cora Evans standing next to Benjy. The music stopped for a moment as Cora handed him something. Hetty didn't see what it was because she got distracted by someone tapping her on the shoulder to ask about drinks.

Hetty pointed in a random direction and turned back, but

Cora had already been swallowed back into the crowd. Benjy was alone once more.

"I wondered where you went," Benjy said as she sat down next to him on the bench. "Did anything catch your ear?"

"The excursion is still going ahead as planned," Hetty replied, "even without Charlie."

"It's probably too late to stop it."

"If we go, we might find out why."

Benjy appeared to be considering her words, but he didn't have a chance to give an answer.

Hetty heard footsteps behind them and she turned slightly to see Marianne moving toward them in the crowd.

"There you are!" Marianne's voice boomed over their heads, louder than the situation merited. "I was looking for you! I wanted to make proper introductions." Marianne swept her hand toward the rather formidable older woman standing next to her. Her eyes gleamed with unspent tears, and her face had echoes of her son's in it.

Benjy stood up at once, and Hetty was on her feet moments later.

"This is Beulah Robinson, Charlie's mother. Mother, these are friends of Charlie's. Benjamin and Henrietta Rhodes. They helped the Vigilance Society bring runaways to Philadelphia and onward. I forget how many trips, but they brought back several dozen people and never lost a passenger. Charlie used to call them the conductors."

Beulah studied them as if they were an untidy stitch on the end of a hem.

"You took my son north."

"Yes, he was one of the first—"

"You should have left him alone," Beulah said, then continued, her voice shaking. "I knew where he was before. That he was just the county over on the Baker plantation. But he gone up and disappeared one night like smoke. You might have done him and others a good turn, but it would have been well to wait for the Surrender. Then our family could have stayed together. All you did was risk death by running. What could there be gained from such foolhardiness?"

"Freedom," Hetty said.

"And what did you give up to get it?"

A vision from the past flashed before Hetty's eyes. The rush of water, and her sister slipping away from her.

"It was a risk well worth it," Benjy replied. His hand looped into Hetty's, placing a gentle but firm pressure on it, pulling her back into the room. "For some, if they stayed, they faced things worse than death."

"Trust me, I know far better than you ever will," Beulah said. "What do you think happened to those that stayed behind? Many suffered the sins of a few. All these conductors. They were looking for a fight and didn't care about the harm it caused, and they still are. Pushing people to vote, staging protests, making too much noise, attracting too much attention, and then they die."

"Nothing changes if we stay quiet and don't raise our voices," Hetty retorted.

"If you stay quiet, you live to see another day."

"Mother!" Marianne exclaimed.

Beulah patted Marianne's hand absently. "It hurts, but what I say is true. My son involved himself in the affairs of the conductors and died before I could see him again. Because of them. He's dead, and nothing will ever change that."

Alarmed, Marianne sputtered out apologies that Hetty didn't heed. She didn't even notice when Marianne and Charlie's mother moved out of sight.

A glass could have shattered above Hetty's head and she would not have moved. All she could hear were those words — harsh words, and sad words, too.

Could it be true?

Could Charlie's association with the Vigilance Society and the direction it took in finding a new purpose in these times of freedom . . . could that have been the cause of his death?

There were deaths in this city—deaths in both the north and south—due to tensions between the races. Was Charlie's death one of them? Or was it simply a case of hate, and that these questions about his gambling, their concerns about him being a terrible landlord, and even the cursed sigil—were all these just red herrings with no relation to his death? That there was no plot, no murderer at all, that what happened was just a random act of violence with no clear answer?

Could his death be Hetty's fault? He wouldn't be here if they left him behind.

Distantly, she heard Benjy calling her name, softly at first, and then with an impatient sigh he tugged her arm. He pulled her along after him as he strode out of the room. Unable to impede his progress, the crowd sprang apart like the parting of the sea.

The crisp air outside brought Hetty out of her daze. Taking several deep breaths, she unfurled her hands from the unsightly fists she had made.

"That was certainly interesting," Benjy remarked. "I know people think things like that, but to say it to our faces, that's certainly a first."

"Perhaps we deserved it. People were punished when others ran away," Hetty said faintly. "Some got their freedom, but those they cared about, that got left behind . . ." She trembled. "They paid the price."

"You're worrying about unknowns again. Don't let what she said bother you. We helped people who were probably going to run with or without us."

"We barely knew what we were doing," Hetty protested, "especially at the start."

"Why do you think I tagged along?"

"You never tagged along." Hetty found herself smiling. "You wanted to come."

"I couldn't let you get killed. Mrs. Evans instructed me to keep you out of trouble."

He chuckled softly at his own joke, the gentle rumble encouraging Hetty's own laughter. She obliged, if only to hide a stab of disappointment. He always gave a different reason whenever the question came up as to why he came along on that first trip. The reason varied depending on his mood and who asked, but he never gave the answer everyone assumed.

It had never bothered Hetty before, because she knew it wasn't true. But it would have been nice to hear, even in a teasing tone, that he followed her that night because he couldn't bear to see her set off alone.

"Hetty," Benjy asked, sobering a bit. "Is something wrong?"

"I'm hungry," she said. It was the first thing that came to mind, but it wasn't a lie. Obediently, her stomach growled, reminding her she hadn't eaten since before they started preparations for the funeral.

"You never did bring back plates," Benjy said.

"Shall we go back?" Hetty hoped he would say no. Food might be freely available, but the cost was walking back into that house to face all those watching eyes.

"No. I know a better place."

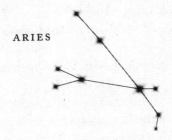

ARIES

16

Benjy took her to an unassuming building with a steaming cauldron painted on its swinging sign.

He came here with Oliver some nights, when he was certain the other man hadn't had a full meal that day. The food was plentiful for its cheap price, and rather decent.

The conversation in the saloon wrapped around them like smoke, plunging them into a more familiar world. People clustered at the tables, doused in candlelight, picking at meals, playing cards, and in some cases drawing glittering star sigils in the air.

A large jolly man behind the bar grinned at their approach.

"Look who showed up—it's Ben Rhodes with a lovely lady at his arm." A grin with two missing teeth bore down on Hetty. "I thought you were a married man."

"He is," Hetty said with a grin of her own. "I know that better than anyone."

"This your wife!" the man hollered. "Why, she's more beautiful than you said she was! Come, come, take a seat. You're here to get something to eat, aren't you?" He turned his head and shouted over his shoulder. "Pat, two plates on the house for these fine folks over here."

"I didn't come here to rob you of business, Fletcher," Benjy said.

"Nonsense—your money is no good here," Fletcher replied, so sternly that Benjy's hand immediately fell away from his wallet. "I can never properly pay you back for the safe return of my sister's daughter from those conniving thieves, but at least I can fill your belly now and then."

"Your niece was among that group?"

"Oh yes, but she only knew your names because the auntie who led the group out recognized your symbol." Fletcher held up his hands, his fingers pinched as if holding up a coin. "The conductors are well remembered in Philadelphia!"

His booming voice got a round of applause in the room and brought attention that sat squarely on Hetty's and Benjy's shoulders the rest of the evening.

They ate amid the pleasant chatter, and between bites of food, people came up to ask questions, or just to say hello, or to request stories of their exploits.

"I heard plenty about you two." A man pulled a chair next to them, resting his elbow just close enough so they could smell the beer off his breath. "Most tales I reckon are true, but there's some I question." He leaned in close. "Is it true about the swamp monsters?"

Hetty glanced over at Benjy.

He nodded, wordlessly urging her on.

"Let me tell you a story," Hetty said, pushing away her plate. "About a place that once entered few people leave. I speak of the swamps found on the Virginia border. Where inside its murky waters are more secrets than you can even dream of. A place where runaways fled into its depths to live out their lives in freedom. A place where slave catchers lost sight of their prey and their lives. Where soldiers sought the impossible." With great relish she added, "They sought a monster to help win the war."

She went on to describe this imaginary monster, liberally taking from stories she heard from the past, as well as mixing her own experiences in the swamp. The more ridiculous the story became, the more the crowd enjoyed it, which only encouraged her.

As she reached the climax of the tale, Hetty spotted Benjy reading a small piece of paper. His amusement faded into a frown and he shoved whatever it was back into his jacket pocket before reaching over and taking a long draw of his drink.

Hetty's voice skipped a beat as she finished the story, though the crowd already taken in by the tale didn't notice this last lurch.

In fact, they asked for more, as if knowing Hetty had cut the telling short of a proper end.

"It's getting late," she said. "We must go home."

"Come around again!" voices called. "We want to hear more stories!"

The voices swarmed around, but when Benjy stood up to leave, people parted to let him past. Hetty gave them and Fletcher a smile before following.

Outside, Hetty said, "If I'd known my stories were so popular, I'd come more often."

Benjy said nothing, striding forward, his shoulders stiff.

Hetty let him walk ahead, counting steps until finally she asked, "What was in that note Cora gave you?"

"That wasn't a note."

"What was it then?"

"It's nothing."

"It's something. Tell me or—"

"It's nothing about your sister. The writer said they hadn't seen anyone of your sister's description pass through."

"Oh no." Hetty shook her head. "I guess we knew it was a bit of a long shot."

"It would have been quite a long shot indeed, since I thought you weren't sending off those letters anymore."

The clang of a trap ran in Hetty's ears. It was one of her own making, from a stack of coins pinched from the piles of clothes she darned, stitched, and enchanted outside her regular work.

"Must be a response to something I sent out a while back." Hetty's voice squeaked in her attempt to brush aside his words. "Something that finally came long after the initial inquiry. News takes a while to travel, you know."

He turned around then. Although he faced her, the darkness made it hard to see his face. That was the only thing in her favor.

"You promised that you'd stop and wait until the last letter returned."

"I can send letters," Hetty said, brandishing her last remaining argument. "I can ask people to look. There's no reason to waste time for something that probably got lost!"

"We agreed—"

"We never agreed—*you* thought I said something that I never did." Hetty started to pull at the band at her neck, rubbing her fingers along inside of the fabric. She never wanted him to blindly agree to her every word, but this was one area she made an exception. The only thing she cared about in the world. "This is my sister we're talking about. The best time to look for her is today, yesterday, and ten weeks ago!"

"It's been years since the war's end," Benjy said, "and nothing came up this way. Maybe she hasn't been looking for you as hard as you have for her!"

Hetty stared up at Benjy, quite certain for a moment she was seeing a stranger. How could he say such things to her, after all they'd been through? All those things he promised her. All those reassuring words. Did he only say such things because that was what he thought she wanted to hear?

"You're wrong! She's been looking too. She just hasn't been able to move freely. We made a promise to find each other. And we *will*, because the only thing we have in the world is each other!"

"Then go look for her, Henrietta," Benjy said, swinging his hand about. "You never needed my permission!"

"Don't tempt me," Hetty snarled.

He said something else then, but his words were lost as a ringing sound caught Hetty's ear.

Although bell-like in quality, it had an echoing sound, one that wasn't welcoming or inviting. A sound that still, on occasion, haunted her dreams. No, it couldn't possibly be that.

"Sounds like a collar," Benjy whispered.

Hetty swallowed. "It does, doesn't it?"

A cheap collar only punished. A slightly more expensive one, common among the small farms with a sizable population of magic users, punished and carried a tracing charm. But the wealthiest slave owners sometimes employed a collar that did all that, plus sounded an alarm that could almost wake the dead.

The bell Hetty heard wasn't quite making such a din. It hardly could be heard over the wind. Hetty turned the corner into the alleyway and stopped short.

There was indeed a collar wrapped around a man's neck.

There were also spots of red on the collar. Flecks that at first glance seemed to be rust. As she leaned in closer, though, she saw the truth.

The red wasn't rust, but blood.

Blood that came from a jagged gash at the base of the dead man's neck.

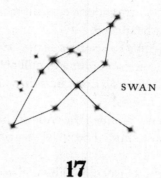

SWAN

17

Hᴇᴛᴛʏ's ᴇʏᴇs ᴋᴇᴘᴛ ꜰᴀʟʟɪɴɢ back to the collar despite the several other pieces of evidence that were just as interesting.

The man's face wasn't mutilated. Aside from the jagged slash along his neck, he was untouched—no fresh bruises or injuries were visible otherwise. There were signs of old wounds and a few puckered scars, and his nose had been broken at least once. But those were marks of the past, and not helpful at all in determining what killed him.

"I think this was placed on him ..." Benjy said, tapping the collar. It fell apart at his gentle touch, splitting into halves right before their eyes. But it went blissfully silent. "With great care."

"More theater," Hetty remarked. She attempted to keep her words light. "Although hardly necessary."

"Someone thought so," Benjy said, picking up the broken collar and frowning as he studied it. He turned it so Hetty could see the pattern of the blood splatters. "This collar was put on him after he was killed, and so was this."

With the end of the broken collar, Benjy pulled back the torn bits of the man's shirt to reveal the sigil of the Serpent Bearer. Like Charlie, it had been cut into his flesh. But the cuts were ragged, with torn skin in places where the cutter moved too quickly.

There wasn't blood around the cuts, more proof that he was already dead when it happened.

"Can't say I'm happy to see that again," Hetty said. Although she was grateful to have something to pull her attention from the collar. "But he's not been set up to be a drunkard. With the collar he's meant to look like—"

"A runaway." Benjy dropped the ends of the shirt aside. "Could this be meant for us to find? The collar was activated long enough for us to hear it."

"By who?" Hetty whispered. "The collar only activates when magic is performed."

"Or when it crosses a boundary."

Hetty's eyes swung around the alley. She saw no one lurking in the shadows, not even glittering star sigils.

"There's no boundary here," Benjy said, poking about. "Someone set this up. I wonder how they triggered the collar's alarm."

"I don't care how it was done."

Benjy's head snapped up at her words, and he reached for her hand. "You're shaking," he said even before she pulled away. Then he looked down at the broken collar in his hand. "This bringing back memories?"

"Only memories." Hetty had to force her hand not to rise to her neck. "Just put it away."

"I have to admit," Benjy said as he placed the collar on top of the dead man, "this is becoming more interesting. One is unusual, but two makes it more than a coincidence. A third would make it a pattern. Add in the theater of these men's bodies being staged, plus the sigil, and we have the start of something truly nefarious. Someone wanted Charlie and—" Benjy paused. "Who *is* this?"

"Maybe there is some clue on his clothes." Hetty knelt and pulled at the dead man's sleeves, rubbing her hands along the seams. "The clothes we found Charlie in were rags. These are a bit nicer, although they are clearly borrowed clothes. They weren't made to fit the body. And"—Hetty held up a sleeve—"there are rips in the fabric where a person might have sewn something personal."

"Like a name?"

"Or a recognizable mark for a household."

Benjy grunted. "Then we might find another body nearby."

"Or we might not." Hetty traced the stitches. "There's another sigil here, imprinted into the cloth. Likely done to keep people in line."

"Like servants," Benjy said quietly.

Hetty nodded. "We're looking at castoffs. From the kitchens, the gardens, the stables, even. Not much to go on. This was stolen, most likely. Why go through such effort?"

"For confusion," Benjy said.

"There's nothing confusing about this."

"To you, perhaps," Benjy said, "but it's supposed to mask motive, and the reason for this death. Very interesting." Benjy tapped the broken collar. "I can't wait to hear what Oliver makes of this."

"He won't like it."

"Well, you don't have to come along to hear him complain." Benjy reached down to pick up the body.

As if she had a choice.

Dark it may have been, but even the deepest shadows would not completely hide him carrying a dead body. For the people he didn't alarm, he would draw attention, and possibly the police, his way. They risked it the other night with Charlie. They could not do the same tonight. They were both distracted, exhausted, and in Hetty's case, hurting from a wound she had never wanted to feel.

As terrible as it was, it was almost a relief to find the dead man. This new murder gave them something to talk about. Something that wasn't about the angry words they tossed at each other. Something to fill the empty air between them.

No lights flickered in the windows, but that didn't stop Hetty from rapping on the door until Oliver jerked it open.

"Who's there?" he called, looking wildly into the night.

Hetty released her spells, and as they appeared on his doorstep, with the dead man hanging suspended in the air by Benjy's spellwork, Oliver sighed. "What did I ever do to deserve this?"

"This isn't on purpose," Hetty said as she shut the door behind them.

Oliver snorted. "I doubt that." He stalked over to Benjy to study the dead man hovering in his front hall.

"Who's this?" Oliver prodded the man with a finger.

"It's another one," Benjy said, "like Charlie."

"Another . . ." Oliver's head whipped back to the body, and he pushed up his glasses to get a better look. "Stars above, it's that same sigil! Why haven't you stopped this?"

"Just keep him until we find more information," Benjy said.

"You'd have more information"— Oliver jabbed a hand at the man—"if you let news about the mark spread!"

Benjy only shrugged. "Someone wanted to make a scene, and I'm not letting that happen."

"You call this a scene, Rhodes?" Oliver's voice broke and he slammed his hand against the wall. The shadows of the light above twisted his features as he turned on them. "Two men are dead! This is murder, not a game!"

"You mean a puzzle," Benjy replied without a hint of a smile. "All you need to do is keep quiet."

As Oliver's mouth flapped open like a fish, Benjy steered the dead man toward the cellar. "If you have questions, Hetty can explain. She's very good at that, after all."

Oliver turned toward her, with more than one question on his face. Hetty answered the easier one.

"We found him in an alley. Someone left a collar on him, and the sound drew us to him."

"Here I thought you two simply went home after leaving the repass," Oliver sighed. "That's what most people would do, but no, you must surround yourself with trouble!"

"You were there?" Hetty's anger cut through his rambling words. "You were there and you let us run around the whole time!"

"I was told there wasn't much to do. That the burial society would handle things."

"Payments and the meal," Hetty said, "small things, not things that mattered. You should have known that. Do you think any of them know how to put together a funeral? Especially in a few days? Why did you even think you could manage it on your own? We always did this together."

"I know." His words were directed at the ceiling. She looked up as well, but if there was anything up there, it was something only he could see. "I was trying to help."

"You disappeared! That was no help. Do you even have a good excuse?"

"Things went well without me, didn't they?"

"I spent the whole time scrambling about."

"Be honest—you don't mind. You never liked staying still, especially when it's about things you don't want to dwell on. No tears for Charlie Richardson from you. Or from any of us who called him a friend."

Hetty turned her attention to Oliver, and for a wild moment considered the extremely unlikely prospect of him being a cause of Charlie's death. But only sadness cloaked his words.

"I was never fond of him, you know," Oliver went on. "He never did a favor without asking for more in return. His path to success came too quickly for a man who started with dust in his pockets. I suppose it doesn't matter now. He's been laid to rest, and you brought me a new body to study."

"You don't have to," Hetty said quickly. "We don't even know if he's connected."

"Of course you don't," Oliver said rather sternly, "because I have yet to take a proper look at him!"

With that, Oliver marched down into the cellar, as if he never had complained about the arrival of the dead into his home.

The man's features were still unfamiliar to her, but perhaps they were thinking too small. They didn't know everyone in town. If they had a picture of his face, they could show it around. See if anyone knew the man. Once they knew his name, there would be one less question to ask.

Hetty drifted into the next room. Unlike the kitchen, the front room stayed neater since Oliver seldom used it.

A large ornate desk shoved in a corner was covered with more papers and books than usual. Hetty riffled through them looking for a clean page and stumbled upon a series of letters written in Oliver's neat script. Letters to Thomas, half written, scribbled over, all conveying sentiments that he drowned in drink rather than put them down plainly on paper. Hetty knew she shouldn't be reading his letters, but she couldn't help herself, couldn't contain her morbid curiosity. She was about to set them back where she'd found them and return to her search for a pencil when she saw her name:

Hetty's back to her old habits again. She threatened to quit her job last week. She called it a difference of opinion, but I wonder if this is just an excuse. She's been itching to leave town, and Benjy says

That was the end of the page, but instead of turning it over to read more, Hetty shoved it back into the drawer, more terrified than she had been at any point that night.

Arguing had started to drift up from downstairs, with Benjy's deeper voice a counterpoint to Oliver's higher tenor. The door muffled the words, but it didn't matter what sparked a disagreement. It could have been about the bodies, or the state the house had been left in. Or her. Hetty knew they talked about her, just as she had done with them when the other was absent. This felt different, though, and she had no interest in learning more than that.

"I'm going home!" Hetty called down into the cellar.

There was a pause in the yelling, but Hetty rushed out the door before Benjy could come up the stairs and stop her.

She kept expecting him to catch up with her at the street corner, or past the cigar shop, or even a few blocks away. He'd run up and then fall into step with her. However, she made it all the way back to their room without sight or sound of him.

Disappointment stirred, but she let it go. If he'd followed, they would have had to talk, and she had nothing she could say without causing more trouble.

Her racing heart made the thought of sleep naught but a fanciful notion, and her restless hands went to the dress that waited for her.

She sewed to keep herself from thinking. Of Benjy's words that were a strange echo of Darlene's. Of Charlie's mother's complaints. Of letters, both read and unread, that seemed to conspire against her. Oddly enough, the murdered man they'd found hardly lurked at all in her thoughts. Not even the collar, crusted with dried blood, and its siren call.

She was tired, she was confused, and she was angry, but that anger was mostly directed at herself.

Benjy had said several things in relation to her sister, but the one thing stuck with her like a small stone in her boot was the last thing he'd said:

Then go look for her. You never needed my permission!

Had it been anger driving his words, or did the anger simply bring up his true thoughts? That he had given up a long time ago and was just pretending? If he was deceiving her about the search for Esther being a worthwhile endeavor, what else might he be lying about?

Hetty wasn't sure how long she furiously dipped the needle in and out of the cloth, but she was nearly done with the dress when the door opened and Benjy came shuffling in.

"Catherine Anne looks ready for a night of excitement," Benjy remarked as the door shut softly behind him. "I didn't realize you had work to do," he added, his words clumsy as he settled into an opposing chair. He avoided her eyes. Instead, he fixed his gaze on the cradle still sitting in the corner.

"I probably have to put it aside, since we have another body to deal with," Hetty said, mostly because she felt she had to say something. "Odd, isn't it, that we bury Charlie and find another? Keeps us busy. Has Oliver accepted that you have no idea who the man is?"

"No, but he will tell us if he finds anything." Benjy cleared his throat and pulled a letter from his jacket, postmarked and weather-beaten, and quite unlike the one Cora Evans had given him.

"This was in the box when I came up," he said.

The letter was addressed to him, and already opened.

Good news would have been the first thing out his mouth, so there was no point in Hetty reading it. But she knew what it was and what it held.

This was the long-awaited letter. The one Benjy had insisted on waiting for the return. He had this idea of a better way to search. He argued that Esther was a healer of some skill, and never shied away from helping others. Benjy narrowed his search on accounts of sicknesses and used them to map out locations where Esther might be found. It was a clever idea, and a plan that spoke of considerable time going over details before he mentioned it to her.

A plan she couldn't see to the end, because she couldn't trust him to wait just a bit longer.

"I guess I was impatient. If I waited just a few more days, I wouldn't have broken my promise." Hetty ran her fingers along the bodice of the dress, seeking any missing stitches, although she knew there weren't any. "I sent a telegram earlier this week," Hetty said to the headless Catherine Anne. "I'm sorry I hid it from you, but I'm not sorry I did it."

"A telegram?"

"Yes." Hetty frowned. "I sent it the other day. You almost caught me writing it the night we found Charlie."

"Only that one?" he echoed.

His phrasing was as odd as his fixation, and she looked upon him curiously. "I only sent one telegram," she repeated. "You thought I sent more?"

"Yes. Mrs. Evans's letter wasn't from the set we sent before."

"But I sent plenty previously," Hetty said, "and I often said the postal system is very flawed and unreliable."

Benjy stared at her.

"I thought you'd been sending letters all this time. I kept thinking we were always short on rent, despite the extra work you took on. I imagined dozens of letters and telegrams you sent because I wasn't paying attention."

"Which you only thought because you lied to me for nearly the same time," Hetty said, although not without sympathy or a flicker of guilt. If she had the means she would have done just that. "We've been short on rent because the landlord keeps changing his mind on what to charge us. I did take on extra work, so I can put money into all those collections and donations everyone goes on about. There's nothing worse when those plates go around and people expect we have nothing to give."

"I'm such a fool." Benjy's voice was muffled as he covered his face with his hands. "I never should have asked you in the first place. Since I've known you, you've searched for your sister, even when you had nothing more than a direction to travel. It was foolish to think mere words would stop you. Nor"—his hands fell away—"was it fair to ask."

"Then why did you?"

"I was worried you'll leave."

The simple words told her everything she needed to know, yet he continued to speak, not quite meeting her eyes. "Every time you talk about your sister, I'm afraid it'll be the last time I'll see you. I know you'll come back, but that promise has been made to me before."

The ghosts of his parents and siblings that Hetty would never meet in this life floated between them.

"I wouldn't go without you."

As that quiet declaration slipped from her lips, Benjy sagged from such relief that if Hetty dared, she might have asked how long he'd fretted about this.

Ages, clearly, and her stomach twisted with guilt.

She never really thought he paid attention to her comings or goings. Had he really been worried she would just disappear without telling him? What could she have done for him to think that after all they'd been through that leaving him behind was something she'd even consider?

Or wanted?

She glanced in his direction. Her eyes met his, and something flickered there for a short moment before he looked away.

Benjy cleared his throat as he studied the letter with sudden intensity.

"Hetty," he started, his voice a soft rumble.

"Yes?"

She must have sounded too eager, for he jerked back a bit.

"Have you thought more about our likely suspects?"

Hetty blinked at the shift in conversation. "Suspects?"

"About Charlie. We had a disagreement of opinion about the matter."

"Which you want to settle now?"

"I have work to finish as well." He pointed to the cradle left abandoned in the corner of the room. "I need to get it out of this room—I nearly tripped over it this morning. You don't mind, since you're going to be up a bit longer, aren't you?" He gestured at the dress.

He was saying the right things, but he was too keen to move to a different topic, even with a cradle he considered mere kindling.

With it next to his chair, Benjy brought out a small chisel, and bent over the cradle.

He worked away, curls of wood falling on the floor that would be swept away when he finished. That surprised her. It felt like a ready excuse to place in between them to keep conversation at bay.

But no, he was diligently working, and after realizing how closely she was watching, she turned back to the dress.

It wasn't long before Benjy stopped and said, "The person who killed the man had to be at the repass."

"What are you talking about? We found him afterwards, and farther away."

"On the streets we would take home from Crone's Cauldron. It isn't far from the Loring home. Only five streets over."

"That's far away," she said. "And if that was true, wouldn't we have noticed we were followed?"

"Don't have to be. All someone needs to do is ask the right questions of people who might have seen us pass. The murderer had to be near—the collar was triggered, and the man was freshly dead. Oliver estimates it occurred after the repass."

"Freshly dead," Hetty echoed. "You sound as if the man was a squash ready to be harvested."

"The body was dropped in front of us on purpose. It was planned just as much as Charlie was, maybe even more, with the collar. You don't see those things around. Most of the prisons bought up the ones that could be salvaged, and the rest were melted down to be reused. This person kept such a thing."

"I can't think of any of our friends who would," Hetty said.

Benjy folded his hands under his chin, his elbows resting on the cradle. "You stole a broken one a long time ago."

"To be used as a disguise. Would any of our friends do such a thing?"

"With murder involved, it's hard to say we know them all that well." A gleam entered his eyes. "Let's consider the suspects, starting with Marianne."

She should be annoyed, but this was a reminder that despite everything, he meant what he said earlier.

He wanted her assistance with the case.

"Marianne is considered because she has ample opportunity and motive. But that only fits for her husband. There is no way she could take the time to perform a second murder with her children, her mother-in-law, and the eyes of the community on her."

"Unless she had help," Benjy said. "Darlene and George?"

"I'm not sure about a motive. They did have opportunity, according to Penelope. For Charlie, and tonight. Both have been acting quite strange this week, and Darlene pulled me aside to warn me off investigating. George is a former soldier—he's familiar with death."

"Magic's been key," Benjy reminded her. "George would rather bite off his arm than use magic that's not needed."

"People say all sorts of things, and Darlene is quite talented with certain spells. But Eunice and Clarence are better with magic."

"Separately or together?" Benjy asked.

"Does it matter?"

"Maybe? Why do you want to add them?"

"Eunice led the charge for a number of things for Marianne, some with a great deal more earnestness than should be expected. It might be good-hearted, or hiding her tracks. Clarence is part of the political club like Charlie and George, and he has some magical talent just like Eunice. As you pointed out, we found the second body on the way from their home. That fool Isaac Baxter is on the list too," Hetty said, "mostly because he tried to bury Charlie with magic."

"That's a good reason," Benjy remarked. "Anyone else on the list?"

"Alain Browne, because he came to us in the first place about Charlie and then lied to me. And then there's the unknown: some stranger tied to all of this we have yet to meet."

"That is your pick," he said, sounding much more like himself. "You don't want to think one of our friends killed Charlie."

"No, I don't," Hetty admitted with reluctance, "but it's not only Charlie we have to consider. That man we found had the same mark. But we don't know who he is or what his connection is to Charlie."

Benjy sat back, considering her words. "You said so yourself," he said. "We haven't exactly been part of his social circle recently."

"But we would know something . . . you would know something. You notice everything! Because you don't, it leaves the places we haven't been part of." Her hands fell away from the dress as a thought occurred to her. "That political club is having an excursion tomorrow. People that Charlie recruited should be there. We might be able to make a connection there if we asked around."

"Or maybe not. All I see is a waste of time."

"Don't you think it's interesting," Hetty pressed. "They're still having an event the day after Charlie was put to rest."

"Life rolls on." Benjy shrugged. "It's too big to slow down or to pause over something as commonplace as death."

FOX

18

Hᴇᴛᴛʏ ᴡᴀsɴ'ᴛ ᴄᴏɴᴠɪɴᴄᴇᴅ by Benjy's argument, no matter how sound he thought it to be. So the next morning she did what she always did when they reached an impasse: She took matters into her own hands.

When Benjy left with the cradle, she headed out to put her plan into motion.

She was going to that excursion even if it meant trickery, lies, and chasing after a train. Tickets would make things easier, and she already had a few ideas how to get them.

Hetty let a streetcar pass, and when it did, across the street was Geraldine. She stood next to a stall and held out her dodgy potions to any passersby who met her eyes. When the last to walk past didn't, she looked away and met Hetty's instead.

Geraldine gulped, and the vial in her hand slipped.

Hetty barreled across the street, heedless of anyone crossing her path.

Geraldine didn't even bother to collect her wares.

She ran.

That might have worked, but this wasn't the first time that Geraldine, or anyone, really, had run from Hetty.

Her finger slid along the stitches at the band around her neck, and Canis Major darted past her. The star-speckled dog dashed through the crowd and lunged at Geraldine's ankles.

The other woman stumbled, falling to the ground.

"That wasn't a smart thing to do," Hetty said as she approached.

"Don't be mad about Alain. He lied to me about the broken water pump, but only to make things look better!"

"What does your husband have to do with these potions you promised not to sell?"

"Don't tell me you came running 'cause you concerned about that?"

This woman was a two-bit thief, but the fear in her face was genuine. Alain had seen Charlie's body and might know more than he would like to admit.

"What did he lie about?"

"I'll tell you if you bring me my wares back." One eye opened slowly. "I'll lose a great deal of money if I don't get them back—you know how it is."

"Tell me now," Hetty said. "What did your husband say?"

Stubbornly, Geraldine shook her head, and not a single word rattled out between her lips.

Hetty was tempted to force the secrets out, but the crowd was growing and she didn't want to draw unwanted attention.

"I'll get your wares. Stay put."

Hetty retraced her steps. But the small stall, the basket, and the jars were all gone.

She turned around, but she knew already the only thing she would see of Geraldine was the trail of her maroon dress as it disappeared into the crowd.

Clever trick, but pointless in the end. Hetty knew where to find her.

Without any further distractions to waylay her, Hetty arrived at a rather handsome building that, despite its best efforts, still looked like a private home instead of the headquarters for E.C. Degray.

As Hetty drew near, she saw the front door open as several men departed.

They passed her, giving her a cursory glance that glided right over her. Hetty waited until they were gone before she approached the door. She made to knock, but a prickle that started at the band at her neck had her jumping back even before the door swung open.

A man peered out and frowned at her.

"Unless you're here to pick up the laundry, you have no business being here."

"That's quite rude," Hetty said, even as she pondered if it was worth it to hit him with a sleeping spell. "You don't even know what I'm here for."

He coolly eyed her. "You're no wife to any member here. Even if you had a reason, no one is here to talk to you."

"You are," she pointed out.

"I'm on my way out." That man patted his coat pocket, nearly crinkling the slips of paper sticking out. Were those tickets? "There's no one else—they're all at the excursion."

"Everyone?"

"Everyone who can go. It's members only, and even if you could, there's no more tickets."

Hetty attempted a grin. "Not even for the right price?"

He sneered. "You can't afford it."

Those words settled how this encounter was going to end.

"Excuse me! That's not fair at all." Hetty jostled forward, placing a foot firmly on the step.

The wards around the building buckled and responded just as she thought they would. Over the shrill alarm she raised her voice. "This is a club to encourage suffrage and participation in elections. It's not some elite club that only accepts a few."

She said more, her voice rising with the alarm, not caring at his attempts to quiet her. She lost the thread of her words after a while and started repeating phrases that sounded decent until the man held up his hands, which were glittering with magic.

"Enough!" he declared, as tiny star-speckled doves darted to the building to settle the wards. The world went quiet, and Hetty stepped back. "I don't make the rules. I just follow them. Go on with your day in peace."

He stepped around and strode off down the street.

"Oh," Hetty said, holding up the excursion tickets she had pulled from his pocket while chaos danced around them. "I most certainly will."

She dashed off before her theft could be caught, slipping through a web of alleys and side streets to the blacksmith's.

There was no one out in the front, but sounds of conversation led her into the back of the forge.

Sy clutched a hammer in his hand as Benjy pointed out a spot on a cauldron resting on the workbench.

"Try again," Benjy said. "Focus right here."

"You should do it—you're better at it," Sy protested.

"And you're not, which is why I'm trying to teach you." Without looking up, he called out to Hetty: "Don't stand over there—you'll be in the line of fire."

Sy swung. He missed hitting the cauldron's rim. There was a flash of light and the cauldron jumped off the table like a startled bird. It bounced, striking the other tools lying nearby and sending everything crashing to the ground.

Benjy only sighed as the last of the crashes echoed in the room, hardly surprised but disappointed all the same.

"Sorry," Sy mumbled. He handed the hammer to Benjy before running to collect the fallen tools.

Benjy picked up the ruined cauldron and tossed it aside. Studying her for a moment, he asked, "What interesting thing brings you here?"

"I wouldn't call it interesting." Hetty held up the tickets. "But I managed to get these for the excursion. I'm going. As I don't wish to go alone, I'm taking Penelope with me."

"Don't be ridiculous," he said. "Penelope won't go." He pulled off his apron with a dramatic sigh. "I suppose if you must have company, I'll simply have to come."

"Not dressed like that." Hetty waved at the soot and grime that covered him. "We have to dress the part."

"Church clothes it is," he said, undeterred. "Sy," Benjy called. "I'm leaving for the day. Bank the fire, don't do any repairs. If someone comes around with something to mend, be vague about when it'll be ready, especially if it's not urgent."

Sy poked his head over the workbench, tools clutched in his arms.

"What if Amos comes around looking for you?"

"Tell him I'm off doing work that got shoved aside for the work I did on the cradle. Practice drawing the sigil, but don't work any magic. I'll tell you what you did wrong tomorrow. I made the same mistakes myself when I first learned."

This assurance lifted the embarrassment in Sy's face, and when he said he'd take care of things, Hetty was certain the forge would be standing the next time she returned.

"That's kind of you to teach him to repair magical objects," Hetty said as Benjy led the way out.

"It's a useful skill. And despite what you saw, he's picking it up better than the last apprentice. Which is funny, since I only took him on because Penelope tricked me into giving him a job."

"Penelope tricked you?" Hetty scoffed. "You don't do anything that you didn't want to do in the first place. Whether it's fixing rooftops or agreeing to go on excursions put on by political clubs." She looked up at him significantly as she said the last bit. "Why did you change your mind about us going?"

With a sheepish grin, Benjy shrugged. "I realized you were right."

"Of course I was," Hetty laughed. "I always am."

"That you are," he said softly as a streetcar rolled by, leaving Hetty uncertain if she was meant to hear his words or not.

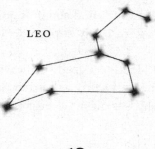

LEO

19

THE TRAIN TOOK THEM across the river into New Jersey. Though there was a location on the ticket, they did not need it. The wind carried boisterous laughter and familiar tunes, and the path before them bore signs of passage of many feet. Soon enough the tops of tents rose up before them, cheerfully beckoning them towards one of the more popular sites for excursions.

The habit of such excursions may have started as a way to raise money for churches and other organizations, but their main appeal was a small break from daily life. Hetty and Benjy had gone on a few of them in the past, but never for long, and they were often working instead of enjoying the activities.

But this time they were here to answer questions about Charlie and ferret out any connections that might lead to the murderer. Yet as they milled about the booths and makeshift stages that lined the boardwalk, the task's urgency faded.

After several overcast days with rain threatening to make an appearance, the brilliant blue sky and the fluffy white clouds that greeted Hetty were enough to push aside all but the most indulgent of thoughts.

She never planned to come alone to the excursion but she expected she would have had to twist Benjy's arm to accompany her. That he agreed without a word was a pleasant surprise. That he appeared contented and at ease was a delight. When he glanced over at her with a smile more relaxed than it had been in days, those pesky temperamental feelings washed over her until she forced herself to look away.

"That looks interesting." Benjy pointed to the man atop a wagon bed delivering a soliloquy to the onlookers gathered at his feet. Illusions of flowers and vines appeared around him as he spoke. "Although his diction is rather poor."

"Don't even think about it," Hetty chided. "We are here to look for answers."

"Where do we look first?" Benjy asked. "Or should I say for who?"

"I—" Hetty began looking around: at the stalls that peppered the boardwalk along with families, at couples, and other groups. All were unfamiliar faces, and all, from the first to the last, seemed to have no clear ties to the murders they had uncovered. She thought she might have spotted the arrogant Isaac Baxter in the crowd, working his charms on the small crowd gathered around him, but even if they could manage to talk to him, there were few spaces welcoming to private conversations.

"I don't know," she admitted. "I suppose that's why you were against coming. It's a waste of time if we don't know who or what we're looking for."

"That's an easy puzzle to solve. Amos paid me for the cradle, we can use the money at that booth." He pointed to a game set up in a nearby stall, where a woman tossed a baseball at milk bottles placed on shelves. "That's a good central spot. We can take turns playing while the other watches the crowd."

"Maybe just you." Hetty absently smoothed her clothes. Her plum-colored dress had been a canceled commission once upon a time. In scattered spare moments she altered it for her figure, adding lace to the cuffs. It suited her just as she hoped, but it came with other worries. "I don't want to ruin this."

"I'm not sure why you wore it, then. There's nothing practical about it."

"Practical is the last word you give pretty dresses, unless it's the manner of their removal." Those words shut him up rather effectively, leaving him so visibly flustered that she couldn't help but add, "It's not like I have a maid to help me with them."

With a laugh she took his arm. "Knocking over milk bottles is not a terrible idea. We'll attract less attention if we're seen taking part instead of just shaking answers out of people."

They did play the milk bottle game, although they quickly learned it was rigged. Benjy managed to hit every bottle except one placed on the highest shelf. He would have gone through all their money to get it, too, if Hetty hadn't discreetly set about a detecting charm to find the magic at work. She pointed it out, Benjy fumed a bit more, and they moved on playing the other games that caught their attention. There were quite a few of them spread out along the boardwalk—guessing the number of beans in a jar, tossing horseshoes, or spinning wheels to collect prizes.

"You are terrible at this game," Hetty laughed, as another dart fell outside the colored rings. The children that gathered to watch scrambled across the grass to retrieve the far-flung fallen darts.

"Why don't you try?" He smirked as he handed the feathered dart to Hetty. "Unless you're afraid of ruining your pretty dress?"

"I'm not." Hetty balanced the dart in her hand, smoothing the feathers. She studied the target for a long moment. Then tossed the dart.

It sailed into the center of the dartboard, not dead center, but right on the edge. A mark that Benjy hadn't been close to meeting.

"Ah," she said, feigning disappointment, "I missed."

"Missed!" Benjy exclaimed. "You almost got it!"

There were giggles from the children, which turned into laughter as Benjy exaggerated his shock and surprise for their benefit.

"Would you like to try again?" The man running the booth plucked Hetty's dart from the ring. "If you hit direct center, you'll get a prize." He smiled as he said this, but the smile was as forced as his cheer.

This game wasn't rigged like the milk bottles, but it was designed to be impossible to win. The board was placed there on an angle, and colors only added to the illusion. Benjy probably would have been able to tell if he stood closer, but he had a harder time than he would admit at seeing things at a distance.

"What sort of prize would that be?" Hetty asked as she picked up a dart.

"Depends if you hit it."

The dart struck dead center a heartbeat later, still quivering even as Hetty smiled very politely at the man.

"My prize?"

"Provided by me." A woman from a nearby stall presented a kite painted on one side with the imagined likeness of a griffin. She leaned close to whisper, "I've been watching him part people from their money all day. It's one thing to raise money, but to cheat people out of a good time! Good job on that."

Hetty held up the kite to Benjy's appreciative eye. "That's fine craftsmanship," he declared. "Did you want me to carry it?"

"No." Hetty turned to the children. "This deserves a good home." She knelt down in front of the trio of children and handed the kite to what appeared to be the oldest. "Enjoy."

They cried out their thanks and skipped off in a cloud of dust.

A hand appeared before her.

"That was kind of you," Benjy said, "considering they were making fun of me the whole time."

She took his hand, letting him draw her up onto her feet. "It was probably the best bit of fun they had the whole time," she said, still holding his hand as she gazed thoughtfully up at him. "Everyone deserves some from time to time. We haven't found any signs of a murderer, but none of this has been a waste of time."

"I'm glad we came," he said quietly.

She was too, but not for the reasons he was.

Hetty let go of his hand but didn't fully pull away. "We should start asking people questions."

"Let me indulge in one more game," Benjy said.

She followed his gaze to a rather abandoned stall. Next to it was a tall vertical pole with a bell set on top, and hand-painted numbers that increased in value as they neared the bell. The person manning the stall sat with a large mallet waiting to be used.

"I'm pretty sure I can win this one." Benjy removed his jacket and handed it to her. His waistcoat, made from the satin scraps of her dress, caught sunlight as he moved to roll up the sleeves of his shirt.

"This one is likely to be rigged as well," Hetty cautioned as she folded his jacket over her arm.

His grin was more than a bit reckless. "If it is, it won't be afterwards."

The man at the stall eagerly took Benjy's money and handed over the mallet. Benjy flipped it in his hand, gave the strength tester a single look, and struck.

The bell rang like a church's bell calling all to its side.

The man at the stall jumped up. Loudly he protested it wasn't set up properly, that its settings had been for kids. He made his voice carry to the gathering crowd as he pulled at levers. Benjy just smiled as he watched this activity.

"Your husband is the first person I've seen to get that thing to ring."

Eunice stood next to Hetty, holding a basket filled with socks. Her pale pink dress had a festive air that suited her quite well, although the roses embroidered along her collar were too large for Hetty's taste.

Of their list of suspects, Eunice was last, just below Clarence. Eunice was too nice, too quiet, too eager to please. But that might only seem true because Hetty didn't know her that well. Nor did she know enough of Eunice's movements to know her whereabouts the night Charlie died.

"What's the basket for?" Hetty asked.

"This? I'm just collecting money for veterans of the USCT. Though I only have a few donations." Eunice shook her head. "There's so much enthusiasm when there's fighting, but no one cares when soldiers come back injured. The government promised pensions for soldiers who fought for the Union, but the Colored Troops got left behind. None of our boys have seen any money. Which is expected, but I had hoped for more from the community. You can't say 'support soldiers' and then turn a blind eye to those that come back injured beyond words."

"I think you might do better some other time. It looks like people are saving their coins for fun."

"That might be true. Are you here to enjoy the day?" There was a bit of a pause even though her words were still quite pleasant. "I didn't even know you two were coming."

"Didn't decide until quite recently," Hetty said as the bell rang clearly over the crowd once again. "I hope we haven't missed anything."

"Nothing much yet. Have you heard they're having a ladies' race on bicycles? With the new bicycles that have become all the rage."

"How exciting!" Hetty did not have to fake her enthusiasm this time. Her interest in bicycles had gone from curiosity to fascination since the new versions arrived from Europe.

Where a bicycle had once been this monstrous thing with a giant wheel that was impossible for most to ride, this new bicycle was much more reasonable in every way. The front wheel was only somewhat larger than the rear wheel, and the frame had a nice sloping angle that was suitable even for skirts. With the pedals moved to the center, and gently curving handlebars, it rode like a dream. Which it very much was. The English inventor had woken up in the middle of the night and declared he had seen the future.

Hetty had ridden a bicycle a handful of times before, encouraged by Penelope, who was both frightened and intrigued by the newfangled machine. They had borrowed it from Penelope's snotty cousin Clarabelle, who had only bought it because it was a growing fashion among the luminary ladies in town. Penelope had fallen off a few times, but Hetty had taken to it like a bird stretching its wings.

Sadly, the bicycle ended up being sold when Clarabelle decided not to chase that particular fashion, so Hetty had few chances to ride one since.

"What's this about a race?" Benjy asked as he joined them. He couldn't quite hide the smug smile on his face as he took back his jacket.

"There's a ladies' bicycle race," Eunice said. "There's a prize of fifty dollars to the winner."

"That much!" Hetty exclaimed. "Where can I sign up?"

"I'm not sure," Eunice laughed. "You'll have to talk to my husband. He's the best person to speak to about, well, about everything, it seems. He arranged all this, you know, down to the last detail. He's been so busy. I know he hasn't had a chance to enjoy himself."

Hetty doubted Clarence could do a simple thing such as that, but kept that observation to herself.

"I'll take you to him," Eunice went on. "I wanted to take part as well, but if you do it, I don't think he'll disapprove. Let me put this down and we'll head off."

As Eunice went to get rid of the basket, Hetty turned to her husband.

"Did you break the game?"

"It still works," Benjy said rather innocently. "The piece he used to keep the test at a certain level is most certainly broken, though."

Which explained the crowd that swarmed the booth now. "You just helped him make money."

"Money he can't keep," Benjy reminded her. "Is there a fee to join the race? I don't think we have much left."

"Eunice didn't mention it."

"Rather odd, isn't that? Eunice said Clarence wouldn't let her take part in the race. He's always glad to show off how indulgent he is."

Hetty knew this of course — it was evident from Eunice's fine clothing and lovely home. But it was also evident from Clarence's monetary support of all the committees and good causes Eunice championed throughout town.

"Maybe he thought it was dangerous." Hetty shrugged. "It's hardly odd. Some treat their spouses like delicately spun glass."

"And not everyone likes such behavior."

This was all the observation he was able to give. Eunice returned and cheerfully led the way.

When they reached the end of the boardwalk and found Clarence, he looked no more bothered than when he was dealing with a catering job for regular customers. He stood aside tallying notes in a small book, and when there was something disagreeable, he yanked the paper right out. Instead of crumpling it, he drew a finger along the page and a sigil flared up on it before flames sprouted from the mark. He held on to it until the orange tongues of the flames tickled his fingertips.

"Clarence," Eunice called, "is the bicycle race still open? Henrietta wants to join and will only do it if I take part as well."

He looked up and blinked as his eyes fell on them. "I didn't know you two would be here."

"Neither did we," Hetty remarked. "We got tickets just this morning."

"After I joined the club," Benjy added unnecessarily.

"Then," Clarence replied, "you should know your dues will need to be paid fairly soon."

"Dues?"

Clarence's eyes didn't leave Benjy's face. "Were you not informed that every member has to pay twenty dollars for the year? Of course," he added, as Hetty and Benjy both started at the princely sum, "if your wife wins the race, that won't be the case." He gave them a lopsided grin. "It's not just you. We had such problems recently with a few of our members. They had fallen on the wayside of paying the proper fees, sad as I am to speak ill of the dead."

"You mean Charlie?" Benjy asked. "That's quite odd, since he was the one that first told me about this club."

"Yes, yes," Clarence said before sparing a glance at Eunice. She hadn't said a word, but Clarence's brow had furrowed with the concerns of a man who didn't want his wife to hear terrible things.

Clarence knew something, if his vague words were any indication. Charlie had gambling debts—this they knew—but they were hearing of debts to the club for the first time. Hetty wanted to learn more, but they wouldn't get a candid answer with Eunice present. Clarence was not the sort of husband who talked easily and openly in front of his wife.

Hetty met Benjy's eyes and nodded ever so slightly. They needed to split up, although she would let him choose which of the Lorings he would lure away.

"I heard piano music on our way in." Benjy turned to Eunice, favoring her with a smile. "Think I can trouble someone to play a few reels?"

"I'm not sure they would let you," Eunice chuckled.

"I think they might," he said easily, "especially if you help me convince them."

With another laugh, Benjy all but swept Eunice away, leaving the woman little chance to ask why Hetty wasn't coming along.

Not that the thought appeared to cross Eunice's mind for a moment. Eunice was so used to carrying people away in her enthusiasm that she probably didn't know how to cope when the opposite occurred.

While Hetty was amused at the sight of their respective spouses disappearing into the crowd, Clarence went stiffer than a dead piece of wood with trouble brewing in his eyes.

Before he could go after them and ruin everything, Hetty stepped into his path.

"I heard from my husband," Hetty said, forcing Clarence to pay her attention, "that Charlie was quite insistent that he join the club."

Clarence's eyes rolled back to her. "He was, but not without purpose. Isaac Baxter likes playing the benevolent god. He promised to forget about some of Charlie's gambling fees if he increased membership numbers. Benjy was just another body to add."

Hetty didn't have to pretend surprise. This was far more than what she expected to learn.

"Would Isaac Baxter send someone around to collect money?" Hetty asked. "Marianne mentioned strange men showing up on her doorstep."

"Of course not." Clarence frowned. "It would be improper so soon. Though I must admit that if he had, I might not have been

informed. I've been busy with the final arrangements for all this.
I had to make do with what I can manage. If I hadn't, I'm afraid
there would have been a light show."

"Fireworks?"

"No, magic. Isaac Baxter wanted to light up the night, but I
had to put my foot down. It was already difficult enough reserv-
ing the area. Anything more would mean we would lose it. And
with it, the chance to escape the city for a bit of fun. I think we
need that, after all that has happened—with last month's elections, with Charlie, and more." Clarence absently rubbed his
thumb around his neck, where his scars, old and faded as they
were, remained.

"Some things are as hard to escape," Hetty said, "as they are
to forget."

"Much like people. Sometimes you think them lost and then
they show up when least expected. I can't stop thinking about
Charlie's mother. If only the first telegrams hadn't gone to the
wrong place, they would have met months earlier."

"Wrong place?" Hetty asked.

"The wrong names were used. Charlie used the name of his
old master and didn't realize there were two Wilsons in the same
area. The Freedmen's Bureau isn't much help, but you know that
better than I do after all your visits."

"I cannot say they are well run," Hetty said softly. "I rely on my
own means these days."

"Then maybe if you consider . . ." Clarence trailed off.

"Consider what?"

"Consider that maybe your sister is already in Philadelphia.
She might not know you have taken on a different name."

"I only added a last name."

"She might not be aware of that."

Hetty had used a combination of names to search for her sister, but never considered the last name she adopted to be confusing. She kept the name her mother had given her, for she had gotten great use of it, and Esther would know it. Names. Could that have been the problem?

"How about you?" Hetty said, remembering the small kindness he had shown her once, waiting in that long line. "Were you able to find something about— I'm sorry, I forgot the name."

"Sofia." The single word melted his usually stern features, leaving only the pain of an old wound.

"Your sister?" Hetty asked, even as she knew the question was wrong. She remembered, at the funeral, how quiet he became when George was making a fool of himself asking about old husbands and wives left behind in slavery.

"My wife." He grunted. "We were fond of each other and got permission to wed. But then her master got wind that I had some skill with magic. I was sold off to a man who gave me my freedom some years later, but before then, I was happy. She had the sweetest voice." Quick as the breach came, he pulled himself back together and became stone once more. "Don't worry. There will be no grand scene to embarrass Eunice. Sofia is dead."

"Dead? You know for certain?"

"I received a response some time ago. Back in 'sixty-three, Sofia and a few others decided to make a break for freedom, going forth on their own without any conductors to guide them. They were caught and chose to fight. It did not end well."

"I'm so sorry to hear that," Hetty said, hearing his sorrows even as he tried to suppress them.

"You should be sorry for those that let it happen," Clarence growled. "Those that do evil things always get their just rewards."

"The past is past," Hetty said.

"If that's true, then why are you still searching?"

"I don't give up easily."

Clarence grunted. "Then I wish you luck for both your search and the race. I'll let the person in charge know you're entering before it's too late. Until then, enjoy the day."

Hetty pushed her way through the crowd, jostling others who flooded the area in every direction. Bits of conversation flitted past her, filled with merriment and an overall bliss that made her feel as if she were an intruder.

People around her spoke about competitions, games, and how many pennies they had to spend on food, and all she could think about was how many people had suffered as Sofia had. Esther could have died in the intervening years and the news would be slow to travel. It was certainly possible. Just as it was possible, as Clarence suggested, that Esther could be in the city already, and it was only their names and the passing of time that left her and Hetty from being unable to find each other.

A man in a poorly cut suit abruptly walked into her path, and she turned to let him pass. As she did, she caught sight of the booths scattered along the way ahead, and on the other side of the flat green where people milled about in clusters, Hetty spied a face she had not expected to see.

Alain Browne was not as nervous and trembling as he'd been the night he had banged on Hetty's door saying he'd found a dead body. He carefully chewed on a steaming hand pie, but he held himself too much like a lightning-struck cat to make it seem like he was actually enjoying it.

What was *he* doing here?

This was a members-only event. While Hetty tried not to judge people and their circumstances, she highly doubted Alain would have the means to afford a membership to this exclusive club. However, neither did they. She had stolen tickets after all, and relied on charm to help smooth their entry. Perhaps Alain had managed the same, or maybe he was an invited guest of another member.

What was it that Geraldine had said? That Alain had lied, but that he had not meant to.

That could mean so many things. It could merely be the prattle about forcing Charlie to fix the pump. Or it could change everything they knew about their investigation.

Alain shoved the last corner of the fried dough into his mouth and Hetty made her decision. She moved through the crowd, skipping past the booths to catch up with him.

But she wasn't the only one making moves across the field.

"Henrietta, I didn't realize you'd be here. Charlie got Ben to join in the end, did he?"

Hetty spun around to face George.

If Eunice had been resplendent, Clarence unbothered by the festive air, George was flushed and sweating like he had just run through the woods with dogs at his heels.

"In a way, I guess he did."

"Surprised by that," George said, puffing up, "given the nasty argument they had before Charlie died."

This wasn't a complete surprise to Hetty.

Her last conversation with Charlie had been because he wanted to use her as a buffer to speak to Benjy. She suspected an argument between the pair, but George's words danced on something that was a bit more than a mere disagreement. She just didn't know what.

At the moment it didn't matter.

George delivered these words as if he meant them to be a surprise, so Hetty gasped, a hand going to her throat as she made her eyes grow wide. "I didn't hear about this!"

For a moment, she thought she overdid it. But then, George's prejudices were easy to take advantage of.

"I suppose he wouldn't tell you," George blustered on. "It was alarming all around. Your husband has quite a temper when pushed past his limits. I don't like to speak ill of the dead, but

Charlie never did know when to stop." George's face twisted. "Especially when he knew better."

Charlie might have known that there was only so far he could push Benjy, but did he know the same of George?

Anger pinched George's face, with a bleakness that reminded Hetty that, of all her friends, he was the only one who saw the war through the eyes of a soldier. Unlike some who rode it out digging trenches for latrines, George had shot several men dead, and proudly, too. It was easy to forget that underneath his schoolteacher's mannerisms, that part was still there, buried deep inside him.

"What did Charlie do?"

"Nothing for you to concern yourself with," George replied. "The man's dead, after all. His big dreams will never come to light now."

"A good thing," Hetty said, drawing out her words with care. "His dreams and schemes always led to trouble."

"You'll find no argument from me."

"I saw Eunice earlier," Hetty said, figuring if George wasn't going to leave her alone, she should at least get some use out of him. "I'll be in the bicycle race later on. Is Darlene here? Is she taking part?"

"I don't think so." George's face filled with worry. "The baby has been rather fussy all day. We probably shouldn't have brought her with us, but Darlene was working a booth and the baby would be in the shade all day. Do you think Lorene might be sick?"

This was a topic of some concern to him, and he stayed on it despite Hetty's efforts to shift things back.

She left George then, her grumbling stomach leading her to a stall with hand pies. Coins exchanged hands. As she took a bite, something bumped her legs. Instead of the table or small child she'd assumed, Hetty looked down and saw a hound made of stars wagging its tail and barking soundlessly at her.

"He sent you?" Hetty asked, and the dog just turned and dashed off toward Benjy. Hetty followed.

She found Benjy standing near the small raised platform at the start of the boardwalk. He turned his head toward her as she approached, and the dog vanished by the time she stepped up next to him.

"No one would let you touch a piano?" Hetty held out the remaining hand pies to him.

He took them eagerly, and barely finished swallowing the first before reaching for the second.

"Only at the dance tent, but if I touched the keys I'd be charmed to that seat until the dancing stops at dawn."

"The excursion runs that late?"

"Would you like to find out? They're having a prize dance."

"A cakewalk would be fun. Think we could win without Penelope and Thomas?"

His answering smile left little doubt of the affirmative.

The cakewalk Hetty remembered as a child had high kicks, jumps, and perfect spins, with couples doing their best to outshine the others. While the gatherings were always fun, the best ones were when Master and Mistress came to watch. Not only was there a chance of a prize, but some people in the quarters got a little bold in their steps. The cakewalk was always about making fun of the bobbing waltzes that went on in the Big House. Over time it became more about what they could get away with without catching notice.

These days it was popular because of the prizes won at the end, which were more often money than cake. With that change, the dance became a fierce competition, and in order to win you had to outshine the other couples with a display of graceful turns and elegant kicks in rhythm to the music.

When Hetty took on a round of the cakewalk with Benjy, illusions danced alongside them, sometimes small things as birds fluttering about, and others elaborate visions drawn from her stories. This was how he persuaded her to dance with him in the first place, and it was how they won the first competition they entered in.

"I went around asking a few questions about the setup of the excursion," Benjy said, with his gaze focused along the boardwalk. "The booths are run by Degray members, usually the more junior members to help pay off the fees. It wasn't by choice, which might have explained some of the rigged games. I chatted with a few of them—not many knew Charlie that well. It doesn't seem like he was an active member."

"Then why did he join?"

"E.C. Degray skews to the well-established. It's a social club mostly. If he didn't join for prestige, he joined to make connections."

"Or something else."

"Or something else," Benjy echoed, "but that's hard to tell. I also asked the junior members if there was anyone who was meant to be at the excursion but they had not seen since yesterday."

"Was there?"

Benjy shook his head. "No suspicious absences. I don't think our unknown man was part of Degray." Benjy brushed away the crumbs from the hand pies. "What did you learn from Clarence?"

"Not much, but he did say Isaac Baxter had him keep an eye on Charlie regarding his debts. If Charlie's debts were large enough to be of concern, why wouldn't there be others?"

"A worthy theory, but it's missing one piece. Dead men can't pay back their debts."

"Unless they were after something bigger. I saw George, and he hinted that there were bigger dreams that Charlie had." Hetty tapped her foot against the ground, considering her next words carefully. "He said a number of other things, too. Including that you had argued with Charlie."

"I did." Benjy eyed the next hand pie. "I told you about it."

"Not the details."

"Did George tell you something?"

"George told me nothing. I think he wanted to distract me. I asked a few questions, then he started talking about his daughter. It would have taken a thunderstorm to change the subject."

Benjy didn't answer right away. "He was trying to distract you. There's nothing to worry—the argument was about nothing you don't know already."

"You found out about the dresses Charlie tricked me into making?"

"Something else," he said.

They were interrupted before he could explain.

"Henrietta!" Eunice called as she ran up to them. "You're going to miss the race if you dally!"

"Go," Benjy urged. "A bit of fun won't hurt anything."

"I shouldn't," Hetty began, but Eunice reached them and grabbed on to Hetty's wrist.

She beamed up at her. "Well, aren't you coming?"

Hetty opened her mouth to protest, and Benjy pushed her forward. "Yes, she is. Good luck to you both!"

With no good reasons for further protest, Hetty let herself be hauled off into the crowd.

Standing elbow to elbow with other overeager women mounted on bicycles, she noticed a few faces that were somewhat familiar—likely members of the Stars of Hope, the ladies' bicycling group that always made sure to wear the most flamboyant hats as they rode.

Hetty carefully mounted her bicycle, smoothing her skirts. Eunice followed, but less gracefully.

Hoping that Eunice would stay safely in the back, Hetty asked, "How far will we have to travel without knocking into one another?"

"That far." Eunice pointed out in the distance. Clarence stood on the end of the field waving a bright yellow scarf. "We are to ride out to him and hopefully not into him."

"I do hope your husband knows a few spells to fly."

Cheers drowned out Eunice's next words, as Isaac Baxter entered the crowd. He moved between the racers, smiling at a few and waving at others as he made his way to the front.

"At my mark, we'll begin!"

Baxter threw his arm into the air. A phoenix burst from his fingertips, leaving behind a trail of bright blue flames.

A few women screamed while others stared like Hetty did.

Only the rattle of wheels brought Hetty back to her senses.

Hetty pedaled forward, as fast as she could. She did want to win. Not just for the money, but because she disliked coming in last in anything. As she passed more of the other racers, she could see her desire becoming a reality. The hats of racing ladies came into view, the gap between them narrowing.

Hetty sped onward, readying to overtake them—

And then the ground burst into the air.

Hetty veered her bicycle away from the initial blast, but the dust and swerving racers made it difficult. Yanking her bicycle handles, Hetty rolled off the path, shrieks filling her ears. Just as she was ready to come to a halt, a second explosion sent her flying in the opposite direction.

She tried to stop the bicycle, but her shoes slipped along the slick grass. Quicker than she expected, quicker than she feared, the grass gave way to the river.

Water suddenly surrounded Hetty. It pulled her into its icy depths. Bone-chilling cold took what air remained in her lungs. She flayed, struggling to reach the surface. But it was out of her grasp. Her skirts tangled with the bicycle and it pulled her under like a sinking stone.

She was going to drown.

The thought swirled in her head.

It had taken just a few years for fate to catch up to her. This was how she was going to die. Water roaring in her ears, cold seeping to her bones, her view obscured, her sister slipping away from her . . .

No. Not today.

She was not going to die like this.

Sweeping her free hand in the water, she ran her finger along the sigils stitched into the cloth band at her neck and focused every bit of her attention to separate herself from the river.

Light from her magic flowed around her, and suddenly, instead of pulling her down, the water began rushing around in a swirling spiral. Hetty found herself rising out of the water, her skirt nearly ripping as the bicycle fell away beneath her. Hovering in the air, quite some distance from the river, Hetty caught sight of the world of dust and smoke below. The figures moving on the ground appeared much like ants. Their faces were hard to tell apart, but she spotted some she knew.

Eunice in the tangle of bicycles. Darlene and George staring, aghast, in the crowd. Clarence on the fringes. Benjy running toward the river.

All this was the last thing she saw before the sigils keeping her in the air faded away and she crashed back into the water.

SEA MONSTER

INTERLUDE

April 1863

GREAT DISMAL SWAMP, VIRGINIA

WITH A CHILD CLINGING to her back and her pistol empty of all its bullets, Hetty returned to the village just as the sun started to set. She lost her scarf to the murky waters, so her braids brushed against her neck. Her trousers were damp to the knees, and there were new tears on her jacket, but her boots had done their job. They were dry and were holding together.

Her way back had been guided by the little fox that darted from tree trunk to tree trunk, its blue-black coat shimmering with starlight. She was glad she had marked sigils on the trees when she had left earlier that afternoon, for as it grew darker, everything grew unfamiliar.

At the entrance of the village the little fox faded away, but she wasn't alone. From the nearest tree, a crow took flight and pierced the wards to leave a tear wide enough for her to walk through.

The star-speckled crow looped around her once more before it flew into the village proper and slid through the walls of a cabin set on the outskirts of the village.

Instead of following, Hetty walked toward Nanette's cabin,

which sat in a position of honor among the loose ring of homes. As she strode along the wooden walkway, doors from the other cabins lining the path sprang open and whispers fluttered past her.

"She's back!"

"I bet she killed them!"

"She's alive?"

"How did she get past the boundary charms?"

"My son!"

This last voice was the loudest.

Olympia ran forward, stumbling across the beams to meet them, her arms outstretched for Hetty to hand over the child.

The young mother pressed her child to her chest, her grip tightening as the child embraced her.

"You brought him back."

"He wasn't hard to find. He's smart. He climbed the trees and stayed well out of the way."

"And the Grays?" Olympia whispered. "We heard gunshots. You weren't hurt?"

"They missed," Hetty said, patting the empty pistol that swung from her belt. "I didn't."

"I'm sorry, Mama," the child said. "I won't run off again."

"No, you won't," Olympia said, her voice too soft to be any stern rebuke. "I'm not letting you out of my sight again."

Leaving mother and child alone, Hetty walked the rest of the way to Nanette's cabin. It was the only door in the circle of cabins that had not opened, although the curtains dancing in the window told her that her arrival had not gone unnoticed.

At the foot of the stairs, she stopped.

"Old woman!" Hetty bellowed. "I did as you asked. I brought the child back alive and well! Enough of your games! My patience has ground into dust. Honor your words or suffer the consequences!"

A force strong enough to be a gust of wind flung open the

door. And in its wake, Nanette stood in the doorway with a pipe clenched between her teeth.

Stark white hair and a heavily lined face were the only marks of her age. Her back was straight, and her body held enough wiry strength to match or better Hetty's own. The leader of this hidden village, Nanette had first made a home here with her husband, her brother, and several others who chose uncertain protection of the swamp in their bid for freedom. Over the years her family grew into a village as others sought safety in the swamp's borders—first from slavery, then from war.

In the few days that Hetty had been here, she had collected stories of Nanette's bravery, cunning, and skill that had kept the little village safe and its people free. The old woman was respected, but the stories Hetty heard went no further than that. Prodding for more stopped the flow of stories entirely.

While Hetty could not deny there was no safer place for miles around, there was no freedom here. People who came to the village never left. And those who chose to leave were quickly dissuaded by any means necessary.

Which was why the old woman was playing games as if this were a fairy tale, giving Hetty tricky and tedious tasks in exchange for help.

It was a nice distraction at first. Answering riddles or sewing together nettles to make a fishing net was hardly a challenge for her. But once Hetty found herself climbing a rotting tree to retrieve an arrow stuck at the top and nearly plunged to her death, it stopped being amusing. Her latest task was finding the child, who the old woman claimed had run away. After a brief conversation with the child, Hetty knew a different story.

"Consequences!" Nanette's voice held a mirth as fabricated as her smile. "What have I done for you to be angry about? I only offered you help."

"Not willingly. My friend is dying, yet you force me to complete these pointless tasks to get medicine. He'll never recover enough for us to leave without your help."

"Recovery is slow for ills like his," Nanette said, not taking the bait Hetty had tossed at her feet. She merely tapped her pipe against her chin. "But if you insist on leaving, I will prepare something a bit stronger. Come inside."

Left with no choice, Hetty stomped into the cabin, not caring if the muck from her boots was left behind.

Dried herbs dangled from the ceiling, leaving the air musky as the scents mixed together. An oil lamp flickered in the corner and the protections sewn into the scarf at Hetty's neck wiggled before settling.

Nanette didn't seem to notice as she pulled herbs from the ceiling. She bent over a small table, grinding them up with mortar and pestle, the pipe between her teeth trembling as she worked. "Why do you want to leave? North, south, or west, you'll run into nothing but trouble. From your scars, you've been doing naught but that." Nanette's free hand went to her own neck. The ringed scars she had there were striking, but not as prominent as Hetty's. "Stay. You'll be safe here."

"There's no safety to be found in this place."

"We look after our own," the old woman insisted. "Your friend's skills are needed, if he's as good of a blacksmith as you claim. And you — you got wits worthy of ten. Stop running, Miss Sparrow. Stay here and be free."

"There is no freedom here," Hetty said. "They're all stuck in a trap of your creation! They can't leave this swamp."

"Why would they want to? They won't find freedom anywhere." Nanette dumped the herbs into a sachet. "The president who so kindly freed us plans to deport us to the Caribbean or Africa, first chance he can get. He only got support for his fancy proclamation because the North doesn't want us folks taking their jobs and making our homes next door to them. Out west there's nothing but stolen land, weeping with blood and sorrows. And the South is as antsy as a cow standing on an anthill. Whatever happens ain't going to be good for us, no matter who wins this bloody war. Living here might not seem like much freedom to you, but us folk have no place to live peacefully." Nanette thrust the medicine at Hetty. "We belong nowhere. Our past is stolen, our present is lost, and our future hangs in the balance. That won't change for a long, long time. This country thrived with our people in chains. You think it'll take just a few years to change all that?"

Nanette thrust these words in Hetty's face. With skill and grim satisfaction that spoke of doing this time and time again with the listeners nearly always conceding. Hetty wasn't the first person to have this lecture, but unlike the others, she had the privilege of being in the company of others who debated every point of this argument backwards and forward. Nanette hadn't said anything wrong, but not everything she said was right.

She looked Nanette square in the eye. "Change happens when you face it directly. Hiding away will do nothing."

"There's no safety out there."

"I never expected it in the first place."

Hetty left the cabin without permission to leave, not even turning when Nanette called back to her.

The villagers were readying for the evening's dinner. Occupied with the task, no one spoke to her, but a few nodded as she went past. None would interact with her with Nanette's watchful eyes on them. Which was for the best. Hetty had enough of wading through lies.

At the cabin they had been given use of, she hesitated outside the door before opening it.

The heat from inside nearly knocked her back. A sweltering wave pressed forward, drying her clothes so quickly that steam rose from them. She almost stayed outside, but she forced herself in all the same.

"I got the medicine," Hetty called, blinking to adjust her eyes to the light.

"Is it tainted like all the others?" Benjy stood above a cauldron, impervious to the heat like any master blacksmith, though the bandage looped around his chest was damp with sweat. Above him, Aries bounced around the cabin, containing the heat and perhaps doing its best to keep the cabin from catching fire as Benjy poured liquid metal into a round mold.

His hands were steady, but Hetty watched all the same, concerned he was not as fully recovered as he claimed.

When the mold was placed on the table to cool, Hetty waved about the medicine that Nanette had grudgingly given her.

"It's different from the rest," Hetty said, opening it up. "She reached for different herbs this time."

Benjy lowered the heat on his makeshift forge and walked toward her, sniffing the air above the cloth.

He coughed and drew back. "It's less this time, but there's Weeper's Delight in there. She puts it in everything."

"It can't be in everything!"

"It is. How do you think she convinced people to stay?" Benjy pulled another casing out of the fire. "It grabs ahold of you and won't let go. And it does it so quietly. My mother started taking it after my sister was sold. It dulled her words, and softened her feelings toward the world. When it stopped working she had to take more and more, until one day she went to sleep and didn't wake up. I'll die first before I let a bit of it cross my lips."

"Well, don't get shot again."

"Not my fault," he retorted, though he rubbed his hand along the bandage.

They had taken a ship down to Virginia, following the latest lead on Esther. Travel by sea was even more perilous than by land, but they risked it to gain time. Other than a queasy day crammed into a smuggling nook, the gamble seemed to have paid off. They arrived on the coast with time to spare, and made the trek inland. But not far into their travels, they ran into a pack of deserters fleeing the fighting.

In the chaos of the encounter, a bullet had grazed Benjy's side. He refused to let Hetty look at it—it was just a scratch he had said, a fiction he kept repeating until he stumbled and fell into the murky swamp water and came out of it feverish and delirious.

The fighting had drawn the people of the hidden village to them. Nanette had generously offered medicine and shelter, which Hetty took without question. But Benjy had smelled the Weeper's Delight and had enough awareness left in him to violently refuse.

Hetty might have forced him to take it in the end if she hadn't remembered something Esther had told her of healing—that fire could purify even the vilest of sickness.

The only fire at hand was a candle in their lantern. Hetty popped it out and set the lit tip against his wound. Her efforts nearly got her set on fire. Benjy pushed and shoved her hands away until he fainted from the pain.

She passed the night fearing she had only hastened his death, but the next morning Benjy awoke cross and complaining to such a degree that she'd burst into tears at the sound.

That was a few days ago, and now the least of their problems.

"We're leaving tonight, aren't we?" Benjy asked. "We're out of food. And the crone's starting to get suspicious."

"She's been that way the whole time." Hetty looked over his makeshift forge and the cooling items next to it. "Did you really need my best sewing needle for this?"

"It needed to be straight. I'll make you a new one ... dozens if you like."

"I don't need dozens. One would be enough." Hetty pointed. "What is this?"

"A compass — it points to your heart's desire."

The pointed end of the needle jutted toward her as he spoke. Hetty lifted her hand away, glaring at him.

"North," Benjy said blandly. "Where else do you think it would point?"

"Very funny," she growled. "Next time you fall into a river, I'm not diving in after you."

"Good, I have no plans to do that again." He held up the compass, studying it for flaws. "Shall we leave tonight? We can still catch up to your sister."

As Hetty made to answer, there was a knock on the door.

Benjy blew out the fire in the cauldron, the star sigils fluttering away with enough speed that they brought cool air with them. He collapsed onto a nearby pallet as Hetty pushed their packs aside. Glancing to make sure he appeared still enough to be mistaken for asleep, Hetty moved carefully toward the door.

When she opened it, Olympia stood there, holding her son. "You're not hungry, are you?" she asked before Hetty could speak.

"I—"

"You don't want dinner? I understand." The woman stepped inside, shutting the door behind her. "Everyone is eating right now. Later someone will bring you what is left. But it will be a while. There are people asking questions of Nanette that she'd avoided in the past, and it will be some time before you are remembered."

"I don't understand," Hetty said, confused by Olympia's appearance as much as her words. People had brought them food, but it had never been Olympia before. "What are you saying?"

"She's saying we should leave now," Benjy jumped in.

They both turned to face him. He sat up, watching Olympia quite closely. "And that she might have even bought us some time to do so."

Olympia blinked at him. "You're well! You have your wits about you!"

"You know about the taint?"

"More than I wish. Not all of us in the village care for Nanette's ways. She knows it, too. Which is why her medicines have it cut into them. My husband injured his leg and I wanted him to live. Now he can't go without Weeper's for more than a few hours these days. You were so sick. How did you manage?"

"I burned a candle into his skin," Hetty said. "Fire purifies."

"It worked." Olympia studied Benjy for a long moment. "Then you are strong enough for travel. I had hoped you would be, for I did not want to burden you further."

"Though you will with your next question," Benjy said.

"If you mean to leave, take us with you. I cannot let my son live here any longer. Nanette was the one that told him to go beyond this camp, all for her little games."

"Your husband cannot leave because of his taste of the taint," Hetty pointed out. "We do not separate families."

"In this case you must." Olympia met Hetty's eyes with a force of will strengthened by her sorrows. "You will not be able to leave this village without me, and I will not get far without you. I know little of the land outside this swamp, but I know it will be dangerous with the armies north of us."

Hetty snapped into attention. "When did you last hear this?"

"Two days ago."

Hetty bit her lip. "Too much of a risk."

"Risk for what?"

"We're here looking for her sister," Benjy answered. "We

hoped to get outside of Richmond before the armies settled into fighting."

"I wouldn't chance it," Olympia said. "Going west would be better than north."

Hetty knew a bald-faced lie when she heard one, but she grudgingly respected this one. The woman was right: They needed the other's help.

"Will you take us?" Olympia asked again.

"Yes, but it means we lead the way once we leave the swamp behind."

Olympia nodded, and then went to the door. "I'll knock when you're clear to go."

"Shall we take her on the path we charted?" Benjy asked once they were alone. "We can take her and her son to a safe place and then press on after your sister. We slipped past armies before. I know we're later than expected, but it'll only cost you three days."

It was *six* days, but she wasn't about to correct him. If he knew he would get upset and offer up suggestions that would be of little help.

Hetty had seen those days come and pass with little more than a sigh and no regrets. She'd made her choice to stay here with Benjy, and it was the easiest choice she had ever made.

"We go south and we keep them with us. The armies are moving faster than expected," Hetty said. "I don't want to get involved in any shooting until it's the only option. I'll have other chances, maybe even better ones, later on."

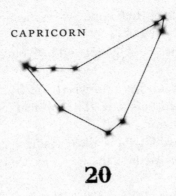

CAPRICORN

20

THE ACRID ODOR of smelling salts had Hetty gagging.

"Get those away from me," she coughed, uselessly waving a hand at the source of the stench. "Get them away!"

"You certainly wake in a cheerful mood."

The source of the vile odor was a vial held in the hand of a neatly dressed woman sitting in a chair next to Hetty. Her hair was streaked with gray, braided into a large plait. She appeared neither friendly nor unfriendly, merely resigned to the task at hand.

Beyond the woman, Hetty could see the canvas of a tent, and other women lying on nearby cots, their faces scratched and their limbs bandaged. Some heavily so, some less. As her eyes focused on them, it dawned on her that they were the other bicycle racers.

"You had quite a nasty fall," the nurse went on. "You're lucky you didn't break any bones. Although the true luck of it is that that no one died."

"How many ..." Hetty forced herself into a seated position. "How many were injured?"

"A half dozen or so. Minor scrapes and bruises. A few broken bones. Though there was one lady who insisted on finishing the race even if there was no one to race against."

"Have you seen—"

"Your husband was sent elsewhere so he could be useful instead of hovering over my shoulder." The nurse drew the sigil for the Arrow into the air. It glowed, and a pitcher fluttered over to her, tipping its contents into a glass. "Drink, and don't fret. You remained unconscious for the better part of an hour." The nurse glanced at the vial of smelling salts. "I did that as a last resort. Drink," she said pointedly.

Hetty sipped the water.

As she did, the nurse reached over and slapped a bandage across Hetty's collarbone. It burned her skin at once, and Hetty half choked on the water even as the heat faded to a cooling mist.

"All better. Can't have your skin marred by that mark."

The nurse snatched the now empty cup away from Hetty as the tent flap was thrown open.

Benjy walked in.

He had misplaced his jacket and he held a basket of laundry the nurse had presumably given him to occupy his time.

His eyes found Hetty's, and before she could even blink, he was already halfway across the room.

"You're awake!" Heedless of the nurse's clucking tongue, Benjy dropped the basket onto the floor and settled on the edge of the cot. All this attracted attention from other eyes around the room, and Hetty wasn't sure if it played any part in his reaching for her hand. As if he was playing up the role many—including the nurse—had placed him in. However, as he held her hand in his, Hetty wasn't sure he noticed anyone else in the tent. It was almost, she thought idly, worth her little dip into the river.

"How bad?" she asked.

"Terrible—you lost the race. In a rather spectacular fashion, I might add." His words were airy, but his grip had tightened around hers. "Next time save the show for when your feet are firmly planted on the ground."

"I'll try," she said, matching his tone. "Tell me what happened."

"The explosion erupted right in the middle. A lot of people were hurt, even some who were only watching the race."

"That is quite unfortunate. Do you know what happened?"

"Only a few things." His pause was long, and likely due to the nurse, who was giving only a portion of her attention to the sleeping patient one cot over. "The excursion is over. They called off all the other events, including the cakewalk."

A moan filled the air at his words.

"Oh, I was so looking forward to it!" a young woman cried, before she turned to sob into her pillow.

"What have I told you about upsetting my patients?" the nurse demanded.

"That was not my fault."

"Off with you," the nurse said, shooing him, "if you're going to make trouble!"

"If he leaves, I'm going with him," Hetty said.

"Are you well enough to leave?" Benjy asked Hetty.

"I feel fine," she replied, even as the nurse rounded on her.

"You just had a nasty fall into a river. You almost drowned! I can't let you walk out of here—"

"Sara!" another nurse called. Whatever else the nurse had to say was lost as she tried to restrain a convulsing woman whose fingers were aglow with scarlet light. With naught but a glance back at Hetty and Benjy, the nurse hurried across the tent to assist with the other patient.

No sooner had the train of the nurse's dress disappeared than Hetty pushed off her blankets.

"Let's hurry while she's distracted."

"I don't think she's going to chase us. And she might be right—you should rest."

"I want to know what happened since you don't have the details . . . or your jacket."

"I ripped it," he said rather vaguely.

The basket on the floor held her clothes, cleaned and neatly folded. Such prompt laundry service meant only that magic was used. And rather poorly formed spells, at that. Her lips pursed into disapproval at the faded color.

"I didn't wash them," Benjy said, pulling out his own jacket from the basket.

"It might have been better if you did," Hetty said. "My dress is ruined."

"What a pity—you looked rather nice."

He meant the color, Hetty told herself, even as her stomach gave an odd lurch. He never spoke about her clothes unless it was about the color, and the dress had been a rather vivid plum. Why would she care anyway? It wasn't like she picked her clothes with the purpose of being complimented on them. Although this time she had hoped . . .

Attempting to abandon her spiraling thoughts, Hetty forced herself off the cot.

Despite Benjy hovering around her, her knees did not buckle. Her fingers did slip along the buttons and fastenings more than she liked. Her slower movement spurred Benjy to ask if he could help, but a few moments of that showed he was better in helping her remove clothing than pulling it on. As she attempted to smooth the wrinkles, Benjy handed her the cloth band.

All the magic was gone from the band, leaving only her stitch-work. Hetty tied it on anyway. Even without magic, it brought a small measure of comfort.

With Hetty leaning heavily on Benjy's arm, they walked out of the tent. Outside, she realized this tent was pitched near the end of the boardwalk, and it was among the only things still standing. In the distance, Hetty could see scurrying figures dismantling tents and stalls. The pieces flew under the power of various enchantments cast by those eager to leave as soon as they could.

Hetty watched them work for a bit, then tugged on Benjy's arm.

"What did you find that you couldn't mention in front of the nurse?"

"That I couldn't get near the explosion."

"Which one? There were two."

"Two," Benjy echoed, as if repeating himself would make it less true. *Two explosions?*

"You didn't see them?"

"I couldn't get close enough. It's blocked off a bit, I'm not sure we can get close enough to check."

"Don't you forget"—Hetty traced a finger in the air, slowly forming the Gemini star sigil. It flashed for a single moment before the magic cloaked them from sight—"this time *I'm* here."

Hidden from sight, they walked through the remnants of the excursion until they reached the grassy plain where the race had taken place.

Several people swarmed the site like ants. Some were cleaning, and some were clearly there to stare and gawk.

The line of defense between the cleaners and the gawkers was George.

"George?" Hetty nearly exclaimed. "You couldn't get past him?"

"Wait a moment," Benjy muttered.

He'd barely spoken before a man strode up to George. Angry words were exchanged. The man tried to push past him. George's fingers moved to form a star sigil. In the flash of light, the ground rippled under the man's feet and sent him flying back to the ground with stunning force.

The man picked himself up. Hetty didn't catch what was said, but it ended with George looking on smugly as the other man retreated.

She could see why Benjy had little success on his own. For someone who didn't like magic, George was quick to cast spells.

Too quick, possibly.

"His spells are employed one by one," Benjy said. "There's no spell lying in wait."

"Then sneaking past should be easy."

Benjy didn't answer her.

Isaac Baxter had just stormed up to George, scattering the lingering crowd. With a bruise and a slightly swollen right eye, he looked far from the polished hustler who sought attention from crowds.

"Where is he?" he demanded. "Where's Loring!"

George pointed. "He's near the river—"

Snarling, Baxter pushed past him.

And like Baxter's shadow, Hetty and Benjy followed. They couldn't get as close as Hetty would have liked. The glamour might have kept them from sight, but the effort to cast it took more out of her than she'd expected. Their slower pace kept them some distance from Baxter, but allowed Hetty to take full note of their surroundings.

The first blast site was a crater, and the burn marks made it appear the work of a fallen star. Around it, the ground was lumpy and deeply gouged from bicycle wheels and boot heels. Chunks of grass and dirt were strewn about, and in the distance, Hetty spied a mound of the twisted metal of broken bicycles.

It was a sad sight.

But it didn't hold her attention for long.

Baxter nearly pounced on poor defenseless Clarence, who barely had time to flee.

"You moonstruck fool!" Baxter hollered. "If you checked everything, why am I staring at a hole in the ground?"

"I did! I checked—"

"Not well enough. People could have died and it would have been on my head! It's my name that people will remember, not yours! How could this have happened?"

"Someone must have slipped in when I wasn't paying attention."

"Stop giving me excuses," Baxter snapped. "I need answers, solutions. Give me something! Your own wife was in there. Surely you care about her?"

At this point in the conversation, Clarence turned away. Hetty could see only a portion of his face. That sliver was not enough for her to tell what emotion flickered across his face. Whatever it was, it didn't appease Baxter at all.

He did some more yelling, but Clarence said nothing more.

In the end, Baxter stormed off, but not to join the men cleaning up. He went in a different direction.

"He's going where the second one was," Hetty whispered.

"Then we keep following him."

They got closer to Baxter this time. He had stopped, and as he reached into his jacket he looked around. His eyes darted in their direction and a ripple of panic crossed his features. Whatever was in his hand was shoved back, and he smoothed out his clothes, grinning broadly at them.

Stars, her spell had worn off!

Though that was alarming, she found herself more curious about his reaction.

Baxter should have started in surprise, but when he greeted them, he acted as if they hadn't popped out of the ground like mushrooms.

"Are you feeling better, Mrs. Rhodes?" Baxter said, locking his gaze on Hetty. "I feared the worst."

"Much better," Hetty said.

"Good." Baxter's smile was thinly stretched and seemed ready to unravel. "Will you be leaving soon? The next train leaves fairly shortly. I'd be happy to buy tickets for you. There's no need for you to linger here. People might think something is wrong."

"Something is wrong," Hetty insisted. "There was an explosion! I saw it with my own eyes—"

"An explosion that was fueled by nothing but hate." Baxter found his footing with these words, easing himself into this lurch of conversation. "A trap set by someone who doesn't want us to have our fun. There's no need for poking or prodding."

"Or asking questions?" Benjy asked.

"Or demanding answers," Baxter snapped. He seemed to be ready to say more, but with one look at Benjy's face, Baxter pivoted. "Surely after everything that occurred you don't want to linger on this side of the river?"

Baxter was being too forceful. He already offered to pay their train fare, and now he was trying to convince them nothing of note happened when the opposite was clearly true. Hetty wasn't sure how much Baxter knew about them. But he obviously knew enough to know he didn't want them poking around.

Very interesting, considering the angry words he had thrown in Clarence's face.

Surely he wanted answers?

That he didn't was a question worth looking into, but one thing at a time.

They needed to look at the blast site. But Baxter was dead set on leading them to the train station.

She had to do something. But what?

Hetty sagged against Benjy's arm, playing up her exhaustion. "We can't leave." Hetty's lip trembled as she looked up at Benjy. "I dropped my locket. I won't leave without it. You promised we'll find it."

"The crew here will find it," Baxter said. "It probably got swept up in the river—"

"It won't take much time to find, as long as people stay out of the way," Benjy interrupted.

Baxter had more sense than Hetty credited to him. Instead of contesting Benjy's words, he just nodded and stepped aside.

"If I didn't know any better," Hetty said as soon as Baxter was out of earshot, "I would say he was trying to get rid of us."

"Just me," Benjy corrected softly. "For the bruise forming on his face."

"You did that?" Hetty echoed. While that explained Baxter's odd behavior, she had other concerns. Namely how such a detail went missing in Benjy's recounting of events following the explosion. "Why?"

"He got in the way." Benjy's voice was flat and expressionless, as if he was reading from a newspaper. "After the blast happened Baxter raised a magical barrier to keep people back, and wouldn't lower it. I suppose I could have used magic to shatter it, but punching him saved time. You were going to drown." He added that part as if he expected her to complain.

"When did the barrier go up? Before or after I fell into the water?"

"I don't know."

Hetty blinked, stunned at these words.

"There was dust and people, and I was further back in the crowd."

Hetty waited for him to continue, but he said nothing more. How strange of him to miss stating an obvious detail. If she didn't know otherwise, it seemed as if he had been the one half drowned in the river.

"Don't you think it strange that he put up a barrier?" Hetty suggested. "He could have put it up in the midst of well-intentioned panic. But if you couldn't break through it without resorting to breaking his focus, it means the spell was firmly set up. If that's true, him trying to get rid of us is less about the punch he deserved and more about reasons he doesn't want us to find out."

"That does make sense," Benjy muttered. "Why didn't that occur to me?"

"Do you wish for me to answer that?" Hetty asked. "Because you won't like my opinion."

"No." Benjy smiled down at her. "I always want to hear your opinion."

He might, but she wasn't about to let him know her thoughts at the moment.

"Good thinking with the locket," Benjy continued. "Now there won't be any questions about me casting spells."

"Or me."

"No spellcasting for you." Benjy turned his eyes to the grass. "You once held a disillusionment charm for half an afternoon while dogs were sniffing around the trees next to us. This one lasted for how long?"

Hetty grunted, her only admission that he had made his point. "Why don't we start looking before Baxter comes back?" she said.

Benjy stepped away from her then, small steps at first as if afraid she'd topple over. When she didn't, he strode further away. "Tell me more about the second blast."

"It was smaller," Hetty said as she followed with care across the ground. "It didn't make as much of an impact."

"It certainly didn't leave a mark." Benjy's eyes roved across the ground.

Compared to the blast site, the area they stood in was unblemished. You couldn't even tell that a bicycle had rolled across it.

"Was your bicycle enchanted?" Benjy drew Capricorn into the air. The form of a goat with a fish tail floated before him, waiting patiently to be set to work.

"It would be a clever trick if it was," Hetty remarked. Off his raised eyebrow she added, "I don't think it was. The protections in my clothes would have reacted."

"Not that dress." His eyes lingered on her for a moment. "You don't wear a dress like that when expecting trouble. Your usual spells aren't stitched in."

"Maybe I should change that habit."

"Maybe." He flicked his hand and Capricorn dove toward the ground. It skimmed along the grass, circling around them. At first the men over by the blast site turned, but none moved toward them. She supposed it did look like Benjy was searching for a missing locket. Only, she knew he was seeking magical residue that might have been left from the second explosion.

As if conducting an orchestra, he guided the star sigil across the ground, leaving no blade of grass unturned. Just when Hetty was starting to think there was nothing to be found, the sea-goat suddenly leapt into the air, then dove back into the ground. The spot where it disappeared shone with a red tinge of magical residue no bigger than a dinner plate.

At once, Benjy bent over as if digging for a fallen object.

"What could this have been," Hetty asked, as he ran his fingers through the grass, "besides explosive?"

"Anything," Benjy remarked. "A reversed summoning spell, a trigger for the explosion, but those are just details."

He stood up holding out a cupped hand. With exaggerated care he took her hand, and made it seem as if he dropped something into her palm.

He didn't let go, but held on to her hand.

"I suppose the details don't matter," Benjy added, "since either way, I couldn't do a thing to stop it."

She squeezed his hand. "Neither could I."

Everything had happened so quickly that her memories could have been jumbled up in more ways than one. Yet she could correctly recall the events of her perilous ride—the veering of her bicycle under her, the rush of wind, the blast appearing right in front of her.

She could see it clearly.

The first blast was planned, but the second was not, even though it was equally deliberate. Deliberate ... and focused on her.

They were right to speculate that someone with the answers they were seeking was here.

And so was the murderer.

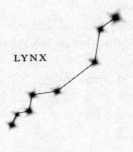

21

WHEN SUNLIGHT STARTED TO CREEP upward on their bed,
Hetty watched as Benjy traced the Shield sigil along the sheets in
front of her. Once the sigil was complete, he flicked it toward the
window. The curtains yanked themselves together and the room
fell back into semi-darkness.

On a normal morning, Hetty would have bumped her shoulder into him and told him to go to work. When the sunlight had
reached their bed, early morning had already burned away. He
was late, she was late, and just lying around wouldn't lead to anything productive. However, this morning she was content to pretend to be asleep just a bit longer.

For all the things they'd had to figure out when they married,
sharing a bed was never a problem. Since their time on the road,
they had grown accustomed to sleeping near the other. Sleeping
close meant they'd be quicker to stir, quicker to be at ease, and
quicker to make sure the other was near. Bits of this habit lingered to the extent that even now she slept better when he was
at her back.

As for other things, well, Hetty would be lying to say the
sleeping was always chaste. She was curious by nature, and being
thrust in danger and uncertainty most of the time only added to

it. When it happened it was more of a relief to put aside a lingering question that would have dogged their steps as they moved about their tiny room. It hadn't occurred often or changed anything in their partnership. But since it had happened, it allowed her to get comfortable around him.

Comfortable to not second-guess motives or to question every word he said. Comfortable to cry into his shoulder, and to dump problems into his lap. Comfortable to admit her fears and share fragile hopes.

Comfortable that even waking up this close next to him stirred up only mild surprise.

She couldn't remember the last time she woke tucked under his arm. Stars, she couldn't remember the last time when she woke up next to him—most mornings he was long gone before she even stirred.

When was the last time this occurred? Winter? It got bitterly cold in their room, and they often turned to each other for added warmth. But that didn't seem right. Last winter she'd sewn spells in their quilt to soften the chill and better hold warmth. Not winter, then? Further back?

She searched her memory. Maybe it was when he started boxing? Did the guilt make him pull away?

"Are you awake?" Benjy mumbled into her ear, his breath brushing against her cheek.

"No."

He chuckled, and sheets shifted as he moved away. "Liar."

"Don't go into work," Hetty said as she rolled over to watch him creep about the room. He hadn't turned on the lamp, but instead conjured a small light that hovered over his head so that the bumpy map of scars on his back looked smooth and somewhat altered.

"Go back to sleep," Benjy murmured.

"You should too."

"I would, but I have work. Unless"—his eyes flew back to her as if her blood had seeped into the sheets—"you're not feeling well."

Hetty playfully coughed into her hands. "I think there might have been something in that river. I don't know if I'll make it."

Benjy leaned back over the bed and pressed the back of his hand against her forehead. Hetty abruptly stopped coughing as she stared up at him, her skin prickling at the intimacy of his touch.

"You don't feel any warmer than usual . . ." he said, and their eyes met for a long moment. "Then again, I'm not a healer."

He slipped away from her again. "I have to go to work," he repeated, mostly to himself. "If I don't show after being absent for the past two days, I'll lose my job."

"Lose your job?" Hetty exclaimed. She sat up, nearly throwing off her covers, more than wide awake now. "After all you done for him?"

"It's me who's taken advantage of Amos's goodwill, not the other way around," Benjy remarked as he shrugged on his shirt. "He always held my job for me during our trips south."

"And all you had to do was bring every member of his family to freedom," Hetty grumbled. She got off the bed, absently tugging her nightgown around her as she turned on the lamp.

Light spilled into the room, illuminating Benjy's somewhat amused smile.

"It's nothing to worry about."

"Nothing? You do all the work at the forge. You're the reason it's still open! Then there are all the odd jobs he just hands over to you, followed by complaints when you can't get your work done. I would have left ages ago."

"Yes, but Amos is absent enough that I can use the forge to work on little projects of my own. Though I suppose I could find work at other places. Maybe even do something different."

"Something different?" Hetty asked. "Do you mean carpentry? Or mason work?"

"Something vastly different." For a moment, Hetty thought that this would be the last word on the subject, but then he added: "When you first pressed Oliver into putting on funerals, I wasn't keen on the idea. Oliver is an embalmer. Everything else is additional work for him, including pretending to be nice to people. Him doing funerals meant we had to help. After doing it a few times, I found I don't mind making arrangements. The settling of the church, the arrangement of the services. Helping give people some peace and allow others to grieve. It's quiet work and it's a job that needs doing."

Hetty smiled. Those words were an echo from the past, and rang as true now as they had back then. "And someone must do it."

"I like working at the forge," Benjy continued, "but I only stayed because one of us needs steady work. But there are other possibilities out there. For me. For you."

"I can find work quicker as a dressmaker," Hetty protested. "I can even open my own shop."

"You could, but I'm keen on a change. It's just a thought." Benjy smiled. "Nothing more."

As he said that, Hetty could see herself, see them, standing in a cellar. There was a body on the table, and there was a casket, and the old man lying there was greatly mourned. But his death, while unexpected, was only the natural end to a long life.

Just a thought, he said. But what a wonderful thought it was.

"I would advise you to stay here and rest," Benjy said. "There is nothing that pressing you need to take care of at this moment."

"Rest," Hetty huffed. "When there is so much to do? I saw Alain Browne at the excursion but did I tell you I saw Geraldine selling her wares on the street? She told me that Alain lied. But I don't know if that's true or if she was just trying to distract me from the wares that I will certainly be throwing out again."

"Distract you."

Benjy moved toward the mantel. He lingered there for a moment, before moving things aside. Tucked behind her box of old pins, the little plant of Moonleaf, and his collection of books was the vial that Penelope had given to her earlier this week. The one Hetty had shown Geraldine, who claimed to never have laid eyes on it despite the label being in her own hand.

He turned it over in his hand. "Your interactions with her always lead to confrontations. You complain about her, tell stories about—"

"To warn people!"

"And such stories get told elsewhere. Do you think you just happened upon this vial by chance? After all the dust you kicked up about her potions, she wouldn't just have them out. This only ended up in your hands because someone came to Penelope's shop. And it's this specific potion." He pointed to the label, which spoke of promises that any person wishing to bear a child would hope for. "Would you have given this a single thought if this was wart remover? The only thing missing is a tag with your name on it. Someone was trying to get your attention."

"This was bait," Hetty said.

"Not bait." Benjy shook his head. "A distraction. Maybe not by this Geraldine woman, but by someone who wants you to focus on this instead. Especially when . . ." He twisted open the cap and poured some into his cupped hand. Clear liquid trickled into his palm, a world of difference from the amber liquid that Hetty had seen before. "It's water."

"You sure?"

"Positive," he said. For a moment she feared he would move to prove his assertion, but instead he dried off his hands with a handkerchief. "This is a fake, and I bet this isn't the only one. Otherwise, tales of people becoming dreadfully ill would have reached your ears."

"It is a clever distraction. I wouldn't have checked the bottle."

"That's what they gambled on." Benjy put the empty vial back onto the mantel. "With this I'm not sure if the Brownes' involvement is an accident or on purpose."

"I could go around to see them. This only adds to my questions."

"I want to go with you."

"But you have to go work."

"Precisely."

Hetty snorted, sensing the other sentiments contained in that single word. "I will not go," she said in the end, "but I will not stay here all day. I have another case to work on." Hetty went to the dress she'd made for Maybelle's daughter. She smoothed the fabric as she gave it one last glance. "The dress is nearly done, and it's the perfect excuse to find out what Penelope or her cousins were able to find out about Judith."

"That doesn't sound too dangerous."

"Worried about me?"

He went quiet for a moment, weighing and disregarding each word before he selected the perfect one. "Only the right amount."

Benjy left then, leaving Hetty to make her last fixes to the dress. Reaching into her sewing kit, her fingers brushed against the cool metal of Charlie's pocket watch.

So that was where it went. She forgot all about it.

She opened it, and flipped it shut like she had seen Charlie do so many times to punctuate his words.

Charlie always had it with him, so why did he not have it the day he died?

Was it forgotten, or left on purpose?

Maybe there was something about the astrolabe. Hetty had disregarded the astrolabe side since it wasn't broken like the clock, but Charlie was up to a number of things they did not know at all. Could the astrolabe lead them to the answers they sought? At any rate, it was worth it to show Benjy, especially if she could persuade him to leave the forge early.

She had little doubt it would be a hard task. He had made it clear he preferred to be with her if she started following leads for this case. And in that she was in perfect agreement.

When Hetty arrived at Maybelle's shoe shop with the wedding dress and little christening gowns carefully wrapped up, the windows were dark. She peered inside for a bit until she spotted a handcrafted Closed sign posted on the door. Not wanting to linger, she debated making her way toward Maybelle's home before she remembered there was a better option.

A few streets more brought her near the herbalist shop. At this hour, the tiny space was quite empty, with only Penelope seated at the stool at the counter as she sorted through a batch of dried plants. The shelves on the walls were laden with herbs, the more common ones near the door. Moving inward the selection increased in rarity, level of poison, and magical properties, culminating with the deadliest of herbs behind the counter. Penelope claimed the latter were kept under lock and key, but Hetty doubted they were actually kept in the shop at all. This was the only herbalist shop that openly displayed its magical wares. Other shops had been burned down in the past by angry white mobs who'd gotten twisted up about brewed magic. But this shop, with wards put in place by Hetty and a bell forged under Benjy's hammer, was protected in numerous ways.

"Morning." Hetty held up the bundle in her arms. "I come bearing gifts."

Instead of looking pleased, Penelope let the herbs slip from her fingers as if a ghost had walked through the door.

Hetty sighed. "Which one of your cousins was at the excursion?"

"Clarabelle," Penelope rasped. "She told me about what happened."

"Whatever she told you is a gross exaggeration."

"You fell into the river! You could have drowned! I should have been there. I bet they didn't have proper healers there."

"It would have been worse if you had. You would've gotten caught in the blast with me. I'm sure I would convince you to be in the bicycle race as well."

"But I would have been there. I should have taken Isaac Baxter's offer."

Thinking of her last encounter with Baxter, Hetty said, "No, best you didn't. Nothing around that man seems right."

"Is that why you were at the excursion?" Penelope asked. "Because of Baxter? Do you think he murdered Charlie? I hope he did — then we can be rid of him!"

"I don't like him either," Hetty said, "but that's not reason enough to accuse a man." Hetty leaned against the counter, staring down at the herbs, before another question rose up in her mind. "Do you think Clarabelle can tell me more about the members of the E.C. Degray club?"

Penelope shook her head. "She wouldn't tell you anything interesting. Her husband is barely involved."

"Too bad — the only other people I know are George and Clarence. And they're not options."

"Why not Clarence?"

"After all that happened at the excursion, he's probably not keen on talking to Benjy."

"Why not? Is he on the suspect list too?"

"He's more a stand-in to be honest to represent someone who might fit the profile of the murderer. He and Eunice have connections to Charlie and Marianne. But I can't think of any good motives, no more than George and Darlene. Although I did ask

Clarence a few questions, but for some reason he didn't seem keen on talking about certain details while Eunice was around. So I had Benjy whisk her off. Which nearly made things worse, since Clarence was going to chase after them."

"You're fine with that?" Penelope asked. "You dislike Eunice."

"For reasons that have nothing to do with Benjy."

"What a strange thing for you to say." Penelope placed deliberate emphasis on each word. "Why is that?"

Caught by surprise, Hetty was still stammering out excuses as Penelope smirked.

"I *knew* something happened! You were acting so strange the other night. I couldn't figure out what it was, but now I know. You've fallen in love!"

Hetty's mouth fell open at this declaration, and for a few moments no words came to her. She felt stripped bare, exposed, even if it was with kindness and genuine delight.

"Don't you dare deny it," Penelope went on. "I can see you searching for the words, and it won't convince me at all! I've known you for a very long time, and I knew you've been lying to yourself nearly as long."

"Lying to myself!" Hetty grabbed these words, puffing up in indignation. "Of all the ridiculous things you have said it's —"

"True." Penelope's eyes danced even as she came closer and closer to the blunt edge of Hetty's temper. "You convinced yourself you married him because of silly gossip, being proper, and whatever excuse you dredged up, anything other than the fact you actually liked him."

"I wouldn't have married someone I didn't like!"

"No, you'd only marry someone you couldn't imagine your life without."

Penelope stood back as she said this, with the firm, calm gaze of someone who had spoken a truth that no twisting words could alter.

"I wanted him part of every story that could be told of my life," Hetty admitted, "and these feelings ruin things."

"Ruin what? There are flowers that bloom after years of lying dormant, and they're beautiful."

"And those last for how many days?"

"Well, good thing you're not flowers. Are you afraid of telling him?" Concern drifted into Penelope's features. "I never seen you look so scared."

"It's easy to be brave when you have someone you trust at your back," Hetty replied.

"But you do—you have me! He breaks your heart, I poison him, and we run off and join a traveling show. You'll have to learn to take care of my plants, but you're very bright and I'm sure you'll pick up on things."

For all the good cheer sprinkled in those words, Hetty knew Penelope was every bit sincere. Poisoning might not occur, but the rest, the rest Hetty knew was a promise that would not be forgotten. A promise Hetty's sister would have made in a heartbeat.

"Thank you," was all Hetty managed to say.

"It's too early for that." Penelope waved a hand. "Oh, and if you need something to get your mind off the troubles of your heart that isn't related to murder, I have just the thing. I was invited to a tea. It was going to be a poetry reading, but after Charlie's death . . . Well, the hostess thought you might like to come."

A hostess that Penelope had gone out of her way not to name, Hetty couldn't help but notice. That pointed to a few likely suspects, some that she would rather avoid. She also assumed the event would mostly consist of gossip without even a whiff of card games or anything exciting.

"Must I come?" Hetty whined.

"I would appreciate the company," Penelope said, "and it would be fun."

It would *not* be fun. It was far more likely to be an utter waste of time. Yet there was no way she could refuse such a simple request.

"What time is it tomorrow?"

Penelope eagerly rattled off the details.

"That gives me the morning." Hetty patted the dress. "The shoe shop might be open then."

"Maybelle's out of town," Penelope said. "Is this the dress?"

"And the little gowns for her baby. I finished it all."

"Already?"

"It was quick work. Maybelle has done me a good turn many times in the past with the information she brought. I hoped to have news from her today. You did ask her about the missing servant?"

"Her and the rest of the family. While you were running around at the excursion, Annabelle, Rosabelle, and I made surprise deliveries of a few basic herbs to families throughout town. Eventually that generosity loosened a few tongues, but only one told us anything useful. This man said he worked for a household where a woman named Judith was turned out about a month ago. The official word was theft of candlesticks and silverware, but whispers spoke of the woman teaching Sorcery. Her employers chose to get rid of her quietly."

Hetty shook her head. "How kind of them. Considering how far a scandal could reach. Do you know anything about the people she supposedly taught?"

"Only that it was a small number—more people were accused about knowing Sorcery than having actual talent. It's actually quite a common thing in households that hire on servants. I asked about where Judith taught her lessons. But all I found was a song." Penelope sang a few bars, stopping only when Hetty expelled a slight gasp. "You know it?"

"It was one of those songs for warning," Hetty said. "Sometimes when collecting passengers, conductors would be drawn near a plantation or a farm. If there was trouble, someone would start singing to warn us of the way to go. Not everyone could make the journey, but they always helped in the small ways that they could—provide us with food, warnings, even distractions."

"And songs," Penelope added.

Hetty turned over the tune in her mind. She had collected songs as they traveled in the interest of comparing them. Her favorite was the one about the People Who Flew. In the song, slaves dropped hoes in the fields and sprouted wings, escaping to new horizons. The slaves' names referred to safe houses or landmarks nearby. Other songs varied from location to location, and once you knew one, it was easy to tease out the meaning of the others.

The song Penelope had heard laid out directions, but there was a line about a bag of flour that didn't make any sense.

Just as she was about to give up, she saw an answer, as plainly as if Benjy had stabbed a pin into their map.

"Is something wrong?" Penelope asked.

"Not at all. You just gave me a bounty of information."

"It was helpful?"

"More than that," Hetty assured her. "And that was clever: Giving people herbs, they'll remember the gift more so than the person doing the giving."

"I may not get directly involved in your cases," Penelope replied, "but I do listen to all your stories."

"Give your cousins my thanks," Hetty said as she pushed away from the counter. "With your help I might be able to find this woman after all!"

"Be careful," Penelope called as Hetty slipped out the door.

The song thrummed through Hetty like the steady beat of a drum. It led her through the familiar streets, making them appear foreign and strange in her rush.

These were songs used to help avoid capture and guide others to freedom, and so it was fitting they were guiding people once more. Guiding her to find a person who seemed to have all but vanished.

Hetty arrived outside of the dry goods store with a swaying sign showing a stack of flour bags. The store was filled with people, but luckily Hetty was more interested in what was upstairs. Slipping around the building, she climbed up a set of stairs to the upper level.

No lights showed in the window, but Hetty reached for the door anyway, knocking once, just to be polite. She waited, but heard nothing, as expected.

There were wards on the door, but they were stacked together using the same sigil. She shook her head and she broke through it. This was the work of someone who knew the basics. Laying spells out like that was no different than using just one, and hardly made it stronger.

The makeshift classroom was quite bare. No desk or tables, just a few scattered chairs and a chalkboard propped against the wall. The only light in the room came from the closed shutters of the window and hardly helped. As her eyes adjusted to the near darkness, she spotted a few empty boxes stacked in the corner. Their edges were dulled and they had marks on the sides as if they'd been tossed about. The only thing that stood out to Hetty as unusual, though, was the strong smell of lavender.

Perfume? She saw no flowers resting in a vase.

She followed the scent, going deeper into the room. As she passed a door, the band at her neck roared into life. Leo burst forth from its stitches to rest at her side. The lioness, whose midnight blue fur shimmered with stars, craned her head at Hetty. Hetty could almost swear she saw a glimmer of annoyance in the pitch-black eyes of the star-speckled creature.

Manifestation of her spells rarely happened without her will, and only ever did when she encountered bold magic. "I know I was careless." With a wiggle of her fingers, Hetty directed the lioness to lie in wait of any other surprises.

Hetty directed her focus on the door. In the shimmering light, a cacophony of colors splashed along it.

The contrast between this sophisticated skill and the pitiful effort on the classroom's door raised the hair off her neck.

One enchantment would be trouble. Two or three, a minor inconvenience. But there were more than a dozen splashed there, and she had no idea if they were protections, alarms, or something worse.

Still, she'd come too far to turn back now.

Hetty set Gemini, Virgo, Sagittarius, and Scorpio at each corner of the door. The sigils glowed with golden light, creating a protective barrier that would keep any destructive magics from spilling elsewhere beyond the door frame. With the power of the simpler Arrow, she sliced at the sigils on the door, breaking them bit by bit as she swung her hands from side to side. When her sigils fell apart, she merely set them once again.

She wished Benjy was with her.

His skill with the delicate work of taking things apart was second only to his ability to remember how to put them back together. Hetty knew she was leaving behind a great deal of evidence that she'd been here. Or if not that, then attracting attention as she worked. She was also growing steadily worried about what might lie behind the door.

No one warded a door this securely when running away. Anything that was of value went with you when you fled. No, someone else had done this. There could be a trap inside. Or a dead body.

There probably was one of both, knowing her luck.

The last sigil came undone with a hiss, the magic turning into mere wisps. As the magic faded, the door swung open. Hetty braced herself for any surprises and the smell of decay, but no particular odor—or person, for that matter—jumped out at her.

Warm light poured into the rooms with enough strength that she needn't create any light of her own. For this, Hetty was grateful. She didn't want any trace of her magic found here after she'd left.

With care, she walked inside. The room was clean. The wall had a large water stain and the rug was threadbare, but it was generally neat and well cared for. It was only slightly bigger than Hetty's own room, but the few pieces of furniture here were of poor quality. A cot shoved in the corner, with a nightstand and a dented bowl atop it. On the table was a stack of books—school primers like the ones that George and Darlene used with the younger set of their students.

Not just like them. She had bound enough to know they were the same.

As Hetty reached for the closest book, the light in the room shifted. As the panes of light moved to show the rest of the room's contents, Hetty forgot all about the primers.

In fact, she forgot nearly everything, as she stared at the wall. It was not spotted with any water stains, but something was there. Something drawn. No, something carved in the wall. A star sigil.

It was Ophiuchus, the Serpent Bearer, the cursed sigil whose presence promised that nothing good ever followed.

Hetty stepped toward it, her hand rising of its own accord. As if touching would prove that the sigil was real and not just some nightmare come to life.

She was seeing threads being attached to pins on the map in their room. Pins that connected the clues, the suspects, and points of interest related to Charlie to a single pin that altered everything.

Judith Freeman.

A woman teaching Sorcery who had gone missing around the same time that Charlie died. Who might have taught at her friends' school. Judith might even know the nameless man they found—could he have been one of her students? Judith could have ties to the political club, or Geraldine's dodgy brewed magic. Or any number of things. Who knows what was connected and what was coincidence? This was a large city, but their community was tight and close. Chance could explain everything, but her gut was telling her that chance didn't deserve that much credit.

The floorboards creaked behind Hetty.

In the open doorway stood a young woman—her surprise turning to fear in the blink of an eye.

Hetty took only a single step forward, and it was enough to send the figure scurrying.

The door slammed shut, but the magic that sealed it might have been paper. Hetty ripped the door open and ran.

She got out in time to see the woman hurtling down the stairs and dashing into the streets.

Hetty watched as the woman's skirt fluttered around a corner —then shook her head before setting off in the opposite direction.

People were so predictable.

When fleeing they retreated in the same direction they came from, keeping along familiar sights and streets.

Easy to follow, especially when the person in pursuit knew the streets backwards and forward.

A few right turns later and Hetty jumped into the path of the fleeing woman. Hetty braced herself, drawing Canis Minor into the air. The binding spell snapped shut around the woman, flattening her arms against her sides as her legs locked together. The woman yelped and fought, until she finally spat swears at Hetty.

"Hello," Hetty said as the woman writhed against the magical constraints. "Is there a problem?"

"Why are you following me!"

"Why did you run?" Hetty countered. "In my experience, people typically only run when they're up to no good."

"They run when they see trouble. Or when they're being threatened."

Hetty snapped her fingers. There was a flash of light and the woman staggered backwards to the ground. Although the woman stayed there, Hetty didn't let herself relax, keeping her eyes vigilant for any sign of sudden movement.

"I like to ask you a few questions about a woman named Judith."

The woman lifted her arm, but Hetty grasped the wrist. She twisted the woman's arm until a long, spindly twig fell to the ground.

A wand.

It was to be expected, but somewhat pathetic all the same. Hetty did not expect that Judith or her students would be grand masters of the craft. Studying magic in secret is hard, and it was far easier to get caught than it was to actually learn anything.

The stranger clutched her arm to her chest but made no move to snatch up her wand or try anything else just as unwise.

"Were you about to use this on me?" Hetty asked. "If so, you're a bigger fool than I thought. Don't you know who I am?"

The woman lifted her chin and stiffened, an action revealing her to be younger than she first appeared. "A busybody."

Hetty pulled at the band around her neck to reveal her scars, letting the crisp daylight show them in all their garishness. A sign of her past, a token of her strength. "I'm Henrietta Rhodes, and when I ask a question, I always get an answer. Who is Judith? You know her. Don't lie to me. You wouldn't have come when I disturbed the wards if you didn't. I advise you to stop protecting her."

"If you got caught using Sorcery," said the woman, "it's your own fault."

"I don't even know the first thing about it."

The woman blinked. "Why are you looking for her then?"

"I'm worried about her," Hetty said, and found it was not exactly a lie. Finding that mark on the wall changed the entire case, and not for good. "Her sister asked me to look for her."

"She has no sister. You're a liar!"

Hetty picked up the twig. When her hands brushed along the wood, Hetty thought she would feel a rush of power, feel something special that made it taboo to anyone who wasn't deemed worthy to even touch one.

Instead, she only felt foolish.

The woman stepped backwards even as Hetty handed the wand back to her.

"Believe what you want, but the truth will not change. If Judith comes around, let her know that her sister is looking for her. And if she's worried it's a lie, send her to me."

"How will she find you?"

"Speak my name and the wind will carry it to my ears."

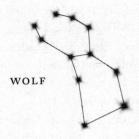

WOLF

22

Wʜᴇɴ ʜᴇᴛᴛʏ ᴀʀʀɪᴠᴇᴅ at the forge, Sy was busy assisting a customer. Lost in her thoughts, Hetty didn't think much of the sight until the older bearded man slapped a hand against the table. The lantern rattled and Sy took a step back.

"That's not what I said!" the customer bellowed. "I brought in a wagon to have the axel fixed last week and I'm here to pick it up!"

"It's not here — there's no wagon."

"Listen to me, young man. Mess with me and the next thing that's disappears will be you —"

"Is there a problem here?" Hetty forced her voice into the conversation. Relief flooded Sy's face, although the belligerent stranger only puffed up as she stepped forward.

"Stay out of this," he sneered. "My business had nothing to do with you."

"What business is that?" Benjy joined them then, his hammer propped casually over his shoulder. His expression was something slightly north of foreboding as the rude man turned to him. "There's no wagon here."

"Then we have a problem. Is it your forge's policy to let people come and take what isn't theirs?"

"Only if they pay us first." Benjy picked up a book off the table. He flipped through the pages until he found the one he was looking for. "You say it was a wagon. The only wagon we have on record for the week had its account paid by Morris Stevens. Is that you?"

"No, my name is Preston Stevens," the man grumbled, "but Morris is my brother."

"I see." Benjy handed the book back to Sy. "Go ask your brother about the wagon. Sounds like he'll know where it is."

"You have no right to speak to me like that!" Preston began, but Benjy had already turned away. He snapped his fingers and suddenly Preston's lips were moving but the only sound Hetty could hear was slightly muffled.

Realizing something was afoot, Preston did the only smart thing Hetty had seen him do. He strode off and slammed the door behind him.

"You didn't sign off on a wagon, did you?" Benjy asked Sy.

"No!" Sy shook his head. "I always make sure to give it to the person who brought it in after what happened with those tea-kettles."

"Then it was Nathaniel." Benjy grunted. "He doesn't care about keeping things in order. Why did Amos hire him?"

"He married Amos's daughter."

"And has been nothing but trouble since."

"Will this man be a problem?" Hetty had her eye on the door, half expecting Preston Stevens to return.

"There's always customers like that," Benjy said. "Not the first, nor the last. Now what brings you here? Again, I should add."

"What do you think?" Hetty asked. "I found something."

"Not *who*?" Benjy led the way back into the forge. The hammer in his hand went onto the table, and he absently rolled a tea kettle forward, stopping when it neared the edge.

"It's complicated," Hetty began.

"That only makes it even more interesting." He flipped the kettle over, revealing holes on its bottom. "Tell me the story."

As Benjy worked on patching the kettle, Hetty described everything that occurred, from Penelope telling her about the coded song to chasing Judith's student through the streets.

"She told me nothing of note, and only grudgingly agreed to pass a message along to Judith if she saw her. But I already found enough before she surprised me. The classroom itself had nothing of importance. But there was a small room in the back." Hetty settled against the bench, rolling the nearest chisel along the surface to hide her shaking hands. "The door was slathered with wards. Carefully done too. I had to pick them away layer by layer. Once I got inside, I knew why. I found"—Hetty licked her lips and she flipped the tool between her fingers—"I found the cursed sigil gouged into the wall."

At her words, the hammer struck a new hole into the kettle's bottom, undoing all of Benjy's careful work.

"The Serpent Bearer!" he exclaimed. "Was it active?"

Hetty closed her eyes, picturing herself standing in front of the wall once more.

"No, the sigil was just a carving," Hetty said. "No magic. Or if there had been magic, none remained."

"That makes sense," Benjy murmured. "You said the door was covered in wards. I wonder how long ago they'd been set."

"I think the better question is by whom?"

"That's tied together." Benjy twirled his hammer between his fingers as he spoke, deep in thought. "How did you dismantle them?"

"Not carefully. I made a mess of the wards. Anyone who returns will know someone had been there, might even be able to trace my magic."

"No. Those wards were set to ring an alarm, nothing more. You would have faced more than that student otherwise."

"Set by Judith?" Hetty wondered.

"If she's teaching Sorcery, I doubt she's that good with Celestial magic."

"Then that discounts her sister, too. Though Alice did do that clever bit with the note she left me."

"That was just a party trick. Someone else set those wards." Benjy let go of the hammer, but it continued to spin, floating in the air next to him. "Could it have been Charlie's murderer? That mark ties Judith to Charlie and the nameless man we found."

"I don't know why!" Hetty threw her hands into the air. "Why do you think I'm here? This changes everything if she's involved in this. And if that's the case, how? Charlie wasn't even interested in learning star sigils, let alone Sorcery."

"The answer to that will explain why she's missing." Benjy held out his hand. The hammer fell into it as he turned back to the kettle. "I only hope we don't find her body."

"I know." Hetty groaned, collapsing forward onto the workbench. "Believe me, I know. I don't like her sister very much, but I don't want to tell her terrible news. I've done that once already this week, and it went poorly."

"Of course it did." Benjy tilted the kettle forward, fingering a hole he'd made by accident. "Marianne lied to you about several things."

"She didn't kill him," Hetty said to the assorted tools facing her. "She gave us Charlie's watch to fix. She could have sold it or buried it with him."

"That's not proof."

"Yet you haven't fixed it."

"I don't have the right tools at home," Benjy protested. "They're all here."

With a smirk, Hetty dangled the watch in front of him. "Any more excuses?"

Eyes on the watch, he asked, "You want me to fix it right now?"

"You aren't doing anything else, are you?"

Benjy glanced at the kettle, which was now even more ruined than when she'd first arrived. He sighed and held out his hand. "Since you insist."

Once he found the proper tools, Benjy dragged a stool over and set to work.

"Why do you want this done now?" Benjy asked as he teased open the casing. "Did you want to give this back to Marianne?"

"No. It's about the astrolabe. I want to use it. The watch should be fixed before then."

"Use it to do what?"

"To look somewhere," Hetty sputtered, her excuses unwavering at his unimpressed gaze. "It could lead us somewhere we haven't considered before."

"Even it does, you'll still have to give it back to her."

"Why don't you?" she countered. "Marianne has made it clear these past few months she doesn't consider me a friend anymore. It's not just one argument or ten—it's just she made it clear she no longer considers me important to have in her life."

"Then don't consider her a friend anymore." Benjy prodded the gears. "I never understood why you did for so long. She hadn't been a good friend to you for years."

"But she was once, a long time ago," Hetty said. "I think that's what makes this so hard."

"Don't let that get in the way of this case. If we're going to solve Charlie's death, you need to let go of the past."

"I can't."

"Try."

Benjy plucked something from the watch's gears and held it up to her. It was a long, slender piece of silver. A pin, she thought at first glance, but then she took a closer look and saw how the end was twisted and curled. It was a key. A tiny key that could unlock a number of secrets.

Benjy placed the key into her hand. "Because I think talking to Marianne has just become very important."

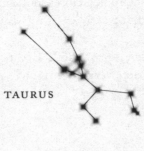

TAURUS

23

When hetty arrived at Penelope's apartment the next afternoon, her friend was in the midst of watering the half dozen plants that sat out on the landing.

"I'm almost done." Penelope held up her watering can. "I'm going to get the ones on the roof. I didn't expect you until a bit later."

"I was curious about this tea," Hetty lied. "You made it sound so interesting."

Hetty had set out this morning to pay a call to Marianne to ask about the tiny key she carried in her pocket, but a block away she lost her nerve. She spent the rest of the morning making attempts to visit people, but remained unsuccessful. She didn't spy Alice Granger in the window of the department store she worked at. Neither Geraldine nor Alain Browne answered the door when she visited their apartment. Judith's classroom remained untouched since Hetty had left it the previous day. The alleys where Charlie and the unknown man were found held no more clues. And she didn't bother making a second try to enter the headquarters of the E.C. Degray club. Even her attempt to visit Cora Evans for a bit of news had been a failure. She had walked up to the door only to meet Cora and Jay on their way out to visit a friend outside the city.

Not wanting to bother Benjy yet again at the forge, Hetty decided there was no harm in arriving earlier than planned.

"Where are we going?" Hetty added. "You never said."

"Eunice's."

"Eunice is hosting? Not one of your cousins?" Hetty pretended surprise. She had pinned her suspicions on Eunice from the start, and had the grim satisfaction of being right.

It was an act lost on Penelope, who merely continued:

"The tea will include a handful of those that were on the Stars for the Union Committee. Although, Darlene won't be there," Penelope added as she went up to the roof. "She and George left this morning to visit Darlene's mother. Go inside. I'll be down in a moment."

Hetty would have taken that suggestion if she hadn't already started for the downstairs apartment.

There would be no better chance to search through Darlene and George's home. Between the classroom and the baby, they returned regularly to the apartment, between and during lessons. While Hetty could get them out for a moment, she needed much more time to do a proper search.

The primers Hetty had seen in Judith's apartment had stayed prominent in her mind since she last saw them. Coincidence or not, there was a connection between her friends and Judith. The only trouble was, she had no idea what it could be.

Darlene kept a tidy home. All the shoes and coats were kept out of sight, and the kitchen had not a single dish out of place. The front room was tidy except that a table held a whistle, one of Lorene's rattles, and, oddly enough, the bell from the classroom downstairs. George's desk was pushed into the corner, burdened with a stack of books, old newspapers, and an abacus.

Poking around the desk's contents revealed nothing other than lesson plans and a few books in Greek.

Hetty opened the door to the small room across a hall. There wasn't much in the room, but it had the best light. A rocking chair sat in a corner, with the quilt Hetty had made folded over its arm so that the diamond trim was exposed.

Finished paintings leaned against the wall, lined up in a row like soldiers. The one on top was a view of the docks from the Jersey side of the river. The first of many landscapes that Darlene sold to make ends meet.

By the window stood Darlene's easel, with a stool and a small table set nearby. There was no paint dabbed on the canvas, but fine lines pointed to her next painting. Hetty didn't have to guess what it was. There was a piece of paper on the easel as well, with a sketch of the intended painting. As she peered at it, Hetty saw herself standing in front of her dress form, measuring the fabric for a dress. Benjy stood on the other side, holding one end of the fabric and gesturing wildly with his other hand.

The lines that captured them were loose and flowing, but done with great care and affection. While she appreciated the art, Hetty's attention fixed on the jagged edge of the paper.

This was the torn page from the sketchbook.

Instead of anything nefarious, Darlene had ripped out a sketch she had started to finish later. Yet the sight did not relieve Hetty.

The more she stared at it, the more she realized she had not slipped into the apartment looking to prove guilt. She was here for the opposite.

Darlene was one of her oldest friends, and even if Darlene was capable of murder, the idea was repulsive. Not because of the act, but because it meant Hetty would lose someone dear to her.

And Hetty disliked losing people, no matter the reason.

Withdrawing from the search, Hetty left the apartment only

to find herself facing Penelope and Eunice Loring on the land-ing outside.

Penelope glowered at her, but Eunice smiled.

"So that's where you went," Eunice said.

"I was watering plants," Hetty lied, rather easily, even if her words got a snort from Penelope. "I thought we were going to your home for tea? Don't tell me everyone's coming here. There isn't enough room."

"It's just me," Eunice said. "Everyone else canceled on me, and I thought to spare you a trip. I rather not be home at the moment, so the walk was nice. Shall we go back upstairs? I think your caul-drons might be close to boiling over."

Eunice went upstairs, but Hetty grabbed Penelope by the arm before her friend could follow.

"I'm going home!"

"Don't be silly." Penelope wiggled out of Hetty's grip. "She'll be offended."

"I don't care. She's lying about three things, and I don't have the patience to figure out what they are."

"She is lying," Penelope confirmed. "This whole thing is about wanting to talk to you. The tea was a roundabout way to get your attention. You can't blame her since there's this rumor about you helping people who bring their concerns to you."

"Is this about the Moonleaf?" Hetty asked, recalling another conversation with Eunice as its focus.

"I don't know—why don't we ask her?"

As that was not something she could protest, Hetty didn't even bother answering. She just stomped up the stairs to Penelope's apartment.

Although, once inside, she forgot all about Eunice.

"What is this?" Hetty exclaimed. Several different-size caul-drons were bubbling on the stove, with brightly colored smoke drifting into the air. There were vials filled with some of these same concoctions, given the smoke rising above them. But somehow the more interesting sight was Penelope's table covered with bullet casings, both opened and sealed.

"The reason my pistol doesn't have bullets is that I'm making my own using some potions I brewed up for the task," Penelope said rather smugly. "I got the idea from Sy, when he joked about putting seeds into bullet casings. That won't work, but I have brewed pellets that might. I won't give you the details on how it works, but when they're fired they do different things. Or should. This is the only one that works." She held up a bullet with a splash of blue paint on one end. "Ice appears when it makes contact."

"Elemental." Hetty nodded. "Very classic."

As there was no place to sit comfortably, they moved into Penelope's small sitting room.

Like the rest of the apartment, there were several plants here, although Hetty never kept up a proper count. If there were five or twenty, she wouldn't know because her attention was always distracted by how much the ivy had grown. Held up from hooks in the ceiling, the vines crossed the room, bunching enough in corners that it looked like a hand ready to reach out from the shadows.

Eunice sat on one side of the couch, but instead of sipping tea, she was idly embroidering a large lace doily.

It was, like the lace collar around her neck, overly frilly.

"What do you think?" Eunice asked as Hetty sat down in the lone armchair. "Be honest."

"The stitching is uneven," Hetty said as she eyed the needlework. "You left the sigils exposed instead of embedding them into part of the design. It's obvious to anyone who looks for them."

Eunice's smile faltered. "It is?"

Penelope coughed into her hand.

Hetty corrected course. "Is this your first attempt?"

"And last, it seems. I made these with Marianne."

"There's your problem right there." The words rolled off Hetty's tongue before she could stop herself. "Marianne was never good with a needle."

These words earned Hetty a frown.

"I do wish you would apologize." Eunice pulled at the cuffs of her sleeves, but her words were firm. "It's poor form to hold a grudge, and all for a silly remark."

"Why don't we—" Penelope began, but Hetty held up a hand to stopper her words.

With her gaze fixed on Eunice, Hetty said rather coolly, "Marianne said Benjy was strange and weird because she didn't understand what he was talking about. I admit I might have said unpleasant things in return and dumped tea on a perfectly innocent rug, but it was hardly a minor slight. Words have power."

"Only when you let them," Eunice said. "You're throwing away a friendship over an offhand comment about your husband."

"It was more than one comment. She's been saying such things for months, forcing others to take sides, keeping the air rife with tensions . . . and then she took you on as her latest project."

"Took me on? What do you mean?"

"You're my replacement," Hetty said bitterly as Penelope covered her face with her hands.

A startled laugh escaped Eunice's lips. "Here I thought her attentions were about my husband's money!" Her smile echoed Hetty's own bitterness. "It's the only reason people care about me at all. I'm on committees because I care, but I'm only asked to join because I can deliver the funds with just a word to my husband. That's my only value."

"That's not true," Penelope said.

"But it is," Eunice replied. Her eyes remained locked on Hetty. "I envy you. You have a wonderful husband, you have a talent with no equal in both magic and dressmaking, and most of all people want you around, even when they're mad at you. Marianne talks about you all the time. She mostly complains, but you don't complain about someone you don't care for. She's hurting right now, and if I can do one thing to help ease that hurt, I am going to do it. I want to help you two make amends. Which is why I brought this with me."

From the bag on the floor, Eunice pulled out a large leather-bound book that Hetty recognized on sight.

It was Marianne's friendship album.

Passed around in their small circle of friends, the book was filled with memories. There were newspaper clippings about a possible Confederate invasion. Several ticket stubs from fairs intended to raise money for the troops. Thoughts written up about the speakers who visited the Institute of Colored Youth. There was even a sketch that Darlene had drawn of President Lincoln's casket when he was on display at Independence Hall. But most of the pages were filled with personal notes, poems, stories, and even little jokes.

Hetty hadn't seen the book in ages, and the sight of the cover brought back a memory of when it had been newly bound and still smelled of fresh glue.

"Why do you have this?" Hetty said, still staring at the book. "Do you want me to add wishes and charms to this, and that will mend bridges that I couldn't manage before?"

"I filled the last pages," Eunice admitted, "but I wanted you to give it back to her. And we'll be with you, to make things less awkward."

"You do know Penelope has never gotten along with Marianne," Hetty said.

"Better than Darlene. She's so concerned about running her school, she's afraid to speak her mind around Marianne. As if Marianne had any influence in that matter."

Hetty smothered a bit of a laugh.

Hetty had spent the last few years dismissing Eunice, prickled by their differences and similarities, and holding a grudge for the other's friendship with Marianne. She knew it was petty of her. It was why she even considered Eunice playing a role in Charlie's murder, even when it hardly made sense.

This gesture with the album didn't make them friends, but it proved how wrong she was about Eunice.

Was that the only thing?

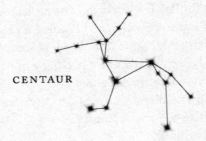

CENTAUR

24

I CANNOT TELL IF ANYONE'S HOME," Penelope remarked as they stood on the steps. Marianne still had black crepe tied to the front door, as well as a wreath. The flowers strung through the ring had started to wilt, as if it too had been touched by the death that had passed through the household. With the curtains tightly drawn so that not even a trace of light could escape, Hetty couldn't blame Penelope for wanting to leave nearly the moment they arrived.

"Maybe," Penelope added, "we should come back another time."

"Nonsense." Hetty stepped forward and knocked. "You can go home if you like."

"I'm not leaving you here alone to get into mischief."

"Mischief?" Eunice asked.

"It's always a strong possibility with Hetty."

The door opened and a cast iron pan swung out in a wide arc.

Hetty ducked to the side in time, and watched as Marianne staggered out with the pan, nearly striking Penelope on the head. She still wore black, but that was the only thing about this situation that could have been expected. Her dress was wrinkled, and her hair, usually so carefully arranged, hung loose and limp around her face.

"Eunice, Penelope?" Marianne blinked, and then she turned to see Hetty safely out of range. "Henrietta, you're here too?"

"We come to see you," Eunice said. "But we don't want to bother you if you're busy."

"I thought you were someone else," Marianne said, glancing along the street, then retreated back into her house. "Come in, can't have you standing out here like a couple of toads sitting pretty on a log."

She disappeared into the house before they could get a word in otherwise.

"I think I just changed my mind," Penelope mumbled, but she followed Hetty inside all the same.

Plunged into darkness, Hetty needed several moments to make out the familiar shapes in the room. With the curtains drawn, the only source of light was a lone lantern in the middle of the coffee table.

Marianne locked the door behind them and ran her fingers along the wood. The sigil of Ursa Major glowed for a moment before fading into a shimmery sheen.

"I wasn't expecting visitors," Marianne said.

"At least, not welcomed ones," Hetty said, her eyes flicking toward the makeshift weapon. "Those men come back around?"

"What men?" Penelope demanded, but Hetty shushed her.

Marianne's shoulders slouched. "I'm afraid you were right to be concerned. Yesterday I came home to find a window in the upper bedroom open and the contents of my room strewn about. Nothing was missing, least not that I could tell right away. This morning the men were back and said they waited this long out of respect for Charlie's passing but in the new week they'd be coming around to settle his debts. They said the contents of the household would be enough."

"How would they know that?" Penelope asked.

Hetty could guess how. It wouldn't be the first time creditors snooped around to check the debtor's wares before they came calling officially.

"Where are your children?" Eunice asked as she placed the friendship album on the nearest table.

"I sent them and Charlie's mother to stay with the neighbors. But I'm afraid to stay here no matter the protections placed around me."

"Anyone would be," Hetty said. "Which room got broken into?"

"Down the hall, last door on the left," Marianne said. When Hetty started for the stairs, she added rather sharply, "You're going to look?"

"Of course I am. You can't stay here if there's trouble. I'll be right back."

Hetty chose the Phoenix sigil, but as she had no source to attach it to, she shifted the sigil to its raw form so a bird with a long plume of a tail flew ahead of her, lighting the way. Odd shadows danced along her head as she walked, the stairs creaking under her weight. Hetty ignored the other rooms for now, choosing to first investigate the one that Marianne had pointed out.

At her first sight of the bedroom, Hetty found Marianne to be braver than expected. Hetty would not have remained in a house with a room left like this.

Ramshackle was not a strong enough word for what lay before her. Furniture was upturned on its side as if flicked away by a giant, the door to the wardrobe wrenched off its hinges, and both the clothes and the linen that littered the floor were torn and ripped apart. Pieces of glass sparkled under the windowsill as the Phoenix flew over it as it toured the room.

Hetty poked her foot into the ruin.

Someone had come in here looking for something. But what?

Eyeing the jewelry box resting on the desk, Hetty ran a finger along the casing.

Nothing obvious had been stolen. But could they have been after something not obvious—perhaps something Marianne or Charlie had hidden? Hetty took out the tiny key she had found inside Charlie's watch. She held the key against the lock on the jewelry box. The lock was too big, but there could be others.

With the Phoenix hovering over her head, Hetty drew the Hare sigil right on the floorboards.

The vertices and lines glowed then pulsed a wave of white light that hit the walls and ceiling at the same time. When it faded, a mosaic of different colors revealed themselves to Hetty.

A line of magic moved from the window, jumping to the wardrobe and then to other parts of the room.

"Someone broke into the room," Hetty whispered to herself, following the line. "Immediately rifled through the desk, the wardrobe, and the bed." From the bed, she followed the jagged magic to the vanity, where it looped around and then darted to the door.

Hetty followed it out into the hallway. The detecting magic grew thin and stretched until it stopped abruptly in front of a closet door. Hetty reached out a hand for the doorknob. It didn't move at first under her hand, but a mighty tug popped it open.

Her victory, small as it was, vanished in a heartbeat.

An arm clamped around her, and something cold and sharp pressed against her neck.

"If you scream," a voice hissed into her ear, "you die."

HERO

25

HETTY STOOD WITH A KNIFE pressed against her neck, mentally kicking herself for being careless. This was what she got for not taking proper precautions, she supposed. If she was lucky, she could wiggle out of this without harm, but she had no idea what this man might be capable of.

"You weren't supposed to be here," the man muttered. "No one was supposed to be here."

"Did you come here to steal something? Something of Charlie's?"

The grip tightened, but the pressure of the knife didn't change. "Is that why you're here? You a friend of his?"

"Yes, a close friend."

The man let go. Hetty stumbled away, keeping her hands behind her back.

He was older than her, with bags under his eyes, and crisscrossed pale scars on his face marred his brown skin. He twirled the knife in his right hand, licking his lips.

"Good," the man said. "Now there are no excuses at all. I thought him being dead would make her see things clearly, but if he had a mistress, that's even better."

Hetty stopped in the middle of making the sigil. "Mistress! Certainly not! I'm a happily married woman!"

"You wouldn't be going through his things if you were."

"Sound logic," Hetty grunted, before switching to the simpler Canis Minor. "But not sound enough."

The flash of magic caught him off-guard, just as Hetty had hoped. The man flew into the wall, and before he could move an inch, Hetty drew Virgo in the air and a woman made of stars stepped forward. Virgo placed a hand on his forehead and the man's eyes rolled back into his head. He slumped to the floor, already in the thralls of enchanted sleep.

Running through the star sigil, Hetty picked up her skirts and hurried down the hall. Nearly stumbling down the dark staircase, she called out as she ran back into the parlor.

"Marianne, I think the intruder—"

Hetty stopped at the doorway. Penelope and Eunice snored on the couch, both collapsed backwards in positions that were far too uncomfortable to fall into naturally.

In front of them Marianne stood, once more holding her frying pan. This time Andromeda glowed along the metal.

"—is someone you might know."

Marianne stepped forward. "I can explain."

"I don't care."

"It merely looks terrible," Marianne said in a rush. "I'm not going to hurt them!"

"And what about me? I had a knife to my throat!"

"Eli wouldn't have hurt you," Marianne declared. Her words brimmed with such confidence that it reduced the last of Hetty's goodwill to ruin.

"Why don't you tell me the truth?" Hetty snapped. "Did you kill your husband?"

"No!" Tears welled up in Marianne's eyes, and the pan shook in her hands. "I could never do such a thing!"

"You have a guest snoozing upstairs that suggests otherwise!"

Marianne's eyes flicked upstairs, and then instead of attacking, she dropped the pan and collapsed into a chair. "Eli is my husband," she said. "Or was, before Emancipation. I was barely more than a girl when we were forced to marry. Eli said he would wait until I was ready before we started acting like man and wife. But it never mattered what we wanted. I was nearly—" Marianne swallowed, and when she continued her voice was firmer than before. "Eli intervened, and they sold him. I was sent away soon after, and then was freed when my new mistress died. I never thought I would see him again. But he found me last year. I thought he'd accepted my marriage with Charlie and had moved on."

"Then Charlie died and he reappeared in your life," Hetty said. "And you didn't tell him to go away this time."

"He had nothing to do with Charlie."

"I believe you."

Marianne pressed a hand to her mouth, pushing back a sob. The star sigil emblazed on the frying pan faded as Marianne collapsed into her couch.

There were signs everywhere pointing toward Marianne having a hand in Charlie's death. Motive, opportunity, even means if the secret lover's ability could be added. Yet, Hetty could not even consider the notion. It was too simple. And nothing with Marianne had ever been simple.

"Did you want him to stay?" Hetty asked.

"I don't know. After those men came here with their threats, I was terrified. For me. For my children. They're all I have left."

"I should have put wards on this house," Hetty said.

"I wouldn't have let you."

"I should have done it anyway." Taking a deep breath, she said what she should have said days ago. "We found Charlie's body mutilated with the sigil of the Serpent Bearer."

"Isn't that—"

"Yes, Ophiuchus, the cursed sigil. He wasn't the only one. We found another body the night of his funeral, and for all we know there could be more. We've been investigating all week, and everything we found just leads to more questions." Hetty reached into her pocket and pulled out the tiny key. "Benjy found this in the gears of Charlie's pocket watch. Do you recognize it? Do you know what it goes to? It must be important if Charlie hid it inside one of his most prized possessions."

Marianne studied the key. After a while, she shook her head. "I can't help you. I have no idea what it might be, and in some ways I'm afraid to find out what secrets he took to the grave."

"We can still find something. Tell me: Is there anything you haven't mentioned before? It doesn't matter how small the detail might seem."

Marianne grew so silent, Hetty braced herself for another torrent of tears. But when Marianne spoke, her words were clear and firm.

"We had a fight the day he died. At dinner with the Waltons, Pastor Evans had pulled him aside to speak. Afterward he wouldn't say what it was about. I wouldn't leave it alone. I kept asking and asking until he snapped at me. We quarreled and then he left. That was the last time I saw him."

"Did you ever find out what he spoke to the pastor about?"

Marianne shook her head. "Does it matter?"

"It might." Hetty slipped the key back into her pocket. "Do you want the watch back?"

"I gave it to you," Marianne said. "Keep it."

"Your son might want it one day."

"I don't want a stolen watch!"

"Stolen?"

Marianne looked away. "I'm afraid with my husband there's a strong chance it was. He wanted to rise to the top, and was willing to do so in ways many did not approve of. Before, I didn't care—I was happy to be pampered and showered with gifts. Who cared if my dresses were purchased from money stolen from another's pockets? I wasn't like you, working my fingers to the bone. I thought myself so much better than you. Yet I know if your husband dies you would not run to the next man you see for protection."

"You don't have to—"

"What choice do I have?" Marianne waved a hand about the darkened room, at all the beautiful things that belonged to creditors now.

"There are always other choices," Hetty said quietly. "Charlie's mother would take you in for the sake of the children. Eunice and Darlene would both lend a hand. I'm also here."

"*You'd* help me?"

"We don't get along well these days," Hetty said, picking up the friendship album and turning to the first page. "But that hasn't always been true."

Although the album had not entered her hands for some time, Hetty's notes and scribbles filled the first few pages, for Darlene, Penelope, and Eunice had come to the city and into their lives much later. Those early pages were filled with silly notes and remarks broken up only by Hetty's first trip south. While Hetty scarcely remembered all the things she'd written or charms she'd left on the pages, the first page stood clear in her mind:

To my first friend in my new life, may we always share good times under happy stars.

Marianne closed her eyes for a long moment before she pressed a hand on top of the book. "I'm sorry for the things I said about you. I didn't think you truly cared, not when the only thing that was important to you was your sister."

"Why not?" Hetty asked, puzzled and a bit lost at this sentiment. "I lost her and I was trying to find her. You know this, everyone knows this."

Marianne smiled then. For a moment, she was the girl that had slipped Hetty a book more interesting than the primers Cora Evans allowed her to read.

"You focused so much on what you wanted, you forgot about what you already had. Why are you looking so hard for a sister when you have plenty of family right here?"

"I left her behind," Hetty said. "I promised to look after Esther, and I failed."

"Then it's not about finding her—it's about your guilt."

"I don't feel . . . I'm not . . . I don't . . ." Hetty protested, but she stopped, unable to argue further.

Marianne gave her a thin smile.

"I should mark the occasion," she said, tapping the friendship album. "The day I outwitted Henrietta Rhodes!"

Marianne's laugh did not make up for the past and the many hurts strewn between them over the years. But it eased Hetty's confusion as she finally understood all the things that had gone wrong between them. Hetty had hurt her friend. Whether it was on purpose or not didn't matter. That hurt cut deep and festered. But now Hetty could see the ending of this bitter and private war.

Penelope jerked awake with a start. She blinked blearily, confused and rattled.

"What was in that tea?"

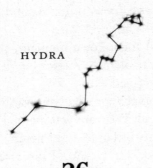

HYDRA

26

I CAN'T BELIEVE YOU THINK she's innocent!" Penelope slammed a dusty bottle of alcohol onto her kitchen table. "She slipped something into my drink!"

"No one forced you to drink it," Hetty pointed out. "It could have been poison instead of a sleeping draught."

"I was being polite." Penelope popped open the bottle and began to pour its contents into the glasses. Hetty's glass got enough to wet the bottom, but Penelope filled hers with a substantial amount. "Eunice took a cup and I had to do the same. Maybe that's why she wasn't that upset. Eunice did offer to stay with Marianne for a bit. Better person than me. Stars, Marianne has been rude to us for ages. You know she's the source of all the nasty gossip around town?"

"I know that." Hetty tapped her fingers on the glass. "It's my fault. I ruined our friendship."

"You certainly did not," Penelope said. "If your leavings and goings bothered her, she should have told you a long time ago. She just let things turn sour on her because she likes playing the victim!"

"I know you never liked her," Hetty said. "Was there any reason why?"

"Do I need a reason?" Penelope asked, swishing the contents of her glass. "I'm sure somewhere deep down she's a good person. I just didn't meet that particular side of her. Besides, didn't you tell me a story once about travelers on the road to Timbuktu?"

"It was not Timbuktu." Hetty wet her lips with a taste of the sweet wine. "It was a place that exists no longer, from the time where scholars visited the Great Library of Alexandria and caravans crossed the Silk Road."

"See, Timbuktu works."

Hetty shushed Penelope. "This story crosses lands near a desert where a traveler picked up companions along the way. Some were by chance. A merchant whose mule could no longer walk, a pair of sisters whose parents perished along the way, and more in unlucky circumstances. Some were needed to strengthen numbers, such as a librarian with a treasury of knowledge and a former soldier who carried swords from his commission and none of the honor. They traveled together and for some time, but they would not all reach the same destination. For while they were true companions for the journey, there were places that not all could go."

"Friends," Penelope concluded for Hetty, "they may stay in your life always, but there may come times for them to go separate ways."

Understanding why Penelope had brought up this story, Hetty considered her own words. "You think this applies to Marianne?"

"Oh," Penelope said, reaching over to fill her glass once again, "you don't want to hear my thoughts about that!"

As they chuckled over this, a knock on the door drew their attention.

It wasn't just a simple knock, but a cascade of knocks that didn't stop until Penelope opened the door.

Sy rushed inside, nearly knocking his cousin over. He bent over the table, gasping for air and yet trying to talk all the same.

"Sy," Penelope exclaimed. "What's wrong? Is Rosabelle ill again? I have some potions prepared for her."

"Not Rosie, something else," Sy managed to say as he looked up. "I need you to find—Hetty!"

"Are you looking for me?" Hetty asked.

"Something happened at the forge. You must see it!"

Sy could have said more then. He could have even explained. But Hetty wouldn't have heard it. Her glass shattered on the floor, splashing the droplets of liquid against her boots.

Sy's words were vague, but in them Hetty saw a stream of nightmares that robbed her of sleep all week.

She stood not bothering with questions.

"Show me."

Penelope went with them to the forge. Quietly following, asking no questions but carrying with her a few healing potions, just in case.

Hetty appreciated the thought. But as Sy scrambled to explain, Hetty suspected they wouldn't be needed.

"I don't know where else to turn. I probably shouldn't have left, but I couldn't stay there longer without doing a thing more," Sy said when they arrived at the tightly shuttered building.

Sy led them not through the shop or into the interior, but around back to the separate shed used to store the tools. The spare tools, Benjy had told her once. The large tools that didn't fit in the shop or the ones they didn't use often. But when Sy opened the door, there was more than just tools inside.

There was a man lying on the ground, his eyes staring, unseeing, into the great beyond.

And she knew him.

Alain Browne laid at her feet.

Behind her, she heard a cry from Penelope as she stumbled backwards.

It should have sounded louder to Hetty's ears, but it was just dull background noise.

Hetty cursed herself for not going around to his apartment yesterday. She should have tried harder at the excursion to speak to him. She should have questioned him more strongly about how and when he found Charlie's body and what else had happened that night. She should have found out what Alain lied about and learned if that lie risked bringing trouble. Now that knowledge was locked away for good.

"When did you find him?" Hetty asked as she looked for any signs of the Serpent Bearer cut into his chest.

"Not too long ago. I went back here looking for a tool," Sy said. "I'm the only one here today."

Hetty looked up at these words.

"Benjy hasn't been here?"

Sy looked away. "I haven't seen him."

There was something else that he wasn't telling her. Something that had him seeking her out instead of Benjy. It should have been Benjy that Sy went running for, not her.

"So you were looking for a tool and found this man," Hetty said. "Was the door locked?"

"No. Nathaniel forgets, and sometimes on rainy nights we get people sleeping back here. At first I thought this man had done the same, then I saw—" Sy gulped. "Then I knew he wasn't just sleeping."

Hetty followed the younger man's gaze back to Alain. She had been focused on his torso and missed what she should have seen in the first place.

A circle the size of a teacup, impressed into the left side of his skull.

"There's only one hammer with that shape," Sy whispered. "And Ben's the only person who can hold it and hit his mark."

URSA MINOR

INTERLUDE

May 1864

SPOTSYLVANIA COUNTY, VIRGINIA

HETTY PLUNGED THROUGH the woods, unable to see the path forward even with sunlight to mark the way.

They'd known it was a risk to continue this route through Virginia, especially as they'd heard gunfire peppering the air.

The fighting must have drifted further west than they'd thought, for they stumbled right into a group of bruised and bleeding soldiers in gray uniforms.

These men weren't slave catchers, but that didn't matter. Once they crossed paths, magic and bullets started flying.

"Stop looking back," Benjy yelled. "It'll only slow you down!"

"They're going to catch up eventually," Hetty said, panting. "And there's more than usual. We need to *do* something."

Benjy slid to a stop. Hetty slowed with less ease, stumbling a bit before she steadied herself.

"Yes, we do," Benjy said. "Suggestions?"

"Split up. Meet me at the cemetery we arrived at."

"Good plan." He nodded.

"Don't make me wait. I'll leave without you."

"I know," he replied, before veering right into the brush.

Hetty went left, the branches tearing at her clothes and skin. She hadn't gone far before she felt the ground ripple under her feet. Hetty spun around and saw the sky light up with Ursa Minor.

The sight nearly sent her stumbling.

They never used that star sigil in any of their spells. Much like how they used the Crow or Canis Minor, that sigil was a message—used only to say: *Run and don't look back.*

There were too many soldiers who were more than eager to stop them.

There was still a chance to get away. But it was a small, fragile one. Benjy chose to make certain she'd had a chance. Even if it meant he himself likely wouldn't.

Hetty ran through the woods. She could curse him later—assuming they both lived. For now it would just be a waste of breath.

Running was all she could do.

As so she did, charging forward through the brush and up into trees where the branches were close enough that she could easily jump between them.

Run, she urged her body, trying to keep her mind focused on the branches. *Run,* keep going forward. *Keep running.* Don't worry about the sounds.

Hetty burst out of the woods in a dead sprint, the shock of it surprising the soldier on rear guard enough that he didn't even react when Hetty slapped the collar around his neck.

Her weight dragging the collar down, she slapped one hand on the gemstones, activating the magic. His body shuddered and arched backwards as the shock ran through his limbs. He swung blindly at her, his strangled cries drawing attention from the soldiers clustered around the bound and bleeding Benjy.

"It's the other one," cried out the nearest.

That was all he managed to say.

A glittery arrow struck at the man, and he fell over backwards as the magic exploded. Flicking her magic off her fingers like sticky seeds, she struck arrows at them all. Sowing chaos with each explosion, becoming the embodiment of every whispered terror that filled their minds.

That terror was usually unjust. Guilty thoughts, Hetty's mother had called it. Guilty thoughts of knowing the harm being done, but trying not to see.

Hetty still didn't understand it—never *would* understand it—but she welcomed seeing that fear in their eyes. Because she'd spent the last few years learning magic just for a moment like this.

A shot rang out, a bullet skimming past her arm. It missed, but slammed into the tree beside her, and the shard of bark that flew into her arm in its wake was enough to momentarily stun her.

She looked over expecting to see a soldier aiming his rifle at her, but found instead that Benjy had one arm around the soldier's neck and kept squeezing despite the man beating a fist on Benjy's arm. The soldier's struggling weakened as his eyes rolled backwards into his skull.

Benjy dropped the man. The body hit the ground with a thud.

He stepped over the body, kicking the gun aside as he strode toward Hetty, storm clouds still brewing in his face.

"Why did you come back! What about the plan?"

"*You* made that plan," Hetty shot back. "I never agreed!"

"You're supposed to leave!"

"I did that before," Hetty replied, "and I will not do it a second time!"

As if she dumped a bucket of water on his head, the fight fled from him entirely and instead he stared at her as if she'd just declared the sun rose from the west.

"Here I thought you only wanted me around to fix things for you."

"That's not entirely true," she admitted. "I —"

Hetty's words turned into a cry of pain as something wrapped itself around her neck.

Benjy lurched toward her, but a flash of light hit him in his chest, sending him flying backwards into the trees and before Hetty could see what happened her vision shifted upward to the sky.

"That's what you get putting this infernal thing on me," a man snarled into her ear. He tightened the rope, cutting into the old scars that lay at her neck. "I'm going to kill you right before your man's eyes, like the dog you are. I should kill him first to make it the last thing you'll see."

"You won't," Hetty managed to sputter, and then slammed her elbow back as hard as she could. It took him by surprise, and the moment he loosened his grip, she twisted out of his hold. Half rolling, half falling, she drew Canis Minor.

The magic flared and he was flung back into the trees, colliding with enough force that an entire branch crashed down on top of him.

Gasping, Hetty ripped off the remains of the rope and staggered over to Benjy. She placed a hand on his shoulder. Benjy moved at once, jerking into a sitting position.

"Are you —"

"I'm fine," Benjy said as he grasped her hand, nearly crushing her fingers. His eyes searched her face before looking beyond her.

Hetty followed his gaze to the man she just felled. "I thought I knocked him out. That's what happened to me when I was jolted by the collar. I think he's dead now."

Benjy let go of her hand. "I'll check."

Benjy went over to the soldier. He stood over the body, staring down at the bearded face for a long moment. Then he picked up one of the tree branches that had fallen.

For a wild moment, Hetty thought as he held the branch he was about to perform Sorcery, but instead he brought it crashing down on the man's skull.

One, two, three times he struck the man, as if wielding one of his hammers, until she heard a sound akin to the cracking of an egg on a pan's side.

"He wasn't," Benjy grunted, dropping the branch. "Now he is. Where to next?"

DRAGON

27

Hᴇᴛᴛʏ sᴛᴏᴏᴅ ᴏᴠᴇʀ ᴀʟᴀɪɴ ʙʀᴏᴡɴᴇ, unsure of where to look first. Sy's last words had distracted her. The blow to Alain's head certainly looked like the work of a hammer. But that wasn't as important as why. Why here? Why now? Why him?

She could almost see an answer to that last question. Alain had found Charlie, and brought them to the alley, and set them on the trail. He was close enough to the case that Hetty kept him in her sights as a suspect. It seems she was right, but not in the way she expected.

If only she had gone to talk to him, she might have noticed the danger swirling around him.

And his wife.

Hetty had no love for Geraldine Browne, but this was such a terrible thing to have happened.

And there was still one more question to ask.

Who did this?

The whispered conversation gave her one answer.

As Hetty studied the body, the cousins argued in the background. While there was an attempt to keep voices low, it didn't last for long.

Penelope stomped her foot. "How can you even suggest Benjy's involved?"

"I'm not saying he did it," Sy protested. "It just looks like it. None of this makes sense. Why do you think I went looking for Hetty? She'll figure out what happened."

Hetty looked between them, seeing the doubts grow in their eyes the longer she stayed quiet. She knew what the cousins wanted her to say, but she couldn't without further proof.

"There will be time for that later," Hetty said. "First we need to move the body."

Since it was broad daylight and Hetty didn't trust her spells to stay in place, they used bricks to cover the body in the bed of the wagon. Hetty laid them herself, the act dredging memories of times when she had been the one carefully hidden under a pile. This time, however, there was no need for breathing holes.

A block away from Oliver's home, Hetty signaled for Sy to stop.

"Wait here." She jumped off. "I need to give Oliver a bit of warning."

But whatever warning she'd planned to give slipped right out of her mind as she came around the corner and found her husband swinging a hammer down on the front steps. His bag of tools sat next to him, and pieces of wood were stacked on the steps of the empty house next door.

He swung decisively, the sound of metal ringing in the air as he hit the nails dead-on. He did it a few times before Hetty couldn't watch anymore.

"Benjy," she forced herself to say, and the hammer paused in the air. "What are you doing here?"

"Keeping myself busy," he answered. "Amos fired me this morning!"

"Fired?" Hetty echoed.

"Because that wagon went missing." The hammer slammed

harder this time, and the collision rang in the air. "Preston Stevens complained to Amos. Amos said the money would come out
of my wages, and I said no because it was Nathaniel who signed
off on it. He asked if I had any proof. I may have lost my temper
at that point. I don't remember what I said, but I won't be getting
the job back."

"What did you do?" she asked.

"Nothing bad. I didn't hit him or anything." Benjy looked over
at her and his smile vanished at the sight of her face. "What happened?"

"Several things," Hetty said. "Is Oliver home?"

Benjy nodded.

"Has he been here all day with you?"

"He has." Benjy lowered the hammer. "And he'll tell you so if
you ask him."

"I only ask," she said, responding to his unspoken question,
"because I found Alain Browne in the spare tools closet at the
forge. His head was bashed open. I brought him with me—he's
in a wagon around the corner."

Benjy absorbed this information without even a flinch. "Is
that all?"

"Well, Sy found Alain first, and then he panicked."

"I imagine he would," Benjy said. "He's not one for surprises.
Which side of Alain's head was struck?"

"The left."

At this, he snorted. "By the stars, what sloppy work! If someone was trying to paint me as a murderer, they should have at least
remembered I'm left-handed. The angle of the wound would be
different if I'd been the culprit. I'm surprised you didn't notice
since you favor your left hand as well."

Hetty sucked in her breath, unsure if she was relieved or not at
this statement. "I never said anything about you being a suspect."

"Your tone did it for you. Hetty," he added quite soberly,

"please tell me you didn't think that I could have killed him? I didn't like the man, but he had valuable information."

"There was quite a bit of evidence pointing at you."

Benjy scoffed. "Would I be foolish enough to kill a man and leave the body in a place I'm known to frequent?"

"Someone certainly wanted me to consider it."

"I should hope you didn't!" Benjy continued. "You should know that if I were to kill somebody, I'd at least be a bit more subtle about it."

"Don't make light of this," Hetty protested. "A man is dead!"

"And before he could tell me anything of value! This is so inconvenient."

"Benjamin!" she snapped as every feeling she pushed down and ignored all week bubbled up to the surface. She turned on him, snarling: "This isn't a puzzle! We're talking about lives! Human lives that are more than pieces on your chessboard!"

Benjy went rigid at her words. He didn't look startled, just scared—and that only made things worse.

A hiccup nearly escaped from her lips. She pressed her hands against her face, embarrassed and ashamed.

"Do you want me to warn Oliver?" Benjy asked gently. "Or would you rather stay here while I—"

"I'll warn him," Hetty said, lowering her hands. "He won't yell as much if I tell him."

Oliver didn't yell at Hetty about body number three crossing the threshold of his home.

He threw his papers into the air and let out a groan that almost shook the rafters.

"Which alley did you find this one?" he said when he finished his theatrics.

"At the forge. His skull was caved in, by a hammer it seems."

"Does he have that mark on him?"

"I didn't see, but I didn't get a chance to check thoroughly. Sy and Penelope were with me, and they were too concerned that Benjy had something to do with it."

"What do you think?"

"It doesn't matter what I think," Hetty began, only to stop as the cellar door slammed shut.

Hetty turned at the sound, but she barely got a glance of who strode out.

"Looks like Benjy's not happy," Oliver observed. His face was creased with concern that didn't lessen as he rubbed his neck. "Although he's been in a foul mood all morning. I put him to work on various small projects to keep him busy, you know how he gets when he's upset."

"Yes," Hetty echoed, not fully listening. "I do."

LIBRA

28

BENJY DIDN'T TALK MUCH on the way back, but Hetty wasn't in the mood for chatter. With each step, all the events of the day tumbled like stones battering a roof. Eunice and the tea that wasn't. Marianne and her troubles. Marianne's betrayal and her belated apology. A key hidden in a pocket watch. That was all just today. This whole week had her rushing from one moment to the next with not long to pause, with nothing but questions. Every time she'd thought she found an answer, she turned around and there were five more questions left to ask.

"Is something wrong?"

Hetty looked up from the lamp that she hadn't turned on yet to see Benjy watching her from the other side of the room.

"I want to take a bath tonight."

Her announcement was met with a nod. "I'll get the buckets."

To fill the tub took fourteen buckets of water, and there was no easy way to get it into their room from the pump downstairs. It was well worth the trouble. The tub, made by Benjy when they agreed that buying one outright was too costly, was Hetty's one indulgence. She had a bath each week, and more often if she could manage it. She even carried on the practice in the wintertime despite nearly catching a cold one night. While they had a system for flying the buckets up through the window, the simplest solution was Benjy carrying the buckets himself. A task he did when she asked, but not without complaints every step of the way.

This evening she heard no complaints.

He remained quiet, and even his footsteps were muffled as he reentered the room, dumped the water into the tub, then headed back to repeat the journey several times more.

When Benjy poured the last bucket, the water came to a rest at the sigil notched inside. Aquarius glowed, and the water began to heat up.

Hetty sat by the tub, waiting for this process to finish.

There were words she could say. A conversation she could start. But she said nothing, did nothing more than nod when Benjy collected the empty buckets and left the room.

Submerging herself, she sank into the tub until the water reached her shoulders. Curled up there, Hetty felt the knots in her belly uncoil. Her troubles, both those of her own making and those beyond her control, still remained of course. But for now all the death and confusion was behind her.

Hetty scrubbed, using the soap to rub away her intruding thoughts as much as dirt. When she got every bit of skin she could reach, she washed her hair too, thinking of her dip in the river. For a day meant to be a break from the excitement, Hetty would have never expected such an adventure at Marianne's. Or even that it would prove without a doubt that Marianne wasn't involved. Marianne and her secret husband. What a shocking and devastating piece of gossip this was! Marianne might move just to avoid hearing the whispers that will arise. Yet there was nothing to fear. Hetty would never speak of such things, not even to Penelope. Hetty kept such secrets. Still, she could imagine Marianne at another tea, with Darlene and Penelope giggling over this gossip, glad to finally have something to lord over the other woman. Except for Eunice, who sat there sewing a doily so big, it was like a blanket in her lap.

Eunice looked in Hetty's direction and then tossed her a large brass key. Hetty reached out to pluck it from the air, but it slipped between her fingers, turning into thread. One strand looped around Darlene and George, entangling them with an empty cradle. Another dangled around Geraldine and her collection of dodgy potions, her expression a bit too innocent and scared to be genuine. There were threads that tangled around Clarence Loring and Isaac Baxter with a banner and a box of money in hand for an election that would never come. The threads thickened to ropes as they choked the tree branches, where, like pendulums, Charlie, Alain, and the unknown stranger dangled, turning in small circles.

Lurking in the tree's shadow was Alice. She pulled at a strand that connected her to a young woman. Judith, Hetty thought, until the young woman turned and her face was Esther's. Esther smiled at Hetty even as blood dripped from the thread around her neck, bright red and burning hot . . .

With a gasp, Hetty bolted upright in the tub, awake before she was completely aware. Water splashed everywhere as she did, including on Benjy kneeling at the tub's side. The fading light around gave her one answer out of the three that occurred to her.

"Are you trying to boil me alive!" Hetty splashed more water at him. He ducked out of the way this time, but didn't completely escape the line of fire.

Hetty slid over to the tub's rim to peer down at him. "What are you doing?"

"The charm on the tub fell apart," he said, not looking at her as he picked up the charcoal he dropped. "I rather you not catch your death in cold water. Or drown. It'd be the second time in nearly as many days."

"Three," she corrected as he finished marking the tub's side. "I fell twice into that river."

"So you did," he said with equal seriousness. He looked up then. "You were muttering about threads. Are you being haunted by dresses?"

"No dresses, just threads. In my dream, there were threads connecting everyone involved with the case. People had different colors. It explained everything, so many things — I'm not sure how I can explain."

"Explaining can wait until later." Benjy jumped up, walking away from her.

"Later? I'll forget all the details."

Already he had shuffled to the other side of their small room. Instead of the map, he settled on the bed, lying on his side as if to go to sleep, but couldn't turn away fast enough to avoid Hetty seeing his face. She might not understand what her dream was telling her, but she understood the distraught expression spread across his face.

"I did not see any threads tied to you," she said. Hetty braided her wet hair as quickly as she could. "You weren't even there. I don't believe you killed Alain."

"Penelope did. Sy did," he said softly.

Hetty grabbed her nightgown off the chair beside the tub, and dressed as quickly as she could.

"They don't. Sy has an overexcited imagination." Hetty settled on the bed next to him. "And Penelope . . . she was in shock. You know how she can get after a bit of excitement."

This should have brought a smile to his face. Instead, he looked as if she'd tossed his favorite hammer into a blazing fire.

"You did believe it, if only for a moment."

"It was designed to be the first thought to cross any mind. Why, even Sy thought it, and he hangs on to your every word!"

"And you?" he asked. "What was your first thought?"

"That it was you that Sy found."

Benjy sat up, and several different emotions flickered across his face, but confusion won out. "That's an odd thought to have."

"You haven't had the conversations I had this week," Hetty said. "Charlie died, and everyone talks about burial societies and planning for unexpected deaths. And they bring up your name."

"Which explains sewing protection spells into all my clothes."

"Not all of them," Hetty said. "Not yet, at least."

"Why are you the one fretting? You've been in far more perilous situations than I have. Not even counting this week."

"I am sorry about that."

"It's nothing less than I expected," Benjy replied. "It's one of the things I've always loved about you."

It took Hetty admittedly far too long to realize not only the words he said, but the emphasis he put on them.

When you've known someone for a very long time, you gain a certain understanding of what they will say or do. You know how they speak. You know when to really listen; you know what course of action they'll take when there's a decision that makes them choose between their life and yours. This happens with people you like, people you hate, and people you once called a friend but now speak with only once in a blue moon. But just because you know this person so well, it doesn't mean they can't still surprise you.

His words were such a surprise. Because as much as she desperately hoped to hear them, she'd never expected it to actually happen.

"'Always'?" she echoed, when the power of speech returned to her.

"Well, maybe not always," Benjy said, and he appeared to have been struck by the same paralyzing spell as she had, frozen where he sat on his side of the bed. "But for quite some time. I was worried if I said something it would upset things."

"How could it upset things when I'm in agreement?"

His eyes widened, and there was such astonishment on his features, it was stunning.

She might have elaborated more, might have spun some elegant sentences that she'd read in books, savoring the turns of phrase that captured emotions so well. She might have shared the details of her own revelation, and they would have a rueful laugh at how terrible things drew them together. She might even say how foolish they had been, and how silly they were to be dancing around a simple truth that they should have both known already. She might have said all those things.

But before she could, Benjy kissed her.

It was pure impulse. Something about the way his hands slid clumsily over her arms and the awkward fumbling that followed as he attempted to enfold her in an embrace told her he hadn't thought that far ahead.

This brought a smile to her lips. She took pride in it whenever she found herself even a slight step ahead of him, but rarely had she had the pleasure of catching him fully unaware.

She savored that pleasure as much as she did the kiss, which completely altered her definition and understanding of the word.

There was honesty in that kiss. Honesty and openness that made her realize that all the little kisses she had collected from him over the years had been counterfeit — token gestures too full of uncertainty to be the real thing.

"How long have you felt like this?" Hetty asked when they pulled apart.

"A little bit after New Year's," he said easily. "We snuck into a party hosted by one of Charlie's friends purely because you wanted to peer through a telescope. You had me out on the roof, chilled to the bone for the excess of an hour, but there was no other place I wanted to be."

Hetty remembered that night—he had been quiet and thoughtful when she looked over at him, but outwardly no different.

"It's not really a moment, but a realization. One I ignored until I couldn't deny its truth. I should have told you earlier. I know I've gone about this all wrong."

"No, you didn't," Hetty said, taking his hands in hers. "Time helps with everything. A year ago I might have laughed at you. Five years ago, I wouldn't have believed you. Every past moment led us here. Changing even the slightest thing could mean risking a different possibility where we never even met. Or where we disliked the other. Or one of us died. Or you moved to Canada."

A smile pulled at his face, a familiar teasing smile, but there was tenderness she hadn't yet seen and his eyes were softer than before as he gazed down at her. "That *is* a big risk," he said. "It does nothing but snow in Canada."

He kissed her once again, putting to an end one conversation as they began another.

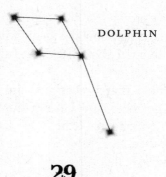

DOLPHIN

29

ALTHOUGH IT FELT LIKE everything was different now, the world had hardly changed overnight. Morning brought skies with spools of gray wool holding the promise of a muggy rainstorm. A woman was still missing, Charlie was still dead. There were two dead bodies in Oliver's cellar, but for the first time all week, Hetty felt prepared to handle it all.

Even a few unexpected things.

Seated on the bench in the courtyard behind the church, Hetty furiously sewed away at Benjy's suit jacket. Damaged from the events at the excursion, it lay on top of a pile of mending until this morning. If Benjy didn't play the piano for Sunday service, it wouldn't be so bad. She would have just done a straight stitch to hold the jacket together. However, the church's aging piano sat in a prominent spot, which called for a proper fix.

The task took more time than she expected. There were more rips than she realized. Focused as she was on her work, Hetty didn't notice anyone near until she heard a small gasp.

Eunice stood in the church's shadow, staring at her as if they hadn't seen each other the day before.

"Good morning," Hetty called.

"And to you," Eunice squeaked.

"You are here early."

"I came around to see how the picnic will be set for later. I will be handling it today. I should leave—I didn't mean to bother you."

"The only thing that bothers me are these rips. I've been sewing since I got here, and I'm not done yet." Hetty clucked her tongue at the garment. "If he didn't have to play piano, this wouldn't be a bother."

"Why not use a spell?"

"I never use repair spells for clothes." Hetty shook her head. "They never fall quite right."

"You can do it for today. It's just piano playing—he's not about to punch anyone."

Eunice slapped her hands against her mouth, horrified at her own words.

Hetty only laughed. "I wished I could have seen that."

"Everyone was so shocked, at least the ones that didn't expect it. Isaac Baxter certainly didn't, and he looked like he was spitting cats afterward. It could have turned into something nasty, but Benjamin had already forgotten him." She paused. "I don't like him. Isaac Baxter has this smile that sends me running out of a room as fast as I can." She shivered.

"Did he do something to you," Hetty asked, as casually as she could, "or say something?"

"No, of course not. Clarence would never allow that to happen." Yet Eunice's smile was far from reassuring. "Forget I said anything."

"Do you want me to give Baxter a matching black eye? I would do that for you."

"For me?" Eunice's surprise was so overwhelming, Hetty wished she showed kindness to the other woman more often.

"If there's anything you need, I'm here for you."

Eunice swallowed, and the fear in her eyes turned into the relief Hetty had seen in many people's eyes when they first approached her. *Here is someone,* Eunice's eyes said, *to get me out this spot of trouble.*

"There is something I need to tell you," Eunice began. "Can we talk——"

"Eunice, there you are."

Clarence's voice drifted into the courtyard.

While his voice wasn't loud, Eunice jumped as if a cannon had gone off.

She rushed to him, apologizing for disappearing without telling him first.

Clarence, however, ignored her words once he noticed Hetty. "What are you doing out here?" he asked.

"I had an emergency repair to make." Hetty tucked her sewing needles and thread into her pocket. As she scooped up the jacket into her arms, she added, "Now I must make a delivery. If you'll excuse me."

Hetty drifted past them. Only at the doorway did she turn back to look at them as she went inside, but they had already moved out of sight.

Interesting as the pair was, it was far from the only exciting thing going around.

Enveloped in warm, rambling chatter, Hetty slipped back inside the church to find instead of earlier, it was later than she anticipated.

A small boy ran past her, hurrying to join the queue of children headed into the church's basement. Darlene stood by the door, calling instructions to the children to not push or knock someone over. She had her daughter in her arms, gently rocking the baby every few moments. As Hetty passed, Darlene glanced over in her direction, but then averted her eyes.

Hetty had determined Darlene had nothing to do with Charlie's murder. This reaction, though, left her thinking there was something else that her friend wasn't telling her. Now wouldn't be the time to find out. Darlene traded off teaching Sunday school classes with another, and this week it was clearly her turn. Hetty would have to wait until the church picnic afterward.

Hetty headed for the piano. Seated back on a slightly raised platform, the faithful instrument of the church was flanked by its main devotees. Given the fingers pointed at sheet music, Benjy and Penelope once again were at odds about music selections for the morning.

Hetty did her best not to laugh.

Nice to know that some things would never change.

About to head to the piano to meet them, Hetty stopped when she heard her name called.

She turned, bracing herself to greet who it was. No one called out to her again. The people standing the closest to her were Frances Fields, Sallie Donnelly, and Gilda Meeks, all who were in deep conversation among themselves. The trio made a newspaper redundant, as they gave information freely, eagerly, and with great detail. The accuracy tempered most of Hetty's annoyance with the older ladies, but hearing her name on their lips was never a good sign.

But if they were talking to her or about her, they made no indication.

So Hetty continued on.

The arguing around the piano was still going on in hushed whispers, but it stopped as Benjy simply took the music from Penelope. "You win—we'll do the pieces you suggested," he said.

Penelope's surprise lasted for a few moments before she noticed Hetty. Eyebrows raised, she said, "I wondered where you went. I thought Mrs. Evans might have gotten you to perform some small errand."

"Just the mending," Hetty said, "although I heard the hens clucking."

Penelope chuckled. "That's what they do. Who was it, Frances or Sallie?"

"All three. I heard my name."

"And what?" Benjy asked.

"That's it, I heard my name. That means there's something to talk about. Because my name wouldn't be on their lips otherwise."

Benjy just laughed. "Let them cluck—they don't have anything important to say."

"That's the problem. Such things are always more interesting to talk about."

If there was time, Benjy might have been able to convince her she was wrong, but there was no time.

Service would start shortly, and they had to prepare. So, Hetty retreated to the pews, and the whispers that followed were louder than usual in her ears.

She had only polite conversation as things began, and no one even looked her way when midway through service Frances Fields gleefully described the events at the excursion during the church announcements.

Hetty began to let go of her suspicions. Clearly she heard wrong. The whispers had nothing to do with her.

Once the service ended, Hetty made her way through the crowd to speak with Cora before the older woman disappeared to help set up the picnic outside. She had just nodded in passing to some people she knew when she looked up to see the trio that Benjy said to ignore were circling him.

"Persistent, aren't they?" Cora's voice floated into her ear.

Hetty looked to find Cora at her elbow. "Have you heard the gossip? What can you tell me?"

"I'm surprised you want to know," Cora said.

"You haven't heard a thing then?"

"I heard a few things, but let them gossip about the excursion. Better than something more personal."

Hetty gave the older woman a second look, seeing a double meaning in those innocent words. Cora's eyes twinkled, and she looked as pleased as the day Hetty told her about her engagement. If they were anywhere else, Hetty might have dared to ask what she meant, but she lost her nerve.

"I'll keep that in mind," Hetty settled on saying.

"I'm sure you will. Ladies," Cora said, as Frances, Sallie, and Gilda approached. "I need your help."

As the gossipy trio passed Hetty, they gave long looks. Although Hetty said nothing, and did nothing more than nod, she knew more embellishments were made in their minds.

Benjy was alone at the piano, tidying up what sheet music lay about.

"They're not hens, they're vultures." Benjy didn't look up as Hetty leaned against the piano. "How do you handle them? Feeding them false tales leads to more trouble."

"Just ignore them," Hetty said, echoing his advice from earlier. "They have nothing important to say."

Benjy scowled at her. "Very funny."

"What did they ask you?"

"Just details about the excursion. It was hard to say if they were checking facts or fishing for more."

"Both at the same time," Hetty said. "They won't give up until they get their answers."

"Then there's only one thing we should do." Benjy reached for her hand. "Let's go home before we get caught in the rain."

"Too late for that." Pastor Evans approached them. "Fat droplets are starting to come down, which means a bit of storm. They'll need help bringing things inside before it's all ruined." The pastor looked at Benjy rather significantly.

"I'll go see if they need a hand," Benjy offered.

"Or two," Hetty added.

"Not you," Jay said to Hetty. "I'm afraid I must ask you a favor. This week's collection needs counting, and with Matthew out sick, I don't trust anyone else to give me accurate numbers."

"Someone stealing?" Benjy asked. "Do you need help with it?"

"Just bad numbers." Jay shook his head as thunder rumbled some distance away. "I hope."

The pastor led Hetty down in the cellar. The cellar itself was quite a large space, used for all manner of events and meetings. There were four rooms down there: a classroom that doubled as a nursery during the week, a small kitchen with a stove that managed to keep a few hundred fed, the church office, and a tiny closet of a room for quiet reflection. It was in this room that the basket of tithes and offerings was locked.

"I hate to ask," Jay said again as Hetty settled onto the stool, "but I know your numbers will be right."

While Hetty was pleased at the compliment, there weren't many bills or coins to go through. He could certainly count this himself. So she wasn't surprised when Jay settled in a chair opposite her, dabbing his handkerchief along his forehead.

"There are far too many wagging tongues in this congregation. Perhaps it should be the subject of my next sermon."

Hetty stopped shuffling through the coins. "You don't need to do that! I must confess, there is some truth to it."

"There is?" Pastor Evans frowned. "Tell me we misunderstand each other, since I'm certain Benjy would never loot graves!"

Her full attention fell to him with those words.

Penelope's cousin Maybelle had said something similar about grave robbing, but only the act and nothing of this nature.

"Looting graves?"

"Told in one flavor of the gossip. The rest is concerned about how little you've done about it."

"We can't stop grave robbing any more than we can any other crime."

"Well, your stories"—here his eyes gleamed with amusement—"make it seem you can do anything."

"My stories are a bit of fun. People can tell when I stretch the truth."

"It's the way you tell them that makes folks believe otherwise. I would like to take credit for that skill, but you had it long before you arrived on our doorstep. You would have made a fine preacher if the job called you. You know how to compel people's attention."

"Then I shall tell new tales to make them forget about this nonsense," Hetty said. "Of all the ridiculous gossip to be had. Why don't people ever spread *good* things about others?"

"I suppose it's not as entertaining," Jay replied, but his amusement flickered out as quickly as it had come. "Though these cases spark such talk, about grave robbing and—"

"It's just talk. Nothing to worry about."

"Then Cora and I should think nothing of how you nearly drowned and didn't tell us?"

"It was just a small thing," Hetty began, but one stern look from Jay stopped her from making excuses. "I didn't think it would be such a popular story to tell."

"There was an *explosion*," Jay said. There was worry in his eyes, and she realized that the rumors chose the most likely culprit for such an excursion, senseless hatred.

"It's not what you think." Hetty shifted atop the stool. "We believe this was done in connection to Charlie's murder. That murderer was there, aware of our investigation, and made me a target. If this is true, it means it might be a member of E.C. Degray."

"That club," the pastor huffed, relaxing somewhat but not completely. "There's something not right about it or those in charge of it, and it's not because every vice and sin can be found there making nice."

"I heard you spoke with Charlie about that before he died."

"I did. He was recruiting people from my congregation. I didn't like it." Jay scratched his chin. "After I told him to stop recruiting, Charlie got real quiet. I could tell he wanted to talk to me about something, but he wouldn't say what it was. He was too anxious. Just kept sweating up a storm and asking me about the state of his immortal soul. I assumed the worst, and asked if what he needed was a friend instead of a pastor."

"What did he say?" Hetty asked.

"We were interrupted." Jay frowned. "I forget by who. At any rate, I said we'd speak at the dinner, but we didn't have the chance since he left early. A pity, since the food was quite excellent. Although the greater pity was that you hadn't been invited as well. Maybe you could have talked some sense into him."

"I suspect we weren't invited," Hetty said, "because we bring too much excitement."

"For some people, yes, but for others you are nothing but a delight," Jay assured her. "Although, that reminds me. Charlie spoke about a building that Degray bought. You remember that school the Quakers ran on Spruce? It closed when they moved across town. Buying it seems to have been Charlie's idea, something that the club would use. Since he died, I haven't heard what will happen to it. I think one of your friends, Needham or Loring, has access. Fine fellows, both of them. Can't believe they're in that silly club . . ."

He kept on this thought for a bit longer, and, being accustomed to the old man's rambling, Hetty listened politely while the pastor spoke, waiting for her chance to make a graceful exit. That bit the pastor had said about Charlie was very interesting, though: What could have happened to make Charlie so frightened?

"You will come to dinner this week?"

"Yes," Hetty answered, before realizing what he had said, and immediately regretted letting the word pass her lips.

Jay grinned, like he always did when he presented her with a clever riddle she couldn't figure out. Except this time there was no riddle, just an old preacher who knew when people had stopped listening to him.

"Cora will be so happy to hear this. It's been awfully quiet since you left us. Make sure to invite all your friends, especially Oliver. Cora's been concerned about him. And so have I. We're quite fond of him and Thomas, and I know he's been heartbroken."

"I'll look forward to it," Hetty said, and found she actually meant it. For it had been some time since she'd sat around the dinner table with them. "Name a night, and we'll be there."

Money counted and put away, Hetty slipped out of the small room to find the church picnic had been fully moved inside. Moving between the tables to the buffet, she had just got her hand on a plate when she heard shuffling behind her, and muffled apologies.

"Hetty!" Penelope rushed up toward her. "Come with me!"

Penelope didn't explain as she led Hetty to the little room where Sunday school was taught. Although the scribbled letters on the chalkboard pointed to a lesson, there were no children presently.

But it wasn't empty.

Darlene shook a finger in the face of the much taller Alice Granger. The other woman's cheeks were flushed with a red that made her look blotchy. As she fussed, Alice drew back her sleeve revealing a wand handle.

"How dare you come here and threaten me! I'll have you know—"

"I'm looking for your husband." Alice drew her wand in a single fluid motion. Darlene jumped backwards into the chalkboard. "I don't care about you."

A bird swept into the room suddenly, blue and glittering with stars. It dove at Alice and brought with it a swirl of wind that sent papers — and Alice's wand — flying across the room.

"Luckily," Hetty said, as the other woman's wand fell into her hand, "I care about you both."

Alice swirled around and a flash of recognition crossed her face before she snarled, "Give it back!"

"Or you'll do what?" Hetty twirled the stick between her fingers. "You can't do magic without a wand." Alice gritted her teeth, but she wisely remained where she was. "Maybe chanting nonsense words without one leads to magic," Hetty continued. "I wouldn't know. I do know you don't understand how magic flows in this world. I'm not sure what's going on here, but you're about to explain it to me."

"You know her?" Alice cried. "I should have known not to trust you!"

"You're the one who contacted me."

"I was told I could trust Henrietta Rhodes, but I didn't know she was friends with a liar!"

"Why don't you explain that bit to me," Hetty said.

"Her sister was a teacher at my school." Darlene drew herself up. "I fired her because in the evenings she taught Sorcery. I have nothing against magic classes, but I draw the line at Sorcery. Do you know what trouble it could have brought us and our students?" She eyed Alice reproachfully. "Especially when the teacher is someone whose entire life is a lie!"

"You're the one who's a li—"

Hetty snapped her fingers. Yellow light flashed around Alice's face. The woman staggered, and when she regained her balance she started talking once more. But while her lips moved, no sound could be heard by anyone. Once she realized that, Alice's pretty little face contorted with rage.

"Stars!" Penelope exclaimed. "I didn't even see the sigil you used!"

"Tell me," Hetty said, ignoring Alice, "how do you know her?"

"George and I ran into her outside of Judith's apartment," Darlene said. "Judith still had some of my primers and I wanted those back. But also, George wanted me to give her the job back. We're shorthanded, which is why he keeps asking you to teach. The door was open when we got there, and we went in thinking Judith was inside."

"Was she?"

"No, she was long gone. But *she* was there." Darlene jabbed an angry finger in Alice's direction. "She thought we scared off her sister. When I saw her at Charlie's funeral, I thought she had come to confront me, but I saw her talking to you and then I got worried—"

"That she was telling me you might be involved with her sister's disappearance?"

Darlene nodded. "Since then you—both of you," she added, including Penelope, "were treating me so distantly. I thought you suspected the worst of me."

Penelope's face flushed with guilt, but Hetty remained serene. "Why is Alice upset with you?"

"She went round to Judith's apartment yesterday. A neighbor said there was a man waiting outside from E.C. Degray, so she's convinced it was George. But it wasn't him—we'd gone to see a doctor about Lorene."

"Lorene?" Hetty's line of thought was disrupted at hearing the baby's name. "Is she all right?"

"Oh, no, nothing's wrong. We've noticed some things that were strange," Darlene said. "The doctor said it's because she can't hear."

Penelope gasped, a hand lifting to her face. "She's deaf? That explains why she always looked so scared when we were out of sight—"

Pink light pulsed in the air, and they turned to watch as Alice broke through the binding on her voice.

"Give me my wand back," Alice rasped.

"Certainly," Hetty said. "I have no use for it." Hetty held it out before her. "When I find your sister, you'll know. I will tell you myself or send her to you."

Alice sniffed but said nothing else as she tucked the wand into her sleeve. She straightened her clothes and exited the small classroom, nearly colliding with Benjy and Oliver in her haste to leave.

Benjy stepped aside, but Oliver remained planted in place to force Alice to step around him instead. She did so with a sniff, too insulted to speak.

"For someone who was too scared to go looking for her sister," Benjy said, "she sure keeps turning up like a bad penny."

"Only in places where she is comfortable. Apparently Judith used to be a teacher at Darlene's school."

He nodded, absorbing this fact, but said nothing more.

"Why did you come down here?" Hetty asked.

"I noticed a ripple of magic and I figured you were the source."

"You always tend to be," Oliver added. He had yet to step into the room, lingering in the doorway. "Which is why I said we're wasting time."

"What's the hurry?" Hetty asked. "And why are you here?" She eyed Oliver, who had certainly not been there for church this morning.

"Good news." Benjy smiled as he said this. "Would you like me to tell?"

"What is there to tell?" Oliver grunted. "Thomas is coming home, hardly anything special."

"Hardly special? This is wonderful news!" Hetty exclaimed, her words echoed by Darlene and Penelope.

Oliver flushed, but tugged at his collar. "He won't be here anytime soon. I just found the letter this morning. I want the cellar emptied out, and it's going to be taken care of today."

"Someone will be coming by tomorrow to give the unknown man a pauper's grave," Benjy added. "Oliver and I are going over to take Alain Browne to his family and tell his wife the news. We're headed off now."

Hetty nodded. "You will go home afterward?"

Benjy cleared his throat. "Not quite. There's another lead about Charlie and his betting that I want to chase."

"I have one of those myself," Hetty said eagerly. "Darlene said there was someone in the Degray club who showed up at Judith's apartment. That's the reason Alice Granger was here. She thought it was George."

"But George isn't involved," Benjy said rather pointedly.

"Thank the stars!" Penelope exclaimed, loud enough to startle everyone, except for Benjy. His eyes danced with amusement, and Penelope hid her face behind her hands.

"Yes," Hetty went on, ignoring this interruption. "I need a list of all the members of the club."

"So you can match against anything else Charlie was involved in. Or any known associates. Brilliant."

"Of course. It's my idea, after all."

She smiled at him, and in response he reached up and brushed back a piece of her hair. "Do try to stay out of trouble."

"Why do you even bother asking her that?" Oliver called.

Hetty turned, having nearly forgotten her friends were still there.

Oliver sighed, gesturing for Benjy to follow him. "I have things to do, places to be, and a house to clean. Although . . ." What could be called a smile made an appearance across his face. "It's good to see you listened to my advice."

"Dare I ask what he meant?" Hetty remarked as Oliver swept out of the room.

"It was mostly nonsense." Benjy leaned forward and pressed a kiss to her cheek. "I'll tell you later."

When Hetty turned to her friends, a bit of her smile lingered even at the sight of their smirks.

"Go on." Hetty steeled herself for the teasing she deserved. "Tell me what you're thinking. Best get it out of the way now."

"To say what?" Penelope asked innocently. "Do you think we spend our time talking about your relationship?"

"Or that we made bets," Darlene added.

"And that Maybelle owes us five dollars?" Penelope said.

Both succumbed to laughter that only grew louder the more Hetty scowled at them.

"I think I missed some very interesting events." George peered into the room. He held his daughter facing outward, so the baby also did her fair share of peering. "I saw Oliver just a moment ago. When did he get up early enough to come to church?"

"He came to fetch Benjy," Darlene said, wiping a tear from her eye. "Something about dead bodies in his cellar."

"Is that all?" George grumbled. "That's not news."

"Thomas is coming home," Hetty added. "I don't know when, but it must be soon enough to have Oliver cleaning the house."

"Well, I'll be—"

"George," Darlene cut in. "Just because the baby can't hear doesn't mean you're going to swear around her!"

"All I was going to say is that I'm happy as a clam," he said rather innocently, which got a snort from Hetty.

"Come on, Hetty, you know more than anyone Oliver has been a bit much lately. He'd be deep in cups more often if you hadn't bullied him into performing funerals, and getting tangled up with your murder things."

"Murder things?" Penelope chuckled.

"What else would you call it?" George said as Darlene shook her head.

"George," Hetty sighed, "you have quite the way with words. You say all the right things, but your tone makes it hard to take you seriously."

"That's right." George nodded, before he stopped. "Hey!"

Darlene took the baby from him. "Sweetheart, Hetty might need your help. She needs a list of Degray members to find out who killed Charlie."

This distracted him. "You do? Why didn't you ask before? Stars, even Benjy was asking me things and this didn't come up."

"He was only asking to find out if you murdered Charlie," Hetty said. "Both of you were on the suspect list for a few reasons, but mostly because of the little gathering at your house the other night."

Darlene and George exchanged a glance. After a long moment they shrugged, hardly bothered.

"Can't blame you," Darlene said. "I had a number of violent thoughts over that unpleasant situation."

"Is this why you ran out the other night," George asked of Penelope, "and were acting stranger than usual? I'm flattered at the thought."

"I'm sure you are," Hetty drawled. "Can you help with a list of names from E.C. Degray?"

George shook his head. "Don't quite have the access. I'm a new member."

"That's wonderful to hear," Hetty said impatiently. "Do you know who can help?"

"Clarence Loring, but you know how he is about rules. He won't help you. And most of the others probably won't point out the moon to you. You might have to sneak in." George started to chortle. "But not even you, Hetty, with all your talent, can manage that one!"

"Why not?" Penelope asked.

Hetty answered, not wanting George to gleefully point it out instead: "Degray's headquarters has wards to keep women out."

Instead of being discouraged, Penelope snapped her fingers. "That's no trouble. That's how we'll get in!"

30

This doesn't sit right with me," Hetty whispered as they lingered on the corner opposite E.C. Degray's headquarters. People walking past them scarcely gave them a glance, but the longer they stayed there, the more notice they'd gain.

"I never said it was a *good* idea." Penelope took out a tiny bristle brush and dipped it into a small tin. Penelope ran the waxy dark red color along her lips, rubbing them together when she finished. "If it was easy, we'd already be inside."

"I told you, I can break those wards from a distance," Hetty said. "There's no need for this foolishness."

Penelope checked her reflection. "You do all sorts of outrageous things every day, but *this* bothers you?"

"There are other ways," Hetty insisted.

"This is simpler."

"It's ridiculous."

"And it's the only plan that will work, unless you can come up with another one. Before I— Wait, here's a likely victim now!"

Penelope tucked her mirror away and sashayed over to the man approaching the club's front door. She called out to him with a giggle. The man turned, and his leer was only slightly worse than the obvious way his eyes swept across Penelope's figure.

"Why, aren't you a pretty one," he said, tipping back his hat.

Hetty's skin crawled, but Penelope only simpered, fluttering her eyelashes. "And aren't you"—she added a rasp to her voice—"a handsome one, looking all important and such." She daringly brushed a hand along his shoulder as if to remove a bit of dirt. "Where're you off to?"

"Just the club. Important business."

Penelope pouted. "That sounds dreadfully dull."

"It wouldn't be, with some company."

"Oh, I've never been inside. Isn't it boring?"

"Not at all. I'm sure you won't find it so." He grabbed at Penelope's waist, pressing her close to him. "Come along and I'll show you."

"What about my friend?"

"What friend?"

Penelope spun around to look for Hetty, but it was a fruitless effort.

The moment this farce began, Hetty had pulled a glamour around herself. She was standing right next to them, impatiently waiting for this nonsense to reach its conclusion.

"What about you?" Penelope said, recovering. "You're not going to get into trouble?"

"We'll go through the back. No one would even know you're there."

The man led Penelope around the back of the building, his hand firmly planted on her waist.

Hetty kept right on their heels as they passed through the side entrance.

No wards stopped her this time, and Penelope's plan managed to work out perfectly.

Though not entirely.

Penelope was still ensnared in a trap of her own creation, but her friend never got into trouble she couldn't get herself out of.

Hetty crept along the room until she reached a door. Peering through the crack along its frame, she saw bright light illuminating a series of tables where games of chance and fortune were in play.

Men lounged at the tables, ranging from tradesmen uncomfortably stuffed into Sunday suits to well-dressed men of leisure. There were no women anywhere on the floor, and even the servers were all men. While they floated indifferently throughout the room, some leaned over to whisper suggestions to certain patrons as they poured drinks.

Hetty spotted a set of stairs in the back of the room. She chewed on her lip as she considered her chances. There must be spells about the room to dampen magic. She could deal with those, but risked drawing attention that created more problems than it solved.

There had to be another set of stairs, she thought. Otherwise she'd have to—

A gentle thud interrupted her thoughts.

In the opposite room, the man they used as their admission ticket lay stretched out on the floor, his lips stained with dark red.

Dragging the back of her hand along her mouth, Penelope stepped carefully over the man and whispered, "Hetty, are you there?"

"Here I am," Hetty said as she reappeared. She nudged the man with her foot. He didn't move, but he did start to snore.

"That wasn't normal lipstick, I take it?"

"A little something of my own creation. I had some hours at the shop and some leftover herbs." Penelope puffed herself up like a cat that surprised a canary. "He should sleep for hours and not remember a thing."

"Well, let's give him a little help with that. Look for a bottle of spirits," Hetty said. "If anyone wonders why this man's dead asleep on the floor, a bottle of booze in his hand will make a convincing cover story."

"Will it work?"

"Hopefully. There's plenty going on here tonight. There's gambling in the next room. A man engaging in some carousing should not look amiss."

Something crashed behind them.

They froze, listening. Moments rolled past with no doors opening or voices calling angrily at them.

"It's probably nothing," Hetty whispered. "But let's find this list."

With the din in the main room covering the sound of their movements, Hetty and Penelope crept through the adjacent rooms looking for the orderly parts of the club. There were a few smaller rooms filled with plush couches and tables, but it wasn't until they reached the end of the hall that they found anything proving this club to be more than a collection of vices and sin.

There were two doors. The one on the right was locked and had Isaac Baxter's name on it. The one on the left had four names neatly lined up in a column:

> Laurence Freemont, Vice President
> Sam Roberts, Lore Keeper
> Clarence Loring, Secretary
> Charlie Richardson, Treasurer

"Well, isn't that funny, Charlie was the treasurer," Hetty said.

"He was always good with money," Penelope whispered.

"Good at taking and losing, but not keeping it."

They entered a room with four desks placed close enough that they'd all have little privacy. While the tops of all the desks held an assortment of papers and books and the like, one desk, while no less cluttered, had the distinct appearance of disuse.

Charlie's desk.

Hetty passed it. "Clarence is the secretary. He would have a membership list. I'll check the drawers. You search—"

Penelope stood next to Charlie's desk, the bit of fading sunlight highlighting a quizzical expression on her face.

"What's wrong?" Hetty asked.

"Something started glowing on this desk when you passed it."

Hetty forgot all about the list as she spun around. In one swift move, she pulled Penelope behind her. Nothing happened. The more Hetty stared at the glass bowl that was the source of the glowing, she realized there was a different sort of spell in place.

"This is a watcher," Hetty whispered. "It will tell the caster if anything has been disturbed. This sort of thing could have been placed there by someone wishing to respect Charlie's passing."

"But it wasn't, was it?"

"No." Hetty tapped the band around her neck. "It wasn't."

The Herdsman took form next to her, joining the two of them as if she was the third member of their cohort. With a sweep of her staff, the woman made of stars struck at the glass bowl and encased it with a blue light. The bowl kept glowing, but its effect would spread no further.

With this fixed into place, Hetty drew the Hare star sigil on the desk. Thin pale gold lines sprang from the sigil, spanning the desk until they arranged themselves and pointed to the topmost desk drawer. Hetty opened it and found that the spell spilled onto a small wooden box. The size of a small book, it was covered in an array of sigils so tightly packed that the individual ones were hard to make out. Warning enchantments, protection charms, alarms . . . any of the above could be there.

While the density of such enchantments was overwhelming, they were done by someone with only basic skill.

With a gesture to the Herdsman, the spell reached over and tapped the box. The sigils vanished at once — leaving behind a very plain-looking box.

A plain box with a tiny keyhole on its side.

Hetty smiled.

Before they arrived at the club that evening, Hetty returned to her home to change into something more practical. As she jammed hairpins into her hair, she saw Charlie's key in the small tin. Without thinking twice, she tucked the key into her pocket.

Setting the box on the desk, Hetty inserted the key into the keyhole, satisfied that it fit perfectly. She twisted it to the left. It didn't budge. She twisted it right, heard a click, and then . . .

The box sprang open.

Papers peered up at her from inside. Receipts, mostly, with a number of stubs for plays, clippings from a newspaper, and pages torn out of a notebook with numbers scribbled on them. Near the bottom of the stack, in the neatest handwriting possible, was a short list of names. And there was the money. Tucked at the bottom and rolled up in bills.

"Look at that!" Penelope whistled as Hetty unfurled the money. "What was he saving it for?"

Isaac Baxter and Clarence had both hinted at Charlie's massive debts. Hints that were seemingly corroborated by Marianne's report of strange men approaching her home, even going as far as breaking in.

Yet if Charlie had such mounting debts, why had he held on to this money? There was nearly a thousand dollars in here, something should be done with it.

Hetty sorted through more papers until she found a small book with a list of nothing but numbers. Some pages had the corner folded over with a word or letter marking the page. The only one she felt confident of was the page corner marked with *Boxing*. That page was filled with numbers. One column was a series of dates, starting in early March and continuing every week since, separated by columns of wins and losses. Some were scratched out and others circled, and the numbers grew bigger the further down the list she went.

If Hetty went through and tallied these numbers, which would be bigger? The wins or the losses?

Hetty turned the page over, but instead of more numbers all she found was a folded slip of paper. She unfolded it and scribbled inside was the following: *You owe me for last week's match.* But the handwriting wasn't Charlie's.

It was Benjy's.

As Hetty stared at the familiar loops and points of the letters, she saw the stuffy boxing venue and remembered the talk of the matches that had occurred since the previous winter. Benjy had known about Charlie's betting and of course Benjy had been taking part in the matches. But he'd never said how closely it was all linked. Surely Benjy knew better than to let Charlie place bets on him. Didn't he?

Then Hetty remembered how persuasive Charlie could be. He tricked her into making a full wardrobe of clothes as a gift and then sold the garments to strangers. If he could trick her, it was possible to trick Benjy as well.

Well, this was no time to dwell on such matters, she thought. Hetty returned her attention to the box's contents and found another small piece of paper. It had today's date on it, along with Benjy's name and his Irish combatant. There was an impossibly large number scribbled on the bottom, and a circle around Benjy's name with a single word in Charlie's handwriting: *Falls.*

Hetty stared at it for a long time before she fully understood that last word.

"A boxing match," she said, gripping the desk's edges. She remembered Benjy mentioning to her about following up on a lead related to Charlie's betting. Not a lie, but not the truth. "There's a boxing match tonight."

"There is?" Penelope's voice floated from half a world away. She held some of the papers Hetty had discarded, but lowered them as Hetty spoke.

"Benjy is boxing tonight. He's in this match that Charlie placed a great deal of money on. Enough it could mean the worst depending on how it goes."

Hetty shoved all the papers and stubs back into the box. She set it back on the table, drew the first sigil that came to mind, and shrank the box down small enough to fit into her pocket. "I have to go there. Now."

"Hetty." Penelope blocked her path. "We can't just rush out of here. It'll cause a stir. Didn't you come to find the membership list? Without that, how will you find Charlie's murderer?"

"Oh, who cares about that!"

"Hetty! You can't mean that. Charlie was our friend. You and Benjy—"

"We helped him, and we're *still* helping him even as I keep finding evidence that suggests he only returned the favor when it suited him! Now my husband's in a boxing match—a crooked boxing match—because of that man. Maybe Benjy's doing it for the money, maybe he got himself tricked, I don't know! If anything happens to him, I'm going to find a way to make Charlie pay."

"But," Penelope protested, "he's dead."

"Yes," Hetty said, "but I've never been afraid of breaking taboos."

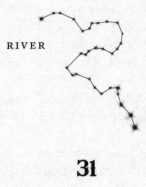

RIVER

31

As HETTY AND PENELOPE made their way through the press of people, Hetty heard snatches of conversation swirling around about the match and the bets riding on it. It was her only clue that they'd arrived in the right place. Although it was the same space Hetty had visited just days earlier, nothing felt familiar about the saloon that housed the boxing match. People packed the room to the brim leaving no space to even jut out an elbow. The crowd was different. It was still a mix of people of different means, but as Hetty and Penelope pushed their way closer, the people around them went from poor laborers to wealthy luminaries. There were quite a few white faces in the room. Hetty had not seen any of those at the previous match. Not only did they all appear to be men, they were arranged together in a neat bloc on the other side of the boxing ring. There was no barrier in place that Hetty could see, and no mixing in the crowd overall.

The combination of the betting and the illegal nature of the event would have generated excitement on any night, but add in the taboo of a Black man being allowed to beat on a white man —why, the air crackled with anticipation. Some excitement was for the money at stake, and some was for the outcome alone.

The thrill of possibilities hummed in the air, but it tempered at the sight of the police lurking in the crowd, their hands not far from the wands holstered at their sides.

They arrived late, Hetty realized, as the loudest sound jostling against her ears was the announcer speaking. His magically enhanced voice nearly drowned out jeers and cries. On stage she could see the Irishman, Jimmy Hart, his pale skin washed out under the bright light. He bounced lightly on his heels.

His opponent stood across from him, cast mostly in shadow. From where she stood it didn't look like Benjy.

Hetty squinted into the light to see, hoping to be wrong. Hoping that someone else stood in Benjy's place, and he was in the crowd instead.

But the announcer started to speak.

"And in this corner the reigning champ, the defender of the Seventh, the bastion of the Fifth Brigade, and tonight's challenger, Bender Ross!"

A roar greeted his name, as well as other calls to place last bets.

Hetty gave none of it her attention. All she could see was her husband stripped to the waist, his body already glistening with sweat, and the lights above shining down at him, highlighting the scars along his back. The arc of a hook on his left shoulder, the tapering whiplashes in the center of his back, older scars crisscrossing the more recent. Here and there the skin puckered from old cuts of glass, and held even more scars she couldn't quite make out at this distance but that she knew were there, as her fingers had trailed along them often, and as recently as the previous night.

His posture was rigid, his muscles tense, and what little she could make of his face was flat and closed off, with nothing of his true character on display.

It was him, yet not him.

This was the Benjy most people chose to see: the brute, the blacksmith, the force of nature. Not the gentle and thoughtful person she had spent so much time with.

Her blood boiled at seeing him standing there, ruining her last hopes that this had all been a mistake. Yet instead of directing her anger at him, she found better targets in the roar of the crowd.

The announcer shouted something then, but Hetty couldn't make out what he was saying. A bell rang with authority, and it began.

No punches were being thrown quite yet, but the men approached each other in the center of the ring and were shuffling about in an awkward dance of advance and retreat. Jimmy Hart stalked Benjy, who withdrew often, barely ducking out of the way of the punches. They engaged a few times, and each time, far too easily, Benjy got himself ensnared in his opponent's grasp.

The first time Benjy fell under a vicious flurry of blows, the sight stunned Hetty so much that she didn't even hear the outcry in the crowd or see the referee move to break them up.

None of this was making sense. Why had he gone down in the first place? He was much better than this!

The referee pulled them apart, and the bell rang.

The fighters retreated to their corners. Hart had water splashed in his face by a cluster of attendants, while Benjy caught his breath.

Hetty hoped it was over, but a bell rang again and Benjy and his opponent were back on their feet, facing each other. This repeated several times over. Not just clinches, but grabs and punches. Hard punches that pushed Benjy staggering backwards until he fell. Every time this happened, she thought it had to be over. Thought she wouldn't have to see him take that punishment anymore. But then the whole thing started up again and kept going—with no end in sight.

Sometime into the seventh round, a jab sent Benjy rocketing to the floor. This time instead of a gong, a new cry came out from the crowd pressed around them.

"First blood," the referee called. "Bender!"

"I thought this was supposed to be a contest," Penelope complained as the crowd howled around them. "Why does he keep getting knocked down?"

"I think it might be a fix," Hetty said.

"A fix?"

"Some matches are decided before they even begin."

"You mean they are rigged? Is it for the money?"

"Probably. There are police here. I think they're worried about what might happen if he wins."

"Then why do this?" Penelope asked. "Why is he even in the ring in the first place?"

Hetty didn't get a chance to answer.

A fist collided with Benjy's face.

He twisted, arching backwards as he fell.

He hit the floor of the ring with a thud, and the ground shifted under Hetty's feet.

A roar went up around Hetty as she flung herself forward through the press of bodies before her, not caring who she shoved aside.

She kept seeing him fall. Saw him clinging to a tree branch next to her, grinning through cuts and bruises. Saw him jumping at the last second before a trap hex activated. Saw him handing her a gun as she positioned herself next to him in the farmhouse with only their wits and magic to protect themselves and the six others with them.

She saw all those things flash before her eyes, but somehow none of that was worse than what she was seeing right in that moment.

Hetty pushed her way to the edge of the ring. She got a view of Benjy sprawled on the mat. She needed only to slide over a bit to reach his line of sight.

When Benjy first told her about all of this, he had explained all the reasons he had to lose. Hetty had teased him about winning matches and her displeasure about losses, but it was not an act. She meant every word. She did not want him to lose. She could not bear watching him take those strikes and blows, especially when she knew he could sidestep, could block, could dodge, and—if he dared—land a square punch that would put an end to this farce.

"Stand up, you fool!" Hetty cried. "Don't just lie there!"

As if her words were carried directly to his ear, Benjy's head jerked in Hetty's direction, and—finally—he began to stir.

Slowly, Benjy pushed himself up to his knees. His other hand moved as he spat out a mouthful of blood. From the crouch, he popped up to his full height just before the bell rang out.

The Irishman, already celebrating, didn't realize the cheers resounding around the room were not for his apparent victory. Jimmy Hart turned, jubilant, only to find Benjy standing.

The fighter's face lost every bit of its color.

They went back to their corners. But that brief rest they had between rounds seemed shorter than it ever was before.

When the bell rang for the next round, Benjy charged toward his opponent. Striking fast, he punched and jabbed at the Irishman, the blows a blur.

It all went too fast.

One moment they were in the middle of the ring, grappling, and in the next Benjy had pinned the Irishman into a corner.

Noise exploded in the room. If she thought it was loud before, she was mistaken—only a bomb would have been louder. Men swarmed around her, blocking her view, trying to push her back as they strained to get a better vantage point. Hetty surged forward and clung to the closest part of the ring, trying to remain planted in her spot. She couldn't miss a moment, not now.

She could taste victory in the air.

But as Benjy moved in for the kill, magic threw itself into the ring.

Like lightning it arched upward, a crack that cut into the air.

It was no star sigil. It was not a potion. It was *Sorcery*.

The bolt of magic arced in the air. For a moment it looked as if its goal was to knock out the light overhead and plunge the ring and the crowd into darkness. But no, it arched down, down and into the ring ... where it struck Benjy.

It thrust him backwards across the ring. He landed, motionless, with a thud.

Police whistles pierced the air, heralding the last traces of order as howls and panic ripped through the crowd.

Hetty nearly lost her footing.

Someone stepped on her dress. Someone else pushed her back. Then the police were storming forward, whistles blowing and wands out.

The crowd was a mob and there was no time to lose.

Hetty needed to get Benjy.

She needed to find Penelope.

She needed to — they all needed to — get out.

But then she caught a glimpse of something across the ring. Illuminated by the swaying light, Isaac Baxter stood still amid the chaos, looking as grim and terrible as the sight unfolding before him.

There could be no coincidence in him being here tonight. Just as there was no coincidence at the way he'd run once their eyes met.

Baxter barreled through the crowd toward an exit, like a fox with a chicken in its teeth. Hetty moved to follow — only to have an arm stretched out toward her, catching her and halting her progress.

With a growl, Hetty drew the Sagittarius star sigil into the air and unleashed it.

The star-speckled centaur charged around the room. The man that stopped her ran even before the first of the spell's arrows launched into the crowd.

The arrows could do just about anything she wanted, the moment she thought it. Right now, that was two things: clear a path and grab Baxter.

The first part was easily achieved with the centaur at her side. But grabbing Baxter proved difficult.

Despite the arrows flung after him, he slipped out of the room. As if to mock her, the last arrows struck the door frame as he left.

While ideas of giving chase blurred in Hetty's mind, the fire went out of her.

She could follow Baxter, but it wouldn't change what had already happened.

Hetty climbed up into the ring without even really realizing how she'd done it. No one stopped her, no one called to her, and if they did it wouldn't have mattered.

Her entire focus was on the crumpled form that hadn't moved at all during all the commotion.

"Benjy," she whispered, patting his face as hard as she dared, trying to avoid the blood spreading from the wound at his collarbone. "Stay with me."

Hetty ripped the bottom of her dress, and pressed down.

His eyes flickered open for a moment. "Hetty," he managed to say. "I . . . I need to tell you something."

"It can wait," Hetty said, as she searched her pockets for a set of sewing needles she didn't have, her eyes fixed on the scrap of cloth in her hand already saturated with Benjy's blood. "It will wait. Because it'll be a garbled mess, and nothing important should be told when—"

"Hetty."

The voice she heard this time was not her husband's, but it was familiar. A voice she missed all these months, that held warmth and comfort.

A voice that she shouldn't be hearing.

Yet when she looked up and saw the bit of a grin that tugged at the deeply scarred side of his face, she knew she was not mistaken.

"Thomas?" she whispered. "Thomas, by the stars, what are you doing here? You're supposed to be in Texas!"

"Penelope said the same thing," Thomas said. "I'll explain later. Which one of you girls is going to give me a hand? I can't carry the big guy on my own."

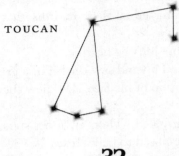

TOUCAN

32

Hᴇᴛᴛʏ ᴘᴏᴜɴᴅᴇᴅ ᴏɴ ᴏʟɪᴠᴇʀ's ᴅᴏᴏʀ until it flew open.

"Hetty," he hissed, "you better not have brought another dead—"

Oliver's snarl slipped away when he looked past her. "Thomas," he whispered. He licked his lips readying to say more, and then he saw Benjy slung between Penelope and Thomas.

"What happened?"

"He got hurt," Hetty said stepping inside.

"I can see that, but why did you bring him here?" Oliver asked. "I'm not a doctor."

"Where else could we go?"

"Still, I want to know—"

"Oliver," Thomas cut in. "Benjy's bleeding. Worry about the rest later."

Oliver swallowed, and then he moved to take Penelope's place, swinging Benjy's arm over his own shoulder. "Let's take him upstairs. Hetty, my old kit is in the cabinet closest to the icebox."

Hetty ran into the kitchen even before he'd finished speaking. She grabbed the frayed kit Oliver had carried during the war. She checked to see what was inside, and then went around the kitchen gathering other supplies, including a candle. Carrying all this with her, Hetty reached the attic room just as they were dropping Benjy onto the bed.

"Here's the kit." Hetty handed it to Oliver. He promptly ripped it open.

"I've never done proper healing," Oliver said, shaking as he drew out needle and thread. "With or without magic. I just sewed up wounds that made it easy to work with the dead."

"It'll be fine," Hetty said.

Oliver said nothing. He sat down to stitch up the wound, but had barely started before he let out a small cry of surprise.

"Stars and shards." Oliver rubbed his fingers against his sleeve. "It was like touching fire."

"What does that even mean?" Penelope said. She picked up the needle, and dropped it not a moment later. Penelope brought her fingers to her lips, more stunned than horrified. "That's not natural!"

Benjy convulsed.

His movements were sluggish but still wild enough that Thomas launched himself forward to keep Benjy from striking Oliver by accident.

"Something's very wrong," Thomas huffed. "And not just because he's still bleeding."

"It must be the spell cast on him," Hetty said, stepping closer.

"I don't know what to do about that," Oliver said. "I don't have anything here."

"You need to get a healing salve," Hetty said.

"I don't have that."

"Penelope does." Hetty turned to Penelope. "You have a batch ready, don't you?"

Penelope nodded. "But will it help?"

"It will," Hetty said. "Oliver, go with her."

"I can't leave you to do this—"

"Go with her and come back quick as you can!"

They stopped arguing with her then, running out the room without further complaint.

"What about me?" Thomas asked.

"Stay there." Hetty took out the candle she'd grabbed from the kitchen. Hetty lit it, although she had to draw Ursa Minor twice to get the flame to start. "I need you to hold him down."

Thomas gaped at her. "You can't be serious!"

"It has to be done. He was hit with a hex. I don't know what it was, but it was Sorcery and it's causing trouble. We can't do anything until I burn it out."

"Why did you send the others away?"

"They'd try to stop me."

"You trust I won't?"

"You know it needs to be done."

Thomas nodded and proceeded to tighten his grip.

Hetty sat on the other side of the bed, the candle flickering as she came to rest beside Benjy.

"Sorry," she whispered, "but this is your own fault for making me repeat history."

She turned the candle over into his flesh. Melted wax hit his skin first and his initial shudder turned into a scream as the flame bit in. Flesh sizzled and the stench made Hetty's eyes water. Benjy writhed around on the bed, but his movements were cut short by Thomas pressing his weight onto him.

"Hold him steady!" Hetty lifted up the candle to check on her progress.

"I've got him," Thomas grumbled. "Don't you worry about—"

Thomas yelped as he was thrown backwards to the floor, falling hard enough that it drew Hetty's attention away from her work.

That moment was enough for Benjy to lurch upward, his hand outstretched toward her.

Hetty didn't move, but Benjy's hand only fell on her shoulder with a touch as gentle as it would have been any other time. But then a searing heat rippled around her throat. Protective charms flowed out from the band at her neck, the Herdsman and her hunting dogs, the Hero, Orion, and Andromeda among them. The sigils shimmered around her for a moment before their light intensified to the point that, unable to bear their brilliance, she shut her eyes.

When she opened them, the light was fading. Her band unraveled and fell into her lap like the simple scrap of cloth it had once been.

Benjy collapsed backwards to the bed. He was still, but he breathed easily and deeply.

The candle had been blown out during all of this, and she gripped it with one hand as she tried to understand what happened.

Had he pulled the magic from the band, coaxing them to fall under his command? Or did he merely activate the charms she kept there that guarded, warded, and neutralized rogue magic?

"After all that, I hope he stopped bleeding." Thomas pulled himself off the floor, rubbing his shoulder.

"His breathing evened off." Hetty made no move to slide off the bed. Instead, she slid closer to Benjy and took his hand in hers. What little strain that was left in his face fled at her touch.

"What happened?" Thomas asked.

"A great number of things."

"Tell me." Thomas settled himself into a chair. "I'll tell the others so you don't have to repeat yourself."

Hetty shook her head, but Thomas tried again, this time his words softer. "Tell me now. I won't interrupt until you're done."

With an exhausted sigh, Hetty gave in and began relating everything that had happened, starting from the knock on their door a week ago about a dead body in an alley. Her voice was tight and the words came fast and in pieces.

True to his word, Thomas never interrupted.

Hetty both appreciated this and expected it. Thomas was the most gregarious of the group, chatting up anyone he thought was halfway interesting. He had jokes, he had funny stories, and did his best to get Oliver smiling at least once a day. But he was also the best kind of listener, the kind that gave you his full attention no matter the topic at hand. Having him listen now, knowing he would later fend off both Oliver and Penelope, was a weight lifted from Hetty's shoulders.

So she talked and talked, to make the long night pass faster and to keep her fears from overwhelming her.

She was successful with only one of those things.

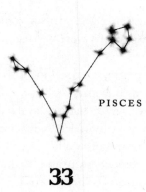

PISCES

33

Benjy was the only one who slept through the night, unbothered by anything that occurred around or to him. While this worried Oliver and Thomas, Penelope didn't bat an eye. She coolly mixed, grinded, and cut various herbs. Not once did she show a hint of worry, even when her most powerful healing potions had no effect. She kept trying things, but never enough to make things worse. Throughout the night she sent Oliver and Thomas away, but let Hetty stay in the room, until after dawn, Penelope kicked her out too.

"I'm going home to get a few things." Penelope cut in to Hetty's protests. "While I'm gone you need to eat and rest, in that order. If you make yourself ill, it's not going to help him get better. More likely he'll get *worse*. Sleep in one of the spare rooms tonight."

That suggestion, as kindly meant as it was, was no solution. No matter where she slept, she wouldn't catch a wink. She might as well stay here and be close at hand.

"I'd rather not," Hetty said as Penelope pulled several vials from her pockets. "This would have been our room if we'd stayed here."

"You sleep in the spare room," Penelope repeated, each firm

word making it clear her friend was gone and only the healer whose practical suggestions were not influenced by emotions remained. "Go eat."

Hetty had no appetite, but one look at Penelope's stern expression drove her downstairs anyway.

The kitchen stove, which had remained unused and ignored all these months, now happily roared with sizzling pans as Thomas worked a different brand of magic.

Hearing her, he stepped away and let the wooden spoon stir on its own while he rummaged around in the cabinets.

"I'm not hungry," she said.

"Which is the wrong thing to tell me," he said. "Sit down and let me fix you a plate. I promise it'll be the easiest thing you'll do all day."

With her protests unheeded, Hetty sat down at the table. But once food was placed in front of her, she found it hard to resist scrambled eggs and fresh bacon. "Oliver just told us you were coming home. I thought I'd have to wait weeks before I got to eat your cooking again."

"I left nearly as soon as I sent it," Thomas admitted. "Though I had been planning to return sooner."

"Trouble?"

"Hardly trouble." He settled into a chair next to her, pulling out his pipe but made no moves to light it. "Deliverance is a nice town most of the time, but there's nothing but ugly outside it. White lawmen roll about pitting everyone against each other. Negro, Natives, poor white folks all calling for each other's blood instead of banding together against the rich." Hetty's face must have revealed her concerns, for he managed a laugh. "I'm making it sound terrible, but it wasn't. There were a few bad spots here and there, but overall it was . . . pleasant." He gave her a sharp look. "I saw my wife and daughter while I was there."

"Your wife?" Hetty echoed.

"And daughter." Thomas's mouth curled over this.

"But," Hetty sputtered, "they're dead!"

"I *thought* they were dead," Thomas corrected. "I got a telegram from them last year. They found out about me and wanted to see me."

"And they live in Texas." Suddenly Hetty understood every shift and movement in Oliver's moods in the months following Thomas's departure. She knew he was upset but thought the reaction a bit excessive, given that Thomas was supposed to be building and protecting schoolhouses. But if Thomas had gone to see the family he had thought lost, why, that explained a great number of things.

Except for one thing.

"Why didn't you tell me?" Then, remembering Marianne's accusations of losing sight of her friends, Hetty added almost defensively, "I would have been so happy to hear you found them."

"I know." Thomas sighed and tapped the pipe against the table. "I said nothing because I was scared. I almost wanted it to be a trick. I thought they were dead for all these years, and never checked if it was the truth. I was afraid they'd know that and hate me for it. I arrived in town, and my darling little girl ran up to me, hugged me as if I'd just returned from a short trip. She's all grown up now—not a little girl anymore, I suppose—and ready to make me a grandfather. And my Bess. She runs the town in every way except in name, and I think her post office is the best run one I've ever seen."

"You had a good time, then?"

Thomas's mouth twisted, pulling at the old scars that covered the right side of his face. "I saw my wife married to a kind man, saw the brightest and clearest sunsets I've ever seen, and . . . and, well, was dreadfully bored the rest of the time! The only time I had fun was when I teamed up with some of the younger men to go after missing livestock."

"Is that why you came back? You wanted excitement?"

"My heart will always have a spot for them, but here"—he swept his hand around the table—"is where my family is. I've missed you all terribly. I only wish I'd come back sooner."

"Your timing is perfect."

"Perfect." He snorted. "I leave you all for a few months, and I return to a mess!"

"Not everything is terrible. Darlene and George adopted a baby."

"Which is one glimmer of starlight!" Thomas went on, "I still don't understand how Charlie's murder connects to what happened to Benjy. Does someone know that you are looking into things?"

"I'm not sure," Hetty lied. Thomas made a sound of disbelief, but Hetty continued as if he said nothing.

"I do know that Charlie's made money off of Benjy's matches. He had a book of figures. It's likely whatever he owned his murderer was coming from last night's match."

"Then why would the murderer attack Benjy like that?"

"Because Benjy was supposed to lose the match." Hetty paused, remembering the swirl of emotions as she stood at the ring, horrified at what she saw and indignant that he would allow himself to be pushed around like that. They had not traveled a long road together for such things to occur. "But then he saw me."

"Changing his mind. Don't blame him." Thomas nodded. "It's a wise move. You don't want to have anyone you care about angry at you."

Hetty started to protest, but found she had no arguments to make in the face of sadness seeping into his features.

"Have you and Oliver exchanged a single word in private?" she asked.

Thomas shook his head. "He does not want to talk to me. He shut the door on my face when I showed up last night. I'm not sure what would happen if Benjy wasn't here to whisk me to the match before I could say something I regretted. Again."

"You just surprised Oliver," Hetty assured him. "Your return caught him with a body in the cellar, and a house in need of cleaning."

"I hope that is all," Thomas said, but did not sound convinced.

Hetty patted his hand. "This is a rather big house, but it's going to become very small if you try to avoid each other."

"I thought he would be happy I've come back."

"We're talking about Oliver. He's *never* happy."

Thomas began to laugh at this only to start to cough so hard she thought he was choking.

Then she saw Oliver leading a man in a rumpled suit toward the cellar. When he turned his head, Hetty knew him at once. This was Preston Stevens, the man she'd seen yelling about the missing wagon.

This truly was a small town.

She hurried after them, ignoring Thomas's start of surprise.

"I don't see why you can't handle—" Preston said, stopping himself as he heard Hetty's footsteps.

"Don't mind her," Oliver said, going around to the table where a coffin lay. "She's just here to clean up." He gestured for her to go back upstairs, but Hetty remained where she was, lurking in the background.

With a sigh, Oliver approached the coffin. "Preston, this is the man I need you to put in a pauper's grave."

"Do you want the coffin back?" the man asked, eyeing the wood greedily. "Because it's mighty nice."

"You can have it," Oliver said. "Do with it what you want." He lifted the lid. "Let me just remove some of the preservation charms."

Oliver barely lifted his hand into the air before Preston let out a small shout. He swayed, nearly keeling over.

"That's ... that's my brother!" he squawked, then pointed at the dead man lying in the coffin. "Morris. I hadn't seen him since ... Stars above, how could this have happened?"

"This is your brother." Hetty stepped up to them. "When did you last talk to him?"

Instead of answering, Preston stared at her. "I've seen you before. Who are you?"

"My name is Henrietta Rhodes," Hetty said. "My husband and I found your brother earlier this week. If we'd known who he was, we would have told you sooner."

"*You* found Morris," Preston said.

"Yes, in an alley off Barclay," Hetty said. "We brought him here since Oliver doesn't mind taking care of things." She hesitated, taking a measure of how grief spilled over the man. The wrong question could push things in a more difficult direction. "Do you know if your brother was involved in anything dangerous?"

"Morris did nothing to put himself at risk."

"Was he a member of E.C. Degray?"

Preston's shock faded suddenly, and his stare turned icy. "What would you know about that?"

"It could be connected to his death."

"'Connected to his death'?" he parroted. "Who do you think you are!"

"Just someone doing their best to help."

Oliver put a hand on Hetty's shoulder, pulling her away from Preston. "If I had known this was your brother, I would have told you earlier. I had no idea. I'm so sorry."

"I'll take him," Preston said. "By the stars," he muttered, drawing the Taurus star sigil. The coffin lifted into the air. "This was not how I expected this day to go." He looked up at Oliver with wet eyes. "Do you know who killed him?"

"No, I'm sorry," Oliver said, with a warning glance to Hetty. "Although I know someone is seeking answers."

LEO MINOR

INTERLUDE

February 1866

PHILADELPHIA, PENNSYLVANIA

THAT'S A VERY IMPRESSIVE MOVE." Hetty eyed the card that Oliver tossed down onto the stack. "But I think this might be a bit better."

She slapped the Ace of Mirrors onto the table.

Oliver's mouth fell open. Across from him, Penelope and Thomas exchanged chuckles as they playfully tossed their cards aside. "How did you do that? How do you even know it's a proper move? I just taught you how to play noughts!"

"Beginner's luck?" Hetty suggested. Her words earned a groan from Oliver.

"That's your problem right there," Benjy called from behind a book. "You expect her to follow them. Hetty sees rules as guidelines."

"You're just afraid of losing," Penelope said. She leaned forward to confide to Thomas. "Benjy always loses no matter what card game Hetty plays with us."

"I think he just lets her win," Oliver growled.

"You're a sore loser." But Hetty dropped her cards, letting them start a new game without her.

She wasn't much of a card player. Her only strategy was playing recklessly until she got results. Which usually meant relying on luck and on the others second-guessing themselves.

Hetty drifted to the other side of the room. Benjy sat with his feet propped up on the table as he read.

He was still pretending to read when Hetty sat down on the windowsill.

"I don't let you win," Benjy said as Hetty reached into her pocket.

"I know that," she laughed. "I wanted to show you this. It arrived in the post today."

Hetty held out the card.

No bigger than the playing cards she just held, it was perfectly blank with not a single mark on it.

Benjy sat up, putting his book aside. "How strange."

"Watch this." Hetty drew the Phoenix star sigil and manipulated the magic so an orb of light appeared in the palm of her hand. She held it under the card, and suddenly the pristine white card changed. Crescent moons appeared in each corner. Then, as if a ghost held the pen, words scratched themselves onto the card.

"A plea for help," Benjy said as his eyes darted along the card. He blinked. "This is the bookseller that was accused of stealing spellbooks! They think something can be done about it!"

"I just wonder why someone sent this to me. Those cases we took on are not that well known."

"Except for one," Benjy corrected. "They must have been at that party last winter when we unmasked the widow who murdered her sister's family."

"But why not send it to you? You did most of the talking that night."

"You're easier to find, since you're still living with Mrs. Evans. Or they assume we work these cases together."

Hetty snorted. "People are always telling tales."

"You can't blame them after all the work we did together." Benjy paused as he always did when a sudden thought occurred to him. "Wouldn't it make sense if we continued on in a different area?"

"I suppose." Hetty flashed a grin at him. "You obviously need my help in these cases. What would you do without me?"

"Would you like to get married?"

The room went very quiet at these words. So quiet that when something heavy fell from upstairs, they all jumped.

The sound echoed in the house, rattling the windows and making the lamps flicker. Alarming on its own, it was made worse by the simple fact that there wasn't anything up there that could have caused the sound. Oliver had just moved into the house last week and the few possessions he owned were scattered around the main level.

Hetty tore her eyes from the ceiling, as Benjy stood up.

"Is this the sound you heard?" he asked Oliver.

"Yes." Oliver sank into his chair. "Thank the stars everyone heard it. I thought I was hearing things."

"Is this why you invited us over!" Penelope exclaimed. "To listen for strange bumps?"

"To have company for strange bumps." Oliver's eyes fell over to Thomas, who was picking up the cards he dropped. "I didn't invite you—you just showed up with Hetty."

"Which I regret," Penelope huffed. "My potions can't do a thing against ghosts!"

"There are no ghosts," Benjy said absently. "It might be an intruder."

"We would have heard glass," Hetty said.

"No," he said, without even considering her words. "Stay here. I'll take a look."

The others took that advice, but Hetty did not.

She followed him up the stairs, loudly stomping behind him so he knew it.

"I'd be careful if I were you," Benjy cautioned. "Go back downstairs."

"To what, three people asking me questions about what you asked me? I'm many things, but I'm no fool. Besides," she added, "it's curious."

Her words only deepened his frown.

"You can forget I said anything."

"Why? It's hardly the worst thing you ever asked me—" Hetty took a step forward and her foot sank into the wood.

"Stars," she swore, "what's this!"

"It's a hex." Benjy studied it with some interest. "I wonder how this was done?"

"I don't care!" Hetty tried to pull her foot out, but she only sank deeper into the wood. When she started to draw a spell her focus broke as her other foot sank as well. "Get me out of this!"

"It does matter." Benjy didn't seem to be aware of her plight as he studied the stairs. "If it's Sorcery, it meant the previous owner had some sour feelings about selling to Oliver. Which explains—"

"Benjy," Hetty interrupted, "if I get swallowed up by a set of stairs, I will be the ghost that forever haunts you!"

That got his attention, like she hoped it would.

Without a word, Benjy set a series of spells around her. Taurus, Capricorn, and Virgo flashed briefly before becoming rays of light that shot down at the stairs. As his magic dazzled around her, Benjy hooked an arm around her waist and pulled.

He lifted her out of there so easily that for a moment she felt like she was flying before her feet returned to the ground.

She glanced back at the wood, but it was smooth.

"How did you do that?"

"Who do you think Oliver asked to help him with this house? He had me do a sweep of the rooms. I found some rogue magic lurking about, but I thought I got them all."

"You clearly haven't," Hetty added. "Looks like you'll need my help."

He clearly wanted to tell her no—she could see it on his face. But after all they'd been through, a little hex like this was nothing. They'd gone too many places, faced too many things. To treat her like a porcelain doll was ridiculous.

But she might be wrong.

In the months since the war had ended and she had settled into life in Philadelphia, she found change all around her. Changes in her search for Esther. Changes in her friends, who were happy to put the past behind them for new endeavors. Changes in the city itself as its people reacted to the promises of new freedoms.

Benjy was the same as always, but even the sturdiest tree bends over in time.

"Having another pair of eyes does help," Benjy admitted. "If we get all the hexes, Oliver won't have to lure us over here again with card games."

"We certainly will," Hetty said. "I'm more talented with magic than you."

"Debatable," Benjy laughed.

There was another thump down the hall, louder this time, and they heard something break. Instinctively they moved together, prepared to face whatever unknown danger lurked ahead.

"You first," Benjy said to Hetty. "I'll be right behind you."

SERPENT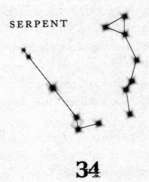

34

BEFORE THE MORNING WAS OVER, Hetty took a nap. She did so by accident, curled up in a chair. One moment she was reading a book, and in the next a blanket had been tucked loosely around her with care. As Hetty stirred, she thought it might have been Benjy who'd done it, but the low murmurs nearby told her it wasn't the case.

Bent over the bed, Penelope changed Benjy's bandages. As she did, she told him about all singing competitions in the coming weeks she expected him to assist with. From the unbroken flow of her chatter, he clearly was still asleep. While Benjy never minded playing for Penelope, the list that Penelope gave was a bit much. Half of them would probably happen, accompanied by a bit of arguing over music choices. But it didn't matter. The lighthearted chatter was all that mattered, because it meant that Penelope was no longer worried about him.

"I forgot to tell you. I think I figured it out," Penelope said as she smoothed out Benjy's bandages. "Of course, you would have figured it out quicker, but it was good for me to try on my own. Otherwise you'll take all the credit. Well, maybe not. You're often quiet about your best ideas."

"Because all he cares about are the ideas." Hetty dropped the blanket on the chair's armrest.

"I know." Penelope sat down on the edge of the bed, picking up a small bowl. "It annoys me sometimes, but others not so much."

"Any change?"

"Only the best kind. There is no swelling, and my remedies are speeding the healing of the wound. I'm not sure how much damage the hex did him, but I'll advise him to be careful. My magic only supports what the body does on its own. It can't perform miracles."

"You say that, but I'm not sure what I would have done without you."

"I think you'll manage." Penelope stood up and stretched out her back. "Burning that candle was a neat trick. I'll have to use it myself one day."

"Will you be here a bit longer? I'm going to the boardinghouse to pick up a few things."

"A few more hours before I head home. I guess you can sleep in here—the spare rooms don't have a proper bed. But don't worry about Benjy. I'm going to give him something that'll put him into a deeper sleep, to help speed up the healing. He won't even know you're gone," Penelope added before she uncapped a new vial. "I'm going to bring Darlene with me when I return tomorrow. She heard Oliver and me scrambling about my apartment last night and refuses to be kept outside of the excitement."

Hetty couldn't imagine what Darlene could do, but there was no reason to turn help away.

After splashing water on her face in the tiny washroom, Hetty left the house and headed south for the boardinghouse.

She had so many questions about last night.

Some Benjy could answer when he woke, but the others would not be easy to come by.

She didn't find a list of club members when she and Penelope had sneaked in, but she did see Isaac Baxter at the boxing match. That Benjy was attacked while Baxter was in the same room wasn't a coincidence. There was a connection there—she needed only to find it.

For now, she'd go back to their room, gather up a few things, and hope that her landlord—

"I want a word with you, Mrs. Rhodes."

Hetty stopped in her tracks, one foot hovering above the stair as she turned to face the last man she wanted to see right then.

Gone was the strangely buoyant man she had run into the other day. Her landlord was back to his usual cheerless self, with a glower that promised trouble.

"Is this about the rent?"

"This is about the ruckus that caused the building to shake enough to break windows. There will be a fee."

"A fee?" Hetty exclaimed. "A ruckus? What sort of—"

"If you can't pay it, you're out of here. I'm giving you a warning. Next time I won't be so generous. I knew you two were trouble."

Hetty stomped up the stairs. But she forgot all about him the moment she caught sight of the door to her room.

The wards had been pushed hard enough to set off an alarm. This explained the noise her landlord mentioned. The wards were thin now, barely holding themselves together in the wake of an obvious frontal assault. It appeared that no one had gotten inside, but someone had tried very hard when they found they couldn't.

With a jerk of her hand, Hetty undid the wards and opened the door.

Waiting for her in the middle of the room was her dress form with a knife stuck in its chest.

Hetty closed the door behind her and took full study of the room.

The window was open, with a crack small enough for a breeze to waft through. Like the door, the wards there weren't broken, but had been pushed to their limits.

Someone had made a considerable effort to break in, but why?

The knife in her dress form gave her part of an answer.

That was frustration and anger. They came here for something, and it wasn't to steal something.

No, that knife told her they'd come looking to cause harm. Finish the job, even, since Benjy was already injured.

The more she looked around, the more she knew it to be true.

Besides the dress form, nothing else was touched. The wardrobe doors were shut. Their trunk was still at the foot of the bed, clothes still neatly stacked on top of it.

Only their lantern showed any change. Sigils that had been carved into the metal to warn against danger glowed so brightly, she thought there might be light contained inside.

Tapping the lantern, she brightened the light to reveal magical residue.

Even as she cast the spell, though, she knew she wouldn't find anything.

How could she?

Magical residue covered everything from the ceiling to the floor in thick layers. But that was hardly helpful. She and Benjy cast spells at such a volume that evidence of anyone else's magic would be impossible to find.

Even tracing it to the window was little help, for the residue splotches melded with all the magic outside.

Hetty shut the window and placed a fresh ward on it, this time the sort of thing that would trigger more than just a mere alarm. They should have been using spells like that in the first place, but they hadn't wanted to upset their landlord.

From there, Hetty started gathering everything in the apartment she could not bear to lose. Clothes, their precious books, the lamps, the pot of Moonleaf, the map, her sewing kit, the quilt off their bed . . . she piled it all into the tub and then drew star sigils along the rim.

It shuddered and lurched upward until it hovered beside her. Hetty started walking and it followed at her heels.

When Hetty came downstairs, her landlord was in the hall complaining to one of the neighbors in the communal kitchen. As the floating tub came into view, voices grew silent.

"Here's your fee." Hetty tossed the can of coins at him. "The rest you can take from selling the furniture," she said. "We're moving out."

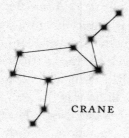

CRANE

35

WHEN HETTY WALKED through the door, Oliver and Thomas's conversation stuttered to a halt at the sight of her tub floating behind her like a duckling.

Both gawked at her, but Thomas jumped up in alarm, his chair scraping against the floor.

"Don't." Oliver put a hand on the other man's arm. "Sometimes it's best not to ask."

Hetty went upstairs and found Benjy still asleep. Penelope must have succeeded in getting him to take a sleep potion, for Hetty was able to drag the tub across the floor without him even stirring.

Penelope wasn't here, but there was a note left next to a half-empty vial of pale blue liquid:

> *If he wakes in pain, two spoonfuls. If he complains, one. And you get some rest. I will know.*

Placing the note aside, Hetty busied herself with settling the items she took from the boardinghouse. In no time at all, each item had found a new home, whether in the wardrobe, a drawer, or in a stack on the nightstand. A few things she left in the tub, like their quilt, but nearly everything was tucked away.

As she stood there with her sewing kit in her arms, the memories she had pushed back returned with great force.

What mess there had been in their room could be blamed on the wind. But the knife was the only proof she needed for an intruder. It was also the reason Hetty had gathered their things with no attempt to return. That dress form was as tall as a person . . . and in low light could easily be mistaken for flesh and blood. Even if the intruder knew otherwise, though, the message was clear.

It was a good thing they weren't home last night.

Hetty placed her sewing kit next to the healing tonic Penelope had left and reconsidered that sentiment.

It had been *lucky* they weren't home, but this wasn't much better.

Whether the enchanted sleep was responsible or not, Benjy's face was peaceful and relaxed. When Hetty lifted the bandages, she saw that the healing salve had done its work. The sickly green veins around the wound had vanished, leaving only the mark where the candle had kissed his skin. She replaced the bandages with care, running her hands slowly along his face before moving away.

Settling on the foot of the bed, Hetty started sorting the slips of papers that had been locked away in Charlie's box. Spreading them around her, she sorted them into little piles based on type: receipts, ticket stubs, notes, flyers, and newspaper clippings. The more she flipped through the pages, the pattern to Charlie's bets became clear. While there was a rich variety of activity, he was most diligent in cataloging the boxing bets. In addition to the page that Hetty had first stumbled upon, other pages broke down the winnings of each week in more detail.

Hetty pored over those pages closely, studying how the lump

sum of winnings broke into smaller amounts, with initials marked beside each cut. While the initials were different week to week — as were the numbers — one initial appeared like clockwork.

Hetty tapped on the looped B. It appeared on every boxing-related note, with the earliest date from late November. This was meant to be Benjy, but out of all the sums listed, his was always the smallest number, no matter how big the winnings grew.

She mentally calculated the difference between the money won in these matches and the amount that ended up in Benjy's pocket. When she landed on the final number, she almost tossed the book into the wall. The gap between owed and paid was a chasm so gaping that if Charlie had still been alive, she'd have tossed him right into it.

How could someone who called them a friend do this?

This was more than selling the dresses that Hetty had made for his wife as a gift. This was more than leaving his tenants to live in squalor. This was stealing. And it did not matter if he had done it out of greed or because he was fending off creditors, or out of fear of losing his fragile freedom. He took money he didn't even earn.

She moved to put the paper down, but there was no more space for a new pile.

"There needs to be a table," she mumbled, staring at the stacks of paper that surrounded her.

"A desk would be better."

Benjy sat with a pillow propped behind his head. He tugged at his bandage as he read the pages in his hand. More papers were piled next to him, but not how she had first arranged them but in a pattern that would only make sense to him.

"How long have you been awake?"

"Since you started going through these papers. What did you find?"

"Nothing that can explain what happened to you last night.

Or that the lead you planned to follow meant you'd be taking a beating."

His hand clenched around the papers. "That's why I didn't want you to be there. I was going to smoke out who'd collected Charlie's bet, and I couldn't throw the match with you watching."

"It's all fake," Hetty grumbled, unmoved by this remark.

"Not everything." His hand reached for hers. "I'm sorry."

"I'm sure you are," she snapped, but didn't move her hand. "Why didn't you tell me about the money?"

"I was embarrassed. Charlie cheated me to such heights that I thought it all a big mistake. I only found out by a slip of the tongue . . . and . . . Well, let's just say there's a good reason he was reluctant to talk to me the last night we saw him alive." Benjy smoothed the wrinkled papers. "He thought paying me part of the money would fix everything."

"And *did* he pay you?"

Benjy nodded. "I got enough to pay off some of our debts and the rent."

That explained their landlord's cheerier mood earlier that week.

"Good, one mystery solved."

Benjy settled back onto the bed with a weariness that had nothing to do with his wound. "You're not mad at me?"

"Not as much as I was last night." She placed her hand on the bandage, pressing gently against his chest. "This makes it hard. I want to know why it happened."

"It was the police." He frowned. "They disrupted the match. I thought that's what happened."

"I don't think it was them." Hetty shook her head. "Isaac Baxter was there. He ran when he saw me, but I couldn't chase him given the chaos that broke out. I think he did it."

"Could have been someone else. Someone who placed a hefty

bet on me losing. A few moments more and it would have been a knockout."

"It better have been a knockout," she teased, but he remained pensive.

"Baxter fits. But I'm not sure if it's because we want him to fit or because it's the truth."

"He wouldn't have run if he was guilty!"

"If he saw even half the glower you gave me, that would have been enough to send anyone running."

"Well, you deserved it." Hetty returned her attention to the papers strewn about. "All this boxing and you never made more than a handful of coins."

"Charlie was always very good with money . . . usually parting people from it." Benjy picked up the book with all of the betting notes inside. He patted the area next to him absently. Hetty slid over, sitting close enough to read the words on the page.

"These are debts he owed white bankers." Benjy pointed to the names. "The initials mark which ones. This is a liquor tab at a saloon he frequented. These are the stores he borrowed from on credit. But this"—he tapped the corner of a page, where a triangle was sketched—"I don't know what to make of this."

"That strikes me as important."

"I agree, but we have no way to answer the question."

Hetty studied the sums amassed before her, all written in careful handwriting. Charlie spent long hours striving to make sure it was all correct. He was always precise like that. Always knew where everything was, even the things he was uncertain about.

"He was making money for something, not just to pay back debts," Hetty said. "He already had so much. Yet he wanted more, even when he had plenty."

"He always saw freedom as the things he owned and the comforts that came with them." Benjy dropped the book, turning his head toward her, moving close enough that he brushed against her. "What happened today?"

"Why do you think something did?"

Without his eyes leaving hers, he pointed to the tub sitting in the middle of the room. "This doesn't belong here."

"Someone broke into our room." Hetty quickly described what she had found, skipping over nothing, though she saved the detail about the knife left in the dress form for last. Sitting next to him, away from the boardinghouse, the whole thing seemed like one of her stories: distant and hardly able to touch her now. "The knife was a message."

"An effective one," Benjy added. "We're not going back there."

He said this as if expecting she would argue with him. She had no arguments. Hetty didn't fear that the intruder would come back or even bring harm, but it tarnished her feeling toward the room and the comfort she often felt within its walls. It wasn't the best place in the world, but it had been theirs.

"Oliver doesn't seem to mind us staying for a while," Hetty said. "Although he might soon change his mind."

Benjy chuckled. "What did you do?"

"I just asked a few questions. A man came by to bury the unidentified body, and it turned out to be his brother. I might have been a bit rude since it was the same man who got you fired over a wagon, Preston Stevens."

Benjy sat up as if lightning had struck overhead.

"The owner of Elmhurst Cemetery. The dead man is his brother?"

This was a question not meant for her to answer.

Benjy shifted papers on the bed, upending the neatly made stacks until he found a card, and he thrust it under her nose.

"ELM four twenty-four," Hetty read.

"Or *Elmhurst Cemetery on April twenty-fourth.* I knew the numbers were a date, but the shortening of the name threw me off. I never thought it to be the cemetery. I never connected it to Charlie. Why would I? The cemetery owner's brother ... Well, that means a great deal left uncovered."

Instead of explaining the importance of this discovery, Benjy rolled off the bed and went to the wardrobe for a change of clothes.

Hetty picked up the paper he'd dropped. *Elm*, she thought, tapping Charlie's handwriting.

Just like Benjy, she'd had a flash of insight, but it did not rouse her to leap from the bed like he had. Charlie had said something about elm that night he'd tried to talk to her, the night before he died. If she hadn't cut him off, had let him speak, would he have said Elmhurst? If he had, would she have listened? Cemeteries were hardly something Charlie had ever involved himself in, so it would have caught her attention. She might have listened. Would Charlie still be alive if she had?

No, not likely—because there was still far more about his death they didn't know, and a single conversation playing out differently couldn't have saved him.

Benjy pulled out their lantern and lit it, and Hetty knew she couldn't stop him from leaving. Nor would she. They were close, and now was not the time for further delay.

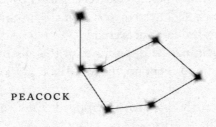

PEACOCK

36

Located on the outskirts of the city, Elmhurst sat on a pretty piece of land that was quite sprawling despite having lost a significant portion of its acreage to the continuing expansion of the city's streets. Elmhurst, like the Lebanon or Olive cemeteries, was one of the few places they were allowed to bury their dead.

It was also the scene where many of Hetty and Benjy's inquiries ended, and, on one occasion, started.

As they approached from the road, the iron gate towered over them, as did the peak of the chapel contained inside. The gates were barred for the night. Hetty had just started to draw a sigil to unlock the gates when Benjy strode away, ignoring her and the gates. He walked the length of the brick wall, their lantern illuminating the way ahead.

"What are you looking for?" Hetty asked.

"Wheel ruts."

Hetty turned her eyes to the ground as well. While she couldn't see anything, there was something strange about the ground. Places that were lumpier than they should have been. Daylight would have made it clearer, but there was a path here, a path that wound to the very back of the cemetery.

Hetty nearly bumped into Benjy when he stopped in front of the wall. He swung the lantern over it.

"Here's the opening," he said, pointing to what looked to be part of the wall. "You first."

The gap was light trickery. Looked at directly, it seemed to be a crack that Hetty could barely squeeze through. But when entered at an angle, it was wide enough to not just comfortably stride through, but to drive a decent-size wagon through with little trouble.

Now standing inside the cemetery, Hetty studied the gap from this side. Others had slipped in here. With a wagon. But why?

The answer to that swirled in her mind for only a few moments before the pieces fell into place.

"Charlie got himself involved in a grave-robbing scheme!"

Hetty knew she'd guessed right from the brilliant smile that spread across Benjy's face.

"How did you piece it together?" he asked.

"Charlie needed money. That was evident from everything we found so far. He had debts he couldn't pay, so he found a way to make it possible. Those willing to be grave robbers can make a tidy sum."

Benjy's gaze fell on the nearest headstone, a plain slab with half-filled bowls of water and other tokens surrounding it. "Charlie was a merciless landlord and a reckless gambler . . . and had mighty big aspirations. A grave robber isn't too far of a leap. What's the benefit of killing him for digging up and selling the dead?" Benjy wondered, more to himself than to her.

"It puts a stop to the whole affair."

"More than that," Benjy mused.

"Charlie wanted to talk to us about something," Hetty started, and encouraged by Benjy's nod, she kept talking. "Which meant he wanted us to *do* something. If he'd gotten himself embroiled in a grave-robbing scheme that spiraled out of control, we'd be the only people who could help him."

Benjy nodded. "He was killed for a reason, wasn't he? He was either quitting, got in deeper than expected, or chose to reveal a secret that in the end cost him everything."

"It was a secret," Hetty said, thinking of her last conversation with Charlie. "He said no one was dying right away, but it was important. A secret would be—"

Benjy pressed his fingers into her arm, abruptly cutting off her words.

Silently, Benjy closed the shutters of the lantern and pulled her behind the headstone.

She ducked down next to him and ran a finger along the band at her neck. The glamour fell gently around them.

She didn't hear whatever it was that had Benjy spooked, but from the way he was clenching her arm, she had an idea what it must have been. Yet all she heard was the pounding of her own heart.

But then—a clink of metal.

Hetty looked around for the source of the sound, but a flash of light filled the air.

Brighter than the sun, it seemed, and reminded her of the flares that slave catchers would toss into the woods to flush out runaways like rabbits. Not only did the flares illuminate hiding places, but they left a person momentarily stunned. By the time a person regained their senses, it was too late.

But this didn't seem to be that—not quite. Hetty didn't see anyone coming near their hiding spot, for one thing. In fact, judging by the pounding of footfalls that sounded in the air, whoever had sent up the flare was using it not to capture, but to escape.

After a few moments the brightness faded and darkness returned.

Blinking to adjust her eyes, Hetty whispered, "Did you see anything?"

Her answer was a soft thump as the lantern fell to the ground, and a rush of air as Benjy gave chase to the shadow sprinting through the cemetery.

She watched him, but decided there was a more sensible way to handle things.

Moving through the gravestones, she traced the opposite path of where she had seen the shadowy figure. She wasn't surprised when, as she swung the lantern around, its light spilled over Charlie's grave. It didn't look like the dirt was disturbed, although it was hard to tell given how recent Charlie had been buried.

Although . . .

Before she could think better of it, Hetty knelt and pressed her fingers into the cold earth as deep as they could go.

And that was how her husband found her, in the dirt up to her elbows. Instead of asking why, he sat down on the other side of the grave, stretching out his legs as if they were at a midnight picnic.

"I see you didn't catch them," Hetty said.

"There wasn't anyone, just a shadow. It ran through the gates. But I don't think it was for us. It was meant for anyone who got too close to the grave we're standing by."

"Someone rigged it? That was risky, given there are rules against spells left here."

"Well, Edward Christopher Degray never cared for those rules while he was living, I doubt being dead changes that opinion."

"Degray?" Hetty echoed, and finally pulled her hands out of the ground. "Like the club?"

"Yes, like the club," Benjy laughed. "You didn't know it was named after someone? I never met the man, but he was pretty important in town. He started the Edmonstone Club, and did a number of important things."

"Which you aren't relating to me."

"Because at the moment you wouldn't care if the man invented a spell to fly to the moon." He tilted his head towards Charlie's grave. "Anything?"

Hetty shook her head. "No traces of magic. We should have brought a shovel with us."

"I'm not sure I'm up to digging up Charlie."

"Not even to see if he's still in there?"

"He has to be. His body was marked with the cursed sigil, so he's useless to the medical schools—no one would have robbed *his* grave. Whoever killed him did him that favor, at least."

"Favor? It's still the cursed sigil!"

"Have you considered that we might have been overly superstitious about it? Sigils have power not just in what they do, but how they are used."

"Are you saying it meant nothing?"

"Power comes from belief. We believe in a curse. It becomes a curse. I think it was a warning to keep us away . . . or draw us in."

"The last was more likely. Stars." Hetty sat back onto the grass. "That's a shade too clever for me."

"It's only a simple trick," he said cheerfully. "Just think, it could have been more complicated."

"How can you find any of this amusing?" Hetty grumbled.

"Because the pieces are coming together." Benjy jumped up to his feet. He gestured around the cemetery and the gravestones that rose up around them. "All of this explains why we haven't figured it out. We were looking in the wrong places. Seeking out the wrong things."

"That's because Charlie was not who we thought he was." Hetty picked up the lantern and strode away from Charlie's grave, putting as much distance between it and her as quickly as she could.

"He's exactly what we thought," Benjy said, matching her

stride. "We just thought him better than that because we still considered him a friend."

"And we like to think we surrounded ourselves with good people?"

"*Interesting* is the word I would use." Benjy shrugged as they headed toward the cemetery gate. "But I suppose that does describe all of our friends."

"Interesting," Hetty repeated, amused at this description, but such a word suited all her friends in one fashion or another. Each who were more than what they appeared at first, with talents that she could only aspire to. "I suppose that is one more reason I stayed in Philadelphia. The people I met made it hard to leave."

"Here I thought," Benjy drawled, "you were just curious about the dead man we found floating in the Schuylkill?"

"I was curious about that," Hetty admitted as she swung the lantern between her hands, "but the mystery was only a small portion of my interest."

"And the rest?"

Hetty could practically see the smug smile that accompanied those words.

This would not do at all.

"I was bored and restless," she said, deliberately giving an answer he would not expect to hear.

"The restless part I understand," he said. "But bored? Didn't you spend an entire season sewing dresses for weddings? When you weren't doing that there were all those charity events and activities your friends insisted you take part in."

"None of it was my choice," Hetty replied. "I did all that to fill the time. But solving mysteries was something I wanted to do. It doesn't hurt that I'm quite good at chasing after answers people like to ignore."

"What about me?"

"You're good at figuring out strange puzzles."

He caught her arm and then twirled her around so they faced each other. This was the first time he done such a thing, but it felt like an old habit and something she could never tire of. "That's not what I meant."

"I know." Hetty didn't even try to hide her grin. "But don't you know that answer already?"

HARE

37

As HETTY STIRRED AWAKE the next morning, she thought the gentle tapping was rain on the window. Opening her eyes, she found it was not rain, but her husband. Sitting up on his side of the bed, Benjy tapped one foot against the bed frame while reading through the papers. The only sign that Benjy had moved since she had fallen asleep was the stack of papers around him.

When they returned to the house, they washed the cemetery dirt away, raided the pantry, and turned their attentions to the papers once more. They went over everything from the grave-robbing angle, trying to see something they had missed. Their efforts gave them no new answers. Isaac Baxter was the most likely suspect in Charlie's death, but Benjy shook his head whenever Hetty suggested confronting the man directly. This was too carefully done, he claimed, and they needed to be careful themselves if they wished to uncover the truth.

At some point, Hetty stretched out on the bed intending to just rest for a moment, but once she shut her eyes, sleep came for her.

"Did you sleep at all?" Hetty absently touched her hair, pushing back hairpins that shifted while she slept.

"A bit." Benjy absently rubbed the stubble on his chin. "If this is about grave robbing, everything changes, including the who and the why."

"Baxter has plenty of motive."

The tapping stilled. "Go back to sleep if that's all you have to say."

"Maybe you're the one that should sleep if you're not seeing the obvious." Hetty moved across the bed and grabbed the closest piece of paper next to him. "Alain is dead. Geraldine has no motive. Darlene and George have ties that are by association and no relation to grave robbing. Same with Eunice and Clarence. Then there's Baxter—"

"Who's your top suspect because of the club, its members, and debts. But anyone else in a high-ranking role could do the same."

"Maybe it's someone we don't know. There's Judith to consider. She's got to fit in there somewhere."

"It's someone we know, just not as well as we think," Benjy said, in a way that left her uncertain if he'd heard her or not. "I feel like I'm missing something, but what could it be?"

"You need to sleep," Hetty urged. "The potions Penelope gave you do not bring true rest."

"How can I rest? It's finally coming together . . . I can see it now. If I hadn't been so distracted, I would have already figured it out."

"We were both distracted," Hetty murmured. "This case isn't like the others. Everything we learn about it strikes close to the heart. When strangers are murdered, we discover their secrets. But when it's someone we know that's dead, we end up learning secrets about ourselves. It's like Charlie dying made me take a look at everything around me, and when I did, I realized finding my sister is no longer important to me."

He stared at her as if she'd sprouted another head.

"I want to find her, of course," Hetty said quickly. "I want to see her again. Searching for her is like me telling stories at parties. I tell them because I don't want to talk about myself. I put on a show to distract, to keep people from getting too close. I want to find my sister, but looking for her gives me an excuse. It allows me to say, 'I can't buy this, I'm saving for a telegram.' 'I can't be a teacher because I need to be able to leave once news of her arrives.' 'I won't move to a better apartment because I can't settle anywhere until I find her.' Excuses — that's what I turned my sister into."

Benjy took her hands, stopping her words with a gentle touch. "That's not true at all."

Hetty shook her head. "You saying those words doesn't make it less true. Our lives would be very different if I hadn't insisted on searching."

"So would have a number of things." He patted her hand before letting go. "You must be specific — haven't you learned this by now?"

As always Hetty found herself slightly stunned at the ease he said such things. "You really don't have regrets?"

"I believe it was you who told me that I don't do anything I don't wish to do." He kissed her cheek and grabbed the set of papers by her side. "Though I can be persuaded."

As he shuffled the papers, he picked up a hairpin. He twisted it so the light caught on the bird perched on a branch.

Benjy held it out to her.

"Try not to lose this," he said. "The rest came out twisted or broken."

"You mean not up to your exacting standards." Hetty stuck the pin into her hair with care.

"If I'm going to give you something, I want it to be the best it can be." He absently patted the bed frame. "Why do you think all this furniture is here?"

"They didn't fit our box of a room."

This set of furniture was better than the set that had ended up in the boardinghouse — as if he had it made and only afterward realized it wouldn't fit. She always knew he liked things just so, but it cast a different light to know it was solely for her good opinion.

"Maybe it's a good thing you were so precise." With certain emphasis she added, "When I saw the hairpin, I realized I love you."

Delight spread across his face, and she made a note to say such things more often, for the sight was divine.

"If that was all it took, I should've made you more of these a long time ago!"

"Maybe," she teased, "given all the pins you ruined."

"Why do you think I made them in the first place? I'm often in great need of them."

The map had gone up while she slept. But it didn't have any of its pins, and not because he had forgotten their placements.

"You could only find my good pins, couldn't you?"

Hetty laughed when he said nothing, and fetched the pins herself.

"Remind me of the places again," she said, moving to the map.

He named the places closest to where her hand hovered instead of the order of how they found them.

"We can't forget this alley." She placed the pin where they'd found the body of the brother of the surly cemetery owner. "That collar." She shivered. "I hate thinking about it. I know we didn't look at it that closely, but I wonder what we could have found on it. Some collars had the name of the slave owners engraved on the inside. I knew some people who even kept them, mostly as a reminder about who reparations should come from. I know you told me most were melted down. I wonder where this one came from?"

She waited, but when Benjy didn't say anything, she turned around. He was looking in her direction, but his gaze had slipped past her.

"Benjy," she said, snapping her fingers. "What's gotten into you?"

He started. "Did Oliver throw it all away?"

Hetty didn't know what he was talking about, but she had seen that expression on his face many times before. Asking him questions wouldn't give her any useful answers.

"Let's ask him," she suggested.

Benjy was already out the door and bolting down the stairs before she could finish her sentence. In the clamor, there was a crash, followed by a yell, then grumblings.

The door to the cellar was still swinging on its hinges when Hetty reached the main floor.

"Aren't you going to run downstairs after him?" Oliver waved a hand absently. Pegasus flashed in the air, and the table moved back into place.

"I'll catch up to him soon enough," Hetty said. "Is Penelope here yet?"

"Haven't seen her. Although she might not be needed anymore. Benjy seems to be recovered enough to nearly run me over."

"I'll let Penelope be the judge of that. Oh, and when she returns she won't be alone. Darlene will be with her."

"Wonderful, more company! Am I running a boardinghouse now? Where people come and go as they please?"

Hetty started at this last bit. "You knew we'd left last night?"

"The wards on the door were perfect. I expected it, to be honest, while you're working a case —" Then, struck by an idea, Oliver gasped and turned toward the cellar door. "Tell me there isn't another dead body down there! If there is, by the stars, I swear —"

"Nothing to worry about," she assured him. "He's just checking a few things. You kept Morris Stevens's things here, didn't you?"

"Figured you'd need it."

"Thank you for that. And for letting us stay." Hetty twisted her fingers, trying to figure the most elegant way to say her next words. "Although, we might be here longer than planned. We moved out of our room."

"I may not be a brilliant detective that solves fascinating mysteries like you, but I was able to deduce that when you came back with the tub, thank you very much. You don't have to tell me why," he added hastily. "I don't think I can handle the reason. Stay as long as you need. Even if it means you never leave."

Hetty blinked. "I thought you said that if we all lived under one roof, one of us would lose our head and it'd be simpler if it was you?"

"Did I?" Oliver grinned, and it was like seeing the sun after days of storm clouds. "Don't recall."

"You're awake." Thomas poked his head in from the next room, newspaper in hand. "If you want something to eat, there might be leftovers in the kitchen. Eunice Loring brought something over earlier this morning. I think there was a card for you."

"She didn't stay?" Hetty asked.

"Had to leave. Said it was important, but not enough to whisper a word to me. More curious how she knew to come here."

"Penelope is the start and end of that question," Oliver said. "But that's not important."

"It's not?" Thomas asked.

"Nope. I need to talk to you."

Oliver pushed Thomas into the next room. "Go get something to eat," he said to Hetty, and then firmly shut the door behind him.

Hetty pressed an ear to the wood. She heard murmuring voices but no discernable words to make the effort worth it.

In the kitchen, she found an empty pot, recently scraped clean of grits. There was some hard cheese and fruit about, but she also found a hunk of dried meat.

As Hetty bit into it and chewed, she saw the dish that Thomas mentioned. It was a pie, although Hetty couldn't tell what fruit made up the filling. Propped next to it was a letter: a belated thank-you to Hetty for sewing Eunice a new dress . . . and then a request to help with a project at Eunice's house, something for her husband.

Hetty stared at the lies. She had never made clothes for Eunice. Eunice had never mentioned a project.

She turned the page around. Scrawled in a corner was a crescent moon and a sun.

Their calling card for those in need of help.

Eunice had reached out to her. Several times. Mostly under guises and small lies meant to attract attention. This was the boldest overture yet. Was it something domestic? Eunice had wanted Moonleaf for a reason. Maybe there was no miscarriage, but simply a desire not to bring a child into a dreadfully unhappy marriage. Or something more.

Something dreadful that left Eunice moving about quietly instead of speaking plainly.

Swallowing her food, Hetty went down into the cellar.

A light, bright enough to be a contender for a small sun, blazed over Benjy's head as he studied the broken halves of the collar they'd found on Morris Stevens.

The burnished silver was spotted with blood, giving the markings along it a rusted appearance.

"I'm going to see Eunice," Hetty announced. "She sent a note. I think she's in trouble."

"I'd say that's a safe bet." Benjy held up the collar and tapped at the name inside:

Meade.

"That name is familiar." Hetty frowned. "Why do I know it?" She looked down at the crumpled note in her hand.

Then she remembered.

She'd been standing in a long line at the Freedmen's Bureau

when she'd heard the name spoken by the man waiting in line beside her.

"Meade is the name of the family that owned the plantation Clarence left behind," Hetty said. "But this can't be his collar. He told me he got free by being sold to a sympathetic owner."

"He might have lied about that," Benjy said. "And a few other things too. How would we know? We don't know him that well. Which explains everything."

Everything that Isaac Baxter could have done, Clarence could have done just the same — maybe even more easily, since no one pays attention to him. And why would they? He had a good excuse to be every place where they'd discovered trouble.

And Clarence had been everywhere, Hetty realized. She'd dismissed him because he was *Clarence:* boring, predictable, harmless Clarence. But maybe not so harmless.

Hetty's hand tightened over the note.

"Eunice can explain things," Hetty said. "She'll give us the answers we need."

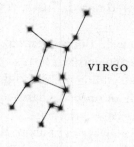

VIRGO

38

THE RAIN HAD PAUSED, but the threat of it lingered enough that Hetty pulled on a rain cape and drew up the hood over her head.

Eunice's home wasn't far, but it seemed farther and farther with each passing moment, each step compelling Hetty to walk faster.

"I'll knock on the door alone," she said. "Eunice is expecting me. If she sees you, she might panic."

"What if Clarence answers? You want me to wait on the street as he stabs you on his doorstep?"

"I can make excuses and stall him," Hetty said. "Go around the back. See if you can sneak in through an open door or something. Do not break down the door."

"Unless I hear screams."

"I don't scream."

"Which is why I'll break down the door if I hear any."

At the corner, Hetty grabbed his hand, swinging him around to look at her. "It'll be fine. We've done riskier things than this . . . and when we hardly knew what we were doing."

"You don't have a plan."

"I don't," Hetty admitted. "Just a couple of hopes strung together."

"That's all we need." Benjy squeezed her hand.

They parted at the corner. Hetty continued toward the front door. She knocked, pulling on her brightest smile.

But when the door opened, Clarence stood there.

Inwardly, Hetty cursed the stars.

Why was Benjy always right about these things?

"Henrietta," Clarence said, pushing up his glasses. "What brings you here?"

"I come to see Eunice." Hetty lowered the hood of the rain cape, wondering how complex of a lie she could spin. Clarence's eyes narrowed a bit, and disbelief bloomed on his face. "I wanted to thank her for the lovely gift she gave Oliver. He appreciated it very much. If Eunice isn't here, I'll just come back another time."

"Oh," he said, relaxing. "How nice of you. Eunice is just upstairs. Come in, sit. I'll go fetch her."

Hetty thought of following him but decided against it. Last thing she needed to do was raise his suspicions.

Making sure Eunice was safe — that was the most important thing right now, not whatever Clarence had done or might do.

Eunice's note burned in Hetty's pocket as if chastising her for the missed opportunity. She should have received this note in person. She should have said something to Eunice earlier. She had noticed something was off but hadn't done anything because it was Eunice. Eunice, who brushed aside any unhappiness that fell her way. Eunice, who was nothing but perfect, and beautiful, and liked by everyone. Eunice, who was in terrible danger if her husband was a murderer.

But it was still possible Hetty was mistaken. Eunice's letter could have been about something else. Benjy could be wrong about Clarence. He seldom was, but he wasn't infallible. The collar wasn't quite evidence. Meade was a common name, and the collar was unlikely to be the only one. Hetty herself had stolen a broken collar once for a disguise. This could be a chance connection, something they'd forced because they had missed the piece that would have brought the whole case together.

If they were wrong, Eunice would be safe. But if they were right ...

Moving into the parlor, Hetty chose not to sit on one of the stiff-backed chairs, but rather paced around the room, counting the seconds that it took for Clarence to return. As she waited, something on the mantel caught her eye.

It was one of Eunice's dreadful lace doilies, oversize and draping like a handkerchief from the ledge.

How odd.

She stepped closer.

There were doilies placed all around, but there was something always placed atop. Without something here, the items on the mantel seemed off-balance. No, there was a gap. Between the oval portrait and crystal figurine, something was missing.

Something that had been a centerpiece. Something she had seen the last time she was here.

Hetty's eyes traced the remnants of a shadow on the wall. Had it been a clock?

Yes, a clock. When she was here after Charlie's funeral, it had been resting there.

As she peered closer, she felt the band at her neck suddenly tighten.

Magic.

Without thinking, she swished her fingers through the air, casting an unmasking spell.

The sigil flared and the cursed sigil, the Serpent Bearer, revealed itself.

They were right after all.

Hetty hurried to the window. At this angle she should see

Benjy. And she did. But instead of lurking around back as they'd discussed, he was moving toward the front of the house. Not going to the front door, but away, and into the streets, striding after a slender figure wearing a rain cape with the hood drawn up.

Eunice.

But if she was leaving, then what did—

"They say you two look alike," Clarence whispered into her ear. "Never saw much of a difference myself. You're both stubborn and dark as sin, but that's where the resemblance ends."

Behind her, Clarence stood with a wand pointed at her throat. Although Hetty had crossed paths with the student of Judith's, that woman had not an ounce of the confidence Clarence possessed.

Clarence smiled at her. Hetty found herself wishing she'd come in here with a better plan.

"Eunice isn't here, is she?" Hetty managed to say.

"No," Clarence said. "And she won't be back for some time."

Hetty's hand moved to the band at her neck, but Clarence was faster. He called out an incantation. The wand's tip turned bright orange before something shot toward her.

Hetty lunged aside, ignoring the pain at her neck. She felt the band slide away. She mourned the loss only for a moment as she threw up Taurus. The star-speckled bull drew itself up in front of her.

It rattled under the force of Clarence's magic and then shattered—the flecks of stars flying everywhere like dust.

Hetty picked another sigil, the sturdier Pegasus, but it withstood a blast from Clarence's wand for only slightly longer than her first cobbled spell. As the next charge of Sorcerous energy came toward her, Hetty threw herself behind the couch. Something burst above her head. Wood chips rained down on her head.

Hetty scrambled to her feet, stumbling, her skirts ripping. She cursed her dress as much as the tight seating arrangements of the room. She had been trapped the moment she'd come in here.

She couldn't fight Sorcery with Celestial magic. It was too fast, too strong, and she didn't have time to properly set the spells that could slow it down.

She needed to get out of there.

She couldn't go toe to toe with a sorcerer.

Sorcery overpowered. It devoured. It put people in chains and destroyed nations in the name of gold. It sucked resources from foreign lands in the name of spices and trade routes and allowed untold horrors to continue unchecked.

But it was an old magic, rigid and unyielding, and unable to cope with newer magic.

Or the unexpected.

She didn't know how much Sorcery Clarence knew, but she knew one thing. She was the best practitioner of Celestial magic in this city.

Hetty ran a finger along the floor, drawing the first sigil that came to mind. The Crow sigil flashed and the couch nearby slid over, giving her cover. Then she drew another to set off a number of flares.

Clarence yelled something. What it was it didn't matter. All the other noise faded to a dull roar as he contended with her distraction.

Hetty plucked Eunice's note out her pocket. As the shields around her began to weaken and crack, she drew the Small Dog sigil in the corner and slid it up under the piano.

The last of the shields shattered. The couch was thrust forcefully aside with a wave of Clarence's wand.

Hetty spun to face Clarence then, a charm on her fingertips, but instead of magic, he blew dust into her face.

"I'm really sorry about this," Clarence said as Hetty's vision began to blur. "Just remember, this isn't about you. This is all your husband's fault."

Hetty reached out toward him. She missed and fell to the ground. Clarence's glasses twinkling above her was the last thing Hetty saw before the world faded away.

URSA MAJOR

39

When hetty woke, her cheek was pressed against cold wooden floorboards.

She moved her tongue about, lessening the cottonmouthed feeling, trying not to let panic take over when she found her arms and legs unresponsive. But moving her toes would be pointless if she didn't even know where she was. She seemed to have control of her eyes, so she swept her gaze around the room, taking in the details of the building. A musty smell. The damp air. High ceilings with exposed beams. Bricks and stacks of wooden beams in the corners. Boarded windows.

The closest door was on the other side of the room. But her path was blocked by a figure stamping out something on the floor.

Clarence.

A surge of rage shot through her and she attempted to get to her feet. She only managed to jerk her head, banging it against the floor.

"You're awake!" Clarence turned. Flecks of drying blood were splattered against his glasses and cheeks. Good. Something in that barrage of magic had managed to hit him.

If she was going down, she was going to drag him with her.

"Wore off already," Clarence muttered as he strode over to her. His face was flushed, his eyes bright behind the cracked lenses of his glasses. His wand, for now, was stuck in his pocket. "I thought I had more time, but this will be good enough." He bent over her. "Don't worry, I'm not going to hurt you."

"Yet," Hetty managed to spit out. She tried to move. Her limbs jerked a bit, but it was not enough movement for her to leap out and strangle him.

The powder he'd blown into her face was some kind of sleeping dust. Magic was keeping her bound, but what was it? Sorcery wouldn't last as long, but it would be hard to break. If it was a sigil, she only needed to distract him. "You can't think I trust you."

Clarence gave her a lopsided grin. "I promise I won't do anything to you, unless you plan to be difficult."

"Have you not heard the gossip? I'm always difficult."

Despite the clash in his living room, it was unlikely he was going to kill her. If he wanted that, they wouldn't be having this pleasant chat.

That left only one other option.

"I'm bait, aren't I?" Hetty asked, although she already knew the answer.

Clarence's smirk faded at her words. The spell loosened its vise. Hetty felt her foot twitch. "You're hoping Benjy will find me."

"I'm counting on it. I can't seem to find him alone. Whenever he's not in a group, he's with you. I couldn't even get him at the boxing match. My first spell hit him, but my next attempts were blocked by your magic. Must you always lurk around him?"

"I like spending time with my husband." Her bindings loosened even more with the twitch that entered Clarence's face.

She'd found a sore spot.

Like prodding with a pin, Hetty pushed deeper. "I pity Eunice for having to live with a man like you. She doesn't even want to bear your child."

With a growl, Clarence grabbed her by the shoulders, hauling her up to her feet before Hetty realized what happened.

"Keep her name out of your mouth!" Clarence shook her, his face contorting in something vaster than rage. "I've done my best by her. I've provided a home and beautiful things. I gave money to every committee she joined, every good cause she started!"

"She's afraid of you," Hetty said when the shaking stopped. She smiled and pressed in for the kill as the last of the binding magics fell apart. "But I'm not!"

Hetty kicked him, striking lower than she'd have liked, but it was good enough.

He dropped her with a yelp.

Hetty finished the Arrow star sigil by the time her feet hit the ground. It flashed in the air, striking a barrier bolstered by his wand.

"You," Clarence sputtered, waving the wood at her, "are being very difficult!"

"I warned you," Hetty replied, and ducked when he returned fire.

Twin snakes of magic spun around her. Hetty deflected the one coming from the right. But the second was close enough to clip her. She darted left, thinking it would miss her, but it looped and —

A dog made of stars leapt into the air, absorbing the Sorcery. It was a hound — not the scrappy spaniel she favored.

Which meant . . .

Benjy was there even before the dog vanished, his clothes spotted with rain and a storm swirling in his features.

"I told you I should have gone to the door with you," he grumbled, as Canis Major flashed in the air, erecting a rudimentary barrier in front of them.

"I'm sorry!" Hetty cried out, as magic clashed with magic. "Where's Eunice?"

"Safe. I sent her to the others." Benjy grabbed her arm and nearly lifted her off her feet.

Benjy's other hand shot out, and the loose bricks on the floor stacked themselves in front of them.

"How did that not stop him?" Benjy said, as brick dust flew over their heads.

"It's Sorcery," Hetty said. "None of this will hold for long."

Benjy didn't even blink.

"Then get the wand. I'll distract him."

Without explaining anything more, Benjy darted across the room. Star-speckled wolves and foxes trailed after him.

Clarence swore, and struck back at once.

He called out incantations, the growl in his voice making each bellow sound like a curse. Benjy darted through the piles of brick and lumber lying about, moving moments before the magic struck.

Get the wand, Benjy had told her, as if Clarence didn't have a death grip on it.

But Clarence wasn't paying attention to her, so she had that to her advantage. With a glance toward Benjy, Hetty slapped her hand against the ground, fingers curled into a familiar star sigil. Her magic took the form of a sweeping Swan. It soared majestically toward Clarence, only to vanish inches from him.

Of course he had a barrier set up. Otherwise this would have been too easy.

Benjy was still darting around the building, narrowly dodging the blasts coming from Clarence's wand. His spells were doing just enough to lessen the damage. But they wouldn't last for long. Benjy hadn't made a full recovery from the other night, and his slower movements were proof of that. He wouldn't last much longer without taking another hit.

But did she really need to take it from Clarence?

No, she realized. All she needed to do was get him to *drop* it.

Hetty ran from the safety of the crumbling brick wall and flung the Phoenix sigil into the air.

As she tightened her hand into a fist, the Phoenix fell apart, releasing a spell that negated the magic Clarence drew around himself.

Clarence didn't drop his wand, but he froze in place.

In that moment, Hetty closed the distance between them. As soon as she drew close enough, she jammed one of her hairpins into his hand.

Clarence dropped the wand with a yell.

Hetty kicked it across the room.

The thrill of victory was still on her lips as something cold and sharp bit into her neck.

"Stop!" Clarence shouted, but his words weren't directed at her. "I'll slit her throat!" He pressed harder and twisted Hetty's left hand, keeping her from drawing any more sigils. "She'll be gone before you even get to me."

"Ignore him!" Hetty urged. "He's trying to manipulate you!"

"Drop the magic," Clarence commanded. "Take three steps back."

A muscle jumped in Benjy's cheek. His arms fell to his sides, and the sigils swirling around him faded away.

"Let her go. Whatever this is about, she's not involved. She didn't even know about the boxing bets."

"Boxing? Is *that* what you think this is about? It was never about the money." The knife slipped away from Hetty's throat. "You really are a fraud!"

"He isn't a fraud," Hetty snapped.

Clarence chuckled as if he hadn't heard her. "Money, boxing . . . is this all you managed to piece together? I thought you two were supposed to be great detectives. The mighty conductors! You don't know anything."

"Charlie's actions put you in debt," Benjy said. "Isn't that why you killed him?"

Clarence laughed. "What does money have to do with anything? I have more than enough of that stuff, and it can't do a thing to bring back the person I lost."

Benjy was quiet a moment. "Who did you lose?"

"His first wife," Hetty said, as a conversation she should not have forgotten suddenly returned to her. Not only did the contents of such a conversation echo in her mind, she saw once more the anger that had filled Clarence's face when they had spoken at the excursion. "Sofia."

The knife pulled away by the smallest amount from Hetty's throat as she said the name.

"Yes," Clarence whispered. "Sofia, my love, my first wife. The one you left to die. She escaped with others during the war, pressing on when you didn't show. She died when she could have lived. Then for years I had to endure staying in your company, listening to everyone sing your praises. Rhodes never leaves a passenger behind! Rhodes brought everyone safely home." His grip tightened on Hetty's arm. "It's all lies! And the stories just kept growing. Growing bigger and bigger, and you didn't deserve any of it. I had to do something.

"But then I remembered your little pastime," Clarence continued. "Grave robbing is condemned by all, so if you were caught doing it, people might wonder what else you were lying about. That maybe these deaths, these cases you solve, were stories no more real than the tales your wife makes up. It was a good plan, except I needed help. That was my mistake. If you want something done properly, you do it yourself. But Charlie knew a man with access to a cemetery. A man eager to make money.

"Charlie did have massive debts, but he didn't owe me money. I'm not a fool to give it to him. I was a fool to trust him. Charlie had been willing to sell you down the river with the boxing matches. My plan was not much different. But he didn't like it. Charlie actually got cross with me over his role in all this, as if he hadn't begged me to be a part of it.

"So he met with me, told me that he was going to tell you everything. I couldn't let that happen. Couldn't let him ruin all my plans just because he finally decided to be honest for the first time in his life. He turned his back and . . . well . . . then I had a mess to clean up. A mess that only grew because he turned into a coward."

"You killed Charlie," Benjy said. "You killed . . . all of them . . . for that? No one even knows about the deaths!"

"But they will. They'll learn what you did to Charlie. To Stevens. And especially to young Alain Browne. There will be a note attached to your body!"

Clarence's grip shifted on her arm.

Hetty braced for the knife, but Clarence shoved her to the ground.

As she fell she saw Benjy rush forward and Clarence flick his hand—

Benjy was in the air. Upside down, he hung like a bat as ropes snapped down from a wooden beam to wrap around his right foot. Another rope had captured his arms, drawing them back. He twisted, swinging around, but his movements soon became small and constrained as the ropes tightened around him.

"No!" Hetty lifted her hand, but light streaked in front of her, forming a cage of magic around her.

"I'm sorry," Clarence said, dusting off his clothes, "but I have no choice. It's the only way out of this."

"It wasn't his fault!" Hetty cried. She pounded on the barrier, sending sparks of magic flying. It didn't budge, but she kept on even as it felt like her hands would shatter. "He didn't know!"

Hetty's eyes were locked on Benjy. Whatever spells Clarence had set, they had missed. Benjy was dangling by his foot. And the ropes around his hands weren't taut. He was still alert. He could break free if he had enough time. He could do it before Clarence stopped toying with him.

A chance was all he needed.

"I know he's your husband," Clarence said, shaking his head, "but how can you defend—"

"It was me! It's my fault Sofia's dead. *I'm* the one who said we shouldn't go!"

"You?" Clarence swung around to her. "*You* said not to go?"

"All those trips. I'm the one who decided where we went. I'm the one who said who we took with us. I made all the decisions. He had no idea about Sofia." She swallowed, exaggerating her remorse to draw him in to her tale. "But I knew."

She had Clarence's complete attention now, and under the weight of his stare, she struggled to keep talking.

She'd managed to break that binding spell earlier because she'd broken his focus. She'd need to pull off that trick one more time.

"You knew?"

"I knew. I knew about them all—about John and Emily and Paul and Edward." The names flowed off her lips, choosing whatever came first to mind. The names didn't matter. They just had to sound right. This was a story, after all. A story she embellished and spun around her to keep Clarence distracted.

And it was working.

"You knew?" Clarence repeated, and the ropes overhead trembled. "*You knew* and you didn't do anything!"

With those last words, the ropes holding Benjy vanished.

Benjy fell.

But before he hit the ground, Benjy flung a spell directly at Clarence.

Clarence was knocked off his feet, but Benjy hit the floor first.

He hit it at an angle. The building shook. Hetty heard something snap, followed by a moan.

The boundary that had been imprisoning Hetty disappeared. She started to run to Benjy, but something floated in front of her, having fallen from above.

A scrap of fabric, spotted with blood . . . and the Virgo star sigil glowing among her stitches.

The band Clarence had ripped from her, with its magic still in play. Benjy must have found it back at the Loring home.

He had kept it with him. Had it protected him?

Hetty grabbed the band and activated the first spell her fingers found. The Crow soared forward. And just in time, too. The star-speckled bird snatched the rope Clarence hurled at her, seeking, no doubt, to string her up as he'd done Benjy.

The spell shook the rope back and forth in its starry beak, until the Sorcery vanished in its grip.

The other sigils stitched into the band burst forth as well.

The Eagle. The Dove. The Crane. The Swan. The Peacock. All glittering like starlight as they fluttered around her like true birds.

The final star sigil that emerged was Virgo. Resplendent in a long flowing dress and an elaborate jeweled headdress mounted atop a crown of braids, the woman made of stars was shorter than Hetty. Her eyes were as black as the mysteries of the night skies, but her features were what Hetty always imagined Esther's to be after all these years.

Virgo smiled at Hetty and stepped forward, shielding her from the hexes that flew, seemingly at random, from Clarence's wand, as he bellowed the same incantation over and over. Virgo batted each one away with her hand, taking the blows until the spell unraveled.

Clarence's rage had so consumed him that he didn't seem to notice. The Eagle and the Peacock battered him with sharp pecks, but he pushed past them, all of his fury focused on Hetty.

"If I'd known it was you, I wouldn't have needed to kill Charlie.

I wouldn't have needed to do anything. Rhodes has a mountainous reputation to chip away at. But yours is made of books and stories, and only needs a good match to destroy it."

"You didn't have to do any of this," Hetty said, as the Swan batted aside another hex. "You could have just posted a nasty letter to the papers. Started a rumor or two. You didn't have to kill anyone. You didn't have to hurt Eunice."

"I told you! Keep my wife's name out of your mouth!"

He raised his arm with the wand. But this time when a spell burst from its tip, it wasn't directed at her. The hex flew at Benjy, where he lay groaning on the floor clutching his arm.

"No!"

Hetty commanded the Crane to intercept, and the bird crashed into the bolt of Sorcerous energy. The collision was a brilliant array of golden light.

Hetty shut her eyes.

When she opened them again, Clarence lunged at her.

Unprepared for this non-magical attack, Hetty swung out her arm. Her nails scratched along his face. He howled, and a fist caught her under the chin.

Hetty fell back to the ground, banging her head against the floor. When the world stopped spinning, Clarence stalked toward her again, drawing a gleaming knife.

He stepped on her left hand, keeping her from working any last spells.

"This ends now. You—"

But whatever foul thing that would have rolled off his tongue never came.

A bang filled the air.

Clarence stopped moving, staring down at himself. Instead of blood, ice sprouted from his right shoulder, jagged and long like a crystal.

Clarence staggered and then tumbled to the ground as ice coated his body.

Standing in the doorway behind him was Penelope. Smoke wafted from the dainty pistol held in her hand.

She was not alone. Behind her were others: Thomas, Darlene, and, for some strange reason, Pastor Evans.

Hetty stared at their worried faces, too confused to ask what had brought them here, let alone at the right moment.

She was just glad, so very glad, to see them.

"Penelope," Hetty said as her friends rushed to her side. "Good thing you finally put bullets in that gun."

PHOENIX

40

IF THERE WAS ANY HOPE that the whole thing would remain a quiet and ugly secret, it died the moment the newspapers reported the wand.

That detail kept tongues wagging all over town, as shock, anger, and, in some cases, disgust captured everyone's attention. Like any good tale, though, more than one version of it emerged, and Hetty heard plenty of variations with small details changed or removed. But in all the tellings, no matter who told them, one detail stayed the same. Clarence Loring, owner of the Good Tidings Catering Company, had been arrested in possession of a wand.

Possession of a wand was a hanging offense in the South, but in Philadelphia, Clarence would rot in jail and never see a day in court. It also meant that his once sterling reputation was in tatters, and every terrible rumor that Clarence had tried to ascribe to Benjy had been deflected back onto him.

But that wasn't the worst of his crimes.

"Shouldn't you be upstairs resting?" Hetty asked, as Eunice picked up the knife she had just dropped. "I have more than enough help."

"It's not really about help," Penelope said. She rolled another improperly peeled potato toward Hetty. "It's to bear witness. You're cooking, and no one has ever seen that before."

"Not true," Darlene said, and dropped more potato skins into the bin. "She's cooked before. But no one's lived to tell the tale."

Her friends snickered around the table. The loudest laughter came from Eunice, though the tears that prickled in the corners of her eyes indicated pain more than mirth.

When Hetty had first entered the Loring house, Eunice crept out moments later, the rain cloak hiding her so well that it had fooled Benjy for a few blocks. But she had stumbled, and Benjy caught sight of her. When he turned Eunice around he saw a blackened eye, a split lip, and a bruise in the shape of a hand-print wrapped around her neck. Eunice told Benjy about Clarence breaking the clock, and finding bloodied and torn clothes that weren't his, and—most important—that Clarence was still in the house and thus Hetty was in danger. Benjy brought Eunice to Oliver's house where she'd be safe. He went back to the Loring house and then tracked Hetty using the trail of magic she'd left behind.

Penelope and Darlene were there to greet Eunice when she arrived. The sight of Eunice's face had spurred them all to action, although they found Hetty and Benjy less by following a trail and more by Darlene's well-placed reminder of the building George, Charlie, and Clarence put money into.

Eunice joked that what had happened to her was worth it. She also refused to let Penelope heal her. Her face, Eunice claimed, was the proof of what Clarence had done. Horrible as it was, she wasn't wrong. Without Eunice's battered face, no one else would have believed their story.

"If you're going to be like that, I'm just going to let you do all the work," Hetty declared.

"You won't do that. You're only doing this because you're bored," Darlene said. She frowned as she adjusted the knife in her hand. "You've been in hiding."

"Not hiding," Hetty said, as the peel curled into a neat spiral around her left hand. "Just wanting to avoid gossip. I'm used to hearing terrible things being said about me, but good things, it turns out, are no better—I feel like I've got spiders crawling along my skin. It makes me nervous that when I really do mess up what you'll think."

"Just remember," Penelope teased, "you can hardly go lower in our opinion."

"I feel so much better," Hetty retorted as she rolled her eyes.

Penelope waggled a finger at Darlene. "Are you still peeling the same potato? Hetty's on number eight and even Eunice, who just got here, had done three more than you."

"It's not a race," Darlene grumbled.

"Hetty," Thomas said, as he popped his head into the kitchen. "Have a moment to spare? I need a voice of reason, and I suppose you'll have to do."

This got more giggles from her friends, but Hetty ignored them as she followed Thomas out into the hall, suspecting she already knew what this was about.

Oliver tapped his foot against the floor as his desk hovered in the air behind him. When he saw Thomas with Hetty in tow, he scowled. "I told you not to bother her."

"We needed another opinion. Benjy gave a vague one on purpose." Thomas turned to Hetty. "Did you want to keep this desk, or can we take it?"

There had been several big changes in the days since the incident with Clarence. Eunice was now living with Cora and Jay. She quietly sold off her household furnishings and gave away the others as gifts, such as the piano, which had found a new home within these very walls. Isaac Baxter vanished after news of his many outstanding debts went public, and the political club he founded disappeared with him. Sy Caldwell quit the forge following Benjy's departure and was trying his hand at a new career. And Marianne had quietly left for Nashville, with an even greater sorrow in her heart.

While some of those events were quite surprising, nothing could surpass Hetty's astonishment when Oliver handed over the deed to his house.

Typical of Oliver, he gave no true reason. He simply said it was a fair exchange. Thomas would later admit, however, it was not a true trade. The money had come in from the boxing match, and when they asked Benjy what he wanted to do with it, he simply told them to keep it. Handing over the house was an attempt to balance the scales.

Hetty didn't know how much money was involved on either side of the equation, but in her opinion, no value would be equal to the gift her friends had bestowed on them.

"You should take it," Hetty said. "You said you were starting up a mailing business? You'll need a desk in your new home."

"Mail-order business," Thomas corrected, and turned to Oliver. "And it will work. People want to buy things without the hassle that occurs when going to the store. I told you—"

"Yes, you told me a great many things, but you hardly tell a good story," Oliver grumbled. He waved his hand and the desk was set down alongside the pile of things they were taking.

Grumbling, Oliver headed upstairs.

"He's right, you know," Hetty teased as Thomas made to follow. "You tell a poor story."

"No worse than the one you told Oliver," Thomas replied. "A little bird said you're going to open a funeral parlor."

"That's no story." Hetty shook her head. "It's a plan. This

house is so big and we've enjoyed putting on funerals with Oliver. It's perfect."

"Well, it was your idea in the first place." Thomas's hand rested on the bannister as he paused his ascent along the stairs. "Thank you for all you did. He'll never admit it, but your frequent visits and the dead bodies gave Oliver something to look forward to."

"We don't deal with murder all the time."

"But they make the most memorable cases."

With that, he went upstairs in search of Oliver. Hetty turned back to join her friends only to find a star-speckled fox guarding the door.

"You want to talk to me now?" Hetty muttered, even though the fox could not answer for her husband. It only stared at her. "Fine, lead me to him."

Hetty half expected to be taken down into the cellar, but the fox merely turned the corner and walked into the parlor, then looked back at Hetty expectantly.

Benjy had disappeared into the room after breakfast, as he had the past few days. He had broken his right arm when he fell, and while it was healing it rested in a sling to keep him from engaging in his usual distractions. It would be a while before he benefited from Penelope's healing tonics, as bone-mending potions took a few days to brew.

Hetty thought he would turn to his books, but soon she realized he needed something to occupy his mind. Without it, he would only dwell on what could have happened if things had gone wrong.

Which meant when Hetty opened the door now, she found him hidden behind a mass of papers. But instead of covering the floor or tables, they floated around like slow-moving butterflies below the glittering sigil painted along the ceiling.

As Hetty stepped closer, she saw drawings of large windows and various pieces of furniture, with measurements all marked.

Renovate the house, she had told him when she pressed the sketchbook into his hand. *Make this our home.*

As Hetty leaned in to study one paper, it flitted away to be replaced by an even more delightful sight.

"Hello," she said. "I see you remembered me today."

"I spoke to you this morning."

"But it's afternoon, and I haven't seen you all day," she teased. "Keep this up and our friends will be wondering if we had a fight."

"Let them," Benjy said, but without the usual lightness that came with such words.

He held up an envelope.

"I found this in the mail that Sy brought from the boarding-house."

She didn't take it.

"You read it?" she asked, although she knew the answer. "Is it good news or bad?"

There was a knock on the front door.

"Let someone else get that," Benjy said. "You need to read this."

"I'll just be a moment," Hetty said, eager to take this excuse. "I'll be right back."

Not content to wait, Benjy followed her into the hall, but he stood aside as she answered the door.

A woman stood in the hallway in fine, if slightly travel-stained, clothing. She was tall, with dark coloring similar to Hetty's. Her head was mostly turned away at first, but when she faced Hetty, it was clear who this stranger was.

Her features were almost identical to Alice Granger's.

No wonder Alice had kept her sister at a distance.

"Are you Henrietta Rhodes?" Judith Freeman asked. "I heard you were looking for me."

"Your sister is looking for you. I was searching on her behalf."

"She actually said she was my sister?" Judith scoffed. "Tell me again how the sun rises in the east."

"She was very concerned about you," Hetty said. "And of the things you'd gotten mixed up with."

"I was just teaching magic to eager minds."

"Like a man named Clarence Loring?"

Judith stilled and shrank back. "Yes"—she swallowed hard— "I taught a few lessons to him. As I did for anyone interested, but he—"

"Threatened you. I bet he wanted to use Sorcery for something you didn't agree with. You refused and he threatened your life. So you disappeared for a bit."

The younger woman said nothing but regret filled her features.

"I know it was cowardly."

"No, it was smart," Hetty said. "Clarence took the life of three people. I'm not sure if he did it with your magic, but it certainly helped him cover his tracks."

"Stars. I read about what happened in the papers. If I had known . . ."

"It wouldn't have changed a thing," Hetty said. "Or you might have ended up dead. No, you did the right thing. But now that there's no danger, you should tell your sister you're alive and well. She'll appreciate that."

"Tell her yourself," Judith shot back. "She went through all the trouble of seeking you out!"

"I could, but she wants to see you," Hetty said. "Your sister will speak to you. Whether it's with anger or with joy, I cannot tell you. Only you can find out for certain."

Judith looked away, her face grimly set. "Then I suppose a visit is in order."

Hetty shut the door and slammed her fist into the wood.

Judith had taught Clarence Sorcery!

Why hadn't she made that connection earlier? Not that it mattered now, but not knowing had nearly gotten her and Benjy killed.

"Don't you think it's funny," Benjy said, "that after all the time you spent asking so many questions, in the end the answer just appears right in front of you?"

"I did go all over town looking for her," Hetty began, only to realize he held the letter out once more.

He wasn't talking about Judith.

The scribbled name on the front of the letter was her first clue. Olympia LaRue had finally responded to the telegram that she'd sent. It was already open, and a few sheets of paper stuck out, as if it contained too much to be properly put back.

With trembling hands, she took it. On the first page were a few scribbled lines:

I apologize for the delay, but you have waited long enough. I reached out to my contacts, and this is the result.

There was another sheet of paper behind it.

Hetty looked up, but Benjy's expression had not changed.

She read on.

The handwriting was different on this letter, with precise care in every stroke of a pen.

Mama used to say magic was the world, and I never believed it until I found a stack of letters waiting for me at home one day, all tattered and rain spotted. Letters I knew that came from you.

Hetty, I have missed you these past years. But it felt like you were with me the whole time. In the stories I remember, in the kindness of strangers helped by a sparrow, and as always when I looked up and saw the stars.

I cannot wait to tell you my stories. You'll find some things funny, I hope, and not judge me too poorly for the things that weren't.

I will not be able to travel to Philadelphia for a few weeks. There is a sickness going around town, and I know I will be needed. Until then I send this letter to convey these words:

You can stop searching. You have finally found me.

Hetty ran her finger along Esther's overly elaborate signature, joy singing in her heart.

Her sister, found!

And on her way!

How wonderful, how amazing, the best of news —

But then Hetty saw another piece of paper inside the envelope, a torn page from a yellowed newspaper dated nearly a full year earlier.

Miss Esther Beale, lately of this town, lost the fight with Yellow Fever after nursing so many through the worst of this dreadful illness . . .

There were more words, but Hetty lost them as the paper slipped out of her hand.

Benjy bent down to pick it up, adding softly, "She was well loved in the community as a teacher, a healer, and a loyal friend."

"She was." Hetty pressed a hand to her face, the words still spinning in front of her eyes. "She always wanted to teach me. It's why I didn't have patience for brewed magic. Esther was going to teach me, was going to change my mind, and now . . ." She drew a breath, then let it go. After all this time, Hetty knew how this story would end. She only hoped it would be different. But there was one thing she knew now. Her sister knew that Hetty had never forgotten her, and that was the second thing she always wanted.

"Now I know the truth," she continued. "I suppose it's a good thing we hadn't made any travel plans."

"We should still go. To prove the letter is true."

"I don't need to prove anything." Hetty tapped her chest, crushing the letter. "I know here."

As Benjy argued his points, Hetty wrapped her arms around him, taking care to not disturb the sling holding his arm.

His words trailed off as she whispered, "Thank you for helping me find her. It took a little longer than I would have liked, but I hope it wasn't too much trouble."

"Don't be so quick to thank me." Benjy's arm circled her, and he drew her close. "That night when you first set off to look for your sister, I only went with you because I was bored."

Hetty snorted. "Bored!"

"Quite bored," Benjy insisted, and Hetty heard the smile in his words. She didn't believe him any more than she did the other claims he made over the years. But it didn't matter. The reasons he gave, the explanations he told, they were just details. Embellishments over one simple truth: he offered his help, she accepted it, and together they accomplished many wonderous things.

"I hope you aren't still bored," Hetty teased.

His laugh was a rumble in her ears. "With you in my life, that is simply not possible!"

When evening rolled around, the house was full of people.

Oliver and Thomas returned from dropping off their belongings at their new apartment. Darlene had brought George and the baby. Cora and Jay arrived, leaving Eunice with no excuse but to stay. Penelope was there, of course. So were the cousins that she liked the best, Sy, Rosabelle, and Maybelle. There was even one of their old neighbors from the boardinghouse and a few others of some importance invited by Hetty's friends.

All these people had arrived for a dinner party, and despite earlier teasing, the meal was quite edible. Everyone agreed, however, that it was a good thing that some guests had brought food with them as well.

They all were gathered in the backyard, seated around several tables shoved together to create the illusion of one long table. A half dozen candles hovering overhead provided illumination, and the stars provided all the decoration required.

Dishes and plates passed from person to person, with a large helping of chatter on the side. There were too many voices filling the air for Hetty to listen in on every conversation, to pluck out the more interesting tales and stories. Instead she let the words wash over her, letting them become a jumble of many parts — which was what all stories really were. One long tale, to which those listening brought meaning and sense to their favorite parts.

Hetty told a few stories of her own, some true and some made up on the spot. As she told them, she caught Benjy's eye more than once. He smiled and nodded, encouraging her to tell the more outlandish tales.

Sitting there, Hetty saw a vision of many more evenings like this in the future. Maybe not always at a table laden with so much good food and company, or even with stars dancing above their heads. But she saw many other times — be they bewildering, sad, or joyous — all with the people she considered family.

Acknowledgments

Let me tell you a secret: *The Conductors* exists because one day I looked at the running list of story ideas I kept and thought to myself, "What happens if I added magic to a story about Underground Railroad conductors?"

Since that spark of an idea, I have filled six notebooks with scribbled notes, used countless pens until the ink ran dry, and written and deleted so many words that I long stopped counting. While all that led to the book you now hold in your hands, I would have never finished it without all the support I had along the way.

Mom and Dad, thanks for giving me that first computer and the space and encouragement to keep writing. It looks like Plan B might work out after all!

To my sisters, Stephanie and Regina, thanks for tolerating all my story talk for years, even when you had no clue what I was talking about. Also, you may or may not have been sounding boards for finer story details — sorry for that.

Aunt Ericka, thanks for all the enthusiasm and excitement for every bit of news I shared in the past, and I promise to remain "still curious" no matter what comes my way.

To all the "J"s, it takes a village to create a book, and I'm glad to have all of you:

Thank you to my stellar agent, Jennie Goloboy. We connected just when I was thinking of trashing this story. It's been a whirl-wind of a time since, and the fun hasn't stopped yet.

Thank you to my editor, John Joseph Adams. You helped me find my vision for the best version of the book.

Thank you to Jamie Levine and the other staff at HMH. You coordinated and arranged more things than I'll ever know about —thanks for all your hard work! Special shout-out to Fariza Hawke, Heather Tamarkin, and Alison Kerr Miller.

Thank you to Jaria Rambaran for providing some very fun art-work and for being 100 percent game for my very silly idea.

To Deborah Oliveira, thank you for being an extra pair of eyes when I needed them the most.

Special thanks to the librarians working in the Norfolk Public Library system who dug books out of storage for me, answered my very particular interlibrary loan requests, and provided a space where I could squeeze in writing over my lunch break. I couldn't have finished this story without you!